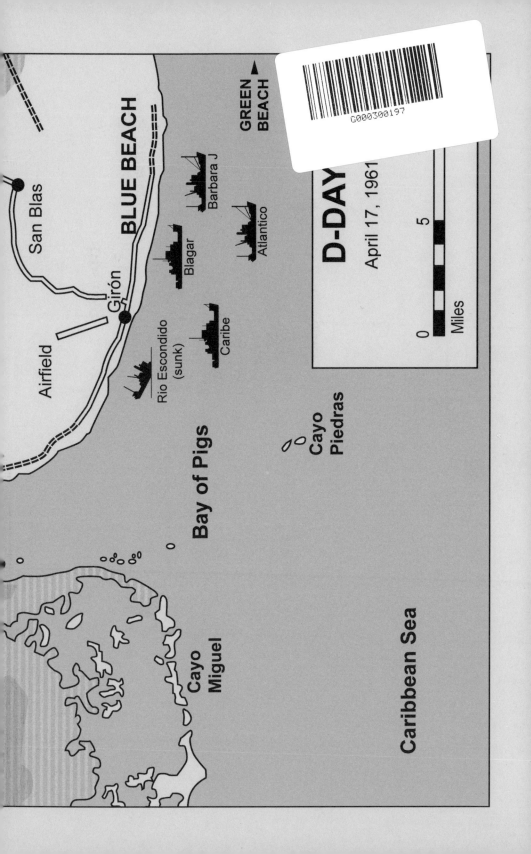

San Blas

BLUE BEACH

GREEN
BEACH

Airfield

Girón

San Blas

Barbara J

Blagar

Atlantico

Rio Escondido
(sunk)

Caribe

D-DAY
April 17, 1961

0   5
Miles

Bay of Pigs

Cayo
Piedras

Cayo
Miguel

Caribbean Sea

WHEN ANGELS WEPT

WHEN ANGELS WEPT

A What-If History of the Cuban Missile Crisis

ERIC G. SWEDIN

Potomac Books, Inc.
Washington, D.C.

Library of Congress Cataloging-in-Publication Data
Swedin, Eric Gottfrid.
  When angels wept : a what-if history of the Cuban Missile Crisis / Eric G. Swedin.
    p. cm.
  Includes bibliographical references and index.
  ISBN 978-1-59797-517-9 (alk. paper)
  1. Cuban Missile Crisis, 1962. 2. Imaginary histories. I. Title.
  E841.S94 2010
  972.9106′4—dc22

                                                                2010002203

Printed in the United States of America on acid-free paper that meets the American National Standards Institute Z39-48 Standard.

Potomac Books, Inc.
22841 Quicksilver Drive
Dulles, Virginia 20166

First Edition

10 9 8 7 6 5 4 3 2 1

To Betty, Kelley, and Kris

CONTENTS

Introduction 1
Prologue: The Bay of Pigs Invasion 3

1   Making Tools: Mushroom Clouds and Dreams of Space 29
2   Survivor: Nikita Khrushchev 61
3   Young Man of Ambition: John F. Kennedy 93
4   Operation Anadyr: The Plan to Protect Cuba 123
5   The U-2 Flight That Never Happened: The Crisis Begins 139
6   Helter Skelter: The World Teeters on the Edge of Sanity 165
7   Desperation: The Spark 199
8   Angels Weep: The Fire Comes 217
9   In the Ruins: Learning to Survive 253

Author's Afterword: Khrushchev and Kennedy 267
Notes 275
Bibliography 285
Index 291
About the Author 307

INTRODUCTION

Counterfactual histories are stories of what could have happened; they are narratives that run counter to the facts of history. That does not mean that such histories are useless. Rather they are useful in the sense that a counterfactual history can potentially give us greater insight into a historical event or time than the actual history. Niall Ferguson wrote that "these 'what ifs' are more than merely the stuff of historical 'parlour games.' . . . They are as much a part of a philosophically educated historiography as 'what actually happened.'" David S. Landes also found counterfactuals beneficial, "not so much because one can ever know the answers but for their heuristic value. . . . Such questions focus attention on cause and effect, help us distinguish between major and minor, direct and indirect influences," and "suggest possibilities otherwise overlooked."[1]

The Cuban Missile Crisis is a perfect candidate for a counterfactual history. Sometimes we forget how important the crisis was because cooler heads prevailed, superpowers backed down, compromises were made, and the only casualty came when the Cubans shot down an American reconnaissance pilot, Maj. Rudolf Anderson Jr. Although the crisis was resolved peacefully, the outcome was not necessarily foreordained by fate nor was it even the most likely conclusion. When analyzing history, we too often assume that whatever happened was inevitable.

When historians do consider this problem—that history had many possible outcomes for decision makers of the time—we use the term "contingency," a wonderful word, encompassing much potential, reminding us of the uncertainty of life, even of lives already lived.

The Cuban Missile Crisis is the closest that the Cold War came to becoming a hot, apocalyptic war, yet the end of the Cold War provides another example of contingency. The Cold War was fought between two power blocs for forty-five years, in wars by proxy, on economic and ideological fronts, and through massive arms buildups. The world formed two powerful, armed camps with tens of thousands of nuclear weapons on a hair trigger to threaten each other.

Two other powerful examples of counterfactuals come to mind. Had a novelist written the end of the Cold War as it really happened, few would have read that book and those who did would have ridiculed it for not being credible. The Cold War ended in 1991 with barely a whimper, astonishing everyone. Never in the history of the world had an empire still in command of its population essentially voted itself out of existence, with the only resistance being a short-lived coup by Communist hard-liners who foresaw their control over one-sixth of the earth's landmass evaporating. Most historians prior to 1991, if they had been forced to make a prediction, would have assumed that the end of the Soviet Union would be filled with blood and fire. That is how empires end.

Similar questions can be raised about the end of World War II. What if the Manhattan Project had been delayed or had failed? Would Japan have continued to refuse to surrender, and would the Soviet Union have conquered more than just Manchuria and northern Korea? Would Japan have been divided between the Soviet Union and the Western powers as Germany was? These questions show how counterfactual inquiries can expand our understanding of the contingencies that existed at that pivotal moment in history.

Because historians and other historically informed people too often neglect contingency, we need counterfactual histories to keep us honest and to find deeper truths. As part of the remedy, this book is an extended exercise in contingency.

|■|

This book is written from the perspective of an American-born historian living in Australia in 1996, in a counterfactual time in which the Cuban Missile Crisis turned out differently.

PROLOGUE:
THE BAY OF PIGS INVASION

When the boat ran into rocks before reaching the beach on April 17, 1961, Francisco Hernández jumped into the water. His heavy load of weapons, ammunition, and equipment pulled him under the surf, but the slight exile still managed to splash ashore at the Bay of Pigs. He hoped to repeat history. Fidel Castro had succeeded by invading Cuba from the sea, so why could Hernández and his fellow exile soldiers not also do the same?

Perhaps it was not a good omen that the first words that Hernández heard on his return to his homeland came from a Cuban militiaman defending the beach: "Long live Fidel Castro!"[1]

FIDEL CASTRO

Only four and a half years earlier, on December 2, 1956, Fidel Castro led eighty-one men in an invasion of Cuba. He had only one boat, an old yacht that took a week to sail from Mexico to Cuba. After failing to find their landing site in the dark on the coast of Oriente Province, the rebels ran aground on the mud bank before a mangrove swamp. The men eventually made their way to firmer ground, but their bad luck that morning continued when a patrolling Cuban B-26 found their ship. The twin-engined B-26 Invader had been built by the Americans during World War II, and the version owned by Cuba mounted six machine guns in the wings and carried three tons of rockets and bombs. Other B-26s joined the first, and they shot up the yacht, preventing Castro's men from unloading their supplies.

The dictator Fulgencio Batista ruled Cuba. He was supported by a forty thousand–man army, elements of which soon arrived, chased the invading rebels into a sugarcane field, and proceeded to decimate them. Under cover of darkness, the twelve rebel survivors, including Castro, his younger brother Raúl, and their friend Ché Guevera, escaped into the Sierra Maestra Mountains. From this position of relative safety, Castro slowly grew his rebel army. He began to receive positive news coverage from American reporters, so much so that he was soon better known in the United States than in Cuba itself. During the ensuing low-intensity guerrilla war between Castro's rebel forces and the Batista regime, Castro set up a clandestine radio station and proclaimed his support for democracy, civil rights, a free press, and a land-reform program.

The usual list of bad attributes of a military dictator applied to Batista: human rights abuse, censorship, murder of political opponents, and corruption in the form of skimming money off the national economy and from the government for himself and his cronies. He had close ties to American organized crime organizations, which built casinos in Havana and used Cuba as a place of refuge from American law enforcement. Batista's only redeeming quality was his opposition to communism, often the only trait necessary in a leader for the United States to provide support to his or her government. Still, Batista left a bad taste in the mouths of many Americans and offended their sense of moral order. Two senior officials at the State Department used the existence of Castro's rebellion to bureaucratically campaign for Batista's departure. Under increasing pressure from the rebels, Batista went into exile on January 1, 1959.

This abrupt victory completely astonished Castro. He made his way to Havana and was acclaimed as the new leader of the nation on January 8. Efforts at democracy in Latin America had regularly been thwarted by the cultural inclinations to continually seek the next strongman to take over and guide the nation; that placed too much power into too few hands. Castro assumed the strongman role and quickly moved to maintain control. During the two years of Castro's guerrilla war, only 867 people had been killed on both sides, but within three months, Castro's tribunals of revolutionary justice had tried and executed more people than that. Televised public trials in Havana's sports stadium, full of shouting crowds, resembled mob justice to foreign observers. Castro's brother Raúl proved to be a ruthless enforcer, while Fidel Castro himself showed his rhetorical strength with powerful speeches. At first, Castro proclaimed his support for political pluralism, concealing his Communist inclinations. Raúl was a secret member of the Communist Party, while Fidel, wanting to keep his options open, had not yet joined.

Only thirty-two years old, Fidel Castro showed himself to be a strong personality and a shrewd politician. He and Raúl had been born into a family of seven children, three sons and four daughters. Though the eldest son is often the most successful in a family, Fidel was the second son and third child, born on August 13, 1926. His father, an immigrant from Spain who became a wealthy landowner through hard work and canny business skills, was married not to Fidel's mother but to another woman at the time of his birth. Fidel's mother was a teenaged maid who had become the older man's mistress, and Fidel's father openly acknowledged the maid's children as his own.

Fidel was baptized as a Catholic at the age of eight, apparently so that he could later attend a Catholic boarding school. Eventually he went to a high school run by Jesuits, who lived up to their reputation in giving him a solid education. An unruly child, strong-willed and obviously intelligent, he seemed to prefer sports and hunting to more bookish pursuits, though he manifested a strong interest in military history and debate. His family intended for him to become a lawyer. Fidel's father and mother married when he was fifteen (it is unclear how his father's first marriage ended). Castro used his mother's surname, Ruz, as a child, and at seventeen he took his father's name.

While in law school at the University of Havana, Fidel became politically active, organizing demonstrations and leading a violent student gang. He is even reputed to have participated in the killing of a rival gang leader. That gangs existed at a university reflected the political chaos in Cuba, where criminal gangs made the streets of Havana dangerous.

Graduating in 1950, Fidel continued his political activism instead of pursuing a career as a lawyer. When Batista, who had been in and out of power as the de facto dictator since 1933, regained power in a coup in March 1952, Fidel and Raúl organized a revolutionary group with the intent of using violence to attain their political goals. On July 26, 1953, they attacked the large army garrison at the Moncada Barracks. Sixty of the 135 attackers died, about half of them after being captured and tortured. Fidel led the survivors into the hills in an attempt to escape, and five days later he was captured. The officer who captured him recognized him from a law class and prevented his soldiers from summarily executing the young rebel. How different would history be had Castro died then?

Castro acted as his own defense counsel at the subsequent trial and, after some impressive courtroom speeches, was sentenced to fifteen years of imprisonment on the Isle of Pines. While in prison, his incipient rebellion crystallized as the 26 July Movement. Castro read voraciously in prison, further educating himself in fascist and Communist ideologies, favoring writers who emphasized nationalism. Communism explained the imperialist injustices he saw, provided an intellectual framework to understand social relations and economics, and prophesied the inevitable evolution from the unfairness of capitalism to a Communist utopia. Both fascism and communism provided prescriptions for rising to power and staying in power by emphasizing the importance of ideology over individual rights. Killing in order to gain and maintain power was morally justified. In 1955 Fidel and Raúl were released from prison and exiled to Mexico. Their exile lasted only a year before they boarded their yacht and launched their invasion of Cuba.

How do we interpret Fidel Castro before the tribunal of history? Was he a man who converted to Marxism early and kept his beliefs to himself in order to give himself more political room to maneuver because he knew that his fellow Cubans were not enamored of communism? Was he a man driven by anti-American sentiment, born from his exposure to the large plantations on Cuba owned by American corporations? The people of Latin America had—and continue to have—a well-earned and bitterly nurtured resentment for the Yankees from the north, who seemed to support any government that offered stability and protected American economic investments and property. When Castro later turned to the Soviet Union as a patron, was he fulfilling his Communist destiny, or was he driven by his innate anti-American hatred? There are good arguments for both points of view, and absent the discovery of new documents that reveal Castro's inner thoughts, we cannot make a definitive assessment. For a man who spoke so much, in speeches that lasted for hours whether delivered before large rallies or intimate gatherings, Castro had a remarkable ability to conceal his inner self and intentions.

It can alternately be argued that Castro was primarily a man of action, not ideology. Such a notion ignores that ideas are an important motivator and that ideas structure both the actions that we choose and how we implement those actions. Regardless, although we lack definitive evidence of his early ideology, we can look at Castro's actions.

Castro came to power on January 8, 1959, by appointing himself commander in chief of the armed forces. The government leadership initially included many anti-Batista politicians, not all of them Castro's allies. When the prime minister resigned in February, Castro added that position to his responsibilities. Within several months of coming to power, Castro began the process of seizing the property of American corporations. In April he toured the United States for ten days and was greeted and admired by Americans happy to see Batista gone. Already suspicious of the bearded man who persisted in wearing army fatigues, President Dwight D. Eisenhower refused to meet with him. In May Castro's government passed a land-reform law that stripped all owners of any land in excess of a thousand acres. This strongly affected the large plantations owned by American corporations. Compensation was promised but at the low rates of assessment that had kept property taxes negligible over the previous half century. Members of Castro's cabinet objected that this law felt too much like communism. Some resigned in protest; others held on to their posts for a while longer, hoping to effect change; and still others went immediately into exile.

At the outset of Castro's reign, Cuba was completely dependent on the United States for exports and most imports. Americans had invested heavily in the island and owned large parts of Cuba, creating extensive sugarcane plantations that dominated the island, leaving little land left over for the peasants that formed the majority of the population. The United States bought most of Cuba's sugar crop, the island's primary export and moneymaker. The Americans also imposed on Cuba a smaller tariff on sugar than it imposed on sugar from other nations, called the sugar quota, making Cuban sugar much more economically competitive in the American market.

In 1960 relations between the United States and Cuba quickly deteriorated. Cuba announced that it was buying crude oil from the Soviet Union. American-owned refineries in Cuba refused to refine the oil, so Castro nationalized the refineries, forcing the Americans out. The Soviet Union also offered Cuba economic and military aid in the form of advisers and weapons. The United States cut the size of the sugar quota. Cuba nationalized hundreds of millions of dollars worth of American businesses and property, and the Soviets agreed to buy Cuba's sugar. In November 1960 the United States imposed economic sanctions on Cuba: no more trade and no more money would flow between the two nations. On January 3, 1961, just two weeks before leaving office, Eisenhower cut remaining diplomatic ties with the island.

OPPOSITION TO CASTRO

As it became apparent that Castro had turned communist and intended to become a close ally of the Soviet Union, the American leadership faced the prospect of its Cold War containment policy being outflanked.* If Cuba, only ninety miles oversea from Florida, became a base for Soviet military power, it would create an enormous security problem for the United States. Cuba could also be used as a base from which to spread Communist revolution throughout Latin America. America had become accustomed to the nations of North and South America being cooperative in the Cold War and did not want to lose that part of its bloc.

The Central Intelligence Agency (CIA) watched in alarm as Castro built up his regular army and organized militia units, supplied with small arms from the Soviet Union. Covert operations to remove Castro and the Communists from power were launched. The CIA had been successful in earlier anticommunist covert operations in other countries. It had funded political parties in Italy to thwart a Communist majority at the polls in 1948 and fomented successful coups in Iran in 1953 and Guatemala in 1954. It had also experienced failures, such as in efforts to support resistance movements in the Soviet Union and Eastern Europe. What the CIA needed, as always, was intelligence and support from indigenous allies.

The Castro group had been only one among many anti-Batista groups, and many of these groups now redirected their opposition toward Castro, whom they saw as even worse than Batista. By the time the CIA became interested, there were already anti-Castro guerrillas in the countryside, and exile groups in Florida had organized against the new Cuban government. The anti-Castro exile groups in the United States were mostly politically, rather than militarily, oriented, each jockeying to become the largest and most powerful so that it would be the one to assume power when Castro was gone.

The CIA persuaded the anti-Castro groups to unify themselves under a single umbrella organization, the Democratic Revolutionary Front. They did so, but it was not a harmonious marriage. Castro's intelligence service, called the G2,

---

* After the Cold War began, the United States developed a strategy of surrounding Communist nations with nations allied to American interests. These nations were invited into military alliances, received economic and military aid, and in some cases had American military forces stationed on their territory. The first nations to receive aid were Turkey and Greece in the late 1940s; they were followed by Western European and Asian nations. The Marshall Plan, which revived the Western European economy with massive amounts of American economic aid, was part of the containment policy.

received training from the Committee for State Security (KGB), and its members proved themselves adept at infiltrating spies into anti-Castro groups, both in Cuba and off the island. The anti-Castro groups' lack of operational security and inability to avoid infiltration by spies frustrated CIA attempts to organize a coup or build up an underground on the island.

Still, the CIA made the effort, training Cuban exiles as guerrillas in camps in southern Florida and the Panama Canal Zone. The plan was to model the Cubans on U.S. Special Forces A-Teams, with five- to nine-member groups infiltrating Cuba by air or sea to set up their own underground operations, bypassing the existing anti-Castro groups and their nests of G2 spies. Training was then consolidated in the high mountains of Guatemala near Retalhuleu, where an airfield was built. The CIA supplied the Cuban exiles with transport aircraft, and exile pilots were trained to drop arms and supplies to the Cuban underground. The Guatemalan Air Force placed some of its own aircraft at the new airfield, pretending that it was its airfield and the Guatemalan Army guarded it. The Cuban pilots practiced making night drops in the mountains of Guatemala in their twin-engined C-46 Commandos and their four-engined C-54 Skymasters. The CIA wanted to use the aircraft because unpredictable weather in the Florida Straits often complicated the normal procedure—using small craft to cross from Florida to Cuba.

Underground teams were successfully sent into Cuba to commit acts of sabotage and to organize subversion. The Cuban exile pilots attempted sixty-eight supply airdrops over the island, of which only three succeeded because of the Cubans' inexperience in night flying. The pilots continued to practice in Guatemala.[2]

The exile air force of transports was supplemented by a squadron of twenty-two B-26 light bombers. The Cuban air force flew the B-26, so some of the exile pilots were already familiar with its operation. The bombers flew out of an airfield near Puerto Cabezas in Nicaragua.*

---

* Two different planes have been designated the B-26, leading to confusion among historians and buffs of military arcana. The first, the B-26 Marauder, was produced by the Glenn L. Martin Company during World War II. Because of early design problems that led to too many crashes, pilots called this airplane the Widowmaker. A redesign made the plane much safer, turning the B-26 into a devastating close-support weapon. The second version, the A-26 Invader, produced by the Douglas Aircraft Company, also fought in World War II. In 1948 the U.S. Air Force changed the designation of the A-26 to the B-26 after the earlier Marauders had been phased out of service.

The underground campaigns in Cuba, executed both by CIA-supported guerrillas and independent groups, yielded some results. One CIA report showed that from October 1960 to April 1961, the seven months leading up to the invasion fiasco, Cuba suffered from

■ 800 sabotage fires, destroying 300,000 tons of sugarcane;
■ 150 other sabotage fires, destroying buildings, including "42 tobacco warehouses, two paper plants, 1 sugar refinery, two dairies, four stores, twenty-one Communist homes";
■ 110 bombings of Communist Party offices, as well as bombings of a Havana power station, a railroad terminal, a bus terminal, and militia barracks;
■ 200 nuisance bombs; and
■ the derailment of six trains and numerous attacks on power transformers.[3]

The attacks were inconveniences that disrupted the Cuban economy, rather than efforts that could lead to Castro's overthrow. The CIA also hatched plots to assassinate Castro but found that more difficult to achieve in real life than it appeared in the movies.

When news reached the CIA that two hundred Cuban aviation cadets were going to Czechoslovakia for training in MiG fighters, the Americans realized that airdrops to the underground could work only until those pilots returned and the Soviet Union delivered their aircraft, expected to be around May 1, 1961. The plan to gradually build up guerrilla forces in Cuba would not work if the MiGs intercepted the airdrops. The idea of turning the Cuban guerrilla fighters into a conventional infantry unit and landing them as an invasion force emerged as a faster solution.

The Assault Brigade 2506 was formed from Cuban exiles trained by U.S. Special Forces. When the first brigade member to die, Carlos Rafael Santana, fell from a high cliff during training, his serial number became the brigade's 2506 designation.[4] José "Pepe" San Román, a former Cuban military officer imprisoned by Batista and released when Castro came to power, commanded the brigade, which was initially fifteen hundred men strong and included soldiers who had fought under Raúl Castro during the revolution. It was supposed to grow to a size of three thousand before the invasion, but recruitment was complicated by some exiles' refusal to serve with soldiers who had earlier served either with

Castro's guerrillas or in Batista's army. The problem was solved by putting different groups of exiles into separate battalions. These units were expected to obtain further recruits after landing in order to reach a full size of five thousand men. The new recruits would come from the Cuban population and from other exiles flown in from Miami.

The brigade's organization reflected the plan for invasion: a paratrooper battalion; three infantry battalions; a heavy-weapons battalion armed with mortars, recoilless rifles, and heavy machine guns; an additional infantry battalion equipped with armored trucks; and a tank company with five new M41 tanks. The tank crews were trained at Fort Knox, Kentucky, where the U.S. Army trained its tank crews, while the other exiles were trained in Guatemala. Initially, each battalion was only the size of a regular company, and the companies were the size of regular platoons; the new recruits, both before and after the landing, would bring the units to full size.[5]

The original plan directed the brigade to invade near the small city of Trinidad on the southern coast of Cuba. The location offered sandy beaches for the invasion craft, a deepwater port, and a nearby airfield. The runway at the airfield needed to be lengthened by three hundred feet to accommodate the B-26 light bombers, a task the exiles were expected to accomplish in a matter of hours with portable steel planks. The 26,000 inhabitants of Trinidad were reported to be anti-Castro in sentiment so the town was expected to provide a fertile source of new recruits. The proposed beachhead was also easily defensible. To the north lay the rugged Escambray mountain range, to the east was the Manatí River as a barrier.[6] Any plausible counterattack would have to be concentrated in a six-mile-wide corridor beyond the river, making the enemy troops vulnerable to air attack. Even better, at the time of the initial planning for the invasion, a guerrilla group was already active in the Escambray Mountains, though Castro's army had destroyed it by the end of March.

Air superiority was the key to the entire plan. Air strikes prior to the invasion by the rebel air force would destroy the small Cuban air force on the ground. Castro's major weapons, in the form of tanks, artillery, and trucks, were mostly parked at Campo Libertad near Havana. Napalm bombs would devastate this equipment. Twenty-one B-26s were to carry out an initial air strike, refuel and rearm at the airfield near Puerto Cabezas, and strike again, landing at the newly captured Trinidad airfield. Flying out of their new location, the aircraft would destroy refineries, power plants, and the fifteen fuel depots that supplied the island, paralyzing Cuba. The planes then would range over the whole island, harassing Castro's forces and encouraging a general collapse of the Communist government. The plan assumed that Castro was hated as much by the general population as by the exiles, and there was substantial evidence that the exiles would garner the necessary popular support. The Roman Catholic Church firmly opposed Castro. The labor unions that were still free of Communist control resisted his rule. And non-CIA-funded guerrillas active in Cuba numbered an estimated five thousand, which implied a much larger number of actual supporters.

The invasion was planned for March 10, 1961, because intelligence sources had revealed that the Soviets were shipping in weapons for Castro's army on March 15. The exiles would establish themselves before the arrival of the Soviet ships and bomb the freighters if they dared to attempt to dock. The invasion plan suffered from having just enough force to do what needed to be done, if everything worked out as hoped, and relied on inexperienced troops. To its advantage, no opposition was expected on the beaches or in Trinidad. A study by the U.S. Joint Chiefs of Staff concluded the plan had "a fair chance of ultimate success," with success defined as sparking a revolt against Castro.[7] Even if everything went wrong, the exiles could retreat into the nearby Escambray Mountains and continue the struggle against Castro as a guerrilla force.

The invasion plan foundered on the transition between U.S. presidential administrations. When a new administration takes power, thousands of jobs change hands, old initiatives are abandoned, new initiatives are created, and only the bureaucrats in the civil service provide continuity. CIA covert operations had gained prominence during the Eisenhower administration; the new administration, composed of politicians and technocrats from the other political party, which had been out of power for eight years, had no current experience with such operations. Though briefed on the invasion plan after the election and before the inauguration, the John F. Kennedy administration did not call an approval meeting until March 11, which was clearly too late, considering the plan's assumptions.

The new leaders in Washington, especially in the State Department, wanted major changes in the plan. They wanted more plausible deniability. The idea of plausible deniability has been around ever since people began to lie, but the term gained currency in the CIA during the 1950s. To effect plausible deniability, when you cause something to happen, you must also create a network of excuses that allow you to argue that you did not cause that something to happen. Plausible deniability is more than the temporary lies used to create operational surprise; it is an attempt to create a lie that will persist for decades. The contradictions intrinsic to plausible deniability destroyed the Cuban operation as it progressed.

The State Department wanted a night landing in order to provide concealment and to make it seem as though it were a clandestine operation that the exiles had developed themselves, rather than a large amphibious landing like those the Americans had perfected during World War II. The diplomats were also worried about civilian casualties in Trinidad, though the invasion planners expected no opposition and one of the major attractions of the site was the anti-Castro Trinidad population. The State Department further asked that the preinvasion strikes by the rebel air force be reduced from twenty-one aircraft to sixteen aircraft because otherwise the air strikes would too closely resemble a conventional operation supported by the Americans, rather than one conducted by the Cuban exiles with their own resources.[8]

The CIA planners scrambled to formulate another plan. They needed to invade southern Cuba because it was farther away from the American coast; they needed an airfield; and they needed a defensible location. The only other qualified location was Bahía de Cochinos, the "Bay of Pigs," ninety miles west of Trinidad and much closer to Castro's center of power in Havana. The airstrip there was long enough for the B-26s, and the Zapata Swamp created a defensive shield for the beachhead. Only three roads, all with easily defendable choke ways, ran through the swamp. As a barrier, the swamp provided protection but also made the area a trap if the operation went poorly and the soldiers wanted to shift to guerrilla tactics. There were no nearby mountains for refuge as there were in Trinidad.

Kennedy approved the revised plan in part because he had no idea what to do with the exile brigade, which had already been trained. He had campaigned against Richard Nixon, Eisenhower's vice president, on many issues, including the Eisenhower administration's failure to contain Castro. On entering office, Kennedy found that he had been wrong about Eisenhower's level of effort on Cuban issues, but he had already made a reckless campaign promise to do more about Cuba. If Brigade 2506 was disbanded, its members could return to the United States and might embarrass the new administration by complaining that Kennedy lacked commitment to his campaign promises. Clearly Kennedy and his aides were not thinking through the implications of their decisions. In the absence of deeper thought, the politician will fall back on the politically prudent course of action. It is just human nature: when faced with a novel situation, and if we fail to engage in innovative critical thinking, we will do whatever we have always done, relying on mental habit rather than critical thinking. Critical thinking is hard.

Two CIA officers would accompany the exile invasion. Grayston L. Lynch had fought in World War II, including during the landing at Omaha Beach, and in the Korean conflict. He had been wounded three times and earned a raft of awards, including two Silver Stars and a Bronze Star with a V for valor. His last Army assignment had been leading a Special Forces A-Team in Laos, training anticommunist forces to support the Laotian government against a Communist insurgency. During that assignment, the Special Forces soldiers traveled to Laos in civilian clothes and worked closely with CIA operatives. Lynch impressed the CIA in Laos, and in January 1961, when he retired from the Army after twenty-one years, the CIA recruited him to be an officer in the paramilitary section. Only days later, he was busy teaching demolition techniques to a small group of Cuban exiles in Florida who had already trained as frogmen. The other CIA officer to accompany the exiles was William Robertson, another veteran with extensive CIA experience, including success in the Guatemalan coup of 1954.

With the invasion approved by Kennedy, the two CIA officers were ordered aboard two landing ships infantry (LSIs) in Key West, Florida. The *Blagar* and the *Barbara J* were built during World War II. Each was 158 feet long, designed to carry up to two hundred troops, and had a ramp on either side of the bow used to off-load the troops when the ships ran themselves up onto the beach. The officers of the two ships were civilian American sailors on loan from the Navy's Military Sea Transportation Service, though the civilian crew members were not Navy employees.*

Loaded with weapons, ammunition, and supplies for fifteen hundred men, the two ships sailed to Puerto Cabezas. The Guardia Nacional, which kept Nica-

---

* Multiple sources refer to the *Blagar* and the *Barbara J* as landing craft infantry (LCI), which is what these ships were called during World War II. In 1949 the Navy renamed the LCI class of ships landing ship infantry (LSI), which made more sense. The smaller landing craft with a bow ramp that most people are familiar with from movies is called a landing craft utility (LCU).

ragua's dictator in power, sealed off the area, closed down communications, and detained the few people thought to be Castro sympathizers. Operational security was so tight that the two CIA officers were informed of the site of the invasion only two weeks before the operation, and the upper levels of the government were not informed that two CIA officers were going along.

Four more ships arrived at Puerto Cabezas: the *Río Escondido*, the *Houston*, the *Caribe*, and the *Atlántico*. These ships had all been leased from an anti-Castro Cuban and were manned completely by Cuban crews. Laden with ammunition, fuel, and supplies, the six ships slipped out of the harbor carrying the men of the brigade, with the exception of the parachute battalion. Each ship took a separate route during the two-day voyage. The soldiers slept on the crowded decks.

While the men of the brigade were confident, the success of their operation had already been compromised by decisions in Washington. In the pursuit of plausible deniability, the number of planned air strikes had been cut down to only two from the initial five, and the number of attacking exile aircraft was cut to only eight of the planned sixteen on each strike. In sum, a total of eighty sorties was reduced to only sixteen. Napalm bombs were also forbidden, on the assumption that such ordinance could be obtained only from the U.S. government and its use would implicate the Americans.[9] An aide to Kennedy persuaded the president to announce on April 10 that under no circumstances would American armed forces be committed to Cuba. Such a prior promise tied the president's hands. Kennedy apparently did not realize that a failed invasion was the worst possible outcome, as it would throw the illusion of plausible deniability out the window.

THE INVASION

On the morning of Saturday, April 15, 1961, eight B-26s of the exile air force, painted with Cuban air force markings to give them an aura of plausible deniability, struck three Cuban airfields. Insufficient damage resulted, though some aircraft were destroyed and some men were killed. The following day, at a graveside service in a Havana cemetery, Castro gave one of his fiery speeches. For the first time, he referred to the revolution in Cuba as "socialist." The time for Castro to hide behind words of sophistry had passed.[10]

The State Department announced its cover story: defecting pilots had made the bombing runs while fleeing the island in their aircraft. To support this story, one Cuban exile B-26 pilot flew to Key West and proclaimed that he was a defector who had bombed the Cubans as he fled. The diplomats expected people to believe this bizarre story or at least credit it enough to be confused about what to believe. Credibility suffered because the exile aircraft was a variant with eight machine guns in its nose, not the type owned by Cuba, which had Plexiglas noses and six machine guns in the wings.

At the United Nations, Cuba accused the United States of being behind the air attacks. The United Nations ambassador for the United States, Adlai Stevenson, was not aware of the CIA plot and denied American responsibility. Stevenson was a prestigious figure in American politics, having been the Democratic candidate for president in 1952 and 1956 but defeated by Eisenhower in both elections. When he learned that the Kennedy administration had not kept him correctly informed, he was livid. After the fiasco, some administration officials maintained that Stevenson had insisted at that point that no more air strikes be made, but this is not possible because Stevenson had no idea that another air strike had been scheduled. Still, in the confusion, Kennedy was told that Stevenson would resign, embarrassing the administration, if there were any more air strikes. On this purely political consideration, Kennedy decided to cancel the single follow-up air strike that had been planned. It is unclear whether Kennedy had completely familiarized himself with the assumptions of the invasion plan and how important the air strikes were.

Castro, remembering what had happened to the socialist Guatemalan government in 1954, had already suspected an invasion might happen. Besides his small regular army, which he called the Rebel Army, he had organized a large militia of over two hundred thousand partially trained men. The substantial Soviet shipment of arms had just arrived: 125 tanks, including T-34, JS-3, and JS-4 models; 167,000 rifles; and 7,250 machine guns, along with other weapons and ammunition.[11] Castro's air force, inherited from Batista, was fairly small: seventeen B-26 light bombers; thirteen Sea Fury propeller-driven fighters, each armed with four 20 mm cannons; five T-33 jet fighters; a single F-51 Mustang propeller-driven fighter; and some unarmed transport aircraft. The CIA estimated that only half of these aircraft were operational, owing to poor maintenance and the shortage of parts for American- and British-made aircraft.

On Sunday evening, a U.S. Navy landing ship dock (LSD) rendezvoused with the exile ships at sea and off-loaded the seven LCUs that the Cuban exiles would use. The exile ships also carried numerous smaller landing boats, useful for landing troops and smaller supplies, while the larger landing craft carried the tanks and trucks. Two American destroyers, their bow numbers painted over, also loitered on the horizon. Farther to the south cruised an American task force with the aircraft carriers *Essex* and *Boxer* and two battalions of Marines.

The exile naval force moved into the bay, heading for two invasion beaches. Red Beach was located at the top of the bay, near the small resort town of Playa Larga. Twenty miles away, Blue Beach, at the mouth of the Bay of Pigs, was located near the airfield and another small resort town called Playa Girón. A Green Beach was also selected farther to the east.

Leading the way to Blue Beach, CIA officer Lynch went in with his frogmen in a rubber raft under cover of darkness. A couple of militiamen in a jeep detected their approach, and Lynch opened fire with his Browning Automatic Rifle. The frogmen joined in with their own weapons, and they stopped the jeep, killing one of the militiamen. Trucks carrying more militiamen moved toward the beach but withdrew in the face of machine-gun and recoilless-rifle fire from the deck of the nearby command ship, the LSI *Blagar*. With the beach cleared, the landing of other troops commenced on Blue Beach. A night landing had actually succeeded.

Lynch went back to the command ship and received a radio message from the CIA that the Cuban air force had not been destroyed. The exile ships could expect an air attack in the morning, so they needed to off-load all the men and ammunition as quickly as possible. The landing at Green Beach was cancelled, and the men assigned to that beach were put ashore at Blue Beach instead. In the rush, two of the landing craft scraped holes in their hulls on coral reefs and eventually had to be abandoned.

By morning, all but one battalion had been successfully landed, the airfield captured, and Playa Girón occupied. A successful paratroop drop by part of the First Battalion north of Blue Beach captured the small village of San Blas, which allowed the exiles to block one of the three roads that led through the Zapata Swamp.

Castro was awakened in Havana and told about the landings. He sent troops to the area, though he was worried that this attack might be a diversion. CIA operatives had put on an offshore light show with noise at another coastal location to encourage this confusion. (Twice during the next three days Castro was distracted by false reports of other landings.) Castro also ordered his air force to attack when morning came. The Cuban air force took off twenty minutes before first light and proved to be the decisive factor in the battle.[12]

Later analysis by the CIA, based on aerial photography and intercepted radio communications, showed that Castro's air force flew only seven aircraft during the entire invasion. Two B-26 light bombers, two Sea Fury fighters, and three T-33 fighters made all the difference. The CIA concluded that if Kennedy had allowed the full air strikes to occur, both in size and frequency, these seven aircraft would have certainly been destroyed because the Cuban government had no effective antiaircraft warning system to prevent their planes from being caught on the ground.[13]

Lynch had earlier insisted on beefing up the *Blagar*'s antiaircraft protection, bringing it up to twelve or sixteen .50-caliber machine guns (reports differ on the numbers), not because he expected to have to fight off Castro's air force, but because he believed that having extra firepower was always useful. When Monday morning came, Castro's air force appeared, but sustained antiaircraft fire from the *Blagar* and the other three ships off Blue Beach drove off repeated attacks.

The exiles claimed to have shot down a Sea Fury. The exile forces also reported many other Cuban airplanes lost to antiaircraft fire during the battle, but the numbers do not match the CIA estimates of how many planes Castro's air force actually flew. Evaluating claims of kills by antiaircraft fire is difficult, because excited and enthusiastic gunners often believe that they have shot down many more planes than they actually have. Even so, the number of Cuban B-26 aircraft reported shot down was so much higher than the CIA estimate of only two B-26s even engaged that the CIA estimate is probably flawed.

The *Río Escondido* off-loaded the troops of the Sixth Battalion on Blue Beach at dawn on April 17. Just after all the troops had landed, a Sea Fury dived at the ship. The aircraft fired four rockets, three of which missed, but the fourth hit a stack of fifty-five-gallon drums filled with gasoline on the deck. The fire spread rapidly. In the hold were twenty tons of ammunition. The crew jumped off the burning ship, and small boats from the other ships quickly raced in to pick the men up.

The *Río Escondido* exploded, generating a mushroom-shaped cloud that spread more than a mile wide in the air high above. In its own twisted way, perhaps fate was forecasting the future, comparing conventional explosives to nuclear weapons. Robertson, the CIA officer at Red Beach, sixteen miles away, heard the explosion and saw the cloud. He frantically radioed Lynch, afraid that the Cubans had used an atomic bomb. Of course, much to Castro's regret, he possessed no atomic weapons.

Half of the invasion force's ammunition was gone, and the rest of it was still aboard the *Caribe* and the *Atlántico*. Washington had been radioing Lynch with suggestions and orders that he withdraw the ships until night fell again and promised, if he withdrew his ships back to outside the twelve-mile territorial water limit, the American naval task force would protect them. Under American air cover, he could have the rest of the ammunition transferred to the three landing craft for a run back into the beach when night returned.

One of the ships from the landing at Red Beach joined the three remaining ships at Blue Beach, and all four ships withdrew, under air attack by the Cubans the whole way. The ships claimed to have shot down one Cuban B-26. A 20 mm cannon shell from a Sea Fury embedded itself in a case of explosives on the *Barbara J*, but fortunately it was an armor-piercing round that failed to arm itself and did not explode. When the ships reached the twelve-mile limit, Lynch called the U.S. Navy for support. The American captain of a nearby warship expressed his heartfelt regrets, but his orders were not to "become engaged in any way." Lynch angrily asked if the captain could pick up survivors after the exile ships were sunk—or was that becoming too engaged?[14]

The two merchant freighters, the *Caribe* and the *Atlántico*, were manned by civilian crews hired for the voyage, not exile activists, and decided to put on steam and move as far away from Castro's airplanes as possible. The two freighters quickly pulled away from the other ships and each other because of their superior speed. The two LSIs and their three landing craft, which stayed to fight, eventually received American naval air protection at 3:30 in the afternoon. While the landing at Blue Beach had not gone according to plan, the other part of the invasion, at Red Beach, had also experienced problems.

RED BEACH

Now we return to the story of Francisco Hernández as he splashed ashore that morning on Red Beach as part of the Second Battalion. At twenty-one years old, he had supported Castro's revolution. But the impact of the revolution hit Hernández's family only after Castro came to power, when his father, who had retired from the Cuban army as a lieutenant colonel and had not been one of

Batista's political spawn, was arrested for refusing to testify against another army officer. After a four-hour trial, his father was convicted and executed. Amid further revolutionary bloodletting, Hernández joined an exile group that sent him to the CIA to be trained as a guerrilla.

The LSI *Barbara J* successfully landed Hernández's Second Battalion at Red Beach at the top of the bay. The commander of the Fifth Battalion, however, complicated the mission by refusing to off-load his troops from the *Houston* until he was sure that Castro's troops did not have artillery. This battalion was composed mostly of former Cuban army members who had served under Batista. When daylight came, the *Houston*, with its battalion still aboard, and the *Barbara J* raced south but did not make it far before Castro's B-26 light bombers arrived overhead. One airplane was reported shot down, but the others shot up the *Houston* with machine guns and rockets. One rocket blew a hole in the bottom of the freighter, and the ship's captain rammed the *Houston* onto a sandbar near the shore to prevent his ship from sinking. The B-26s dropped bombs near the *Barbara J*, springing its hull plates, and it began to take on more water than its pumps could handle. It was forced to leave the stricken *Houston* in order to reach the other four ships off Blue Beach, where it could obtain more pumps. The *Barbara J* then fled out to sea with the rest of the small fleet.

The troops of the Fifth Battalion on the *Houston* managed to get ashore despite strafing runs by Castro's light bombers. Once ashore, they received orders to march six miles north to return to where they were supposed to land originally. The exile soldiers set off, ran into a machine gun manned by only six Cuban soldiers, and retreated. The battalion commander had completely lost his nerve.

The exile air force's transport aircraft were scheduled to make a paratroop drop at first light. While the drop mission near Blue Beach was successful, the two aircraft that were supposed to drop about forty men north of Red Beach ran into trouble. Upon sighting a Cuban B-26, the transport pilots turned away, then tried to return to their drop zones from a different direction. The ground points they had memorized to guide them were not the same on the new approach path, so they dropped the paratroopers in the wrong places, scattering them and their heavy weapon containers. For most of the battle, the paratroopers fought as small groups or as individuals, unable to fulfill their assignment of helping to block the road to the north. The commander of the paratroopers was a real fighter; isolated from his men, he used all his ammunition, went into hiding, and made his way to Havana, where a friendly embassy spirited him back to the United States. He returned to Cuba in 1962 on a sabotage mission and disappeared during the Fire that year.[15]

Fortunately, Hernández and the men of the Second Battalion had already moved inland from Red Beach and had taken positions alongside the road that ran between swamps. The Castro government called the local defense area the Zapata Zone. Eighteen miles north of Red Beach was a thousand-man battalion of Cuban militia stationed at a large sugar mill complex with the odd name of Central Australia. On Monday morning, the Cuban battalion quickly moved south in trucks, running into an ambush set by the exiles of the Second Battalion. The survivors limped away. That Monday afternoon, another Cuban battalion charged down the road. By now the exiles had two of their M41 tanks in support. The government militia troops attacked and were slaughtered; by some accounts more than 900 of the 968 men died.

As the government militia fell back in disarray, two exile B-26s arrived and strafed them. The exiles were thrilled to see that they had air support. The entire plan hinged on air support making up for their limited numbers. As they watched, a Cuban government T-33 jet arrived. The T-33 was an American training jet, armed with a pair of .50-caliber machine guns and sold to Batista's Cuba and numerous other countries around the world as an inexpensive, easy-to-fly jet fighter. This T-33 shot down one B-26 and damaged the other one severely enough that it was trailing smoke as it tried to make the three-and-a-half-hour flight back to Nicaragua. Hours later the second B-26 disappeared after radioing a message that it was going into the sea.[16]

Another government force tried to push its way down the road toward Red Beach and was again repulsed with heavy casualties. The government military leaders were not showing any tactical imagination, perhaps believing that dogged determination would be sufficient. Prisoners captured during this battle told the exiles that the Cuban military was planning a night attack. After the Second Battalion received reinforcements from the troops at Blue Beach and a third M41 tank, the exiles prudently withdrew near the village of Playa Larga and dug trenches and foxholes before night fell.

The government began its push with an artillery barrage, dropping hundreds of rounds from 122 mm howitzers on the entire area. Though few casualties resulted from the artillery fire, the exiles huddled in their foxholes, terrified that the next shell would find them and take their lives. As the barrage subsided, the government launched its main attack with Soviet-supplied tanks leading the way and infantry following. The exile M41 tanks and bazookas took care of these T-34 and JS-3 tanks, surplus from World War II, by hitting them in the sides. Soon six government tanks had been knocked out. The government forces then launched a large-scale infantry attack. This was beaten back. The government later lost two more tanks that had apparently stumbled into the exile lines. Such are the random chances of nighttime fighting.

The Second Battalion and its reinforcements, a force of almost four hundred men, had defeated a force of two thousand men in the series of night attacks. Now the exiles at Red Beach, exhausted from twenty-four hours of almost continuous action, faced a serious ammunition shortage. They were ordered to abandon the effort at Red Beach and withdraw to Blue Beach. Leaving behind two hundred prisoners, trucks successfully conveyed them to their new positions at Playa Girón.

BECOMING A FIASCO

On Monday night, six B-26s of the exile air force launched a strike on the Cuban airfields, only to be thwarted by ground haze and blackout conditions below. The luck that a marginal military operation needed in order to succeed was deserting them. Fate had begun to frown.

The *Blagar* and *Barbara J* spent Monday night searching for the two fleeing freighters loaded with the exiles' ammunition. The crew of the sunken *Río Escondido*, now aboard the *Blagar*, attempted a mutiny rather than have the *Blagar* return to the battle in Cuba. The mutiny was quickly put down. The U.S. Navy joined the search and located both of the wayward ships: the *Atlántico* was one hundred miles out from Cuba, and the *Caribe* was two hundred miles out. The latter freighter heaved to only when an American destroyer fired a shot across its bow. Both were instructed to return to the battle.

The plan to return with ammunition had failed, as the *Atlántico* and the *Caribe* had gone too far to make it back to the island in a timely manner. The besieged exiles were running short of the supplies that they had initially carried ashore. On Monday night, two transports dropped ammunition by parachute. On Tuesday morning, an exile C-46 transport landed at the captured airfield and off-loaded 850 pounds of cargo, mostly ammunition. The transport was also supposed to evacuate the wounded, but the wounded were not at the airfield because the airplane had been delayed. Rather than waiting they had gone back into Playa Girón. The C-46 left with only an exile B-26 pilot, who had earlier survived a plane crash by being thrown clear.

All day Tuesday, April 18, the *Blagar*, the *Barbara J*, and the three landing craft waited for the freighters' return while the exiles fought to maintain the beachhead. In the evening, the *Atlántico* showed up, and the exhausted crews loaded the landing craft with ammunition. When night came, the *Blagar* headed toward Cuba, shepherding the three landing craft. The *Barbara J* remained behind to meet with the other returning freighter. Heavily laden with ammunition, the landing craft could make only six knots, forcing Lynch to realize that they would arrive with only one hour of darkness left—not enough time to unload and retreat back out to sea. They needed air cover.

Lynch radioed Washington to say, if "jet cover is not furnished beginning at first light, expect to lose all ships." His goal was to force Washington to provide air cover. Instead, he was ordered to turn around and head back out to sea.[17]

As the invasion unraveled, Kennedy searched for alternatives. The U.S. military argued for intervention. Air strikes were suggested and rejected because the American government could not deny involvement in the invasion if its aircraft flew over Cuba. Gunfire support from the American destroyers was considered and rejected. Simply flying air cover was also rejected. Sending in the two battalions of Marines was not even considered in light of the other rejections. In the end, Kennedy decided not to dig a bigger hole for his administration, but the men on the ground were not aware of this betrayal. "Betrayal" is a harsh word, and plenty of administration defenders would object to it, arguing that the Cuban exiles had no right to expect more support than what had been promised. The reality is that, in the glare of sunlight, the defenders of plausible deniability clung to their illusions, telling themselves that they owed nothing to the men of Brigade 2506. The CIA had created Brigade 2506, and when it got into trouble, a bewildered Kennedy stood aside.

Since Monday afternoon, the exile paratroopers at San Blas had come under pressure from militia forces pushing down from the north toward Blue Beach. The Third Battalion defended the third road into the area, which ran along the coast from the east, and on Monday afternoon, they had also come under fire. On Tuesday, the government forces closed in on Blue Beach, pushing back the defenders on all three roads with artillery fire.

On Tuesday evening, six exile B-26s caught a large convoy of government forces moving down the road from Playa Larga toward Blue Beach. They roved back and forth, exhausting their ammunition loads. Some reports put the Cuban casualties at eighteen hundred men and seven tanks.[18] Three of the pilots were Americans, CIA instructors who had stepped in to relieve their exhausted students. The flight from Puerto Cabezas to Cuba and back lasted seven hours, excluding the time spent over the target. The flight time and the preflight and postflight activities combined to make for long days, especially when pilots flew two sorties a day. Some exile pilots had refused to continue making sorties, terrified of flying over the beach without fighter cover.

Kennedy finally agreed to a big aerial push on the morning of Wednesday, April 19. The exile air force would fly their B-26s from Puerto Cabezas while the U.S. Navy provided fighter cover. The CIA officer who wrote the order confused the time zones so that the B-26s arrived an hour before the Navy fighters. The exile air force had been so depleted by losses and mechanical breakdowns that only four aircraft could be launched. One was forced back by engine trouble. Castro's T-33 jets jumped the three remaining B-26s, shooting down two of them and sending the other home riddled with thirty-eight bullet holes. The two unlucky B-26s were each piloted by a pair of Americans. One crash-landed, killing one pilot, while the other pilot came out with his pistol blazing and died under the guns of the militia. The other two pilots crashed into the ocean, were captured by Castro's militia, and were each executed by a single bullet in the forehead.

Castro's Prensa Latina, the state-controlled news agency, sent out a picture of the two dead airmen, claiming that they had died in the crash and demonstrating that Americans had been part of the invasion effort. The photographs showed the men with their life jackets inflated and their boots off. The Cubans realized their mistake and took a second picture with the life vests deflated. The CIA obtained both pictures, and newspapers friendly to the United States published both and explained the Cuban deception: pilots who are alive after a water landing remove their boots and inflate their life jackets.[19]

All day Wednesday, the government troops applied pressure to the exile forces defending the Blue Beach area. The *Caribe* returned with its ammunition, rendezvousing with the other exile ships outside the twelve-mile limit, and the exile ships prepared to make a night run in with fresh ammunition. At noon on Wednesday, Lynch received word that the American government had decided to abandon the invasion. That night the Americans would come in, using Marine landing craft to evacuate the exile soldiers. Two destroyers were authorized to open fire if necessary. Plausible deniability had finally collapsed, and the American government was willing to enter the fight, if only to facilitate a withdrawal.

At two in the afternoon, Cuban tanks broke through the defense perimeter and began to overrun the exile troops. The exiles had run out of ammunition. Breaking into small groups, they tried to make their escape into the surrounding Zapata Swamp, leaving their dead behind. At least the dead had fallen in their homeland.

Two days later, the U.S. Navy entered the Bay of Pigs in force and spent three days searching for exile survivors. They especially concentrated on finding men from the Fifth Battalion who had survived the *Houston*'s forced beaching, since these men were located across the bay from Blue Beach, where the final battle had been fought. Destroyers cruised the bay, Navy aircraft flew in air support, and landing craft and smaller boats scoured the beaches and nearby swamp. The two CIA officers and their remaining frogmen helped in the search. Dozens of survivors were recovered. Patrol boats from Cuba's navy watched from a distance, and U.S. Navy fighters chased off a flight of two Cuban Sea Furies. Had this level of American effort been expended during the invasion, the beachhead would certainly have been maintained.

Just two pairs of jet fighters from the nearby American aircraft carriers flying combat air patrol over the exile beachheads in rotation would have completely driven Castro's air force from the sky, allowing the exile air force to relocate to the captured airfield as planned and deal devastation on the enemy. The exiles had landed enough fuel and ammunition to refuel and rearm the exile B-26s at the captured airfield, but while Castro's fighters dominated the sky, the exile pilots did not dare try to use the airfield. This fuel and ammunition could have easily changed the entire course of the battle, especially if deployed from the beginning. Of course, sending American fighters on sorties over the Zapata beachhead would have violated the hallowed principle of plausible deniability.

AFTERMATH

On April 20, 1961, Castro gave a four-hour televised victory speech. Six days later he appeared in another four-hour television event with more than a thousand of the exile prisoners from the invasion. He said to them, "To execute you, which all our people would agree with, would only shrink our great victory."[20]

Of the 1,474 men in the brigade, 141 died and 1,189 were captured. A few of the prisoners were tried and executed, but most were sentenced to long prison terms for treason. Castro never published accurate loss figures for his forces, but estimates range from fifteen hundred to five thousand dead. While the government had won, their straight-ahead tactics had cost them numerous casualties.

Castro's secret police arrested tens of thousands of Cubans during the invasion and afterward, tightening his grip on the island. He was desperately afraid of another invasion, not by exiles, but by American troops. Looking at his casualties against those of Brigade 2506, he knew that he did not stand a chance against a determined American military effort. As a consequence, he urged the Soviet Union to accelerate its support for the Cuban Revolution. Khrushchev had already sent a letter to Kennedy: "There should be no misunderstanding our position. We shall render the Cuban people and their government all necessary assistance in beating back armed attack on Cuba."[21]

Many historians have used the term "fiasco" to describe the Bay of Pigs invasion. CIA officer Lynch rejected the word; it was a tragedy to him, and this veteran of American wars was ashamed of his country.[22] For the men of Brigade 2506, it was a tragedy; for the people of Cuba, it was a tragedy; and for the hundreds of millions dead from the Fire, it was a tragedy. For the American government, it was a fiasco characterized by poor decision making on all levels, by a failure to think through the consequences of different outcomes, by a strategy hampered by the failure to ascertain the facts, and by a lack of centralized command. In the end, the American government was blinded by the false promises of plausible deniability.

In an address to American newspaper publishers on April 27, Kennedy said, "This administration intends to be candid about its errors. For a wise man once said, 'An error does not become a mistake until you refuse to correct it.' We intend to accept full responsibility for our errors. . . . We're not going to have any search for scapegoats. . . . The final responsibilities of any failure are mine, and mine alone." Kennedy had finally found some backbone, though in all fairness many members of his administration had also made serious mistakes in the advice that they gave their president.

Kennedy commissioned the Cuba Study Group to learn from the mistakes of the debacle. It concluded, "A paramilitary operation of the magnitude of Zapata should not be prepared or conducted in such a way that all US support of it and connection with it could be plausibly denied."[23] The use of the word "should" instead of "could" showed that the American government had not learned its lesson about the uselessness of plausible deniability. The study group also failed to explicitly state the obvious conclusion: the key mistake occurred when the president limited the preinvasion air strikes. Kennedy was not willing to be his own scapegoat.

To his credit, Kennedy was willing to negotiate for the release of the exile prisoners through private channels. Castro proved receptive. The only question was how much it would cost—perhaps up to fifty million dollars in food and medicine. The negotiations had not concluded by the time the Fire came the following year.

The study group also had another effect. Gen. Maxwell Taylor, commander of the 101st Airborne Division during World War II and U.S. Army chief of staff from 1955 until his retirement in 1959, was invited to serve on the group. Taylor shared with Kennedy his belief in flexible response, as opposed to massive retaliation, in the event of a nuclear war. His work on the study group so impressed the president and his brother, Robert F. Kennedy, that in July 1961, the president created the position of military representative of the president for Taylor. This allowed Kennedy to hear military advice from a person he trusted, rather than from the Joint Chiefs. On October 1, 1962, just before the Cuban Missile Crisis, Taylor became chairman of the Joint Chiefs of Staff.

While the Bay of Pigs invasion was a long shot, the Trinidad plan had merit. What if the exile air strikes had not been limited by the illusions of plausible deniability and had destroyed Castro's air force on the ground? What if the exile invasion had succeeded, whether at Trinidad or at the Bay of Pigs? Such counterfactual questions illuminate our understanding of history. They show that history is not set in stone, but contingent on the decisions of real people doing the best they can with limited understanding and abilities. If different decisions had been made, if the winds of fate had blown in the right direction and the exiles had succeeded, then perhaps hundreds of millions of people would not have died in the Fire.

But it was not to be. Francisco Hernández and his fellow exiles had failed, and now the winds of fate brewed up a hurricane.

Further sources: Leycester Coltman, *The Real Fidel Castro* (New Haven: Yale University Press, 2003); Haynes Johnson, *The Bay of Pigs: The Leaders' Story of Brigade 2506*, with Manuel Artime and others (New York: Norton, 1964); Peter Kornbluh, ed., *Bay of Pigs Declassified: The Secret CIA Report on the Invasion of Cuba* (New York: New Press, 1998); Grayston L. Lynch, *Decision for Disaster: Betrayal at the Bay of Pigs* (Washington, D.C.: Brassey's, Inc., 1998), a delightful book with a strong point of view; and Victor Andres Triay, *Bay of Pigs: An Oral History of Brigade 2506* (Gainesville: University Press of Florida, 2001).

1

Making Tools: Mushroom Clouds and Dreams of Space

Numerous writers, drawn to this terrifying spectacle like moths to a flame, have described the first atomic bomb explosion. Fifteen seconds before 5:30 in the morning of July 16, 1945, a new era was born when a five-foot sphere containing fifty–three hundred pounds of high explosives compressed fifteen pounds of radioactive plutonium to create a nuclear chain reaction and a massive fireball at the Trinity Test Site in the New Mexico desert. Albert Einstein's famous equation, $E = mc^2$, had been proved correct: a small amount of matter could be converted into an enormous amount of energy. The bomb's explosive power was equal to twenty thousand tons of the conventional explosive TNT; hence the reaction was referred to as a twenty-kiloton explosion. The mushroom cloud—the classic signature of a nuclear explosion—reached 7.5 miles into the atmosphere, and the shock wave was felt over 100 miles away.

Fifteen Nobel laureates worked on the Manhattan Project, which was directed by the physicist J. Robert Oppenheimer, making it perhaps the single project in human history with the greatest concentration of brainpower. The idea of using nuclear fission in a chain reaction to make a bomb had not even been broached until 1938, and only the United States had the resources to devote to realizing what seemed to be a fantasy. After spending $2 billion, the United States succeeded, using scientists and engineers from America, Great Britain, and other countries in Europe.

In addition to the test bomb, two other atom bombs had been built. The components for Little Boy, the atomic bomb intended for Hiroshima, had already been shipped out of Los Alamos and would be placed aboard the heavy cruiser USS *Indianapolis* for a secret voyage to Tinian. B-29 bomber crews had trained at Wendover, on the Utah-Nevada border, for this specific mission. Built from a design different from that of the test bomb, the Little Boy used the iso-tope uranium-235, rather than plutonium. The third bomb, Fat Man, was made with plutonium and was used on Nagasaki.

The Manhattan Project was not only an American success. One of the physi-cists working on the project, Klaus Fuchs, had been born in Germany. He had fled his homeland when the Nazis came to power and settled in Britain before traveling with British scientists to Los Alamos, where he made important con-tributions to the success of the effort. Fuchs had Communist sympathies, and during the war, he began transmitting Allied military intelligence to the Soviets as a spy. George Koval, a Soviet intelligence officer, also managed to infiltrate the Manhattan Project. He had been born in Iowa, moved to the Soviet Union with his parents as a youth, and was raised in Siberia, before being recruited by Soviet military intelligence. Trained as a spy, Koval was sent back to the United States and had considerable success in collecting intelligence from 1940 to 1948, including working in the atomic bomb manufacturing facilities at Oak Ridge, Tennessee.[1] Fuchs and Koval were not the only Soviet spies who either penetrated the Manhattan Project or loitered at its fringes, but both passed key information that helped the Soviets explode their own atomic bomb in August 1949.

That the Americans decided to build an atomic bomb while in the midst of a world war was only prudent. They had to make sure that they had such a weapon in case one of their enemies also acquired it, but the moral decision to use the bomb requires a longer inquiry.

JUSTIFYING HIROSHIMA AND NAGASAKI

On February 13, 1945, almost eight hundred British Lancaster bombers hit one of the few remaining entries on their list of sixty German cities slated for area bombing, Dresden. The Royal Air Force often tried to create a firestorm that would consume the heart of the city on these bombing assignments but had suc-ceeded only once before, at Hamburg in 1943. On February 14, three hundred American B-17 bombers added to the misery begun by the British the night be-fore, and the firestorm at Dresden consumed tens of thousands of civilians, many of them refugees from the Soviet armies to the east. This firebombing has gone down in history as an act that skirted the edge of being defined as a war crime. Even before the bombing of Dresden began, U.S. Lt. Gen. Jimmy Doolittle protested that it would amount to terrorism.[2] How had military and political leaders decided that deliberately bombing civilians was justified?

World War I introduced the airplane as a weapon of war. While aircraft had not been decisive in that conflict, airpower advocates in the interwar period argued that they would be decisive in future wars, and as such they deserved proper funding and a separate service branch of their own, equal to the army and navy. In Great Britain, the Royal Air Force was established even before the end of World War I. Hugh Trenchard, the first British chief of the Air Staff, argued in 1928 that bomber fleets "can pass over the enemy navies and armies, and penetrate the air defenses and directly attack the centres of production, transportation and communication from which the enemy effort is maintained."[3] Other prophets of airpower included Italian Gen. Giulio Douhet and Maj. Gen. Billy Mitchell, an American. These theorists believed that bombers flying in formation and bristling with machine guns could defend themselves against fighter aircraft, enter enemy airspace, and destroy the enemy's ability to continue the war. Armies and navies became subordinate branches of the military in the minds of strategic bombing advocates.

So firmly did Trenchard believe in the bomber that he neglected the development and production of fighters, arguing that only British bombers could protect the island nation by destroying the enemy first. We see the beginnings here of what later became the doctrine of mutual assured destruction (MAD) during the post–World War II era of nuclear arms.

The moral problems of airpower were apparent early on. Warfare has always been hard on civilians in the vicinity of combat, but a moral belief had grown in Western civilization that killing civilians was wrong. Civilian casualties during World War I were about 5 million, compared to 10 million combatant dead.* But with the rise of mass conscript armies and the industrialized societies to sustain them, strategic bombing advocates argued that all citizens of a country could now be considered combatants. The soldiers on the front actually fought, but the factory workers built the tanks, guns, and ammunition that equipped them,

---

* Over half the civilian casualties came from the Russian civil war and the Armenian genocide in Turkey.

and the farmers grew the food that fed the factory workers and the soldiers. All elements of industrialized warfare had to work together for a country to make war, and thus all elements were legitimate targets. This shift in thinking was not widely accepted. Before World War II, the American government issued a statement that it "strongly opposed the sale of airplanes and aeronautical equipment" to any nation that deliberately bombed civilians from the air, a sentiment common to many governments of the period.[4]

The 1936 movie *Things to Come*, based on the H. G. Wells novel *The Shape of Things to Come* (1933), prophesied a future in which airpower ruled supreme. Bombers destroy cities and civilization in Europe collapses, to be rebuilt by noble pilots from the sky and their fearsome aircraft. Eventually civilization advances to the point that space travel is possible. The movie drew heavily on the theories of the strategic bombing advocates.

As World War II loomed, British politicians and the British public learned to fear the coming of enemy bomber fleets to lay waste to their country. A similar phenomenon occurred in France. Ironically, Hermann Göring built the German Luftwaffe, soon to become the possible fulfillment of British and French fears, with a heavy emphasis on the tactical ability to provide close support to the German army, not on strategic bombing. All sides believed that precision bombing of factories and transportation facilities would be unnecessary; a few attacks on cities would crack the morale of the civilian population, and the people would surrender.

After World War II started, the British slowly began to use their bomber force. When President Franklin Roosevelt called on all belligerents to avoid bombing civilians, the British, French, and German governments agreed. Initial attacks were carefully planned to avoid hitting civilians, partially out of moral qualms and partially because the British feared that if they started bombing German civilians, the Luftwaffe would retaliate by bombing British civilians.[5] As the war progressed, British airmen learned to their surprise that their bombers were not flying fortresses, but quite vulnerable to German fighters. If they flew too low, German antiaircraft defenses also took their toll. Furthermore, precision bombing remained a fantasy, especially if the bombers flew high enough to avoid the antiaircraft flak.

When the Germans bombed Rotterdam in May 1940, killing perhaps a thousand Dutch citizens, initial newspaper reports claimed thirty thousand dead, confirming the worst fears that people had. The British began bombing German factories with mixed success, losing too many bombers and failing to hit the targets. In August 1940 the Germans launched the Battle of Britain, an attempt to use airpower to force the British into submission. Failing that, the Germans hoped to suppress the Royal Air Force long enough to allow a cross-channel invasion. This was the purest test of the prewar bombing theories. At first the Germans concentrated on airfields and aircraft factories, but as Hitler's frustration increased, the Germans turned to bombing the cities. Believing the theorists, Hitler assumed that this would force Britain to submit. The Blitz killed more than 43,000 civilians and caused enormous amounts of physical damage, all without significantly damaging British morale or their ability to continue the war. Hitler called off the Blitz in frustration and turned to his real long-term goal, as described in his prewar book *Mein Kampf,* and prepared to attack the Soviet Union.

As the British bombing effort progressed into 1941, bombing theories foundered on the rock of practical experience. British prime minister Winston Churchill and other leaders realized that only night bombing missions could protect the bombers from excessive losses. Navigating at night was difficult; even finding cities was difficult, especially after the Germans instituted blackouts. Still, cities were the only targets possible to find at night. A report by Churchill's scientific adviser, Lord Cherwell, recommended area bombing of cities in order to "de-house" the population; by breaking "the spirit of the people," Germany would collapse. Cherwell even mathematically calculated that by bombing the fifty-eight largest cities in Germany, a third of the nation's population would be rendered homeless. The government agreed and in February 1942 authorized area bombing of cities to "be focused on the morale of the enemy civil population and in particular, of industrial workers."[6]

Dropping bombs on civilians from tens of thousands of feet in the air allowed government leaders, the military leadership, and aircrews to retain psychological distance from the reality of the killing. Certainly Churchill would never have countenanced British soldiers on the ground de-housing German cities by burning houses and shooting the civilians. That form of killing was too intimate, face to face, stripping away all psychological barriers.

The man who assumed the position of commander in chief of Bomber Command in February 1942 was a perfect fit for the new government policy. Air Marshal Arthur "Bomber" Harris had begun flying in 1915 during World War

I, and people who knew him found him dogmatic and self-assured. A clearness of purpose and deep reservoirs of self-confidence are important ingredients for a leader, but the ability to learn is also important. Britain's own official history portrays Harris as a man with a "habit of seeing only one side of a question and then of exaggerating it. He had a tendency to confuse advice with interference, criticism with sabotage and evidence with propaganda. He resisted innovations and was seldom open to persuasion."[7]

As a disciple and protégé of Trenchard, Harris ardently believed that with a force of four thousand bombers he could end the war solely through strategic bombing. He never wavered from this belief and argued that he failed to succeed because he never had access to a bombing force of that size, even though Britain devoted a third of its wartime economy to building strategic bombers. The regular loss rate precluded reaching four thousand bombers, and the peak strength of Bomber Command in the spring of 1945 was 1,609 aircraft. Harris always overestimated the effects of his command's bombing efforts. Up until the spring of 1944, he ardently proclaimed his belief that Bomber Command would win the war by itself. His supporters maintained that morale was the "joint in the German armour."[8] A plan called Rankin was even drawn up for the rapid occupation of Germany and Western Europe in the event that Germany suddenly collapsed under the pressure of strategic bombing or from separate pressure on the Russian front.

When the Americans joined the strategic air war, building up their own force of B-17 and B-24 bombers in the Eighth Air Force in Britain, they also brought their own ideas of how the air war should be fought. The Americans persisted in believing in daylight precision bombing, hitting Germany during the day while the British flew at night. The Americans also wanted to concentrate on key industries, attacking in turn ball-bearing plants, then oil facilities, and finally, transportation. They sought the vital link in the German economy that would cause everything to collapse if it were destroyed.*

---

* The key problem that confronted Hitler throughout the war was limitations on his supply of oil. Even as German industrial production peaked in 1944, turning out 19,000 tanks and 40,600 planes, there was scant fuel to use the weapons effectively. The December 1944 attack in the Ardennes, the Battle of the Bulge, ground to a halt for lack of fuel more than any other factor. In some cases, the Luftwaffe turned to using teams of horses to move planes from the maintenance area to the runway, rather than use precious aviation gasoline. German planes did not reach their peak performance because of the lack of high-grade aviation fuel, and new pilots could not receive sufficient training in the air before going into combat.

In April 1944 Harris and his American counterpart, Carl A. Spaatz, were brought to heel when command of the strategic bombers was turned over to the Supreme Allied Commander Europe, Dwight D. Eisenhower. The American general directed the strategic bombers to concentrate on bridges, roads, and rails in France so that he could isolate the Normandy Peninsula before D-day. After the successful invasion of France, Harris was allowed to return to bombing German cities.

Harris was obsessed with destroying German cities by area bombing. Even when the Joint Chiefs agreed to concentrate on destroying German oil and synthetic oil production facilities, Harris continued to use the British bomber fleet to work toward his goal of turning sixty German cities into rubble. He argued that weather and tactical factors often prohibited attacks other than area bombing of cities. Chief of the Air Staff Sir Charles Portal "wondered" in a letter to Harris if the "magnetism of the remaining German cities" had drawn Bomber Command back to Harris's goal of area bombing the Germans into submission, rather than the excuses that Harris was offering.[9]

Harris's personal popularity with the British people, a result of government propaganda, made it too difficult to fire the air marshal for insubordination. Instead, at the end of war, he was released from service and denied the peerage and other honors that men of his rank received. Members of Bomber Command itself were denied their own campaign medal, even though Bomber Command lost 56,000 men during the war. On average, only about one out of every four aircrew members survived a tour of thirty missions. A grim toll, but in the end, the promises Harris and other advocates of strategic bombing made were too extravagant and soured perceptions of what they did accomplish.

During the course of early 1945, both the British and Americans continued to pummel Germany with their strategic bombers. Losses to Luftwaffe fighters fell as the German air force found itself starved for fuel. The British even began to regularly fly over Germany during the day. Hitler refused to let his nation surrender, and the Allied bombers continued their work, though now the destruction was much more effective. The alternative to strategic bombing would have been to ground the bombers, an option that no nation could consider in light of German reluctance to even hint at surrender. German economic productivity peaked in September 1944 and fell precipitously after that.

Before leaving for the Yalta Conference in February 1945, Churchill looked for a way to show the Soviets that the Allies were supporting their offensives. The

British Air Ministry came back with a proposal to bomb certain cities in order to inhibit the ability of troops to move through the cities. Dresden was among the selected cities. Though Dresden was the seventh most populous city in Germany, up until then it had experienced little bombing. The bombing of the city was approved, and the awful firestorm led to a public outcry. Dresden became a symbol of futility and moral blindness.

After the war, it became apparent that the German economy had actually steadily increased production up until the last few months of the war, and during the war there was never any good evidence to show that area bombing was hurting the Germans. An American survey after the war concluded that fewer than half of all bombs dropped by the strategic bombers fell within five miles of their target. Precision was an illusion that the frustrated bomber barons clung to. Ironically, as Allied armies entered Germany in the last few months of the war, Allied bombers turned most of their efforts from area bombing (Dresden was an exception) to concentrated efforts against rail and barge transportation networks and oil production. Railroads were particularly vulnerable because they could not be moved or readily hidden, and the German economy could not afford the fuel for truck transport. Germany needed locomotives burning the plentiful coal of the Ruhr to move the raw materials and goods that are so essential in making a modern economy function. The German transportation system collapsed. At last, at the very end, the strategic bombing campaign had found the Achilles' heel it had so yearned for.

As the war progressed, the German people could not supply enough workers for their factories, so workers were enslaved in conquered countries and brought to Germany to work. Part of the work shortage stemmed from the Nazis' refusal to draw more heavily on their population of adult women as workers (unlike the Allies, who found in women an untapped labor bounty). The slave workers died with the Germans under the rain of British and American bombs.

Churchill was well aware of the moral uncertainty of strategic bombing and strongly doubted that bombing alone could be decisive in ending the war. But when the British were confined to their home island and fighting desperately in North Africa to protect the oil and strategic position of the Middle East, strategic bombing provided one of the few ways to hit the German homeland and cause some damage. Churchill also sponsored commando raids and other efforts to help the resistance movements in German-occupied countries as a way to keep the pressure on Germany. Regular bombing of Germany also helped sustain British morale when news of victories was hard to come by.

The strategic bombing effort compelled the Germans to ring their cities with ten thousand antiaircraft guns, especially the dreaded 88. These weapons could have served a much more useful purpose as antitank guns on the Russian front, and so could have the enormous quantities of ammunition expended on trying to hit high-flying bombers. Fighter aircraft that could have fought on the front remained to defend the home cities. Personnel and effort spent on rebuilding and working around the destruction wrought by the bombs could have fielded more divisions and increased industrial production.

The strategic bombing effort also enabled Churchill to resist calls by the Soviets and Americans for an early invasion of northwestern Europe to create a second front. The second front, he argued, was being fought in the air. Churchill wanted to delay the invasion of France as long as possible, until the Western Allies had built up overwhelming force. The real struggle against Germany was fought on the Russian front.

Curtis E. LeMay was an American air division commander in the European war known for his innovative tactics and proven ability to solve problems. He transferred to the Pacific in 1944 and took over the strategic bombing effort against Japan, using the new long-range B-29 bomber. LeMay realized that Japan was different from Germany. The Japanese economy had already partially collapsed because of an effective campaign by the U.S. Navy to destroy merchant shipping. Because Japanese antiaircraft defenses were weak, LeMay abandoned the American doctrine of attacking in daylight from high altitude. He stripped the guns off his B-29 bombers so that they could carry more bombs and sent them against Japanese cities at night and at low level. The bombers did not attempt precision targeting because they carried napalm and incendiaries, not high explosives. It was hard to set German cities on fire, but the greater proportion of wood construction in Japanese cities made them more vulnerable to firebombings.

On March 9, 1945, over three hundred of LeMay's B-29 bombers struck Tokyo and caused a mass fire that burned sixteen square miles of the city and killed up to a hundred thousand people. The fire created its own weather, sucking in wind for oxygen and feeding on itself. This was only the most notorious of the firebombings. Two million Japanese civilians died as other cities were methodically burned to the ground. In just four years of war, the Americans had slid down the moral slope from thinking that targeting civilians was never justified to aiming for total war, in which they tried to kill enough of the enemy—men, women, and children—to force a surrender.

Another fact weighed heavily on the consciousness of the American policy makers as they tried to end the war. On April 1, 1945, a massive invasion fleet of thirteen hundred ships landed a half million men on the island of Okinawa. The island was considered part of Japan, and the Japanese fought a tenacious campaign with a hundred thousand soldiers, including kamikaze pilots. The Americans lost 79 ships and 12,513 men, with almost another 39,000 wounded. It was a hard fight that lasted almost three months.

Okinawa was a preview of a possible invasion of the Japanese home islands, and the American leadership learned sober lessons. What would an invasion of Japan —where there were so many more Japanese soldiers, a civilian population armed with bamboo spears, thousands of suicide aircraft waiting for one final flight, and even suicide watercraft—be like? The Americans prepared Operation Downfall, the final invasion of Japan for X-day. Casualties would certainly be heavy.

Dropping the new atomic bomb was not a significant moral leap from this point. Many scholars have argued that dropping the bomb was not justified, that the war would have ended anyway, or that other ways to end the war could have been found. Most of the men involved in making the decision, however, saw no difference between dropping an atomic bomb and firebombing a Japanese city with hundreds of airplanes. The former option took fewer airplanes and cost just as many lives.

A B-29 bomber named the *Enola Gay* dropped Little Boy on the Japanese city of Hiroshima on August 6, 1945. The city was selected because it was one of the few that had not been firebombed by conventional air attacks. Out of a population of 245,000, 70,000 people died in the blast immediately, and perhaps another 60,000 died in the following months from their injuries and radiation. Three days later, on August 9, 1945, the city of Nagasaki was destroyed by Fat Man. Forty thousand people died immediately, followed by another 34,000 in the subsequent months. In fact, deaths from these atomic bombs were proportionally greater than deaths from conventional bombings earlier in the war because the effects of an atomic bomb blasts happened nearly instantaneously, giving the victims little time to take shelter or flee.

The Japanese sent the head of their own small atomic bomb program to Hiroshima after the bomb had been dropped. He found unused X-ray plates, developed them, and saw that they were black. He also used a Geiger counter to test bones of the dead and concluded that an atomic bomb had been used.

The Americans had used their only two atomic bombs (the Trinity test had used the third) in the August blasts but calculated that they would have six or seven more by X-day in November. Plans were created to use the bombs to clear the invasion beaches. The long-term effects of residual nuclear radiation, called fallout, were not yet appreciated. Fortunately for the American soldiers and the Japanese people, the government of Japan decided to end the war by surrendering.

Both the Hiroshima and Nagasaki bombs were detonated while still high in the air, which maximized blast damage and minimized fallout damage. Fallout is the highly radioactive particles of matter that have been vaporized by the atomic explosion. Since an airburst's fireball does not touch the ground, only the matter of the bomb and the surrounding air are available to create fallout. A groundburst, in which the atomic explosion carves out a large crater in the earth, has a lesser blast effect, since the blast has to travel along the ground rather than through the greater area affected by a comparable airburst. However, a groundburst generates the most fallout because all the matter vaporized from the crater becomes radioactive particles, which are sucked up in the mushroom cloud and scattered by the winds. Sometimes fallout lands thousands of miles away, where it continues to emit dangerous radioactivity until it decays. The decay rate of fallout depends on the type of isotopes involved and can vary from a few days to centuries. Some isotopes have half-lives—that is, the time it takes the isotope to lose half of its radioactivity—measured in thousands of years.

Because the first two atomic bombs used in war were airbursts, neither Japanese city was poisoned by fallout, and thus both could be rebuilt. In fact, Hiroshima and Nagasaki became thriving cities after the war. The Japanese remembered that they were the first victims of atomic weapons and felt a sense of self-pity in their status, erasing from their national memory that they had started the war with their expansionistic military conquests.

MAKING MORE TOOLS OF DEATH

The genie was out of the bottle, and the Americans continued to build more atomic bombs. With a monopoly on the technology and the expectation that it would be at least a decade before any other nation developed this ability, American strategists pondered their responsibilities and opportunities. A proposal to turn their weapons over to an international body was even considered, but eventually the U.S. government decided that it enjoyed having a nuclear monopoly.

When the Soviets exploded their own atomic bomb in 1949, the startled Americans decided to build a superbomb. The hydrogen bomb used fusion, rather than the fission process of atomic bombs. The hydrogen bomb, also called the thermonuclear bomb, could be a thousand times more powerful than an atomic bomb, and thus its force was measured in megatons, with one megaton equivalent to one million of tons of TNT. The Hungarian-born physicist Edward Teller led the American effort, which exploded the first hydrogen bomb on Enewetak Atoll in 1952. The Soviet physicist Andrei Sakharov designed the first Soviet hydrogen bomb, which was exploded only a year later. The nuclear arms race began in earnest, with the two superpowers pouring billions of dollars and enormous resources into making thousands of nuclear weapons. Surprisingly, and unknown to the Americans, the Soviets at first found it hard to manufacture more bombs quickly, and by 1953, four years after they had exploded their first atomic bomb, the Soviets actually had fewer than a dozen atomic bombs small enough to deliver by bomber.[10] By 1962 the Americans had built more than six thousand nuclear weapons. We do not know how many the Soviets had made, but it probably was no more than a third of the Americans' total.[11]

Britain exploded its first atomic bomb in 1952 and followed that with its first hydrogen bomb in 1957. British scientists had worked on the Manhattan Project, and the Americans supported their ally's entrance into the nuclear club. In 1960 the French exploded their first atomic bomb in the Algerian desert. They were still working on a hydrogen bomb in 1962. Both Britain and France desired their own nuclear weapons, separate from the American arsenal, in order to give themselves more independence in their foreign policies, though this impulse was much stronger in Charles de Gaulle's France than in Britain, which had a "special relationship" with the United States. The Soviet Union had agreed to give the necessary technology to build an atomic bomb to China but aborted these plans when the Sino-Soviet relationship deteriorated in 1960.

The United States and Soviet Union experimented with putting nuclear weapons not only in bombers and atop ballistic missiles but also into depth charges, torpedoes, antiaircraft missiles, air-to-air missiles, and artillery shells.

A considerable amount of effort went into developing nuclear weapons small enough to place atop missiles or in large suitcases. Some weapons maximized their electromagnetic pulse (EMP) in order to destroy electronics and electrical systems, while other weapons were designed to minimize their radioactive fallout.

Both nations conducted dozens of tests as they built ever more powerful weapons. The United States used islands in the South Pacific and a test range north of Las Vegas, Nevada. The Soviet Union favored the Central Asian deserts of Kazakhstan and Arctic islands north of Siberia. Some of the tests were ground-bursts, others were airbursts, and the United States also conducted at least one water burst, using a fleet of obsolete World War II warships as targets, to measure the effect of a nuclear weapon on ships.

Both the Americans and Soviets behaved foolishly during the tests, directly exposing hundreds of thousands of soldiers, sailors, and civilians to the effects of the nuclear explosions. For instance, in 1951 an entire regimental combat team of five thousand American soldiers was stationed next to an open-air test in order to evaluate the psychological effects of the test on the men. The United States acted so carelessly in part because it lacked concrete information about how much radiation the human body could safely absorb without serious side effects. As the 1950s progressed, the agreed-upon limit regularly shrank as scientists realized that radiation and fallout were much more dangerous than they had initially assumed.

Two effects created most of the destruction at Hiroshima and Nagasaki: blast damage from the initial explosion and the fires that followed. Because fallout had such a minor impact in those blasts, subsequent nuclear weapons tests concentrated almost exclusively on blast damage. Test buildings, constructed using various materials and located at multiple distances from ground zero, were built in Nevada. Cameras were used to document the damage caused to frame houses and the other structures. Post-explosion analysis enabled the American scientists to develop sophisticated mathematical models that explained how many buildings would be destroyed based on how far they were from ground zero, the strength of the nuclear weapon used, and whether the buildings were made of concrete, lumber, or a combination of materials.

Along the way, the damage created by post-explosion fires was ignored—not in a deliberately negligent way but because fire damage was harder to evaluate than blast damage. As a result, government predictions of the damage from nuclear weapons were based on underestimates. The Fire, in its own way, was a grand experiment under real conditions. More people died than expected, cities were more thoroughly destroyed than expected, and the subtle long-term effects of so much fallout were a surprise.[12]

All this testing led to a measurable increase in radioactivity in the atmosphere, which the jet stream spread around the world. By the late 1950s scientists were calling for a ban on open-air testing, suggesting that it be restricted to explosions deep underground. Such testing would contain the radiation by preventing the explosions from breaching the earth's surface. The American chemist Linus Pauling was a leader in the campaign for underground testing. During World War II he had declined to work on the Manhattan Project, and after the war he became a vocal opponent of further development of nuclear weapons. After winning the Nobel Prize in Chemistry in 1954 for his work on chemical bonds, Pauling grew more aggressive in his antinuclear activities, enough so that the federal government and some other scientists suspected he was a Communist sympathizer. His 1958 book *No More War!* emphasized his pacifist convictions. Pauling campaigned for the United States and Soviet Union to stop open-air testing in the interest of public health, and by 1962 he was rumored to be under consideration for the Nobel Peace Prize for these efforts.

The amount of money flowing into nuclear weapons research meant that the demand for nuclear physicists increased sharply after World War II, especially with the superpowers. Graduate programs in nuclear physics at universities expanded to accommodate the demand. The physicists used their newfound connections to government to successfully lobby for additional funding for other big science projects, such as particle accelerators and other large devices to detect and study ever smaller pieces of matter and energy, including solar neutrinos and cosmic rays. A downside of the increased prominence of physicists was an emerging sense that scientists were irresponsible in developing science and technology that could destroy all life. This ambivalence toward scientists is readily apparent in postwar movies, books, and popular culture.

While conquering the atom had led to a climate of global fear, nuclear technology had other uses. A team led by Enrico Fermi built the first fission-based nuclear reactor in 1942 as part of the Manhattan Project, and more nuclear reactors to create the fuel for the atomic bombs followed. During the 1950s nuclear scientists and nuclear engineers eagerly pursued applying nuclear reactors to every possible situation. In the military arena, the first nuclear-powered submarine, the USS *Nautilus*, was launched in 1954. Nuclear power plants also replaced oil engines on aircraft carriers and cruisers, especially on American ships. Experimental vessels included a nuclear-powered airplane and a nuclear-powered merchant freighter.

Scientists also recognized the potential for nuclear reactors to supply electricity, and a small experimental breeder reactor in Idaho generated the first nuclear power in 1951, though only enough to light the reactor building. In 1953 Eisenhower announced his "Atoms for Peace" program; within two years a thousand residents of Arco, Idaho, were receiving their electricity from an experimental nuclear power plant. The first commercial nuclear power plant was completed in 1957 in Shippingport, Pennsylvania. The Soviet Union and United Kingdom built similar plants.

Expensive to build because of safety measures, nuclear plants supplied cheap electricity without polluting the air but at the cost of generating large amounts of radioactive waste. Nuclear engineers spent considerable effort to make the reactors safe. They designed light-water reactors that would automatically shut down if controls failed. But occasional accidents, such as the Windscale reactor fire in the United Kingdom and the Kyshtym disaster at the Mayak nuclear facility in Siberia, both in 1957, led a few to question the wisdom of nuclear reactors.

Were nuclear weapons merely more destructive weapons, or had they rewritten the rules of war? Military theorists on both sides of the Iron Curtain argued over this question. Both the Soviet Union and the United States built extensive air defense systems of radar, fighters, and surface-to-air-missile batteries. As so often happened, military spending accelerated advances in technology. To coordinate U.S. air defense, the Air Force built the Semi-Automatic Ground Environment (SAGE) system. At one point, one out of every five employees at the largest computer company in the world, International Business Machines (IBM), worked on the SAGE system. IBM AN/FSQ-7 computers were the largest computers ever built, each with over 49,000 vacuum tubes, weighing 250 tons, and occupying a three-story building. The SAGE software eventually totaled over a million lines of programming code, and at one point, over half of the programmers in America worked on this single project. By 1953 a single SAGE system could simultaneously track forty-eight aircraft. The system was to be fully completed by 1963, with a total of twenty-three direction centers and twenty-four

AN/FSQ-7 computers and having cost about $8 billion. Most of these centers were up and functioning in October 1962.

Bombers required hours to reach their targets and could be shot down. Thus, to be even more useful, nuclear bombs needed a faster and more reliable delivery mechanism than a bomber. The marriage of a nuclear warhead to a ballistic missile created that new tool.

DREAMS OF SPACE

Three men made the rocket. Appropriately enough, one was a Russian, another an American, and the last was a German. The first man, Konstantin Tsiolkovsky, was born in 1857 to a Polish farmer and his Russian wife. A bout of scarlet fever at age ten left him partially deaf. Not allowed to go to school because of his deafness, he taught himself from books in his father's library. His father was not wealthy, but being literate and owning books were advantages that many in the Russian Empire did not have. In his later teens, Tsiolkovsky lived in Moscow for three years and went to the libraries there to further his self-education.

The eccentric Russian philosopher Nikolai Fedorov worked at the Rumiantsev Museum, the leading lending library in Moscow, housed in a magnificent complex of onion-domed buildings, and Federov tutored the young man. An odd religious thinker, little noticed in the history of ideas, Fedorov argued that humanity should dedicate itself to developing the science and technology necessary to overcome death, which he considered to be the ultimate evil. This new science, he believed, should also be used to resuscitate the dead. Fedorov thought that once a person died, the particles that made up his or her body floated into space, and that in order to recover those particles and reconstitute the bodies, scientists would have to develop space travel. The people who were brought back to life would then overcrowd the earth, so other planets would need to be colonized to make room for them. This variant on the Christian resurrection, in which science stood in for the power of Christ, appealed to Tsiolkovsky and greatly influenced his later work. The writings of this thinker affected not only Tsiolkovsky, since "Fedorovism" became quite popular in prerevolutionary Russia and the early Soviet period, before Stalin suppressed it as being contrary to Communist thought.

Tsiolkovsky obtained a teacher's certificate (it was a true irony that a man barred from school as a child was now allowed to teach children) and became a high school mathematics instructor. He married, had children, and delved into the question of space travel. Since space was thought to be a vacuum, or at the very least an ether, Tsiolkovsky believed rockets were the answer. Rockets, invented by the Chinese over a thousand years earlier, were at the time used as fireworks, as signaling rockets, and as weapons, with limited usefulness in warfare. The novels of Jules Verne also inspired him. In his 1865 novel *From the Earth to the Moon*, Verne used rockets for guidance thrusters on a space capsule after it was launched into space by means of a massive cannon. Ironically enough, the cannon was placed in Florida, later the location of the American space program.

In 1903, the same year that the Wright Brothers invented the airplane, Tsiolkovsky published his seminal work, *The Exploration of Cosmic Space by Means of Reaction Devices*. The book is a serious treatment, presenting equations that describe how rockets work and equations that describe how an artificial satellite could orbit the earth. Tsiolkovsky's other works described the effects of zero gravity, the use of gyroscopes to change the attitude of spacecraft, airlocks through which space travelers could enter and leave their vessels, a cosmic greenhouse to grow food for the space travelers, multistage rockets, and the design of a liquid-fueled rocket engine. He also described his vision of humanity colonizing the asteroid belt, other planets, and other stars of the Milky Way. After the Communists came to power, enamored of all things scientific, the aged Tsiolkovsky was honored as a scientific hero, awarded a pension, and even given a state funeral upon his death in 1935.

It is simply amazing how much Tsiolkovsky conceived far before the technology could be developed. Most important, he used mathematical rigor to show that space travel was possible—it was not fantasy, but merely a matter of engineering.

In America, Dr. Robert H. Goddard, a professor of physics at Clark University, was similarly inspired by the works of Jules Verne and H. G. Wells. In 1919 the Smithsonian Institution published his book, *A Method of Reaching Extreme Altitudes*, describing the physics of rockets and how they might be useful. Goddard was ridiculed in the press for his ideas. Though harboring secret dreams of space travel, Goddard decided to concentrate on the practical problems of how to build a liquid-fueled rocket. He had no idea that he had a Russian counterpart who was exploring the same subject; his ideas about rockets were all his own. On March 16, 1926, on a snow-covered field in Auburn, Massachusetts, Goddard flew the first liquid-fueled rocket for two and a half seconds. A mixture of liquid oxygen and gasoline pumped into the rocket's combustion chamber, and the resulting gases, expelled from a nozzle, created the propulsion.

Goddard faced increased notoriety with his continued experiments and found it difficult to obtain funding for his research. The Guggenheim family came to his rescue, providing funding and allowing him to relocate to the desert near Roswell, New Mexico, where he continued to build ever larger rockets.* Though he received numerous patents, Goddard could attract little interest in his research. His greatest achievement came in 1937, when one of his rockets reached approximately 1.7 miles in altitude above the New Mexico sands.

In Germany, the gift of a telescope turned the thoughts of a young aristocrat to science. Wernher von Braun was the second son of a wealthy landowner and baron who served as minister of agriculture in the Weimar Republic before the rise of the Nazis. In boarding school, von Braun read the book *Road to Space Travel* by the German rocket pioneer Hermann Oberth.

Oberth's ideas were his own, also initially inspired by the writings of Jules Verne, though he later drew on the work of both Tsiolkovsky and Goddard. A German from Romania, Oberth submitted his theoretical work on liquid-fueled rockets as his dissertation and was rejected. He privately published the work in 1922 as *By Rocket into Planetary Space*. Another professor accepted it as Oberth's dissertation, allowing him to earn his doctorate. In 1929, he published an expansion of his earlier book, which von Braun read.

Oberth's ideas fired the ambitions of von Braun, encouraging him to bring up his failing grades in physics and mathematics so that he could enter the Technical University of Berlin in 1930. At the Technical University, von Braun joined the Verein für Raumschiffahrt (Society for Space Travel), made up largely of others who were inspired by Oberth. Through the society, von Braun met Oberth himself, though the physicist was in Berlin for only a short time before he returned to his job teaching high school in Romania. Lacking further funds, Oberth only later worked his way into minor academic posts in Germany. His

---

* Guggenheim funding in the late 1920s and 1930s also went to aeronautical research, the education of aircraft engineers, and the operation of a model airline between San Francisco to Los Angeles used to develop the best technical and business techniques necessary to create the airline industry. This funding was essential to developing the U.S. aviation industry and is an excellent example of technological philanthropy. See Pat Bahn, "A Guggenheim Fund for Spaceflight," *Space Review*, October 22, 2007, http://www.thespacereview.com/article/986/1 (accessed on January 2, 2009).

protégés continued researching his dream without him. The society rented some land, a former ammunition dump they named Rocket Airdrome Berlin, and began to build small liquid-fueled rockets.

The society's work attracted the attention of the German army, which supplied it with funding and convinced von Braun to continue his education. At age twenty-two, von Braun earned his doctorate in physics, presenting a dissertation on liquid-fueled rockets. What had been unacceptable for Oberth's teachers a decade earlier was now quite acceptable, especially for an aristocrat with army backing.

The Nazis' rise to power increased government interest in the society's efforts. Expecting war and enthusiastic about technology, the Nazis viewed rockets as a potent new weapon. The army and Luftwaffe built a rocket-development facility in Peenemünde on the Baltic coast. The workforce there eventually grew to four thousand scientists, engineers, and technicians. Von Braun was patriotic and quite willing to work on turning rockets into weapons, though his ultimate dream remained using them for space travel. The military effort was only a means to an end for him. Von Braun joined the Luftwaffe and learned to fly while continuing his research. In 1937 he joined the Nazi Party. In 1940 he became an SS officer and eventually rose to the middle grade rank of *Sturmbannführer*, literally "Storm Unit leader," equivalent to an army major.[13]

In 1942, three years into World War II, von Braun's team successfully flew the A-4 rocket a distance of 120 miles. Forty-six feet tall and weighing almost fourteen tons, the rocket was designed to fly 200 miles, carrying 2,150 pounds of high explosive. By this time Oberth had joined the effort, though von Braun was clearly the leading light. The A-4 (later renamed the V-2) had numerous engineering problems that needed to be fixed before it could be considered a reliable tool.

Hitler saw the war going against him and desperately sought to reverse the tide by building new wonder weapons. The V-2 became one such weapon. Extra resources were funneled to the project, and an increased effort was made to turn the research vehicle into a reliable production vehicle.

The British were also worried and, on the night of August 18, 1943, sent a large bomber force of 497 aircraft to attack Peenemünde. The goal was not just to destroy the island base but to kill the scientists and engineers. The British recognized that the real target was the knowledge and skills in brains, not the physical factories. The raid was a failure on both counts, as it did only minor damage to the V-2 factory and did not kill enough experts to make a difference.

Alarmed by the raid, Hitler ordered V-2 manufacturing be relocated to central Germany. The SS was ordered to expand a mine into an underground rocket factory as quickly as possible. For the expansion, it used slave labor, housed in a concentration camp called Dora-Mittelbau. An additional concentration camp in the nearby city of Nordhausen also supplied labor for the factory. During the two final years of the war, sixty thousand inmates worked on the factory or in the two camps; twenty-five thousand died.

During this time, the Gestapo arrested von Braun and some members of his staff, including his younger brother, and accused them of putting their dreams of space flight above the immediate needs of the Third Reich. Released after two weeks, von Braun returned to work. He remained at Peenemünde, designing bigger rockets, though he visited the underground factory at least fifteen times and was well aware of the labor conditions there. Among the new rockets under design were a winged version (actually launched as a prototype, but its wing broke in flight), a multistage rocket capable of hitting the northeastern United States, and even a rocket capable of putting a satellite in orbit.

Some three thousand V-2 rockets were built in the factory before the end of the war. More than thirteen hundred of these rockets fell on England, almost as many fell on Antwerp, and hundreds more were launched at other targets. Perhaps six thousand people, almost all civilians, died in the blasts. A guided cruise missile that used a jet engine, the V-1 "buzz bomb," was also developed at Peenemünde, though not by von Braun's team. The British developed methods to shoot down the V-1, but there was no defense against the V-2, other than pushing Allied armies to overrun the launching sites. The lack of any defense against the V-2 turned the weapon into a terrifying monster in the public's mind, even though aircraft killed millions more during the war.

In the war's closing months, Hitler and his people pinned their hopes on the development of secret weapons. Success in war requires economy of scale. A few pennies spent on a bullet can kill a soldier. A bomber can repeatedly rain destruction on enemy cities and troops. The V-1 and V-2 rockets were impressive technological achievements, but they violated the rule of economy of scale. The expensive and inaccurate V-2 rocket delivered only 2,150 pounds of explosive. The Germans also fielded the world's first operational jet aircraft, giving the Allied air forces a scare, but it was a case of too few, too late.

When the Red Army approached Peenemünde in 1945, von Braun organized an exodus of his technicians and tons of documents to Bleicherode in central Germany, near the underground factory. Von Braun was already thinking about life after the war. He and his key team members wanted to be captured by the Americans, because that economic powerhouse had the resources to help them continue their rocket research. Von Braun had not forgotten the dream.

Von Braun and his technicians surrendered to the U.S. Army. They negotiated for access to their knowledge but were also interested in moving to the United States themselves. The Army collected enough parts from the underground factory to build a hundred V-2 rockets, recovered fourteen tons of documents that von Braun had hidden, and rounded up as many members of von Braun's staff as it could find. While excited by the treasure trove of technical materials, which would allow them to build their own rocket program, the Americans were appalled by the Nordhausen and Dora-Mittelbau camps, where they found thousands of corpses, the victims of starvation and cholera, in various stages of decomposition littering the ground because the crematory ovens could not dispose of the dead quickly enough.

The Americans created Operation Paperclip to bring German specialists into the United States. If necessary, their Nazi backgrounds were concealed, though some of the Germans were sent back to West Germany to stand trial for war crimes. While interested in the pursuit of justice, the American government was even more interested in obtaining German expertise to use in the emerging Cold War. Von Braun and his specialists, their association with the underground factory conveniently forgotten, were moved to America and went to work for the Army at Fort Bliss near El Paso, Texas. Though von Braun worked with the Army, the Americans did not arrange for a visa for him until 1949, when they took him across the border into Mexico so that he could reenter the United States and have his passport stamped. Until then, von Braun had been in the United States illegally in the eyes of immigration officials.

The Army did not really know what to do with the Germans, other than have them assemble and launch the captured V-2 rockets at White Sands, New Mexico. Robert Goddard had a chance to examine a V-2 before his death on August 10, 1945. He found that the Germans had surpassed him, a frustrating inevitability considering the disproportionate amounts of funding that von Braun and Goddard had received, but he maintained hope in the idea that their shared dream of space travel might one day be realized. Goddard had filed over two hundred patents on different elements of rocket design, which the patent office accepted and then the government classified. None of this information was available to the Germans before or during the war. In 1950, familiar with the work the German scientists were doing for the Army, Goddard's widow filed a suit against the U.S. government for patent infringement. Von Braun reviewed the patents and agreed that many of the patents had been infringed upon, though the Germans had developed the technology completely independently of Goddard. A decade later the government settled with Goddard's widow for $1 million.

As he waited for the American government to realize how important rocket technology was, von Braun wrote a novel, *The Mars Project*, describing how a mission to Mars might realistically be accomplished. An eighty-page technical appendix described the rockets and other vehicles required to realize this vision. Seventeen publishers rejected the book. Once his work in the field garnered notice, a German publisher printed the technical appendix, and then in 1953 the University of Illinois Press picked it up for publication in the United States.

In 1949 a German V-2, with an American-developed Wac Corporal atop it as a second stage, reached an altitude of 244 miles. Rockets were showing potential, and the Cold War was heating up, as China fell to the Communists in the same year. In 1950 the Army ramped up its rocket development program and moved it to the Redstone Arsenal of Army Ordnance near Huntsville, Alabama. Von Braun was moved to Huntsville, along with the hundreds of other technicians working on rockets, including the 130 Germans on his team. Von Braun became the technical director of the Guided Missile Development Group. A biographer has pointed out that the organization at Redstone was remarkably similar to the organization at Peenemünde.[14]

Von Braun continued to promote his dream of space travel with a series of articles in *Collier's* in 1952. His writing was accompanied by Chesley Bonestell's magnificent paintings showing the promise of rockets reaching orbit, astronauts in space suits, satellites, a mission to land a man on the moon, and a doughnut-shaped, permanently manned, orbiting space station with a free-floating telescope, viewing the heavens free of the atmosphere's interference. In one article, von Braun described how "small winged rocket missiles with atomic warheads could be launched from the station."[15] Though not designed as such, the articles were a sober reminder that peaceful efforts at space exploration had a darker use.

In 1955 the weekly Disney television program *Disneyland* broadcast a segment called "Man in Space." Von Braun consulted on the program. Such media attention, combined with the popularity of science fiction in magazines and movies during the 1950s, accustomed the American people to the idea that space travel was a real possibility.

BALLISTIC MISSILES

Dreams of space travel did not inspire the Army to fund von Braun's rocket team, nor did they prompt the parallel rocket development programs run by the Navy and Air Force. Rockets promised to be a new frontier in weapons, and the American defense establishment in the 1950s funded numerous programs to build rockets—small ones, medium-sized ones, and big ones. Von Braun's team built the Redstone rocket, a surface-to-surface missile with a range of two hundred miles, similar to the V-2. This became a medium-range ballistic missile (MRBM) when it carried a nuclear warhead. In 1958 Redstone rockets were used in the first launch tests of ballistic missiles carrying live nuclear warheads. The two nuclear weapons in the tests exploded over the Pacific Ocean. Redstone missiles were then deployed in West Germany, ready in case the Cold War turned hot.

Von Braun also developed the successors to the Redstone, the Jupiter series of rockets, as intermediate-range ballistic missiles (IRBMs) with a range of fifteen hundred miles. The Air Force wanted to deploy its new Jupiter missiles in France, but Charles de Gaulle refused, so two squadrons totaling thirty missiles were deployed in Italy, with another squadron of fifteen missiles deployed in Turkey, within range of Leningrad, Moscow, and most of the European portion of the Soviet Union.

The Army had asked von Braun to put his development of a satellite launcher on hold, but von Braun knew that a modified Redstone would make an excellent launcher with the addition of upper stages. He set to work on this modified Redstone, calling it the Jupiter-C, though it had nothing to do with the Jupiter series. The Pentagon was so suspicious of its German genius that it sent a high-ranking officer to inspect the fourth stage of the rocket to ensure that von Braun did not plan to launch a satellite during a test and apologize afterward.[16]

When the Soviets launched their *Sputnik* satellite in 1957, the United States suddenly wanted to launch its own satellite. The Vanguard rocket from the

Naval Research Laboratory was tested for this purpose first because it had been designed only to launch satellites and had more of the appearance of being a tool of science, whereas the Redstone was clearly a weapon of war. After the Navy prototype failed, with a spectacular explosion on the launchpad, von Braun's Jupiter-C was used to launch the first successful American satellite, *Explorer 1*, on January 31, 1958.

The National Aeronautics and Space Administration (NASA) was established as a civilian agency to run the American space program later that year. In 1960 NASA opened the Marshall Space Flight Center in Huntsville, Alabama, and von Braun and his development team were transferred from the Army to NASA. Von Braun became the center's director. His Redstone rocket was used to launch the first two American astronauts into space on suborbital flights.

For full orbital flights, NASA needed a larger rocket. The Air Force had developed the Atlas, the first American intercontinental ballistic missile (ICBM). With a range of over ten thousand miles, the Atlas changed the strategic equation completely. Beginning in 1958, Atlas squadrons were deployed in Colorado, Wyoming, California, Nebraska, Washington, Oklahoma, Kansas, New Mexico, and New York. Beginning in 1960 another ICBM, the Titan, was also deployed in squadrons in Colorado, South Dakota, California, Washington, and Idaho. These ICBMs could be launched from the continental United States and hit any target in the Soviet Union by flying over the polar regions.

Though the Atlas rocket was used to launch the later Mercury astronauts, the first seven Americans chosen for spaceflight, NASA wanted a new, civilian rocket capable of lifting large amounts of weight into orbit. While with the Army, von Braun and his team had begun to create such a family of rockets. With the start of NASA's Apollo program, von Braun's Saturn rockets had a purpose. No longer would NASA have to use rockets converted from military use. The largest planned, the *Saturn V*, could have put a man on the moon. Von Braun's dream of working on rockets solely for space travel had been realized. Too bad the final result was never realized.

The marriage of nuclear weapons to ballistic missiles created a deadly combination. Ballistic missiles by themselves were not accurate enough to be reliable conventional weapons. Engineers measured a missile's accuracy by its circular error probability (CEP) rating. The Atlas ICBM had a CEP of 4,600 feet. This meant that at least half of the time, an Atlas warhead would land within 4,600 feet of its target. That distance would have made a conventional warhead useless, but a rocket with a nuclear warhead could still destroy its target if it landed less than a mile away.

A large nuclear weapon, such as a one-megaton warhead, even if delivered by an inaccurate ballistic missile, could easily destroy a city or another nuclear missile standing out in the open. But what if your target was a missile placed underground in a silo of reinforced concrete? A near miss might not destroy the silo, meaning that missile would still be available for use by the enemy. The United States began to build silos for its ICBMs so that it would be harder for Soviet missiles to knock them out during a nuclear war.

New military strategies and terminology were developed for nuclear wars. A "first strike" was a preemptive nuclear attack, in which one side would launch all of its nuclear weapons in order to destroy so much of the enemy's nuclear forces that any retaliation would be minimal. Such a strike required accurate delivery systems, either bombers that could penetrate enemy air defenses or missiles that hit close to their targets. The best answer to a first strike was to maintain nuclear forces large and robust enough so that no matter what happened, enough nuclear forces would be left behind to launch an effective retaliatory strike to obliterate the enemy. To make the threat of retaliation more viable, a nation's nuclear forces had to be well dispersed: ballistic missiles placed in hardened silos, bombers scattered in numerous airfields, and submarines carrying ballistic missiles hidden in the oceans. (Silos and effective submarines were in only the early stages of development by 1962.) All of these strategies coalesced under a single term: "mutual assured destruction." In essence this term meant, if you nuke me, I'll nuke you back, and we'll both lose.

By the early 1960s, in addition to its large bomber force, the United States had Jupiter IRBMs in place in Europe. Squadrons of Thor IRBMs, developed by the Air Force, were also deployed in England. The Atlas ICBMs had already been deployed around the United States, and the next generation of ICBMs had been developed and was ready for deployment in the form of the Minuteman ICBM.

Before the Minuteman, all ICBMs were liquid fueled, meaning that the missile stood empty until the highly toxic and corrosive fuel was added just before launch. This procedure meant that it took hours for missiles to be readied in the event of war. There was another way.

SOLID-FUEL MISSILES

Early rockets, from the time of their invention by the Chinese, had been made using solid fuel that burned to create the propulsion. The great innovation of Tsiolkovsky, Goddard, and von Braun was the use of liquid propellants. All the MRBMs, IRBMs, and early ICBMs relied on liquid fuels. Rockets, especially tactical versions, were still being made using solid fuel, and the Air Force saw the potential of using solid fuel for ballistic missiles also. Solid fuel could last for years, and such a missile could launch within minutes.

In 1955 the Air Force started the Minuteman program, designed to deploy a hundred solid-fuel ICBMs by 1964 and another four hundred the following year. The missile was called the Minuteman because it was expected to be able to launch within a minute of being alerted, rather than within hours, as with the liquid-fueled missiles. The first ten Minuteman missiles became officially operational at Malmstrom Air Force Base (AFB), Montana, in late October 1962 (these were not used during the Fire). The Minuteman silos were eighty feet deep, just twelve feet in diameter, and covered by blast doors that weighed a hundred tons to protect the missile from a near hit by a Soviet nuclear weapon. The doors would be blown off by conventional explosives just prior to missile launch.

Thiokol was one of the major companies contracted by both the Army and Air Force to work on solid-fuel missiles. To make the first and third stages of the new Minuteman, a new plant was built in the desert of Utah, chosen because it was far enough from population centers to cut down on complaints by the locals over the noisy rocket tests, and it was far enough inland to avoid hits by submarine-launched ballistic missiles (SLBMs) or by submarine-launched cruise missiles.

Solid rocket propellant is mixed in large bowls, like something out of a giant's kitchen, and early Thiokol test rocket projects actually used commercial kitchen appliances as mixers. The mixed chemicals form a paste, which is poured into a mold and allowed to harden. Eventually, rockets became so big that multiple mixes were poured to create a single rocket. The mixtures remained viable for years until ignition.

By the mid-1950s development of ICBMs was well under way in both the United States and the Soviet Union. The Americans and Soviets sought to build missiles with sufficient range to reach across oceans so that they could base these weapons in their home countries. As the missile race became public, Americans came to fear that both a "bomber gap" and a "missile gap" had developed, with the Soviet Union pulling ahead of the United States in the development and deployment of bombers and missiles. The Eisenhower administration could not quell these fears, even though it knew that such gaps did not exist, because their knowledge of the true state of Soviet progress was based on secret overflights of the Soviet Union by American spy planes such as the famed U-2.

Lacking the ability to conduct their own overflights of the United States, the Soviets used other means to keep track of American developments. Oleg Kalugin, a former Soviet intelligence officer, wrote in his memoir that he had been contacted in 1959 by a Thiokol engineer based in New Jersey who offered plans for solid-fuel rocket motors and even a sample of the solid fuel. Kalugin eagerly accepted the offered intelligence, and the Thiokol engineer was never caught.

SOVIET MISSILES

Von Braun's counterpart in the Soviet Union was Sergei Pavlovich Korolyov, born in Ukraine in 1907, five years before von Braun. We know little about this brilliant engineer and organizer. An aircraft engineer in the famed Tupolev Design Bureau, Korolyov became active in the Group for the Study of Rockets, which experimented with liquid-fueled rockets in a manner similar to the German Society for Space Travel. In 1933 the group launched a rocket to an altitude of thirteen hundred feet. The Soviet government made the group into a state organization, and the military funded further rocket development. In 1934 Korolyov even visited Tsiolkovsky, a passing of the flame from the great theorist to a younger generation.[17]

In 1937 Korolyov was arrested during Stalin's purges. A confession of guilt was beaten from him. Unlike so many others, he was not immediately executed but sent to work as forced labor in a surface gold mine in eastern Siberia. This was effectively a death sentence, since 30 percent of the laborers died in the mine each year. Korolyov lost all his teeth, had his jaw broken, and almost died of scurvy. After a year, Soviet aircraft designer Andrei Tupolev managed to have Korolyov transferred to a prison with him and other aeronautical engineers. Although they were prisoners, they were expected to continue their research, even as World War II came.

In 1945, with the end of the war, Korolyov was released from prison and made a colonel in the Red Army. The Stalinist system had decided that it needed him. The Soviets were annoyed that von Braun had taken the documents from

Peenemünde and that the Americans and British had stripped the underground rocket factory. The Soviets picked through the pieces; recruited former workers, including two top engineers who had not fled with von Braun; and reopened the rocket factory. They wanted to build V-2s for themselves. Korolyov was put to work as part of this effort in the Soviet-occupied zone of Germany.

A year later the Soviets moved the rocket research and production, including the German engineers and technicians, to the Soviet Union. Their new home was located at Kapustin Yar on the Volga River. Korolyov developed a Soviet version of the V-2 called the R-1, with a range of about 168 miles. In 1948 Korolyov may have spent more time in prison, an illustration of how precarious survival was in Stalin's Soviet Union, especially for the most capable people. By 1953 all the information had been drained out of the German experts and the last of them were allowed to return home.

In 1950 the first military unit equipped with R-1 missiles was deployed. This mobile MRBM was very complex, requiring twenty vehicles and four kinds of liquid propellants (liquid oxygen, alcohol, hydrogen peroxide, and permanganate catalyst) for the main engine, for turbines to pump the fuel into the engine, and for ignition. Red Army generals were unhappy not only with this complexity but also with the inclusion of alcohol among the fuels, since soldiers were known for their skill in making their own liquor.

In 1955 the Soviets began to use a second development and test center at Baikonur in Kazakhstan, much farther away from the American surveillance posts in Turkey that collected radar information on test flights. Korolyov continued to develop new rockets, roughly keeping pace with the Americans in the liquid-fueled variety. His R-7 rocket, with a range of five thousand miles, was the world's first ICBM. His first three test flights failed, but a fourth effort succeeded on August 21, 1957.

During all this time, Korolyov continued to nurse his original dream of space travel. He proposed launching an artificial satellite using the R-7, and on October 4, 1957, *Sputnik* was launched. While honors and prestige came Korolyov's way, they were privately awarded. His name was a state secret, and he was known only as the "chief designer," though apparently there were also other chief designers conducting rocket research.

With the success of *Sputnik*, Korolyov was able to turn his attention from weapons to the new Soviet space program. Satellites and the Soviet manned space program all launched out of Baikonur. Successes followed, including obtaining the first photographs of the far side of the moon with the space probe *Luna 3*, launched in 1959, and putting the first man into orbit in 1961. There are unsubstantiated rumors that four earlier attempts at launching a man into orbit had resulted in three deaths and one severely injured cosmonaut. More cosmonauts followed the first success.

In 1959 the R-7 (called the SS-6 Sapwood by NATO) was deployed as an operational weapon. The launch complexes for the ICBM were so expensive to build, even though all the construction was aboveground, that only six launch sites in total became operational. Four of these were at the Northern Cosmodrome, a new launch center near Plesetsk, five hundred miles north of Moscow, with the remaining two at Baikonur. Only the missiles at Plesetsk had the range to hit the continental United States.

On December 14, 1959, the Soviet Union created the Strategic Rocket Forces, an independent service responsible for all land-based strategic ballistic missiles. The bombers remained with the Soviet air force, and the missile-carrying submarines remained with the Soviet navy. In 1948 the Soviets had created the Air Defense Forces, separate from the regular air force, with the sole responsibility of defending the Soviet Union with fighters, antiaircraft missiles, and antiaircraft guns against American bombers.

At the time of the Fire, the Soviets were far behind the Americans in solid-fuel rocket technology, despite the intelligence they had gathered from the Thiokol engineer. This meant that all Soviet missiles, even those on submarines, were still liquid fueled and required hours of preparation before launch. The Soviets also had not put any of their missiles in silos yet, perhaps because silos were so expensive to build and fueling a missile in a silo seemed to be an awkward process in theory.

BALLISTIC MISSILES ON SUBMARINES

Wanting to protect their nuclear missiles from both first strikes and retaliatory strikes, the United States and the Soviet Union developed the SLBM. The first effort came in the form of a cruise missile with stubby wings, a variation of the German V-1 rocket from World War II. The United States converted or built five submarines to carry these Regulus cruise missiles. One submarine could carry between two and five missiles, each with a range of 575 miles, and at least two submarines were on patrol at any time.

The Soviets developed the same ability. Four Echo-class nuclear-propelled submarines were built, each equipped with six SS-N-3 Sepal cruise missiles. Each cruise missile could carry a 350-kiloton warhead for 345 miles. The Soviets also developed the first submarines to carry ballistic missiles, using an innovative storable liquid fuel. Some of these submarines were nuclear powered, while others relied on older diesel-fueled engines.

The first of the nuclear-powered Hotel class, *K-19*, suffered a reactor accident on July 4, 1961, in the Atlantic off southern Greenland. Twenty-two crew members died from escaped radiation, and the submarine was towed back to base. The Soviets usually kept their submarines in port to reduce costs, and this accident encouraged them to keep their other nuclear-powered submarines in port in order to fix any problems with their nuclear reactors.

The problems that the Soviet submarines experienced were not confined to nuclear reactors. In general, Soviet weapons were afflicted with poor workmanship and poor quality control. Parts did not work as expected or failed more frequently because the Soviet system had always rewarded quantity—via designated production quotas—and not quality. This was true even though defense industries made an effort at quality control that was absent in the civilian economy.[18]

While a definitive count of total Soviet submarines is disputed, we do know the following: At the time of the Cuban Missile Crisis, the Soviet Union had eight Hotel-class submarines, including the ill-fated *K-19*, which had the nickname "Hiroshima" among Soviet sailors. Each Hotel submarine carried three SS-N-4 Sark missiles, which store their liquid propellants internally. Fired from the surface, each Sark could carry a megaton warhead for a range of 370 miles, requiring the Soviet submarines to move uncomfortably close to the American coast before firing. Up to twenty-two diesel-powered Golf-class submarines were also each equipped with three SS-N-4 Sark missiles.

The U.S. Navy decided not to pursue the liquid-fueled rocket option any further, leapfrogging the technology forward. Lockheed Corporation built the Polaris fleet ballistic missile, a solid-fuel rocket that could be launched while submerged, for the Navy. Solid-fuel rockets not only could launch much faster but also took up much less space. A new submarine was built to carry sixteen of the missiles. On July 20, 1960, off Cape Canaveral, Florida, two Polaris test missiles were launched from the submerged USS *George Washington* within two hours of each other. By the time of the Fire, the Americans had five of this class of submarines available, each carrying sixteen Polaris A-1 missiles with a range of 1,380 miles. Another four Ethan Allen–class submarines were also newly commissioned, and each carried sixteen improved A-2 versions of the Polaris missile, with a range of 1,725 miles. The A-1 carried a 600-kiloton warhead, while the A-2 warhead doubled the destructive power to 1.2 megatons.

All of these American submarines were nuclear powered and thus not required to surface for any reason except when in port. Each of the American "boomer" submarines had two complete crews assigned to them, a Blue crew alternated with a Gold crew, so that the submarines could stay at sea almost continuously. These men lived under the sea, waiting for the moment that orders would come, praying that their purpose would never be realized.

|■|

Now that nuclear weapons had been joined to the ballistic missile and the long-range bomber, the technology was in place to make the Fire. But it is humans who make moral choices, not machines. Without fingers on the launch buttons, the ballistic missiles would remain inert on their launching pads and bombers would remain on their airfields—potential, not actual, destruction.

Two men confronted the most important moral choices ever made: Nikita Khrushchev and John F. Kennedy. What sort of men were they, and how did they make decisions? Through their lives, we can also see how the United States and the Union of Soviet Socialist Republics reached the point of confrontation over Cuba.

Further sources: David A. Clary, *Rocket Man: Robert H. Goddard and the Birth of the Space Age* (New York: Hyperion, 2003); Richard G. Davis, *Carl A. Spaatz and the Air War in Europe* (Washington, D.C.: Center for Air Force History, 1993); Max Hastings, *Bomber Command* (London: Joseph, 1979); Oleg Kalugin, *The First Directorate: My 32 Years in Intelligence and Espionage against the West*, with Fen Montaigne (New York: St. Martin's Press, 1994); Geoffrey Perret, *Winged Victory: The Army Air Forces in World War II* (New York: Random House, 1993); Dennis Piszkiewicz, *Wernher von Braun: The Man Who Sold the Moon* (Westport, CT: Praeger, 1998); Norman Polmar and Kenneth J. Moore, *Cold War Submarines: The Design and Construction of U.S. and Soviet Submarines* (Washington, D.C.: Brassey's, Inc., 2004); Richard Rhodes, *Dark Sun: The Making of the Hydrogen Bomb* (New York: Simon & Schuster, 1995); Richard Rhodes, *The Making of the Atomic Bomb* (New York: Simon & Schuster, 1986); and Ronald Schaffer, *Wings of Judgment: American Bombing in World War II* (New York: Oxford University Press, 1985).

2

Survivor: Nikita Khrushchev

Nikita Khrushchev remains an enigma to us. Even the manner of his death is still a matter of heated speculation among historians. We are fortunate that his son survived the Fire, because he was on vacation in Switzerland when it came, as he later wrote a biography of his father that is mostly reliable.

UKRANIAN PEASANT

Nikita Sergeyevich Khrushchev was born to peasants in Kalinovka in the spring of 1894. He likely lived in a hut called an *izba*, made of rough lumber and a thatched roof, with dung spread on the walls in the winter to keep its occupants warmer. A bland diet of bread, cabbage, onions, and *kvas* (nonalcoholic drink brewed from bread) was supplemented by fresh vegetables when they were in season. Khrushchev recalled that he wore no shoes during the summer and had only shoes made of bark during the winter. (Oddly, the most vivid image of Khrushchev for many people in the West came from an incident at the United Nations on October 12, 1960, when he brandished his shoe and banged it on the desk before him during a speech that he did not like.) He claimed that his grandfather had only two baths in his life: when he was christened as a baby and when he was prepared for his burial. Khrushchev's parents were so poor that they did not own a horse, which meant that they could not plow the fields, and so their existence was precarious. Only by moving far away to the coal-mining town of Yuzovka (later named Donetsk, Ukraine) in the Donbas, czarist Russia's primary mining and steelmaking region, and working as a railroad laborer or as a miner was Khrushchev's father able to effectively support his family.

In Khrushchev's own words, "After a year or two of school, I had learnt to count up to thirty and my father decided that was enough of schooling. He said that all I needed was to be able to count money, and I would never have more than thirty rubles to count anyway."[1] Receiving so little education was common among most peasant children, and at this point he had only a rudimentary literacy, which he developed further as an adult. His father tried to apprentice Khrushchev to a shoemaker, but the young man refused. Then the father tried to make him a store clerk, since he was so good with numbers; again, failure. Even at a young age, Khrushchev had higher ambitions.

At age fourteen, Khrushchev moved to Yuzovka with his family and went to work. At first he worked cleaning out mine boilers, which left him covered with soot and ash, but soon he apprenticed as a metal fitter and found that he enjoyed the work. Metalworking paid comparatively well and was a high-status job among the social hierarchy of the factory and mines. Khrushchev built himself a bicycle and later added a noisy motor to it so that he could roar about the town. This was a completely different life than working the fields as a peasant.

The young metal fitter began to read radical newspapers and soon became involved in socialist politics. This behavior was duly noted by the police, and Khrushchev was fired and forced to find another job. Fortunately fitters were in demand, and the area had many factories and mines. Khrushchev met an older man, Ivan Pisarev, who operated the main elevator for the Rutchenkovo mine, a job that required diligence and organization, and went to his house often for conversations about socialism and union activities. Pisarev also had five daughters, all of them educated. Khrushchev married the oldest, Yefrosinia, when he was twenty years old and she eighteen, a significant social step up for him. The couple moved into a nice apartment, something his parents, who often had to live with relatives, could never afford. Khrushchev had a reputation as someone who could fix anything and a seriousness that encouraged him to seek out the company of people older than himself. He was obviously a young man seeking to better himself. He was grateful when he started to show gray in his closely cut hair at the age of twenty-two because too often he was taken for being younger than his age.

As a skilled fitter, Khrushchev was too valuable to be drafted into the army for World War I. During the war, he was active organizing socialist-inspired strikes in the mines and factories. He did not join the Bolsheviks immediately after the Russian Revolution, perhaps because the more moderate socialists, the Mensheviks, were more to his liking, since more of the skilled workers favored them. Khrushchev joined the Communist Party in 1918 and sometime later joined the Red Army, where he served as a political commissar, indoctrinating the troops in Communist ideology, maintaining morale, and ensuring that the regular officers followed the party line. The civil war, during which the Red Army fought different White armies, was a vicious time, characterized by many atrocities. The Donbas industrial region is estimated to have lost a third of its workers, many of them slain as the armies moved back and forth during the fighting. Khrushchev's role during this time is hard to properly document, as a consequence of his own effort to obscure his own past. As he later advanced in the party, he tried to hide the fact that he was not an early party member and tended to embellish his supposed role in the initial success of the early party.

Early in the civil war, Khrushchev fled with his family from Yuzovka back to his home village of Kalinovka. He left his wife and two children with his parents while he went to fight. Disease, malnutrition, and death stalked the land, and his wife succumbed to typhus, exactly when and how we do not know. His son and daughter survived.

After the war, Khrushchev worked as a manager, getting the mines and factories of the Donbas running again. The mine owners and engineers (most of them foreigners) had fled, leaving the workers to literally take the coke ovens apart to see how they worked. Khrushchev proved to be a hardworking, hands-on leader who could accomplish much with little. When he was selected to assume the management of a mine on his own, he begged to be allowed to attend two years of additional education instead. For Khrushchev, as for many of the Bolsheviks, education was not just reading, writing, and arithmetic, though those were important; nor was it just political education, also important. It was also cultural education: learning to appreciate a good ballet, read a classic Russian novel, maintain good hygiene, use a modern toilet, and act at the table or in company.[2]

During this time, Khrushchev married a seventeen-year-old woman named Marusia with an infant daughter. She neglected caring for his two children in favor of her baby, and Khrushchev's mother persuaded him to put the woman aside. He did so, though his attitudes later in life showed that he was a man who disliked divorce. This second marriage was kept a family secret, though Khrushchev is reported to have helped out Marusia later in life.

Khrushchev quickly moved on to his third wife, Nina Petrovna Kukharchuk, a Ukranian and the daughter of well-off peasants. She was better educated than he and an equally ardent Communist. In a way, she was his teacher in ideological matters. Oddly enough, though they were husband and wife in all ways, living together for the rest of their lives, they never married. They had three daughters and a son together, though one daughter died at three months old. Perhaps a marriage ceremony was too bourgeoisie.

After Vladimir Lenin died in 1924, Leon Trotsky and Josef Stalin struggled to fill the void in leadership. Trotsky was focused on continuing the socialist revolution internationally, while Stalin wanted to concentrate first on the Soviet Union. While the doctrinal differences excited true believers, the foundation of the dispute was a power struggle that Stalin eventually won. Khrushchev had subscribed to Trotskyite ideas and as a consequence could have been killed in the great purges of the 1930s, but his family effectively kept his leanings secret.

While Khrushchev claimed to have finished his two years of further education in 1924, we have no independent verification of this. He remained active as a political leader while in school and in 1925 became the party boss for a district near Stalino. He climbed steadily up the Communist Party ladder, working hard and resorting to intrigue when necessary. The details of his life at this time are sketchy at best, but he quickly moved to Kharkov, then to Kiev, the capital of Ukraine. While there, he campaigned for permission to go to Moscow to further his education again. According to a friend of his wife's, his dream was to be a factory director. He liked the hands-on work of running a factory and despised having a job where he moved paper all day.

Only a hundred students were accepted each year to the elite Stalin Industrial Academy in Moscow. Khrushchev's political patron in Ukraine, Lazar Kaganovich, had already moved to Moscow in 1928, and he arranged for Khrushchev to be admitted to the academy in 1929, despite his poor academic background. Khrushchev never finished the three-year course of study, however, because his political career continued to soar. Within just a few years, Khrushchev had become the effective political head of Moscow. Perhaps Khrushchev's greatest success, beyond personal survival, was the completion of the initial phase of the Moscow Metro, an underground subway system for the capital that served as a showpiece of Communist achievements. His quest for an education, three times diverted in favor of political pursuits, was over.

Khrushchev brought his parents to live with him in Moscow in order to care for them and to have them care for his children. His wife worked long hours as a party official at a factory until the birth of her last two children; when her husband became a high party official, she turned to occasional party work and teaching evening courses. Khrushchev was often not home, a consequence of one of his greatest assets: a strong work ethic that kept him on the job for long hours. While Khrushchev's family was prospering, the rest of the Soviet Union suffered from the twin horrors of collectivization and the purges.

In early 1930 Stalin demanded the complete collectivization of the nation's agriculture by the end of the year, moving peasants from their own property and forcing them to join agricultural collectives. He was motivated by Communist ideology and a desire to destroy the potential power of the peasants to be an independent political and economic force. Food production in Russia was a fragile effort, easily disrupted, and the result of collectivization was such a dramatic drop in production that millions died from starvation.

In the midst of this national calamity, many party members on both the national and local level spoke out about the errors. Anyone who opposed Stalin was considered an enemy and was called a rightist, oppositionist, deviationist, or enemy of the people. At this point such labels meant expulsion from the party, a prison sentence, or exile to Siberia. As the decade passed, however, punishment turned to torture and execution not only for the party members but also for their families.

At the Industrial Academy, Khrushchev was a strong Stalin supporter, an eager participant in the fight to expose anyone who disagreed with the leader. Perhaps his enthusiasm was motivated by a desire to prove his own loyalty. The academy was a premier institution in Moscow and Stalin's own wife was a student there. Khrushchev soon deposed the local party leader and replaced him. When Stalin took notice of this poorly educated peasant, Khrushchev responded like a puppy getting attention from his master. Khrushchev's campaigns against enemies of the people continued as he moved up the political ladder. As head of the Moscow party, he made fiery speeches in support of Stalin, called for the harshest measures, approved the arrests of some of his closest friends and colleagues, and was involved as a bureaucrat in the death of thousands. With a prudent sense of his own survival, Khrushchev did nothing to help friends and colleagues. Refusing to sign death warrants was a quick way to bring suspicion on oneself and one's family.

In his paranoia, Stalin had a keen sense of how to incorporate others into his web of destruction, implicating them by forcing them to help and creating shared guilt. At its height the purge was driven by lists of people to be arrested, tried, and, in most cases, executed. These lists were sent down from higher officials, along with quotas for the number of victims to be found. To help achieve a national quota of thirty-five thousand in June 1937, Khrushchev found two thousand former kulaks (prosperous peasants who, before collectivization, owned their own land) living in Moscow to be offered up as enemies of the people and as a sacrifice to their god, Stalin. It got to the point that party members made spurious accusations against each other in a desperate attempt to curry favor with the authorities.

Khrushchev later denied that he knew that many of those arrested were executed. He said that he assumed they were imprisoned, though he also made sure that he did not find out any more; as with Germans during the Holocaust, willful ignorance was a way to prevent a crisis of conscience. When close friends were arrested, Khrushchev told himself that they must have been secret traitors. Signed confessions were often wrung from the arrested before their sham trials and executions, though later in the purges, trials were dispensed with completely. Khrushchev clung to these confessions to preserve the self-deception that he practiced in order to continue to function and to survive. So ready was Khrushchev to submit himself to this system that in 1937 he actually confessed his 1923 infatuation with Trotskyism to his patron, Kaganovich. He was sent to have the same conversation with Stalin, who advised him to confess to a party conference. Khrushchev did so and survived, and this only cemented his deep adoration for the Soviet leader; Khrushchev himself used the term "worship" when referring to his relationship with Stalin. It has been rumored, though not proved, that in the 1950s, Khrushchev ordered that death lists or warrants that he had signed be removed from the state archives.

While no one can know the mind of Stalin, a twisted psychological labyrinth, we must ask ourselves why Khrushchev survived. Khrushchev was an agreeable man who liked most other people, even pathological killers such as Nikolai Yezhov and Lavrenty Beria, who served as heads of the People's Commissariat for Internal Affairs (NKVD, or secret police). Khrushchev was also quite garrulous, and this eased Stalin's suspicions that his disciple might be scheming.

Stalin and Khrushchev were a study in contrasts. Stalin disliked making speeches, whereas Khrushchev enjoyed public speaking, especially impromptu addresses to workers, and was considered a good orator. He was not articulate in a literary way but could effectively speak to the common man. Stalin was five feet, six inches tall and always strived to look taller, wearing lift shoes and speaking on elevated platforms; Khrushchev was only five feet, one inch, and seemed not to feel a need to compensate. Khrushchev's lack of education probably made Stalin feel more secure, since Stalin was a powerful intellect in his own right but lacked the education of Lenin and his great rivals, such as Trotsky.

In January 1938 Stalin sent Khrushchev south to be the party head of Ukraine. While ambitious, Khrushchev balked at the assignment, arguing that his knowledge of Ukrainian was too poor for effective speeches, but he also obeyed Stalin, his master in all things. No doubt Khrushchev was aware of what had happened to the previous leaders of Ukraine, who, along with their immediate families and even more distant relatives, had died in the purges.

When he arrived in Kiev, Khrushchev found the party in tatters from purges and the region still traumatized by collectivization. He continued the purges, as Stalin had instructed, and under his guidance at least fifty thousand more people lost their lives. Almost every Communist leader in Ukraine and in local Red Army units was replaced, with half of all the party members in Kiev itself denounced, arrested, or executed. Khrushchev had arrived at the same place that so many other ideologues morally inhabited: he justified present brutal actions with a vision of a future socialist utopia. Only the coming of World War II slowed down the executions, and the invasion of the Soviet Union itself actually stopped them. The secret police still hunted and tortured politically unreliable people, but the atmosphere of paranoia was calmed—at least to the extent that anything could be calm when Stalin was in charge.

THE GREAT PATRIOTIC WAR

The first act of World War II was a conspiracy: the Nazi-Soviet Non-Aggression Pact, signed in 1939, which promised that neither side would attack the other and which covertly divided up Poland and Eastern Europe. A week after the pact was signed, German forces fell on Poland, quickly conquering the hapless nation in only a month. Two weeks into the campaign, the Soviet Union moved in to occupy its share of the spoils. Part of Poland was renamed Western Ukraine, and Khrushchev took the lead in integrating this new territory into his Ukraine. About 10 percent of the population was deported into the Soviet interior, and 350,000 people were either executed or died as a result of deportation. The Soviets accomplished this much in less than two years before they were interrupted by the German invasion on June 22, 1941.

The winter before the Germans attacked, Stalin began insisting that everyone who attended his late-night gatherings had to drink. The gatherings were an essential part of Stalin's method of government, and all of his closest advisers and fellow party leaders participated. Khrushchev had avoided alcohol his entire life, a legacy from his mother, but at the age of forty-six he learned to drink. As war came to the Soviet Union, Khrushchev also took up smoking to deal with the trauma.

Weakened by the purges that had removed almost the entire high command and perhaps half of the officer corps, the Red Army collapsed under the German assault. Fortunately, a few experienced leaders had been spared, and within months they were rehabilitated from prisons and exile in Siberia. During the war, Khrushchev continued to serve as the top political leader in Ukraine, where the Soviets experienced some of their greatest defeats—at Kiev and Kharkov. After the defeat at Kharkov, in which a counteroffensive strongly advocated by Khrushchev ran into a German trap that led to the loss of almost a half million soldiers, Khrushchev was summoned to Moscow, where Stalin fought the war from his supreme headquarters in the Kirov Metro underground station. Khrushchev expected to be arrested, but Stalin apparently enjoyed prolonging the agony of suspense instead. A few months after Khrushchev arrived, Stalin actually tapped his pipe on Khrushchev's bald head to knock out the ashes, explaining to the other commanders in the room that ancient Roman generals who had been defeated in battle would pour ashes on their own heads as an act of humiliation.

The Battle of Stalingrad, in the city on the Volga River named after Stalin himself, became the turning point on the eastern front and redeemed Khrushchev. He was in the city from the first of the battle—encouraging the troops, always engaged, and developing a reputation for personal courage. When the war ended with a Soviet victory and the military occupation of Eastern Europe, turning the Soviet Union effectively into one of two superpowers, Khrushchev found his faith in the Communist cause renewed. As with so many Communist accomplishments, the victory had come at enormous cost.

Estimates of how many Soviet soldiers and civilians died in what they called the Great Patriotic War vary in detail but not in magnitude, with the best research arriving at the chilling number of 27 million. Ukraine suffered a disproportionate share of this total, losing one out of every six people. This loss does not include the punishment that Stalin imposed on Soviet prisoners of war returning from their harsh treatment in German camps. Stalin sent most of them directly to the gulags in Siberia, since he viewed all of his soldiers who became prisoners of war as traitors. We do not know his opinion of his own son, who died while a prisoner of the Germans in 1943. In a June 1944 letter to Stalin, Khrushchev urged lenient treatment of the prisoners of war, most of whom had not yet been liberated. Stalin ignored him.

Khrushchev hated the carnage of war, as does every human being with any sensibility, and he suffered other personal costs. His oldest son, Lyonia, was an undisciplined merrymaker, who left women pregnant in his wake, had abandoned his first wife, and had killed a naval officer during a party while drunkenly trying to shoot a bottle off the officer's head. He died during a dogfight in 1943. Lyonia's wife, Liuba, was later accused of being a spy and spent ten months in an NKVD jail, where the guards deprived her of sleep, though they otherwise did not physically torture her. Four years in a labor camp followed for Liuba, during which time her weight dropped to about seventy pounds, and then she spent five years of exile in Kazakhstan. The Khrushchevs raised her daughter as their own, and according to our best source—a dissident with access to NKVD files—Khrushchev saw Liuba only once in person, and she saw her daughter only once after she transferred custody to her in-laws, in 1956. We do not know why Khrushchev did not rectify the injustice of Liuba's treatment, even after Stalin's death; perhaps he believed the NKVD charges against her. Certainly it was easier to believe what the NKVD said than to confront the numerous miscarriages of justice. Khrushchev was lucky compared to other members of the ruling Politburo, who lost wives, siblings, and children to purges.

Liuba also had a son from a previous marriage, and the Khrushchevs sent the nine-year-old child to an orphanage after his mother's arrest. He escaped and found the Khrushchev family, whereupon Khrushchev's wife gave him two sausages and sent him to another orphanage. His story grew grimmer and involved nearly starving to death, living as a homeless youth, spending time in a correctional colony, and finally joining the army as an adult. He met his half-sister again in 1955, and the two were a study in contrasts: she was an educated woman who was the adopted daughter of the leader of the Soviet Union and he was impoverished and immediately recognized the enormous gulf between them. Fortunately, Liuba reconnected with her son after returning from exile, and they had no further contact with the Khrushchev family.

During the war, Khrushchev began to lay the groundwork for his adminis-tration of postwar Ukraine. As part of that effort, he requested the whereabouts of earlier leaders and intellectuals and was shocked to find how many of them had been executed. This should not have been surprising, especially to a person who had participated in the purges. Yet in a country where all information was treated as a secret and where there was no free press to encourage the flow of information, even a leader in the Politburo could be unaware of many things.

The war had reduced Ukraine to ruins, and rebuilding consumed Khrush-chev's energies. He also directed the brutal repression of nationalist guerrillas in Western Ukraine, during which at least two hundred thousand people died. Despite Khrushchev's efforts, acts of sabotage, assassination, and terrorism by the guerrillas continued into the mid-1950s. Another two million Western Ukraini-ans were forcibly moved to other parts of the Soviet Union, a tactic that Stalin favored to handle restive minorities. The Ukrainian Greek Catholic Church sup-ported Ukrainian nationalism, so Khrushchev struck at it by sending an assas-sination team that rammed the car of Bishop Theodore Romzha off the road and beat him with iron bars. When a post office truck approached, the attackers withdrew, and later Khrushchev himself met with a toxicological expert and ar-ranged for the wounded bishop to be poisoned at the hospital. Other church of-ficials also died, but we can only assume Khrushchev's knowledge of these cases.

In 1946 Ukraine again experience famine, prompted by a drought, Commu-nist insistence on collectivized agriculture, and a national policy that compulsory quotas be met before any crops were diverted to local needs. The quotas fed the cities and the new Eastern European satellite nations. Khrushchev had agreed to the quotas, but after the famine started and he heard reports of cannibalism, he urged Stalin to give assistance. Some assistance came, though Khrushchev was sure that he was skirting the possibility of being arrested for his impertinence. For a time he was dismissed from some of his duties as the party leader in Ukraine, though he remained the head of the Ukrainian government, and his name disap-peared from the press in May 1947, usually a sign of impending doom in the Soviet system. By the end of the year, however, Stalin had forgiven Khrushchev and his party posts had been restored. The 1947 and 1948 harvests were good, even with collectivization including 60 percent of peasant households by 1949.

As head of the party in Ukraine from 1938 to 1949, Khrushchev witnessed his own minor cult of personality. Stalin awarded him medals, and the press wrote such fawning profiles that only an egotist could avoid embarrassment. Khrushchev claimed to dislike flattery, but he did nothing to discourage the cult, a feature of Stalinist communism, though his cult was a pale shadow of Stalin's.

Khrushchev had reached the end of his work in Ukraine. Stalin summoned him to Moscow in 1949 so that he could once again head the party in Moscow. Khrushchev also became one of the four Central Committee secretaries (a post that Stalin also held). Khrushchev had already been made a member of the eleven-person Politburo in 1939. Stalin was in physical and mental decline, but his paranoia was still alive and well and now focused even more on his closest colleagues. In the year Khrushchev returned to Moscow, two members of the Politburo were arrested—and then shot a year later—while the Jewish wife of another Politburo member, the foreign minister, Vyacheslav Molotov, was sent to a labor camp.*

There is some evidence that Stalin had already suffered two strokes; his arteries were hardening, sapping his energy, and there was no doubt that he was a lonely man. His management style of bypassing official procedures so that he could conduct business directly continued. Much of his direction came during marathon sessions in which he invited his inner circle to watch movies at the Kremlin and then go to his dacha to spend the rest of the night drinking, eating, and talking until dawn. Afraid of poison, Stalin insisted that others taste each dish of food before he ate.

In this nest of intrigue, Khrushchev proved himself as cunning as any of the others, though they underestimated the poorly educated peasant from Kalinovka. It certainly took an iron will to participate in Stalin's overnight sessions and find the energy to go to work the next day. The stress of seeing his fellows accused, sometimes arrested and sometimes killed, and knowing that he might be next forced a man to live in a daze of fear and uncertainty. Lesser men would have collapsed with ulcers. Khrushchev did more than survive; he slowly moved his protégés into key positions and protected others from Stalin's paranoia by sending them to positions outside Moscow.

---

* During the Soviet-Finnish War of 1939–40, Finnish soldiers built improvised explosive devices (IEDs) by filling glass bottles with gasoline and maybe tar, soap, oil, or other substances to make the burning gasoline stick to its target; using gasoline-soaked rags to plug the bottles; and then lighting the rags and throwing the bottles. These IEDs were somewhat effective antitank devices. The Finns called them Molotov cocktails to mock Vyacheslav Molotov's claims that the Soviets were dropping food parcels, not bombs, on Finland.

In 1952 the Politburo of the Central Committee of the Communist Party of the Soviet Union was replaced by the Presidium of the Central Committee of the Communist Party, a twenty-five member group.* This change was probably part of Stalin's plan to replace most of his older cronies with newer recruits. Around this time, Stalin also discovered a "doctors' plot" to poison the top Soviet leadership and ordered the arrest of the medical doctors who served the Kremlin, most of whom were Jewish. Even in his old age, Stalin seemed to be gearing up for a new round of arrests among his closest supporters.

Two months after the doctors' arrests, in March 1953, a stroke felled Stalin, who lingered in an incoherent stupor for several days before finally succumbing. Initially, Lavrenty Beria, as head of the secret police, assumed effective control and placed his ally Georgy Malenkov at the head of the Soviet government. In the Soviet system, titles often concealed more than they revealed. Khrushchev, still in awe of his socialist hero, despite having seen the dark side of the mercurial man, mourned the loss of Stalin. With Beria in charge, Khrushchev's rank on the list of Presidium members was lowered to fifth, whereas under Stalin he had been either second or third, with Stalin listed as first. His fellow Communist leaders had clearly underestimated the peasant.

Considering his role as Stalin's henchman in the purges, Beria's whirlwind of policy changes were a surprise. Hundreds of thousands of political prisoners were immediately released, including Molotov's wife. The Kremlin doctors were released, and Beria publicly announced that the evidence of the doctors' plot had been fabricated. The Soviet policy toward East Germany, which was near collapse as hundreds of thousands of workers fled to the West, also took a sharp turn. Beria indicated that he was willing to see the satellite collapse and reunification of the two German nations in return for economic payments from the West. Beria often announced policies without consulting other members of the Presidium, a trait that he shared with Stalin but that was guaranteed to alienate the other Soviet leaders.

Beria's actions alarmed his colleagues. Releasing the political prisoners so quickly implied that the entire leadership had been party to false accusations. Beria also released petty criminals, causing an increase in urban crime. Primarily

---

* There was also a Presidium of the Council of Ministers, in keeping with the Soviet system of having parallel systems of governance, a Communist Party system and a formal government system. Communist leaders often held equivalent posts in both systems.

though, the other Communist leaders were terrified of Beria and his brutal personality. They knew that he had personally taken part in torturing prisoners as head of the secret police, and rumors that he had raped dozens of women also circulated. Their main fear, though, was that Beria would begin a new purge and come after them.

ASSUMING CONTROL

In a move completely contrary to what his colleagues on the Presidium expected of him, Khrushchev orchestrated a coup only three months after Stalin's death in 1953. Beria arrived at a meeting of the Presidium of the Council of Ministers to find himself verbally attacked in turn by the other members, including Malenkov. Malenkov announced Beria's arrest as a group of military officers allied with the plotters entered the room. They hustled him to an air defense base outside the city, avoiding Beria's bodyguards in an adjacent room and the secret police units that controlled the city. All of the plotters had gambled with their lives; had Beria had even an inkling of their intentions, his control of the secret police would have allowed him to react quickly. With Beria securely under their control, the plotters formed a new government, with Malenkov retaining his position and Khrushchev becoming first secretary of the party. Six months later, after interrogation and a show trial, Beria and six others were executed as enemies of the people.[3]

One of the most telling indicators of the changed nature of the new regime came when Khrushchev opened up the grounds of the Kremlin to visitors and tourists. Unlike Stalin, he was not afraid of the people, in whose name the party always claimed to act. One of Khrushchev's greatest strengths was his willingness to go out among the people and see what was really happening. Khrushchev enjoyed visiting peasants and workers. This dose of reality helped him to see a situation as it actually was, not so colored by the lenses of Communist ideology, though he still relied on Stalinist thought to provide goals and methods to run the country.

In 1953 Khrushchev launched his Virgin Lands proposal to transform semi-arid regions in western Siberia and Kazakhstan with intensive agriculture. By the end of the decade, the effort had significantly raised agricultural production, though naysayers predicted that it would not last and that it would result in an environmental disaster. Half of the nation's livestock was raised on the small personal plots that Soviet policy allowed, an indication that there was a more effective path to agricultural success, but Khrushchev remained adamantly wedded to collectivization.

Khrushchev eased Malenkov out of power in 1955, demoting him from prime minister to minister of electrification. While Khrushchev was quite willing to use execution against dangerous enemies, he did not do so against political opponents whom he had outmaneuvered and marginalized. Malenkov even remained as part of the Presidium.

In 1956, at the end of the Twentieth Congress of the Communist Party of the Soviet Union, a secret session was held only for Soviet delegates, excluding the many international delegates who had attended. Khrushchev's speech to these delegates lasted almost four hours, with a short intermission, and left party members in shock. Their new leader described the excesses of Stalin: the arrests based on false evidence, the purges, even the mistakes during the Great Patriotic War.* The Presidium had labored for days over the text of the speech, and Khrushchev overrode many of its objections. Khrushchev dictated his speeches to stenographers, recognizing his own lack of good penmanship and spelling skills. One must keep in mind that he felt sorry only for the Communist victims of Stalin's excesses, never for those hapless souls who were not true believers. The speech was subsequently read to Eastern European Communist leaders at the conference. Copies were read to all the members of the Soviet Communist Party in their local meetings as well as to all 18 million members of the Komsomol (the Soviet youth organization). In Poland, the Communist Party printed up eighteen thousand copies for distribution to party members. One Polish copy was obtained by Israeli intelligence and passed on to the CIA, which arranged for the *New York Times* to publish the speech on June 4, 1956.

Why did Khrushchev make this speech? He later claimed that he had been in Ukraine during the worst excesses in Moscow, but in fact he had ordered tens of thousands slain in Ukraine itself. Many of the other members of the Presidium were implicated in Stalin's crimes, and Khrushchev made a point to note that it was a different time and that they had not known most of the details of their leader's plans. By revealing its crimes, Khrushchev felt that he was cleansing the Communist system of its Stalinist poison. He still believed in the socialist vision

---

* Yet, even after this speech, with Stalin vilified, his body remained in its place of honor in Lenin's mausoleum until 1961, when it was removed and buried under cement.

of changing the world for the better and thought that the party had simply taken a wrong turn with Stalin and needed to return to the right path. The honest historian, however, cannot help but notice that most Communist governments came to power in a shower of blood and destruction and maintained their power by regularly bleeding their people through political repression. This was true in the Soviet Union, China, the Eastern European countries, North Korea, North Vietnam, and Cuba. Despite this moral myopia on Khrushchev's part, the speech was clearly a courageous act.

Khrushchev was also prompted to make his speech by the issue of what to do with the hundreds of thousands who remained in labor camps or in exile, even after Beria's mass releases. Commissions from the Supreme Soviet, the thirteen hundred–member national legislature, traveled through the labor camps, examining records and releasing hundreds of thousands of prisoners. How awkward was it for men and women to return home, now rehabilitated, and come face to face with Communists who had perhaps given evidence against them and escaped the purges? A subsequent investigation on the behalf of the Presidium found that 688,503 people had been executed out of the 1,920,635 arrested for anti-Soviet activities.[4] Khrushchev admitted in his speech that evidence against the prisoners had been fabricated; not a single incident involved real political crimes, other than opposing Stalin. The millions who had died from famine as a result of forced collectivization were not considered victims by Khrushchev, since he himself still supported the need for collectivization.

While Khrushchev's speech prompted a crisis of faith within the Soviet Union, the revelations heated up the situations in Poland and Hungary, where anti-Russian sentiment mixed with nationalism. These two countries were led by Communist governments in large part because they had been occupied by the Red Army after World War II and the Soviets still kept armed forces within their borders. The Communists did not have sufficient popular support in Poland and Hungary to obtain legitimacy from any source other than the gun, and the unpopular governments teetered on the edge of widespread popular unrest. Khrushchev and the Presidium vacillated between sending in Soviet troops to reassert control over Poland or letting the new leadership they had selected for the country reassert control by itself. At one point, Soviet troops actually started to move on Warsaw, but eventually the Presidium decided to stay the troops and Poland calmed down.

The opposite occurred in Hungary when the people rose up and fought the Soviet troops in a 1956 uprising. Evidence later surfaced that showed that the Presidium initially agreed to let the Hungarian Communist Party try to solve its own problems, rather than use Soviet troops. The Communist leader of China, Mao Zedong, urged Khrushchev to crush the uprising so he would not appear weak. Some members of the Presidium complained that the Hungarian Uprising was the work of "imperialist agents" from the West. Such paranoia was unjustified, since the CIA had only one agent who spoke the language in all of Hungary and he spent most of his time performing duties related to his cover at the embassy. The Americans were just as astonished as the Soviets by the uprising, even though the Soviets had hundreds, if not thousands, of intelligence assets in Hungary.[5]

Coincidently, the French and British, in collusion with Israel, attacked Egypt at this time in an attempt to reclaim the Suez Canal, which Egypt had recently nationalized. This was one of the last gasps of imperialist arrogance by these two European powers. Khrushchev assumed that the Americans would back the British and French in order to push back the socialist-oriented Egyptian government. To everyone's surprise, the Americans did not back their two allies but demanded that they remove themselves from Egypt. The Suez Crisis was only a minor consideration for Khrushchev, but the diplomatic and public turmoil of the crisis provided a distraction from his efforts in Hungary, as he finally decided to crush the Hungarian rebels. The Soviet tanks rolled and Hungarian insurgents fought back with rifles and Molotov cocktails. While reliable statistics are hard to find, some twenty thousand Hungarians may have died; the Soviets lost about fifteen hundred soldiers. About two hundred thousand refugees fled Hungary to the West.

What is surprising about the twin crises in Poland and Hungary was the erratic nature of the Soviet decision-making process. Khrushchev was only one of many voices in the Presidium, all arguing with each other, though his voice counted more than the others. He did not seem to have a methodology to his decision making, other than to follow his gut instincts, which changed with each new wrinkle in the evolving situations. He had risen to the top because of his well-honed survival instincts, which allowed him to continually gauge Stalin's mood and to detect treachery in his colleagues. Such cunning was not well suited to making sound diplomatic choices.

Prompted by the anti-Soviet speech, by the experience of the Hungarian Uprising, and by the instincts that Stalin's Soviet system encouraged, Khrushchev's rivals in the Presidium made a bid for power in June 1957. Molotov, Kaganovich, Malenkov, and Dmitri Shepilov led the attempted coup, which involved eight of the then-eleven full members of the Presidium. The plotters talked during walks, not in houses, cars, or offices because they knew that those were bugged by the KGB (which, at this point, had taken over the bulk of the NKVD's responsibilities). There are some indications that Khrushchev anticipated the coup, although he did not visibly prepare for it.

The plotters were not in a position to wrest control from Khrushchev as it had been wrested from Beria—with an immediate arrest—because they had little power outside their membership in the Presidium. The heads of the KGB and armed forces remained loyal to Khrushchev. After two days of verbal struggle, during which the plotters repeatedly criticized Khrushchev and tried to browbeat him into submission, Khrushchev and his supporters found an alternate way to fight.

The Presidium was technically drawn from a larger group of 130 members called the Central Committee, made up of party leaders from around the Soviet Union. In the past, the Central Committee had simply approved whatever the Presidium decided. Now Khrushchev used his support from the military leadership to rush Central Committee members to Moscow by military air transports.

A Central Committee plenum met for six days, the climax of a struggle that lasted for a total of eleven days. In the Soviet Communist tradition, short of arrest, the goal of a plenum was for one side to argue long enough to force its opponents into such abject submission that they would actually vote to condemn themselves. Marshal Georgy Zhukov, head of the armed forces, a prominent and brilliant commander during the Great Patriotic War and now a Khrushchev loyalist, led the charge by strongly condemning the plotters for their complicity in Stalin's purges. By the end, only Molotov refused to submit; the four leaders of the coup were removed from the Presidium but not ejected from the party. The other four members of the Presidium who had opposed Khrushchev remained in their positions because publishing their names would have revealed to the public that Khrushchev had not retained majority support. Though Khrushchev proved himself to be a petty man, he believed that brutality was no longer the way to deal with vanquished political opponents. The plotters were stripped of their dachas and privileges, sent into obscure government postings, and humiliated in various ways over the next several years, including eviction from the party and retirement on regular worker pensions. Zhukov was promoted from candidate status to full member of the Presidium after this display of loyalty, only to be removed four months later when Khrushchev came to distrust him. The head of the KGB, Ivan Serov, another key Khrushchev supporter, was also later dismissed.

Khrushchev had learned that his anti-Stalin campaign threatened the authority of the Communist Party to lead the Soviet Union, so he toned down his rhetoric, trying to differentiate between Stalin's effective leadership and his unfortunate mistakes. Friends and the family of Khrushchev also detected a change in him after this episode. He became more authoritarian and less willing to listen to advice. Multiple sources have commented that Khrushchev surrounded himself with mediocre individuals to serve as aides or assistants. If true, this shows that the man lacked self-confidence, and those who lack confidence sometimes take reckless actions to show themselves and others that they are worthy.

As was typical of Communist dictators, Khrushchev's assumption of near-absolute power had corrupted his mind and spirit. He regularly offered his opinions on the worth of art, movies, or literature and assumed that his opinions had value. He considered himself an expert on agriculture and boasted more than once that the Soviet Union would soon surpass the United States in per capita meat production. He became an enthusiastic proponent of corn, encouraging farmers to plant millions of acres of the crop. This had mixed results, since most of the Soviet Union is too far north for effective corn production.

A CIA study in 1960 described Khrushchev as a "hypomanic." This is a lesser form of mania in which a person is subject to sudden changes of mood—quick to feel anger or depression yet just as quick to feel elated and energetic. Khrushchev had a tremendous capacity for work and allowed his hyperactive nature to drive him to exhaustion. Others found him "overtly cheerful" and "highly social," and the head of the KGB characterized Khrushchev with the following terms: "firmness of will, quick-wittedness and capacity for fast, careful, thinking."[6]

Like Stalin, Khrushchev displayed a tendency to believe scientists and engineers who spouted the correct ideological terms, especially if the ideas agreed with what he wanted to believe. The biologist Trofim Lysenko argued that plants adapt to their environmental conditions by acquiring the characteristics that they need, a kind of Marxism in action among the grass and flowers. Lysenko rejected the science of genetics as pursued in the West and claimed that he would dramatically increase Soviet crop yields. This appealed to Stalin and Khrushchev because it was a quick fix that did not require them to rethink their ideology, the implementation of which had actually produced low crop yields. Stalin vigorously supported Lysenko, going so far as to arrest scientific opponents, some of whom died in custody. Khrushchev also supported Lysenko but allowed scientific opponents to voice their objections without punishment.

FOREIGN POLICY

His position at home consolidated, Khrushchev became more aggressive in leading Soviet foreign policy. Following his own interpretation of Communist dogma, Stalin had believed that another world war, pitting the Communists against the forces of capitalism, was inevitable. Khrushchev disagreed, creating an opportunity for increased understanding among the adversaries in the Cold War. Unlike Stalin, who traveled outside the Soviet Union only twice, to the World War II conferences in Tehran and Potsdam, Khrushchev traveled regularly and widely after becoming the Soviet leader. Nothing in his background, as he lacked education and travel experience, had prepared him to see the world as anything but a class struggle. Stalin occasionally reminded his inner circle that it did not have the muscle and cunning to handle foreign affairs in a hostile world; he once allegedly declared, "After I'm gone, the capitalists will drown you like blind kittens."[7]

We have one account of a Stalin-era foreign policy decision that Khrushchev weighed in on. According to Politburo records, in June 1945 Khrushchev was the only member to support a Soviet invasion of Hokkaido, the northernmost of the four main Japanese islands, to follow the invasion of Japanese-occupied Manchuria that August. The attack on a home island was intended to create a situation similar to that in Germany, where joint occupation led to more Soviet influence on the conquered nation's internal politics and, later, creation of East Germany. Khrushchev's colleagues rejected the idea as foolhardy from a military standpoint and as a violation of agreements with the United States.[8] This episode demonstrates that Khrushchev was inclined toward an aggressive, even reckless, foreign policy even before he became Stalin's successor.

Khrushchev, often acting the buffoon, lacked the polish to be an urbane world traveler. He was concerned about overdressing for the part and sensitive to even the slightest insult. Foreigners were unimpressed by him. Early in his leadership, Khrushchev made a special effort to court Yugoslavia and China, the two Communist nations without significant numbers of Soviet troops stationed within their borders. Both efforts eventually failed. Yugoslavia remained wedded to its idea of a separate path, with each Communist nation choosing its own way of implementing the ideology. Similar ideas had encouraged the rebellions in Poland and Hungary. The Soviet Union courted China by initiating enormous technology transfers, including building hundreds of factories, sending thousands of advisers to China, and even initially agreeing to help the Chinese nuclear bomb project. In the end, national interests proved more compelling than Communist solidarity, and the Soviet Union and China began to drift apart, each striving to be the international leader of the Communist movement. Also aggravating their differences was the emphasis on industrial workers in Leninist-Stalinist thought, as opposed to the emphasis on rural peasants in Maoist thought.

The most important foreign policy issue for Khrushchev was the relationship between the Soviets and the Americans. Nuclear weapons had changed the nature of war. Just as Eisenhower had decreased the size of American conventional forces in favor of relying on nuclear weapons, Khrushchev decreased the size of his nation's military in favor of nuclear weapons. While the Americans frantically built more nuclear bombs, more bombers, and more ballistic missiles, the Soviets proceeded at a slower pace, emphasizing missiles over bombers. Khrushchev believed that nuclear weapons were so destructive that no nation would use them and that the Soviet Union did not need an overabundance of nuclear weapons to create a credible force.

At the 1955 Geneva summit, a gathering of the leaders of the United States, the Soviet Union, France, and Britain, Khrushchev listened to President Eisenhower make an impassioned speech about how nuclear weapons had made engaging in war a futile endeavor. A nuclear war would destroy the Northern Hemisphere.[9] The speech convinced Khrushchev that the Americans had no intention of attacking the Soviet Union, and it encouraged him in thinking that the Americans feared nuclear war too much. Using an opponent's fears against him was a vital tactic in Stalinist politics and Khrushchev took this experience and made the tactic of bluffing a central tool in his intellectual arsenal for foreign affairs. During the conclusion of the Suez Crisis, for example, Khrushchev dictated a letter to the British that subtly implied the Soviets would use nuclear weapons to protect their Egyptian allies. The Americans forced the British and French to leave Egypt, but Khrushchev saw his own threat as the primary reason for the withdrawal—a most disturbing conclusion for the future health of the world.

There is evidence that Soviet bureaucrats manipulated Khrushchev, who failed to inspire in them the kind of fear Stalin had relied on, by feeding him false information and withholding intelligence. Khrushchev's efforts in Yugoslavia and China, for example, were damaged in part by such manipulation. The Soviet leader found it difficult to combat this problem. How could he demand honesty in a culture that had been built on lies for decades? Not only did Khrushchev receive bad information, but he also displayed alarming arrogance by acting as his own intelligence analyst, often ignoring the advice of the Soviet experts on America and China.

Sino-Soviet relations turned more than sour; they completely collapsed during Khrushchev's tenure. This resulted partially from Khrushchev's inept diplomatic efforts, though he visited Beijing at least twice to personally negotiate with Mao. In 1960 the leaders began to show their antagonism by using those slurs unique to Communist ideology; they called each other nationalists, adventurists, deviationists, or revisionists. Such words revealed a real antagonism. Perhaps the split was inevitable, as national interests superseded brotherhood in communism.

The situation was exacerbated by the Great Leap Forward, Mao's plan to rapidly develop his nation's agricultural and industrial capabilities. A key component of this effort was creating large communes and rapidly collectivizing China's agricultural sector. As in the Soviet Union under Stalin, the result in China was famine. An internal government document put the deaths from famine at 14 million, while other experts have doubled or tripled this estimate. Mao also demanded that steel production double and required that peasant households smelt down scrap metal in small backyard furnaces. The result was large amounts of useless pig iron. The Great Leap Forward collapsed from its own internal contradictions by 1962, and we have some indications that Mao's hold on power was damaged by these efforts. This failure also offered the potential to damage China's prestige with other Communists.

Soviet prestige received a wonderful boost in 1957. Scientists from around the world had organized the International Geophysical Year (IGY), which would last for eighteen months from July 1, 1957, to December 31, 1958, and would amount to a concerted scientific effort to learn more about the planet. Only China refused to participate. During the IGY, eighty-six vessels took measurements of the planet's oceans and seas. In the run-up to the IGY, explorers swarmed onto Antarctica, setting up dozens of camps and monitoring stations. An IGY committee also coordinated "world days," specific times when scientists at numerous places around the globe made simultaneous measurements, such as during the total solar eclipse on October 12, 1958. The fallout from open-air nuclear testing was more carefully monitored during the IGY, leading to alarm over how much more widespread the effects of nuclear testing were than expected and contributing to the international movement among scientists advocating a ban on open-air tests.

In 1954 a committee had agreed to an American plan to launch artificial satellites to orbit the earth as sensor platforms during the IGY. Sergei Korolyov, the chief designer of the Soviet ballistic missile program, used the impending IGY to persuade the Soviet government to build a launcher and satellite to preempt the United States. The project was kept secret, and the United States did not even know that it was in a competition until the Soviets surprised the world by launching *Sputnik*. In their haste to beat the Americans, the Soviets created a very simple satellite, with few scientific instruments. On November 3, 1957, the much larger *Sputnik 2* was launched with a dog, Laika, aboard, as well as many more scientific instruments. Laika died in orbit since there was no way to retrieve her.

The launch of *Sputnik* electrified the world and vindicated the Soviet effort. Khrushchev bragged publicly that the Soviet Union had "outstripped the leading capitalist country—the United States—in the field of scientific and technical progress."[10] He may have even believed his words, and many throughout the world and in the United States wondered if the Americans were falling behind.

In a secret memo, obtained by a dissident, Khrushchev confessed that the Presidium members felt like "technological ignoramuses" when Korolyov showed his ballistic missiles to them.[11] The leaders of the Communist world tentatively touched the rocket, not believing that it would fly. It looked nothing like an airplane or a bird. Fortunately for the Soviets, their leaders needed only to believe in the missiles and to supply funding; Korolyov and his technicians provided the rest.

Yuri Gagarin became the first man in space on April 12, 1961. The American Alan Shepard flew less than a month later, though only in a suborbital flight, not the complete orbit that Gagarin had flown. America's first orbital flight did not come until February 1962. When Gagarin arrived in Moscow, Khrushchev met him at the airport with the entire party leadership, and a newsreel showed the Soviet leader wiping away his tears of pride. Being ahead in the space race gave Khrushchev an inflated sense that the Soviets were about to pass the West in scientific and technological progress. He felt the urge for Soviet communism to flex its muscles.

THE BERLIN CRISIS BEGINS

As World War II ended, the four great powers divided Germany into four zones of occupation: Soviet, American, British, and French. They also divided Berlin, Germany's capital, into four zones. The division was considered a temporary arrangement, and it was expected that the country would soon be reunited. But the Soviets feared a reunified Germany and, as a matter of habit, rarely gave up what they already possessed. As the Cold War developed, the Soviet zone became the communist German Democratic Republic (East Germany), while the three Western zones combined to become the democratic Federal Republic of Germany (West Germany). Berlin remained divided, with rail, road, and air access through East Germany guaranteed by wartime agreements. In one of his oddest foreign policy moves, Stalin blockaded the Western zones of Berlin in 1948, assuming that he could starve out the West Berliners. A massive airlift by the Americans, British, and their allies kept Berlin stocked with food, fuel, and other supplies, and after almost a year, Stalin opened ground access again.

West Germany flourished under a democratic free-market economy, while East Germany struggled to recover from wartime damage and Soviet reparations, which sometimes required entire factories to be dismantled and moved to the Soviet Union. East Germany also suffered from large numbers of citizens leaving the country for the political freedom and better economic conditions of West Germany. The Soviets viewed Berlin as an enemy outpost deep in the territory of their satellite, a base for spying and perhaps even a base for nuclear weapons (though none were ever placed there). The Soviets wanted the West to diplomatically recognize the East German government and thus acknowledge the de facto separation of the two Germanys, whereas the West insisted that free elections be held and the two Germanys be reunited. The Soviets were also concerned that West Germany would develop nuclear weapons of its own—a feat that the Germans were quite capable of—and use them to retaliate against the Soviets for the 1945 defeat.

On November 27, 1958, Khrushchev delivered a note to Western ambassadors that demanded the West sign a treaty recognizing East Germany and turn Berlin into a demilitarized "free city." Otherwise, the Soviets would abrogate their wartime agreement and turn over the authority for road and rail access to the East Germans, who, not bound by the postwar agreement, could cut off access to Berlin. Khrushchev gave the West six months to decide whether to accept the the new arrangements.[12]

There are two accounts of how this diplomatic note came to be written. The first story is that Khrushchev developed it entirely on his own and delivered it to the West without consulting the Presidium. The second story is that Khrushchev developed it entirely on his own and then presented it to the Presidium, the members of which were too cowed to object to it. In either case, Khrushchev made this decision on his own. When Hubert Humphrey, a U.S. senator from Minnesota, visited the Soviet Union in 1958, Khrushchev told him that he had "given many months of thought to the Berlin situation."[13] Other sources indicate that these were solo thoughts, rejecting any advice on the matter from the relevant ministries. When Khrushchev's son asked him what he had expected to achieve with the diplomatic note, he said that he did not know. There was no plan. Khrushchev expected the situation to develop and he would see what happened before deciding on his next move. He was not a gambler in the traditional sense, but any man who had survived the Stalin period had to have a high tolerance for risk. With his power unchallenged, the deepest aspects of Khrushchev's personality came to the fore, unrestrained by outside influence.

Oddly enough, it seems that Khrushchev was largely motivated by his desire for a summit meeting with Eisenhower in the United States. Khrushchev had been pursuing a policy of reconciliation with the West ever since he rose to power in 1953, but he sent such mixed signals that Western leaders did not trust him. The U.S. secretary of state John Foster Dulles was especially suspicious. Based on his long experience as a diplomat, he believed that the Soviets would lie and break any treaty. Khrushchev was concerned by the Americans' aggressive "containment" policy. The North Atlantic Treaty Organization (NATO), created in 1949, had unified the United States, Canada, the United Kingdom, France, and other Western European nations in an anticommunist alliance, while the Southeast Asia Treaty Organization (SEATO), created in 1954, did the same for the United

States, Britain, France, Australia, New Zealand, Pakistan, the Philippines, and Thailand.* To the Soviets, containment looked like encirclement.

Eisenhower had no intention of inviting Khrushchev to America without substantial progress on negotiations in Geneva, Switzerland, over the Berlin issue. An undersecretary of state was instructed to convey a message to this effect to a Soviet contact, but the American diplomat passed on an unqualified invitation instead. Records show no explanation for this bizarre mistake. Visits by foreign leaders were less common back then, and Khrushchev considered the invitation a major coup, showing that the Soviet Union was important. Eisenhower felt that he could not withdraw the invitation, as the move would make his administration appear incompetent.

Khrushchev demanded that he fly to America on the most impressive airplane that the Soviets possessed, a prototype of the new four-engined Tu-114, the largest airliner of its time. Soviet officials were so worried about the new plane that they wanted to station navy ships along the flight path to rescue Khrushchev if he were forced to ditch. Khrushchev thought this too expensive, so the rescue line was made up of freighters, tankers, and fishing trawlers. An onboard group of engineers and technicians monitored the aircraft during its flight.

In September 1959 Khrushchev traveled to America for a thirteen-day tour that included Washington, D.C.; New York City; Los Angeles; Hollywood; San Francisco; a farm in Iowa; Pittsburgh; and then a return to the nation's capital. One of Khrushchev's more endearing traits was his natural curiosity, especially when seeing new things and meeting new people. He decided to deliberately rein in his curiosity because he did not want to act too impressed with America. American reporters' embarrassing questions about the Hungarian Uprising and Soviet political repression were a continual irritant, and he found them person-

---

* The initial members of NATO were the United States, Canada, the United Kingdom, France, Belgium, the Netherlands, Luxembourg, Portugal, Italy, Norway, Denmark, and Iceland. Three years later, in 1952, Greece and Turkey also joined. West Germany joined in 1955 to show its recognition of the de facto division of Germany and to antagonize the Soviets. Because of geography, Australia and New Zealand were not part of the North Atlantic organization, so in 1952 the United States signed the Australia, New Zealand, United States Security Treaty (ANZUS) with those two Southern Hemisphere democracies. The Warsaw Pact between the Soviet Union and its Eastern European satellites was not formed to counter NATO until 1955, a reaction to West Germany joining NATO. The Warsaw Pact was less necessary because Soviet marshals already controlled the satellite armies and Soviet troops were still stationed in most of the satellites from their conquest during World War II.

ally insulting. Any personal insult was an insult to the entire Soviet Union. And when he saw anticommunist demonstrators in the larger cities, he assumed that the protests were staged; as he candidly admitted to an American official, demonstrations in the Soviet Union happened only with Khrushchev's permission.

Khrushchev tended to overcompensate for his insecurities, quickly resorting to boasting about Soviet achievements. He did behave better in America than he had during earlier experiences with other Western leaders. British prime minister Harold Macmillan and the American vice president Richard Nixon had both separately visited the Soviet Union, where conversations with Khrushchev were a bizarre mixture of substance, jokes, flattery, and threats. Khrushchev's boastful confidence was not only for the benefit of foreign leaders; in 1961 he presented a study to the Soviet people that he had personally directed and predicted that the Soviet economy would surpass the American economy by 1970 and a full Communist utopia would be achieved by 1980. In this Communist utopia, workers would work because they would want to, free housing would be available for most, and plentiful consumer goods would be available for all.

At the end of the trip, Eisenhower took Khrushchev to Camp David for negotiations that bore little fruit. Khrushchev declared that he was not afraid of a nuclear war; Eisenhower responded that he was afraid of such a war and thought that everyone else should be also. Khrushchev withdrew his Berlin ultimatum and invited Eisenhower to visit the Soviet Union. Eisenhower accepted the invitation and agreed to another four-power summit. Khrushchev would not allow his concession to be written in a joint communiqué, only agreeing that Eisenhower could mention it verbally to the press and Khrushchev would not disagree. Khrushchev considered his trip to America to be a great success, though he left mostly bewildered Americans in his wake.

A similar trip to France soon followed, and Khrushchev thought that he carried himself well in his meetings with President Charles de Gaulle. De Gaulle found the Russian cunning and intelligent, pleasant except for his tendency to "somewhat violent speech." De Gaulle was frustrated that Khrushchev used "a set piece formula for each question which he continually repeated." The Frenchman offered numerous ideas, as if sampling them, and proposed the notion that the United States was not necessary in European affairs and that the Europeans could come up with their own solutions to East-West problems. Despite his willingness to follow a path different from the Americans', de Gaulle was certain that West Germany had to remain firmly on the side of the West.[14]

These meetings with his peers made Khrushchev feel giddy with pride that he was a world leader. Any timidity that he might have felt in foreign affairs was gone, and he was ready to try to reshape relations between nations to suit his own needs. Eisenhower was scheduled to tour the Soviet Union in June 1960, and Khrushchev personally supervised the preparations. These included the construction of new dachas for the American president to stay in, even if for only one night as he traveled about the country, and of the first golf course in the country for the golf-crazy American leader. In neighborhoods that Eisenhower might see, and even in places he probably would never see, buildings were repaired, roads fixed, and new paint applied. Eisenhower's June visit was to be preceded the month before by a summit in Paris between the leaders of the Soviet Union, the United States, France, and Great Britain.

THE U-2 CRISIS

In 1955 an extraordinary new plane flew for the first time. The U.S. Air Force and the CIA needed a new high-altitude reconnaissance airplane, and the brilliant aerospace engineer Clarence "Kelly" Johnson at the Lockheed Skunk Works facility in Burbank, California, designed the U-2 for that purpose. The plane was just under fifty feet from nose to tail but had an unusually large eighty-foot wingspan, which made it act like a sailplane, able to fly at the high altitude of seventy thousand feet, with long range. Powered by a single jet engine, only the most skilled pilots could fly the aircraft, which at high altitude had a thin margin of only ten knots between maximum speed and stall speed. Drop below stall speed and the aircraft could spin out of control.

Since 1946 American and British reconnaissance aircraft had probed the edges of the Iron Curtain. In 1952 they began to deliberately cross the Soviet Union's border in order to obtain intelligence in the form of photographs and readings of radio and radar signals. Over a hundred aircrew were lost over the years as the Soviets shot down their aircraft, but the Americans and British felt that the cost was worth it in order to gain intelligence. The Soviet Union and its satellites were such effective police states that gaining intelligence through other means was challenging. The new U-2 joined the game in 1956, first flying out of Wiesbaden, West Germany.

The U-2 gave the Americans another advantage in the Cold War struggle for information. Eisenhower personally approved each flight, and while the American leadership recognized that the overflights violated international law, they felt that they needed to know the extent of the Soviet ballistic missile program. The Soviets objected through diplomatic channels but stopped doing so after a while, as each complaint was only a humiliating admission that they did not have the ability to defend their own airspace. Khrushchev did not even mention the topic in his meeting with Eisenhower at Camp David. By that time, feeling more secure in their knowledge of Soviet strategic strength, the Americans, not wanting to spoil diplomatic efforts, had already scaled back the level of incursions.

On May 1, 1960, International Workers' Day, an important Communist holiday, a U-2 piloted by Francis Gary Powers took off from Pakistan to fly a loop across the Soviet Union and land in Norway. A U-2 had never flown so deep into the Soviet Union. One of the goals of the effort was to fly over Plesetsk, six hundred miles north of Moscow, where the first Soviet ICBMs were being deployed. The trip was made then, only six weeks before Eisenhower's planned visit to the Soviet Union, because of the low positioning of the sun—it had to be in the right position for the missiles to stand out in the high-altitude photographs.

The Soviets were livid. A specialized high-altitude interceptor happened to be along the U-2's flight path, and the pilot was ordered aloft with instructions to ram the U-2. Fortunately, he could not get close enough to the enemy aircraft and did not have to decide if such a personal sacrifice was warranted. The Soviets launched one flurry of surface-to-air missiles (SAMs) that managed to explode close enough to break the U-2 apart and also hit a MiG-19 fighter in pursuit. The Soviet pilot was killed. The CIA initially believed that no pilot could survive the destruction of a U-2, but Powers parachuted to safety.* When informed of the successful interception while viewing the annual parade in Red Square from atop Lenin's Mausoleum, Khrushchev reacted with elation.

The Americans had a cover story—another example of plausible deniability —and announced that a research aircraft had been lost over Turkey. Khrushchev assumed that Eisenhower had not authorized the overflight and thought it was a rogue operation. Four days later, in a speech before the Supreme Soviet, Khrush-

---

* In early 1962 the Soviets exchanged Powers for a KGB colonel whom the Americans had caught spying in the United States.

chev announced that the aircraft had been shot down. Why did he reveal this information when other overflights had not been discussed publicly? Did he want to demonstrate Soviet military prowess? Did he want to embarrass Eisenhower in order to weaken his political position so that he would make concessions to the Soviets?

The Americans added to their lie by publicly suggesting that the Soviets may have been referring to the missing research aircraft over Turkey. Then an American diplomat overheard at an Ethiopian diplomatic reception in Moscow that the pilot was still alive. The Eisenhower administration had not expected Powers to survive and was embarrassed to be caught in its lies. Khrushchev clearly wanted Eisenhower to disavow any knowledge of the flights and stoked the crisis to see whether it might turn out to his advantage.

When Eisenhower announced that he had authorized the overflights, without mentioning that he actually authorized each individual flight, Khrushchev felt betrayed. He called the reconnaissance missions an assault on the "pride and dignity" of himself and the Soviet Union.[15] His plan to embarrass the United States and its president began to unravel, and by the time he arrived in Paris for the four-powers summit he was in the grip of a tantrum that lasted for days.

In the initial meeting of the four leaders, in a large room at the Élysée Palace, Khrushchev insisted on speaking first and proceeded to subject Eisenhower to an impassioned forty-five-minute lecture. According to the British prime minister, the Russian's hands trembled and his left eyebrow twitched as he clutched the papers of his prepared speech. As Eisenhower listened to the translation, his face turned red with anger. When his turn to speak came, the American said that the overflights would be suspended. De Gaulle asked Khrushchev why he was so worked up over the overflights when a new Soviet satellite had just passed over France numerous times.

Khrushchev denied that the new satellite had cameras on it, which was probably a lie, but we are not certain about that specific satellite. Later satellites certainly carried cameras. In any case, the new technology of satellites was making the need for overflights obsolete. Already the American Corona satellite program was launching satellites to overfly the Soviet Union, take pictures, then send the pictures back to earth in a reentry vehicle that deployed a parachute. An aircraft snagged the film package in midair. Eventually satellites that could directly transmit images from space would be developed.

Satellites by their very nature have to orbit the earth, passing quickly over countries every ninety minutes. The principle of requiring permission for aircraft to fly over sovereign territories was well established, but no such rule had been instituted for satellites. Some countries complained, but the two superpowers (the only two nations capable of launching satellites) quickly realized that they had no choice in the matter: they had to agree to other satellites if they wanted other nations not to complain about their own satellites.

Khrushchev refused to continue with the summit and disinvited Eisenhower from visiting the Soviet Union. Before leaving Paris, the Soviet leader held a two-and-a-half-hour news conference for three thousand journalists. It turned into a raucous session, with Khrushchev shouting his complaints and the journalists responding with catcalls and hisses. Khrushchev enjoyed a good verbal brawl and declared to the journalists, "I like coming to grips with the enemies of the working class and it is gratifying for me to hear the frenzy of these lackeys of imperialism."[16]

Members of the Presidium, Khrushchev's staff, and Soviet diplomats all expressed dismay at their leader's tantrum. Some even doubted his sanity. Anastas Ivanovich Mikoyan, an important member of the Presidium, whispered, "Khrushchev engaged in inexcusable hysterics" and "he simply spat on everyone." Of course, these sentiments were all relayed in private, to family and close friends, never in public. It was as if all the self-control that Khrushchev had displayed during the years under Stalin, necessary for survival, had eroded away and the exact opposite psychological condition now existed: a man who could barely assert any intellectual control over his emotions. In plainer terms, Khrushchev was an unstable decision maker.

A month later, at a conference of the Romanian Communist Party, Khrushchev launched a vicious personal attack on Chairman Mao. The Chinese spat back in a war of words that sounded more like name-calling by children on a playground than by grown men who aspired to be statesmen. Khrushchev retaliated by yanking all the Soviet advisers out of China and canceling all the joint projects. These 1,390 experts had been invaluable to the Chinese efforts to industrialize, but their removal hurt the Soviets even more, depriving them of an important source of intelligence on the other Communist titan. How Khrushchev's actions served the interests of the Soviet Union in any way is a mystery; they served only to placate his raging emotions.

Khrushchev continued his international travel, visiting Austria for nine days, followed by three days in Finland, before going to New York City in September 1960 for a meeting of the United Nations General Assembly. As host to the UN headquarters, the United States could not deny him entry, but when he arrived by sea, the pier was mostly empty of well-wishers and the longshoreman's union boycotted the ship so the Soviets had to dock themselves. The famous shoe-banging incident occurred during this visit, and the Soviet leader further continued his streak of bizarre behavior at press conferences and in impassioned speeches at the UN and elsewhere. Khrushchev also demanded that the UN headquarters be moved to a different country and that the UN secretary-general be replaced by a troika: one person from the West, one from the Communist countries, and the third from a neutral country. Neither proposal attracted much support. According to his son, Khrushchev considered his time in New York to be a triumph personally and for the Soviet Union.

Khrushchev also met Fidel Castro, whom he referred to with affection as "the bearded one," in New York in 1960.[17] The 1959 Cuban Revolution had caught the Soviet leadership completely by surprise. Latin American affairs had always been a backwater behind more important considerations for the Soviets. Reports differ on how the two men reacted to each other; regardless, the march of history was to fatally intertwine their lives and decisions. Khrushchev almost always liked a fellow Communist, and though Castro had achieved much without outside aid, now he needed help.

An agricultural crisis awaited the Soviet leader on his return home. Crop production promised to slip back to numbers not seen since 1953. For five months, Khrushchev worked vigorously, using his normal solutions: changing local leaders, encouraging more cultivation of corn, and transferring private cows to collectives (while doggedly refusing to recognize that these single cows and private gardens provided a significant part of the diet for Soviet citizens). Khrushchev also worked on other domestic issues, such as housing.

Ever since he had run the Moscow party in the 1930s, Khrushchev had worked on the problem of insufficient housing for the workers that flocked to urban areas, especially Moscow. The succession of five-year economic plans had emphasized building factories and exploiting resources, not creating consumer goods or housing. In 1956 housing construction doubled, thanks to Khrushchev's favored solution of rapidly building five-story apartment houses out of prefabricated concrete blocks. This partially solved the problem, but resulted in shoddy buildings that turned the outskirts of Moscow into endless rows of drab buildings, depressing the spirits of the workers who were supposed to be grateful for their new homes. Khrushchev recognized that the buildings would last only twenty years or so, and at that point he expected them to be replaced by better structures. This emphasis on quantity over quality, creating incredible long-term waste and inefficiency, was a problem endemic to Soviet communism.

Khrushchev watched the 1960 American presidential election with interest and was delighted when Kennedy was elected. He saw the Democrat's win as a slap in the face to Eisenhower, since his vice president had lost the contest. Khrushchev also saw the election of a new American president as an opportunity to change the tone of negotiations with the West. In 1960 the Soviets had shot down an American patrol airplane—not a reconnaissance aircraft—that strayed into Soviet airspace in Siberia. This was not one of the deliberate reconnaissance flights. Two crew members survived the crash, and Khrushchev released them a few days after Kennedy's inauguration as a peace offering for the new president.

From his roots as a peasant, Khrushchev had risen to head the Presidium, the chief governing body of the Communist Party and the Soviet government. As with any great leader, the positive aspects of his personality were magnified by his power, as were his negative attributes. He once told a close friend that if his actions were placed on a scale after he died, "I hope the good will outweigh the bad."[18] In the hands of this man rested profound responsibilities.

Further sources: Anne Applebaum, *Gulag: A History* (New York: Doubleday, 2003); Stéphane Courtois and others, *The Black Book of Communism: Crimes, Terror, Repression* (Cambridge, MA: Harvard University Press, 1999); Sergei N. Khrushchev, *Nikita Khrushchev: Creation of a Superpower* (University Park: Pennsylvania State University Press, 2000); Simon Sebag Montefiore, *Stalin: The Court of the Red Tsar* (New York: Knopf, 2004); and William Taubman, *Khrushchev: The Man and His Era* (New York: Norton, 2003), an excellent work.

3

Young Man of Ambition:
John F. Kennedy

The inauguration of the youngest president ever elected in the United States occurred on a cloudless day in January 1961, with temperatures below freezing and a biting wind that refused to abate. A severe storm the previous day had left Washington, D.C., covered with snow, and soldiers used flamethrowers to melt icy drifts around the inaugural stand. Robert Frost had composed a poem for the occasion. While the light was too poor for the aged poet to complete reading his manuscript, he had written prophetic words: "Of young ambition eager to be tried . . . In any game the nations want to play."[1]

Foreign policy and national security policy are in many ways a game, even more so to economists and theorists enamored with numbers and the new innovations of game theory. It is also a deadly game, as John F. Kennedy already knew. He had personally faced the dangers of war; his older brother had fallen to those dangers. Only forty-three years old, Kennedy stepped forward to recite the presidential oath, administered by the Chief Justice Earl Warren, becoming the chief game master of his nation.

YOUNG MAN OF PRIVILEGE
Whereas Nikita Khrushchev was born to poverty as a Russian peasant, his opponent, John Fitzgerald Kennedy, was born to a life of wealth and privilege in the Boston area. His ancestors on both sides had fled the potato famines in Ireland and found success in business and politics in Massachusetts. Born on May 29, 1917, the second child of nine and the family's second son, John "Jack" Fitzgerald

Kennedy was named for his mother's father, who served three terms in Congress and multiple terms as the mayor of Boston.

Both of Kennedy's parents were the oldest children in their families and both were ambitious. Joe Kennedy showed a talent for making money, growing a small stake into a large fortune, moving from opportunity to opportunity, whether as a bank president, stock speculator, or the owner of a chain of movie theaters and a small Hollywood production company. After the end of Prohibition in 1933, the liquor distribution business made him even wealthier. When Franklin D. Roosevelt came to power, Joe Kennedy turned to public service, serving as chairman of the Securities and Exchange Commission and then in other posts. Jack's mother was devoutly Catholic, while his father (and later Jack himself) maintained the proper observances, though not necessarily the morality implied by the Christian faith.

Jack grew up with an intense sense of competition with his older brother, Joseph Kennedy Jr., who excelled in athletics and earned good grades.[2] Jack loved to play sports, but he was plagued with numerous odd physical ailments that sometimes required hospitalization. His infirmities annoyed the young boy, and he pushed himself to be as strong as possible, never making excuses or feeling sorry for himself. At boarding school he showed himself to be a leader, mostly in making mischief and challenging the schoolmaster and teachers. His IQ of 119 failed to translate into anything more than mediocre grades.

Jack had no personal experience of the Great Depression that scarred so many others during the 1930s. His wealthy lifestyle manifested itself in other ways. He rarely carried cash, as he expected other people to pick up the bill; his father would reimburse them later. The Kennedy children were used to having servants around, and Jack developed sloppy personal habits because he always had someone to pick up after him. He dressed casually, not just for comfort but because he believed the rules of decorum that others had to follow did not apply to him.

After graduating from boarding school, Jack traveled to London for some European seasoning. He intended to stay for a year, but illness again struck. Following friends from boarding school, he went to Princeton for a short time. When he fell ill again, he went for two months to a ranch in Arizona, where the warm climate helped him feel better. On his return to New England, he decided to follow his father's wishes and attend Harvard. Admission was not a problem, even with his mediocre grades, because his father was an alumnus and had the wealth and social status to guarantee entry.

His older brother was also at Harvard, cutting a path of accomplishment toward his goal of becoming the president of the United States. The Kennedy family breathed the highest ambitions. Jack Kennedy spent his time socializing, playing sports, and perfecting the art of seduction. The men of his family had a strong tradition of womanizing, and Jack followed their example with enthusiasm.

In his home life, Jack found his mother to be a distant, rigid woman, with firm Roman Catholic beliefs. Jack was very rebellious and his own religious orientation quickly became surface observances rather than inner conviction. A particular burden for the family was the third child and oldest sister, Rosemary, who was mentally handicapped. The family insisted on including her as much as possible in family activities and treating her as normally as possible, at a time when family shame was often associated with mental disorders. As an adult Rosemary became aggressive and violent, and her father followed the advice of doctors and had her lobotomized. A botched operation forced the family to institutionalize Rosemary, a failure that haunted the close-knit family for decades.

During the summer of 1937, just two years before the outbreak of war, Jack and a friend spent two months traveling in Europe, visiting France, Spain, Italy, Germany, and Britain. He kept a diary of the journey and, very much the arrogant American abroad, recorded his annoyance with other countries, but at the same time he made an effort to move beyond his personal experiences, reading books and talking to journalists in order to create an informed opinion based on a more objective look at the situation rather than his narrow emotional reactions. This trait marked him as a mature form of an intellectual, despite his youth, who seeks to understand and analyze why something was the way it was, rather than create justifications for an attitude already arrived at through emotion or ideological commitment.

The Kennedys were social climbers and overcame the barriers in class-conscious Boston to become American aristocrats themselves, though America had no noble titles to confer such status—only money, education, and social connections. Despite their achievements, as Irish Catholics the Kennedys suffered from social discrimination and were barred from entering the highest levels of Boston society. In 1937 the family was thrilled when President Roosevelt appointed Joe

Kennedy as the ambassador to Great Britain, the most prestigious diplomatic posting for the Americans. For the descendent of Irish immigrants to attain this position showed that the family had finally arrived. In the Anglophile high society of Boston, the ambassadorship broke the last barriers. One of Jack's sisters later married the son of a wealthy English duke.

In 1939 Jack persuaded Harvard to give him a semester off to travel again to Europe, as an assistant to his father, in order to collect material for his senior thesis on European politics. The young man enjoyed the social life of the privileged in Europe and even accompanied the family to the coronation of the new pope, Pius XII. Jack did not do much work for his father but did throw himself into his own research, traveling to the American consulates or embassies in Leningrad, Moscow, Kiev, Bucharest, Turkey, Jerusalem, Beirut, Damascus, Prague, Munich, Italy, France, Germany, and Athens. He also visited Danzig and Warsaw in May, only four months before World War II began there.[3] He talked to senior American diplomats and journalists and read diplomatic dispatches. Jack later traveled throughout South America with his mother and sister in 1941. These experiences stand in marked contrast to the education of Khrushchev, who had little ability as a diplomat and whose exposure to other countries was so affected by ideological blinders that the experience served little positive use.

As a Kennedy, Jack was determined not to be a playboy; instead, he was anxious to make his mark on the world. His continuing unresolved health problems complicated these ambitions. He had abdominal pains and colitis, which required frequent hospitalization and uncomfortable medical tests. Multiple visits to the Mayo Clinic in Rochester, Minnesota, did not help, but Jack continued to confront his health problems with the stoicism that his parents had taught him. In 1940 he began to experience back pains, perhaps as a result of the steroids that doctors had prescribed for his colitis. As a consequence of being ill and in pain so often, Jack was determined to live life fully in case he did not receive a full measure of years.

Kennedy's father vocally supported the appeasement policy of the British prime minister, Neville Chamberlain, as a way to deal with the aggressive foreign policy of Germany's Adolf Hitler. This support, consistent with his lifelong isolationist beliefs, destroyed any hope that Joseph Kennedy Sr. had of becoming the U.S. president. That ambition would be left to his eldest son.

Appeasement failed, and World War II began while Jack was still in Europe. Jack returned to Harvard and wrote his senior thesis, which was later published with the title *Why England Slept.* A journalist helped him with his writing style, but the content was all his own. The timely book sold remarkably well—eighty thousand copies in the United States and England—showing that Jack had a career as an academic or journalist if he so chose.[4]

With the start of World War II in Europe, America roused itself into preparation by implementing the first peacetime draft. Jack was due to be drafted and wanted to serve, though he could have easily avoided the military because of his health problems. In fact, when he volunteered for the Navy in 1941, he failed his physical exams, so his father intervened to request that a medical board pass him. Jack became a Navy ensign in the summer of that year. He was assigned to a desk job at the Foreign Intelligence Branch of the Office of Naval Intelligence in Washington, D.C. A heated affair with a Danish journalist named Inga, a twice-married beauty, led to Federal Bureau of Investigation (FBI) concern because it considered the woman a possible security risk due to her journalistic work in Germany before the war. Inga later disappeared from his life, another in a long train of women who he left in his wake, like so much flotsam.

In June 1942 Jack successfully transferred to a training program for future commanders of motor torpedo boats. These patrol torpedo (PT) boats were eighty-foot-long craft made of plywood that could race across the water at speeds up to forty knots. Each PT boat carried four torpedoes, with a 20 mm cannon at the rear and a pair of twin .50-caliber machine guns for antiaircraft defense. With a complement of only seventeen, a junior officer could have his own command, and that appealed to the twenty-five-year-old Jack. The idea of the PT boat never quite lived up to the expectations of advocates, but it was an exciting opportunity for dangerous work. Only his father's intervention got Jack selected, 1 of 50 selected from 1,024 applicants.

After training, Jack was selected as a training instructor in Rhode Island, though his performance had not warranted such an assignment. Again his father had intervened, wanting to keep his son closer to home and out of harm's way. Jack went to his grandfather, the former mayor of Boston, who contacted the right senator, and Jack was transferred to PT boats patrolling the Panama Canal Zone, far from the actual fighting. Again Jack asked his grandfather to intervene. The young man was then posted into the thick of the action in the Solomon Islands in the South Pacific, at Tulagi, just across the water from Guadalcanal.

Was Jack's persistence just a young man's lust for adventure? Some cynics might argue that Jack was already looking forward to a political career and war experience went over well with voters, but there is no evidence for this point of view. Joe Jr., not Jack, was the designated future president in the family. World War II was a great moral crusade that inspired many Americans to enlist. Nine months in the war zone destroyed any illusions that Jack had about war. He saw enough death to know that dying is just dying and not usually an act of nobility. He soon shared the disdain of his sailors and fellow junior officers for the competence of generals and admirals, though he admired William "Bull" Halsey, the admiral in charge of the South Pacific theater at that point. He found that his fellow sailors just wanted to return home alive.

Jack also found that PT boats had no armor and burned nicely when hit by enemy fire. He assumed command of PT-109 and was transferred with his boat squadron to different islands in the Solomons as the Americans pushed the Japanese back. Because control over airspace was contested, the Japanese resupplied their garrisons at night with fast-moving destroyers and transports in what the Americans called the Tokyo Express. Fifteen PT boats were sent to ambush a force of Japanese destroyers during the night of August 1–2, 1943. Confusion, a breakdown in radios, and a lack of defined tactics created a complete debacle. Thirty-two torpedoes failed to hit a single target, and the concept of the PT boat flunked its biggest test.*

Some of the PT boats returned to base, while others were left on patrol. In the early morning hours, PT-109 was in the middle of the strait, idling only one of its three engines to keep down the white froth of its wake, which could draw the attention of a night-flying Japanese aircraft. A Japanese destroyer came out of the night and sliced PT-109 in two. This incident was the only occasion in the war when a PT boat was rammed. Two crew members were killed, and the rest of the men found themselves clinging to the forward part of the hull, which remained afloat. The boat's engineer had been seriously burned.

The next afternoon the sailors decided to make for a small island, a swim that took five hours, with Kennedy towing the boat's engineer. The island had no food or water. That night, the exhausted Kennedy swam back out into the strait, hoping to signal a passing PT boat by lantern. No boats came. His squadron had

---

* Five nights later, a force of American destroyers tried the same tactic in the Battle of Vella Gulf and sank three Japanese destroyers. The larger destroyers were better weapon platforms than the PT boats were.

given up the PT-109 as lost. The following night, another crewman tried the same tactic with no success.

Only some rainwater slaked their thirst. Swimming to a nearby island, the men found coconuts. Kennedy and another officer swam to still another island, where they found a canoe, fresh water, and some crackers and candy. Native islanders also found the crew, and Kennedy carved a message into a coconut to be taken by a native to the PT base. After seven days stranded on the islands, Kennedy and his crew were brought to safety.

Journalists ate up the story when two PT boats picked up Kennedy and the crew. The crew had only praise for their commander, and the account of his heroism made national headlines. The newspaper editors liked the idea of a son of privilege fighting for survival, affirming the egalitarian ideals of the nation. Kennedy was surprised to suddenly be a national hero and viewed his own actions as normal and the result of pure chance. After he became president, a journalist published a book on the incident, *PT-109*, cementing Kennedy's heroism in the public mind.

Despite his physical illnesses, Kennedy had been on the Harvard swim team, and that training had served him well. Among all the accounts of the incident, no one mentioned his bad back, though his men knew about it because Kennedy continually wore a corset-style brace and slept with a plywood board under his mattress for support. After only ten days of recuperation, Kennedy insisted on returning to command another PT boat.

In December 1943 stomach problems, including an ulcer visible in an X-ray, sent Kennedy back to the States for care. An episode of malaria complicated his other medical problems. Back surgery in 1944 for a ruptured disc found instead that the cartilage in his spine was degenerating. His colitis also acted up, though he allowed the Navy doctors to believe that this was a new problem, not something he had concealed in order to enter the service. The Navy decided that Kennedy was medically unfit for duty and retired him.

The medical problems continued even though Kennedy spent early 1945 in Arizona trying to recover. With the end of the war in Europe, he became a correspondent for the Hearst newspapers, covering the founding of the United Nations in San Francisco and events in Europe. In June 1946 Kennedy collapsed after walking in a parade. To complicate his complex medical problems, Kennedy had also probably contracted gonorrhea, a problem cured with newly available antibiotics. In 1947 another episode in London led to a hospitalization, during which he was informally diagnosed with Addison's disease. This explained the brownish yellow color of his skin, stomach problems, fatigue, and inability to gain weight. Modern doctors have speculated that the Addison's was caused by the steroids he took for his earlier diseases, though we will never know. Hormone replacement therapy was prescribed to combat the Addison's, and Kennedy elected to keep the diagnosis secret; he even lied about it later in life when directly asked.

Kennedy's physical misery was complicated by a greater sorrow. On August 12, 1944, Joe Jr. died when his bomber exploded in midair. It had been packed with explosives for use as a flying bomb, aimed at V-1 launch sites on the Belgian coast. The pilots were trained to bail out after a trailing bomber crew took over as pilot via remote control. Kennedy took the loss of his brother hard, not just because he loved him, but also because he had lost the competition that had defined his life to that point. The following year, he compiled a book of reminiscences of his brother by family and friends, *As We Remember Joe.*

ENTERING PUBLIC SERVICE

With the end of the war, Kennedy set his sights on public service. When his father saw his initial hopes for a future politician die, he transferred those ambitions to his next oldest son. At first the plan was for Jack to follow his father in accepting important government appointments, rather than becoming an elected politician. His regular exposure to political leaders throughout his life and his acquaintance with the top leaders of the day as a journalist reinforced his natural self-confidence and belief that he could join their ranks. Kennedy believed that a journalist merely reported what was happening, whereas a political leader was "making it happen."[5]

In 1946 Kennedy changed course and decided to run for Congress. His father had subtly laid the groundwork for the campaign, in part by persuading the incumbent Eleventh District congressman to run in Boston's mayoral election instead of for reelection to Congress. In return, the older Kennedy helped pay off the incumbent's campaign debts. Not disposed to the traditional Boston-style campaign of mingling with people, Kennedy still managed to come across as friendly, likable, and always well informed. He spoke with an easy confidence, though his delivery was stiff until leavened by more years of political campaigning. He looked younger than his twenty-nine years.

A Democrat in a strongly Democratic state, Kennedy needed to win in the party primary election. He emphasized his veteran status and campaigned vigorously, overcoming his natural tendency to be disorganized and late for appointments and engagements. His father spent up to $300,000 on the campaign, a startling sum for those days, and all his siblings worked hard to see that he won.

In the midst of a national Republican landslide in 1946, Kennedy won his seat in Congress. Though genuinely devoted to the concept of public service and motivated by idealism and a desire to do what was best for his country, Kennedy found being a junior member of the minority party in the House of Representatives boring. His father paid for an office staff larger than that of any other member of Congress, and Kennedy was mostly shielded by the staff from the day-to-day details of dealing with constituent demands. Lacking sufficient understanding of domestic issues, he studied intensively, and, because unions were important in his working-class district, he became versed in labor law.

Kennedy's domestic agenda relied on a continuation of New Deal liberalism, while in foreign policy he was stridently anticommunist, an early cold warrior. As his own political beliefs developed, Kennedy did not follow his father's continuing taste for isolationism. His father encouraged independent thought, a trait that he admired in himself and in his son, and Kennedy lived up to this ideal.

Kennedy was skeptical of ideology and assumptions, nonideological in his taste for pragmatism, and a realist in his approach to foreign affairs. He supported Truman's containment policy, which started with massive foreign and military aid to Greece and Turkey in 1947 to resist communism, and then voted for the Marshall Plan to rebuild the economy of Western Europe. In 1949 Kennedy also supported the formation of NATO. As a consequence of his ardent commitment to anticommunism, Kennedy supported the hunt for American Communists by Senator Joseph McCarthy and his colleague Richard Nixon. After McCarthyism was discredited, Kennedy was embarrassed by his prior enthusiasm.

In 1948 Kennedy's sister Kathleen died in a plane crash; now the two siblings closest to him were gone. In 1951, accompanied by his sister Pat and brother Robert, Kennedy went on a seven-week trip through Asia. With an eight-year gap in their ages, boarding school, college, and careers, the two brothers did not know each other as well as one might expect. They now bonded with the trust that only brothers can have, and Bobby Kennedy became his older brother's most important adviser and confidant. As with most of Jack's trips abroad, his political status and wealth allowed Kennedy to meet with national leaders and important members of the governing elite in each country.

The trip also convinced Kennedy that the United States must forge stronger ties with the newly emerging nations of the third world. Most of these new nations had just achieved their independence from European empires and wanted to follow a new path. Because the Soviet Union had effectively held onto the old Russian empire, the Soviets did not have any contrary colonies-turned-nations to contend with, and many nations emerging from Western colonialism showed interest in communism as a means of bolstering their independence. Kennedy recognized that converting these new nations to democracy could not be achieved by military might; instead, it would be an ideological and economic struggle against "poverty and want," "sickness and disease," "injustice and inequality."[6]

Kennedy saw the House of Representatives as only the first step in his political career and served for only three terms before running for the Senate in the 1952 election. Even at this point, the goal for him and his father was the presidency. Kennedy had contemplated running for governor of Massachusetts instead but preferred the Senate because as a senator he could be involved with foreign policy. It is surprising, considering his ultimate goal, that he chose the Senate. Presidents usually came from the ranks of governors or vice presidents, and before Kennedy, only Warren G. Harding had ever been directly elected from the Senate. Bobby Kennedy managed his brother's Senate campaign, and their father funded a lavish effort—including a half-million-dollar loan to Boston's largest newspaper—against the distinguished Senate incumbent, Henry Cabot Lodge Jr. Kennedy won a narrow victory, taking office during a Republican landslide year occasioned by the election of the popular World War II general Dwight D. Eisenhower.

The McCarthy crusade to find secret Communists in the government, which ruined careers and failed to unearth a single disloyal American, came to a halt after televised Senate hearings showed him to be the lout that he was. The Senate voted to censure the wayward senator, but Kennedy chose to abstain from the vote, concerned about the continuing popularity of the rabid, red-baiting McCarthy in Kennedy's home state. He had to regularly explain this failure of political courage for the rest of his life and ultimately settled on the weak excuse that he had been in the hospital for yet another back surgery during part of the process leading up to the vote. The surgeons placed a metal plate in Kennedy's back, which became infected, requiring another surgery to remove it.

As a sort of penance for his blunder on the McCarthy vote, Kennedy wrote a book called *Profiles in Courage*, describing six senators in American history who took unpopular stands on important issues that threatened their political careers. In a way, Kennedy was defining himself as being in the company of those great men. The 1956 book became a national bestseller and won a Pulitzer Prize. While his literary output paled in comparison to that of his great idol, Winston Churchill, Kennedy clearly aspired to be respected as an intellectual and a politician. Almost immediately whispers and outright accusations of fraud surfaced, suggesting the book had been ghostwritten. While it is true that Kennedy had substantial research assistance and aides who even drafted chapters, the final drafts and conclusions are clearly Kennedy's.

In 1953, knowing that further political aspirations required a wife, Kennedy married a glamorous socialite, Jacqueline Lee Bouvier. Her astute political skills complemented his own, and the couple made a good match, though the marriage was not always happy and often strained by Kennedy's continued compulsive womanizing. After Jackie suffered a miscarriage and a stillborn daughter, the couple had a daughter in 1957 and a son in 1960. Jackie was photogenic and publicity-aware, and she made the two of them into celebrities. They were profiled in numerous national magazines during the next decade. The glamour helped Kennedy become known countrywide, but at the same time, the senator had to work to show that he had intellectual depth and that he was not a superficial publicity hound.

Kennedy campaigned behind the scenes for the vice presidential spot on the 1956 Democratic presidential ticket. In the process, he effectively took control of the Massachusetts Democratic Party. Other Democrats feared that a Catholic would doom the ticket, reflecting the anti-Catholic bias that had been so prominent in much of American history. As part of the national party convention maneuvering, Kennedy even put his name forward for the presidential slot. He came close to claiming the vice presidential nomination, which would have been a mistake as Eisenhower won reelection against Adlai Stevenson by a decisive 15 percentage points.

Kennedy and his family kept his illnesses a tight secret, even though he was hospitalized an average of four or five times a year. Daily injections of the steroid cortisone as an anti-inflammatory kept the Addison's disease under control, but unknown to medical science of that time, the steroid contributed to the continued compression of his spine. Colitis, urinary tract infections, abdominal pains, diarrhea, and throat infections continued to plague him, and all were aggravated by the cortisone, which depressed his immune system and made it harder for his body to fight off infections. After a poor performance at a speech, Kennedy resolved to take extra steroids when he needed to be more alert. Only his stout constitution and an iron will allowed Kennedy to push on toward his goal.

The senator regularly sought to engage issues that would give him national exposure. He opposed the defense reductions by Eisenhower, who wanted to rely on the nuclear deterrent rather than large conventional forces. But even with the cuts, only the Soviet Union and China had larger militaries than the United States had.

The civil rights movement and the desegregation movement promised a new day for the descendants of African slaves, and Kennedy had to take a stand on the issue. He had little empathy for the plight of blacks, whom he had encountered mostly as domestic servants, and he tried to establish his liberal credentials as a supporter of civil rights while trying not to alienate white southerners, the backbone of the Democratic Party. Commenting on his eagerness to appeal to all possible constituencies, one of his fellow senators asked, "Why not show a little less profile and a little more courage?"[7]

Robert Kennedy ran his brother's 1960 presidential campaign. When asked about his youth, the senator emphasized that he had been serving as either a naval officer or member of Congress for the past eighteen years. He issued a statement denying the rumor that he had Addison's disease, a lie that was technically true since he had refused his endocrinologist's request to run the tests necessary to confirm the diagnosis. One of Kennedy's aides carried a special bag with all of the senator's medications, and when it was misplaced during a campaign trip to Connecticut, Kennedy was in a panic until it was recovered. Anyone going through his list of medicines might have been dismayed at the idea that such a near invalid wanted to be president. In addition to keeping his illnesses quiet, Kennedy had to combat irrational accusations that a Catholic president would take instructions from the pope and not put his nation first. Also, numerous journalists had heard rumors of Kennedy's womanizing, but no one followed up on them because at that time such private behavior was not considered worthy of reporting.

Kennedy chose the majority leader of the Senate, Lyndon Baines Johnson, as his vice presidential running mate. He did not like Johnson, but he thought that he would make a good president if Kennedy failed to live out his term, and as a southerner, Johnson could help deliver crucial votes in the election. Kennedy ran on the slogan of a New Frontier, a phrase that harkened back to the day when America had an expanding frontier of settlements, but this new frontier consisted of social and economic challenges.

The security challenges posed by nuclear weapons and the Cold War also became prominent campaign themes. Kennedy ran in 1960 on a platform that accused the Eisenhower administration of allowing a "missile gap" to emerge between the United States and the Soviet Union.* After the launch of *Sputnik*, Americans came to believe that the Soviets were ahead in both missile technology and in the number of nuclear-tipped missiles manufactured and deployed, all ready to destroy the United States and its allies in a flurry of mushroom clouds.

On the issue of civil rights, Kennedy had to choose between the two factions in the Democratic Party, and after he chose to promote civil rights, he stuck firmly to the decision. When the civil rights leader and future vice president Martin Luther King Jr. was arrested in Georgia on trumped-up charges and sent to a labor camp for four months, Bobby Kennedy called the judge and got the sentence suspended.

Kennedy also challenged his opponent, Eisenhower's vice president Richard M. Nixon, to four televised debates, the first in presidential history. While radio listeners thought Nixon had won the debates, television viewers reacted more favorably to Kennedy, who had a relaxed style in contrast to the lumpy Nixon and his attack-dog methods.

The vote was close, with 64.5 percent of the electorate voting and Kennedy winning by only 118,574 votes. The margin in the Electoral College was wider —303 votes to Nixon's 219. Many commentators were shocked at how close the vote was considering that Nixon's campaign was poorly run while Kennedy's was disciplined. Perhaps anti-Catholic bias played a role in reducing an electoral mandate to a mere win.

---

* In the mid-1950s Americans had first been alarmed by a "bomber gap," when they feared that the Soviets had more bombers than the Americans had. The truth was exactly the opposite, although the Air Force played up the gap in order to reinforce its requests for funding. One of the reasons for thinking that there might be a bomber gap was the Soviet practice of intentionally skipping numbers in serial designations on bombers that were displayed in public, such as during the May Day parade. Foreign observers naturally assumed that when they had seen a 15 on an airplane the previous year and then a 58 the following year, then there must be forty-three intervening aircraft, which was not necessarily true.

AS PRESIDENT

At age forty-three, Kennedy was the youngest man ever elected to the presidency, though Teddy Roosevelt had assumed the office at forty-two after the assassination of President William McKinley. He had only seventy-two days between the election and inauguration and had to choose his cabinet and other top government officials quickly, but the campaign had exhausted the frail man. On the day following the election, his hands, out of view of the cameras, trembled during a press conference. According to an aide, during the family's two-week vacation that followed the election, Kennedy's mind seemed neither keen nor clear.

Kennedy met with the outgoing president only twice. The second time, Eisenhower met with him privately to show him how to respond to a nuclear attack. A Marine helicopter was to whisk the president to the secret command facility at Mount Weather so that he could direct the war. Eisenhower also emphasized that the United States was far ahead of the Soviets in strategic forces, especially with the new Polaris missile submarines being built and commissioned. On the international front, Kennedy's immediate concern was the deteriorating situation in Laos, where a three-way civil war included a Communist faction and an American-supported royalist faction. Cuba was discussed but only as one of many problems.

As a new president, Kennedy held weekly press conferences, broadcast on television and radio. His intelligence and wit impressed audiences. He included Republicans in his administration, offering the opposition important cabinet posts, taking care to appoint men who would cooperate with him. Kennedy chose to act as his own chief of staff, and his inner core of aides worked on a variety of issues, rather than specializing, as Kennedy ran everything with a hands-on approach.

Showing the idealistic tone that he wanted his administration to promote, Kennedy quickly established the Peace Corps by executive order. The program sent young people to third world countries to live and work alongside those whom they tried to help. Peace Corps volunteers were forbidden from engaging in diplomatic and intelligence work, yet the Soviet Union quickly condemned the program as a way of sending spies abroad. The Soviet Union did not follow up with a similar program: the governments of Communist countries did not want their citizens returning from other countries with subversive ideas, nor did they want them to discover a world that did not match the carefully crafted propaganda of the party-controlled press.

A month into the new administration, Kennedy's secretary of defense, Robert S. McNamara, announced that the missile gap did not exist and that in fact quite the opposite situation existed: the Americans had more ICBMs than the Soviets had. The overflights had shown that the United States, despite *Sputnik*, was far ahead of the Soviets, especially in the number of deployed nuclear-tipped missiles. Nixon had been unable to address the missile-gap controversy during his campaign because it would have meant revealing the illegal source of the information.

Kennedy strongly supported a nuclear test ban treaty. In the late 1950s measurements in the atmosphere showed that the effects of nuclear testing were much more dramatic than had been anticipated and that worldwide radioactivity had risen as fallout circulated along the jet stream in the upper atmosphere. With a strong scientific case for stopping open-air testing, the Americans and Soviets had been negotiating for years, but an actual treaty had been held hostage to the fluctuating temperature of their diplomatic relationship. Advances in seismographs had made it possible to tell the difference between earthquakes and nuclear tests, making it almost impossible to cheat on a test ban. Aerial monitoring of radioactive particles could also catch violations.

Kennedy approached foreign policy with a mixture of idealism and realistic pragmatism. Americans have always had dual motivations behind their foreign policy—idealism and self-interest—and while America often preached the gospel of democracy and individual rights, the question became how to conduct a moral foreign policy in an immoral world.[8] This problem became acute during the Cold War, as America could no longer reject the dirty tricks of self-serving foreign policies by retreating into isolationism. Communism verses democracy was a worldwide struggle, with battlegrounds in economics, in Europe, in the newly emerging third world, in domestic politics, and in the world of ideas.

When scholars view the moral nastiness of the Cold War, in events such as the overthrow of legitimate governments in Iran in 1953 and in Guatemala in 1954, the reaction is often disgust. Such acts violate a sense of fair play and the American ideal of being a "city on a hill." These coups and other policy maneuvers demonstrate that America found the cause of anticommunism to be more important than the promotion of their more idealistic values. But perhaps these excesses should be understood in the context of the times and should serve as lessons in how a struggle can become so intense that morality is sacrificed.

Scholars on the right end of the political spectrum tend to minimize the sins of American-supported dictators, and scholars on the left tend to accentuate those sins and minimize the sins of the Communists. Because the Communists told the world and themselves pervasive lies, it is often difficult to find and understand the historical truths of Communist regimes. We do know that communism as practiced by Stalin, Mao, Castro, and other national leaders always ranked power and ideology over the individual person. Individuals who stood in the way of agricultural collectivization, sought political pluralism, or wanted basic human rights were eliminated as obstacles. Communism killed more people during the twentieth century than any other ideology, upward of a hundred million dead, if one excludes the Fire as being motivated by any particular ideology.[9]

Most nations look to their own needs when creating their foreign policy and make self-interest the most important value in dealing with foreign governments. No one expected the Communists to exercise a foreign or domestic policy on moral terms, though observers often held the Americans to a higher standard because the Americans claimed a higher moral ground. The Cold War was viewed by all concerned as an apocalyptic struggle, with the winner taking all and the loser being totally vanquished. In such a struggle, morality and rules based on anything other than self-interest fell to the wayside. In trying to preserve the world for democracy, America's anticommunists came close to losing the nation's soul.

Kennedy was well aware of these moral quandaries in foreign policy. As mentioned above, his first crisis was in Laos. The Joint Chiefs urged him to commit American military power to the country, arguing that if Laos fell to communism additional pressure would fall on Thailand, South Vietnam, and Cambodia to succumb to the ideology. Kennedy rejected this advice, considering Laos too remote and the political situation too difficult for American troops to make a difference, but he did increase American funding for South Vietnam, where the post-French dictatorship was fighting a Communist insurrection with the help of six hundred American military advisers.

Kennedy had a poor opinion of top military leaders from his time serving in the Navy, and he maintained this opinion through his presidency. He especially disliked the Air Force chief of staff, Curtis E. LeMay. Every meeting with the general agitated him. Aggravating the situation was LeMay's prestige as a general in World War II; his conservative, aggressive nature; and his refusal to listen to a point of view he did not share. Kennedy was frustrated that LeMay and his military brethren often provided a single, unified source of information; he wanted many sources of information to compare and contrast before arriving at his own opinion.[10]

Kennedy's lack of experience as an executive became brutally apparent during the planning process that led to the Bay of Pigs fiasco. For several months he pondered what to do with Assault Brigade 2506, which had been bequeathed to him by Eisenhower, and listened to conflicting advice from many sources. The CIA director, Allen Dulles, told the president that he thought the chances of victory were better than they had been for the successful 1954 Guatemalan coup. The young president also was impressed by the patriotic courage of the Cuban exiles who wanted to invade their homeland and free it from the Communists. He apparently did not go over the details of the plan carefully enough and did not adequately consider what he would do if the invasion failed. He floundered, trying to treat it as a political problem and preserve plausible deniability, and weakened the plan by delaying it long enough that the invasion site had to be moved from the original Trinidad site. Then he compounded his error by cutting back on the number of air strikes. It is hard to imagine how Kennedy could have made a poorer string of decisions.

During the crisis the president was afflicted by chronic diarrhea and a urinary tract infection. After the fiasco, he was depressed. He actually wept multiple times and called it the "worst experience of his life."[11] He learned hard lessons about how to make better decisions and be sure that the right information flowed to him. He also learned to distrust the CIA and Joint Chiefs, who had both endorsed the invasion and whom he held partly responsible for its failure. To his credit, he also considered himself to share in the responsibility. In public, he blamed only himself.

The failure did not mean that Kennedy had reconciled himself to Castro remaining in power. Though he ruled out an invasion by the American military, which would have caused massive public relations problems in Latin America, Kennedy maintained the economic sanctions and continued to seek other ways to oust Castro. Kennedy also feared that an invasion of Cuba would lead to an attack on West Berlin by the Warsaw Pact countries, a trade of territory that could easily lead to a general war.

The space race also worried Kennedy. Only a few days before the Bay of Pigs fiasco, the Soviets had put the first man into space. Kennedy looked for a way to leapfrog the Soviets in this race for prestige, and so on May 25, 1961, in an unusual direct address to Congress, a second State of the Union address, Kennedy urged the nation to commit the United States to landing a man on the moon and returning him safely to earth before the end of the decade. Large budgets to support this effort were drawn up.

One wonders if this Apollo project would have succeeded. Would the American people have been willing to put so much money into such a project? Would the technological hurdles have been overcome? The end-of-the-decade deadline left only about eight and a half years to accomplish what people had never even dared dream of until recently. Because it was so important to international prestige in the context of the Cold War, there is a strong possibility that the necessary funds would have been available. Other great technological triumphs had already been achieved in the areas of aircraft, computers, and nuclear technology, so perhaps the Americans would have succeeded. Imagine that, a man walking on the moon.

In early June, Kennedy flew to Europe for a two-day summit with Khrushchev in Vienna, Austria. Khrushchev eagerly looked forward to the meeting. From a distance, he had already taken his measure of the younger man after the Bay of Pigs invasion; he had been astonished at the failure of the Americans to follow up with a landing by U.S. forces. Khrushchev decided that Kennedy was no different than Eisenhower; whether Democratic or Republican, presidents were still Americans. Khrushchev also thought that Kennedy was weak and indecisive by nature.

At the summit, the Soviet leader gave Kennedy the usual treatment, haranguing the younger man over ideology, making repeated threats, refusing to discuss the issues, and failing to establish a personal connection. Khrushchev seemed to believe that he could browbeat Kennedy into submission in the same manner as one of his Communist underlings. Kennedy told a confidant that up until Khrushchev, he had never met "somebody with whom he couldn't exchange ideas in a meaningful way and feel that there was some point to it."[12] Perhaps the only positive development was Khrushchev's promise not to resume nuclear testing. Both nations had suspended testing since November 1958 in an attempt to build up trust toward a limited or comprehensive nuclear test ban treaty.

The Soviet leader also warned Kennedy not to "humiliate" the Soviet Union.[13] That he used the word "humiliate" provides the greatest insight into

Khrushchev and his deep insecurities, both personally and on behalf of his nation. Khrushchev left the summit convinced that he could continue to bully the younger man. He had been astonished when Kennedy admitted to mistakes, such as U.S. surprise at the Chinese intervention during the Korean conflict, and to political limitations, such as the close election that brought him to power without giving him an electoral mandate. Khrushchev would never have admitted to making a mistake or having a personal failing; those were the kind of self-critical words that Communist officials spoke only in desperation as they were forced from power.

THE BERLIN CRISIS

As related in chapter 2, Khrushchev began the Berlin crisis in 1958 without any definite ideas about how the confrontation would play out. In Kennedy's mind, one of the purposes of the June summit was to try to resolve the crisis, but Khrushchev wanted instead to increase the pressure on the Western allies. The Americans felt that if they surrendered their treaty rights to Berlin, none of their allies would trust them to maintain their other treaty obligations. For the Soviets, East Germany was an economic drain, especially because of Berlin. So many skilled workers had left the Communist country that the leader of East Germany had even asked for Soviet workers to replace them. In the first half of 1961, more than a hundred thousand East Germans took advantage of Berlin's open borders to permanently migrate to the West. In July the rate dramatically increased, with thirty thousand East Germans fleeing in just one month.

Soon after taking office, Kennedy had announced a large increase in the defense budget. He intended to move away from Eisenhower's reliance on nuclear weapons and toward fielding larger conventional forces. In July Khrushchev countered by announcing a one-third increase in his military budget, reversing his earlier efforts to decrease the size of the Red Army by a million soldiers and rely more on nuclear weapons. Kennedy responded with his own announcements, during a nationally televised address from the Oval Office, proposing an expansion of the Army from 875,000 to 1 million soldiers through an increased draft call-up and even the activation of reserves to immediately make up manpower needs. These were the actions of nations moving toward war.

In his speech, Kennedy had also urged that Moscow engage in negotiations. He was surprised at the positive response to the speech in America and Western

Europe, where polls showed the majority of the population unwilling to yield on Berlin and expecting the Soviets not to yield. In some ways, Kennedy felt that all this support was stampeding him toward selecting a military solution. The Pentagon offered multiple military options, and Kennedy even carefully considered whether a surprise nuclear attack could cripple Soviet forces. In truth, a surprise nuclear attack would have devastated the Soviets, but there would have also been some damage to Western European cities and millions of Westerners would certainly have died along with tens of millions of Soviets.

On August 13, 1961, the East Germans began to construct a wall sealing off West Berlin from the rest of East Germany. At first the wall was just barbed wire, but gradually efforts were made to construct a more permanent barrier. The Berlin Wall solved East Germany's chief problem—emigration—by prohibiting East Germans from easily fleeing their country. Building the wall was such a significant move that Khrushchev had earlier visited Berlin in secret and toured the city in an automobile to more clearly understand the nature of Berlin on the ground, another example of Khrushchev's penchant for hands-on management.[14]

The West was completely surprised by the Berlin Wall's construction, and it took some time for political and military leaders to decide what it meant. A week after construction began, the United States decided to move a battle group of fifteen hundred soldiers to Berlin to join the two battle groups already in the city. The solders, in a convoy of 491 vehicles, had to cross East German territory by highway to reach the city, a move permitted under the Yalta Conference agreement. Kennedy was so certain Communist troops would try to stop the convoy that he requested updates every fifteen minutes during the twelve-hour trip.[15] The Soviets did not object to the movement of the battle group, however, showing that the rest of the agreements would remain in force. The wall itself violated the agreements on four-power administration of the city, but as it happened, it also provided a way to solve the ongoing crisis. The adage "good fences make good neighbors" actually applied here; in essence, the Soviets had found a way to address their most pressing concern and resolve the crisis: they dropped their demands.

On August 30, 1961, the Soviets renewed nuclear testing, ending a three-year moratorium and breaking the promise Khrushchev had made two months earlier at the Vienna summit. In the following three months, the Soviets conducted thirty-one nuclear tests, including the largest nuclear explosion in history, at fifty-eight megatons. The large bomb was called Tsar Bomba, or "King of Bombs." It was actually designed to generate a hundred-megaton explosion, but Soviet scientists substituted lead for some of the uranium in order to keep the yield down. Fortunately, the bomb was an airburst at four thousand meters rather than a groundburst, which would have caused an enormous amount of fallout. From a military perspective, such a large weapon was no more useful than a bomb a tenth of that yield, but it sent the political statement that Khrushchev wanted to make.[16]

These tests were a bald attempt at intimidation. A frustrated Kennedy, believing that the "logic of a thermonuclear war demands that we exhaust every effort to find a peaceful solution consistent with the preservation of our vital interests," persisted in his diplomatic efforts. In a September speech to the United Nations, Kennedy also said that "mankind must put an end to war—or war will put an end to mankind."[17] The Americans quickly resumed underground tests on September 15 and later resumed atmospheric testing on April 25, 1962.

While the Berlin Wall calmed tensions over Berlin and Khrushchev opted to make no additional moves, the overall level of Cold War tension continued to increase. The Kennedy buildup added two more divisions to the fourteen divisions that the U.S. Army already possessed. During the Berlin crisis, the Kennedy administration brought enough ships out of mothballs to carry a full division in the Atlantic for a beach landing.* After the crisis, the Navy kept this amphibious capability.[18]

One of the reasons that Khrushchev decided to end the Berlin crisis, after the wall solved his most pressing problems, was a sense that Kennedy was so weak as a president that he might not be able to resist the demands of the right wing in the United States. The slogan "Better Dead than Red" exemplified the right-wing attitude, motivated by fervent anticommunism, a belief in military power as the best guarantee of American interests, and persistent distrust of the Soviets.

---

* During the 1950s the United States allowed its ability to launch amphibious invasions to atrophy. Specialized ships from the World War II era necessary for amphibious operations grew obsolete and were replaced slowly, so that by the end of the Eisenhower administration the United States had the ability to lift one division in the Pacific and only half a division in the Atlantic for amphibious assault. These meager numbers, so much smaller than the American capability during the height of World War II, when perhaps a dozen divisions could have been lifted simultaneously, are mitigated by the facts that the United States possessed the world's largest and most powerful Navy and that the only other nation with the ability to lift even a brigade for amphibious assault was its close ally, Great Britain.

While the right wing was a potent force in American politics, Khrushchev overestimated its influence on government policy and no doubt was alarmed by its more extreme statements.

In reality, the Soviet nuclear forces were substantially inferior to America's, a fact that the Kennedy administration decided to publicly describe in an October 21, 1961, speech by Deputy Defense Secretary Roswell Gilpatric. The Soviet GNP was estimated by the CIA to be 39 percent of America's GNP, almost certainly an overestimate, perhaps even by a factor of two. One of the ways that the Soviet economy was able to compete with the Americans in turning out weapons was that the Soviets produced few consumer items, forcing their people to live in effective poverty for the greater good of international communism.

Even with the easing of tensions over Berlin, incidents continued to occur. At the Berlin Wall's Checkpoint Charlie crossing point on October 27, 1961, a disagreement led to a standoff with dozens of Soviet and American tanks lining up, their loaded guns pointed at each other across the barbed-wire fence. The standoff lasted until the next day, when negotiations resolved the tension, and each side withdrew one tank at a time. Soviet fighters also occasionally harassed Western flights in and out of Berlin.

As its first year in office came to a close, the Kennedy administration looked at the Berlin crisis as a victory. West Berlin remained free, Kennedy had stood up to the Soviets, and the Berlin Wall became a propaganda albatross for the Communists, an ever-present reminder that when given a free choice, people opted out of communism.

SIOP-62

On September 13, 1961, President Kennedy and his closest civilian military advisers, including Secretary of Defense McNamara, received a top secret briefing from the chairman of the Joint Chiefs of Staff, Gen. Lyman Lemnitzer. We do not know if this briefing occurred in the morning or the evening. The middle of the day was occupied with a state luncheon in honor of President Sukarno of Indonesia and President Modibo Keita of Mali, who were visiting Washington, D.C., after attending the first summit of the Non-Aligned Movement in Belgrade, Yugoslavia. This movement sought to provide a forum for nations that did not want to align themselves in the East-West ideological confrontation that characterized the Cold War.

By virtue of his position as the top military officer in the nation, Lemnitzer gave the briefing personally. The subject of the briefing was SIOP-62, an example of the military necessity of the continuous use of acronyms. The Pentagon even issued a military manual, the size of a book, cataloging the accepted acronyms that American naval and military forces could use. SIOP-62 stood for Single Integrated Operation Plan for Fiscal Year 1962.[19]

In the event of a general nuclear war, the United States would rely on a variety of vehicles to deliver nuclear weapons to the home territories of the Soviet Union and its allies. The Air Force's Strategic Air Command (SAC) provided bombers and ballistic missiles. The Navy provided ballistic missiles via its new Polaris submarines and aircraft launched from carriers in the Atlantic, Pacific, and Mediterranean. The Army's tactical nuclear weapons, used in artillery shells and short-range missiles, were not expected to play a significant role in a general nuclear war.

American strategic forces included in the SIOP were scattered around the world on a total of 112 bases, though most of these were in the continental United States. Other SAC bases included installations in Puerto Rico, Newfoundland, Labrador, the United Kingdom, Morocco, Spain, and Guam.

In 1960 the Joint Chiefs of Staff realized that each separate military command had developed its own bombing plans in the event of a general nuclear war, with little coordination among the various commands and not enough political guidance. A planning staff was put together and tasked with designing the SIOP, and the first plan went into effect on April 15, 1961. Every fiscal year the plan was revised to take into account new American weapons and new targets. Unfortunately, we do not have a complete copy of SIOP-63, so we must rely for our analysis on the one remaining copy of SIOP-62.

The SIOP was obviously needed. The initial planning staff found that if the Air Force and Navy had carried out their service-specific plans, two hundred time-over-target conflicts would have occurred. Such a conflict meant that a ballistic missile could arrive in an area at the same time an Air Force bomber was scheduled to be there, or an Air Force bomber could have dropped its bomb on a target at the same time that a carrier-based Navy bomber was supposed to drop a bomb on the same target.

The SIOP developed a National Strategic Target List of more than eighty thousand possible targets in the Sino-Soviet bloc countries. After analysis, this list was narrowed down to 3,729 essential targets. Fortunately for the planners, many of these targets were near enough to each other that obliterating the 3,729 targets required only 1,060 nuclear weapons. Because the planners expected some ballistic missiles to fail and some bombers to not always get through Sino-Soviet air defenses, they created a mathematical model of how many weapons should be allocated to which targets to achieve the greatest possible certainty. The seven most important targets faced a 97 percent assurance, 213 targets faced a 95 percent assurance, and another 592 faced up to 90 percent assurance.

A tally created on July 15, 1961, showed that the United States had 1,530 nuclear weapons on alert, mostly in bombers that were already in the air or standing by on runways, with aircrews waiting nearby, ready to be airborne within fifteen minutes. If given more warning, within fourteen hours, the Americans could deliver a grand total of 3,267 weapons. These numbers had only increased by the next year, when the Cuban Missile Crisis occurred. Because of the cost, Soviet bombers were not kept on alert, and most Soviet submarines were kept in port. This contrast between the two superpowers ran throughout their entire military forces: whereas the wealthy United States built weapon systems and constantly kept them in use, the impoverished Soviet Union built numerous weapon systems but could not afford to continually practice with them. Soviet pilots had substantially fewer flight hours than their American counterparts; their ships spent most of their time in port, while U.S. Navy ships spent at least half of their time at sea; and many Soviet tanks and other weapons were effectively in long-term storage, while American equipment was usually in use.

The SIOP allocated about 80 percent of the nuclear weapons for military targets and the other 20 percent for urban-industrial centers, though it acknowledged that numerous military targets were near urban centers and would ultimately kill many civilians. The plan did not address the nuclear fallout that would affect the entire world.

It is important for us to note that the SIOP expected a general worldwide nuclear war between the East and the West, so China would be included in the destruction even if China were not involved in the political causes of the war. While the strains in the relationship between China and the Soviet Union were becoming obvious, the SIOP planners did not account for tension between the Communist powers; both were targeted regardless of how the war started.

The number of nuclear weapons that the Soviet Union could deliver was not calculated in the briefing, but the Soviets were thought to have only ten to

twenty-five ballistic missiles that could reach the United States, about two hundred bombers, and twenty-eight submarines that could launch a combined
seventy-eight nuclear-tipped missiles. The Pentagon staff had run military exercises and found to their dismay that they could not guarantee that all Soviet
bombers could be stopped by American and Canadian air defenses; and that
while they would destroy many of the submarines, some would get through.

While this data was not included in the SIOP, other Pentagon studies had
shown that in the event of a first strike by the United States, where they expected
to destroy most Soviet strategic weapons before they could be used, American
casualties would still be between two million and fifteen million people, with
many more lost among their allies in Europe.

General Lemnitzer emphasized that if the plan were followed, it would allow the United States to "prevail" in a general nuclear war, whether or not the
American military launched a first strike. "Prevailing" was apparently defined as
achieving the military objectives of the plan. Such a conclusion showed how difficult it was to apply conventional military thinking to the scale of destruction
that nuclear weapons introduced to military operations. Back in 1945 strategists
had considered nuclear weapons to be just big bombs, and in that sense they did
not have to change their intellectual paradigms; but as the bombs became more
powerful and more plentiful, the complete annihilation of a nation became possible. Though at first this thought was difficult to swallow, as the 1950s passed,
the military became more accustomed to the idea of millions dying. The casualties became just numbers in war games, mathematical quantities passed around
amid other numbers that represented delivery systems, kilotons or megatons of
destructive potential, launch failure rates, and circular errors of probability.

General Lemnitzer also emphasized that the plan contained fourteen different options. The first option was the targeting to take place if the Soviets launched
a surprise attack with only fifteen minutes of warning; this option would allow
the use of only alert forces. The last option assumed at least fourteen hours of
warning, which allowed the use of all American strategic forces. The other options assumed somewhere between fifteen minutes and fourteen hours of warning. Missiles coming from submarines and bombers coming from aircraft carriers
were expected to need two hours of warning to be included in the SIOP strike.

The SIOP provided fixed targets and quantities because the Pentagon believed a more flexible plan would be more difficult to follow during a general

nuclear war and could cause inefficient use of the U.S. nuclear arsenal. The key term is "efficiency." The Pentagon also argued that there was no effective way to quickly redesign the plan to meet political instructions during an actual war— for example, to limit strikes to military targets. Besides, even if the Americans wanted to limit collateral damage to civilians, with the awful power of nuclear weapons and so many military targets located near cities, how would the Soviets know that the Americans were trying to avoid civilian casualties?

The Pentagon had written one shred of sanity into the SIOP. All commanders, whether a bomber pilot or a missile-launch officer or a submarine commander, had to maintain positive control. This meant that they had to receive an explicit code in order to proceed with their missions. This was most important for the bomber crews. They could take off and fly toward their targets, but they could not actually penetrate enemy airspace and drop their bombs until they received this code. In the words of the briefing: If the bomber crews fail to "receive a message ordering the execution of the SIOP before they reach hostile territory, they will return to bases."[20]

Even with this "fail-safe" system to maintain positive control, the Pentagon planners were clearly concerned that the political leaders of the nation would tamper with their finely tuned plan and request more options. They were right.

Kennedy was appalled by the rigidity of the plan and showed his irritation by tapping his thumb on his front teeth and running his hand through his hair during Lemnitzer's briefing. After the briefing, McNamara described the inflexible SIOP as a plan for a "spasm war."[21] The president agreed and made his attitude public in his next State of the Union address, delivered to the combined Senate and House of Representatives on January 11, 1962. "Our strength may be tested at many levels. We intend to have at all times the capacity to resist non-nuclear or limited attacks—as a complement to our nuclear capacity, not as a substitute. We have rejected any all-or-nothing posture which would leave no choice but inglorious retreat or unlimited retaliation."

The American way of war, as defined by its successful experience in World War II, was for the political leadership to define the war and for the Pentagon to run the details of that war. What the generals and admirals failed to understand was that a nuclear war was a dance with national suicide, a political act requiring the utmost finesse in order to push to the brink, maybe dip your toe into the water, but to step back in time to prevent unnecessary casualties. The SIOP was about using all the expensive weapons that had been developed and manufactured after so much effort; unused weapons were wasted weapons.

The Pentagon planners were ordered to do a better job and apparently did so. Sadly, we do not have a copy of SIOP-63, the master plan that was put in place on August 1, 1962. The president was briefed on this plan on September 14, just over a month before the Cuban Missile Crisis. We know that this plan included five additional options, allowing the president to maintain more political control and to escalate the nuclear war gradually. The ability to exclude China or other Soviet allies from destruction was also included. McNamara also got his wish for an option in which the Soviets launched a counterforce strike in response to an American attack. In this scenario, a smaller force of American nuclear weapons would be kept in reserve in case the Soviets did not then surrender.

KENNEDY GROWS

The worsening situation in South Vietnam demanded Kennedy's attention. A nationalist movement led by Communists had succeeded in driving out the French colonialists, and the country was divided in 1955, with the Communists ruling in North Vietnam and a Western-supported dictator, Ngo Dinh Diem, taking power in South Vietnam. Communist guerrillas in the south began to make life difficult for Diem, and the United States steadily increased its military and economic aid to the country. In the fall of 1961 Kennedy commissioned various studies to examine what to do next.

Many advisers, including Secretary of Defense McNamara, the Joint Chiefs, the CIA, and other presidential aides, wanted a massive increase in aid, including sending eight thousand to ten thousand American ground troops. Even with such efforts, the advisers acknowledged that Diem was too corrupt to be a good ruler and that even more aid might be needed in the form of six divisions (205,000 troops) of American military support. The concern was that a Communist takeover in South Vietnam would lead to Communist takeovers in Thailand, Cambodia, Indonesia, and Malaysia. This idea was called the domino effect. The same effect had been seen after China had fallen to the Communists, emboldening the neighboring Communist government of North Korea and leading to successful support for the Vietnamese Communist movement in the south.

All over the world, European colonial empires were collapsing and forming new third world nations. In some cases, the liberation of a colony happened peacefully; in others, a war of liberation was necessary, and often Communist guerrillas were the best prepared to take advantage of the situation. The American advisers thought that letting South Vietnam fall would dishearten anticommunists everywhere.

Other advisers to Kennedy argued that American support to South Vietnam should be limited to economic and military aid. The old adage "Do not get involved in a land war in Asia" still applied. The Korean conflict, which had ended only eight years before, had left the U.S. government with an abiding respect for how large the Chinese population was and how many casualties the Chinese Communist leadership was willing to take. In Korea, the Chinese lost between six and ten soldiers for each American soldier in addition to all the dead among the North and South Korean armies and civilian populations.

Even though Kennedy was reluctant to commit further resources to South Vietnam, the alternatives were even less palatable. He decided in November 1961 to send more aid and to increase the number of American advisers to over 3,500, but he stopped short of sending American combat troops. As the situation developed over the next year, U.S. Army advisers and aircrews found themselves in covert combat. Some have argued that the American advisers exceeded their instructions and that Kennedy was not fully in control; however, one can understand why American soldiers, who bonded with the Vietnamese soldiers whom they advised, failed to resist going on patrols and missions just to help out.

As part of his reaction to the Berlin crisis, Kennedy had announced a three-fold increase in spending on civil defense. Civil defense included preparing to survive a nuclear war by building public fallout shelters—a nice idea in theory. Some private individuals had already built personal fallout shelters. In some ways, Kennedy saw supporting civil defense as an easy way to gain political points and reassure the population. In September, he even wrote a letter for *Life* magazine to print alongside the article "You Could Be Among the 97% to Survive If You Follow Advice in These Pages." More sober scientists told the president that it was unlikely so many would survive. Kennedy eventually found that the enthusiasm of fallout shelter advocates was a financial black hole, since fallout shelters for every citizen essentially meant building alternative housing for the entire population, and that the existence of fallout shelters even encouraged Americans to accept the idea of going to nuclear war. He backed off the civil defense initiative and allowed it to dwindle during the summer of 1962. That interest in the program had peaked just months before the Fire cannot be ignored by any reader; if more people had possessed fallout shelters and sufficient food storage, certainly more would have lived.[22]

In December 1961 Kennedy's father suffered a stroke that left him impaired for the rest of his life. He could no longer speak clearly, and he struggled with walking. This was only the most recent in a long series of personal tragedies and reminded Kennedy that his own life was fragile. Despite his health problems and the pressures of the presidency (or perhaps to cope with them), Kennedy increased his womanizing. He told the British prime minister that he needed a woman every three days or he would get a terrible headache.[23]

While president, Kennedy often took five hot showers a day to find some relief from his physical pain. He also sat in a rocking chair, finding its stiff wood much more comfortable than a cushioned chair. He relied on many doctors for his care, and they did not know how many drugs he was taking; as one biographer put it, "Kennedy was more promiscuous with physicians and drugs than he was with women."[24] A regime of exercise had strengthened his back, but his condition was still deteriorating. Despite all the pain, Kennedy retained a keen intellect and his sense of humor.

As an amateur historian himself, Kennedy was acutely aware of how historians might judge his administration. Because he understood the need for primary sources, he had secret recorders installed in the Oval Office, in the Cabinet Room, and on his office telephone. He could record any conversation that he chose to record, including phone conversations. Dozens of hours of tape were recorded, and all were lost in the Fire—just one of the painful gaps in the historical record that we must cope with.

Throughout the summer of 1962, Kennedy continued to enjoy high public approval ratings, though his domestic policies foundered on a slowing economy and rising civil rights tensions in the South. It is unfortunate that Kennedy found it politically difficult to make progress on civil rights. He shied away from tackling the problems of racism and racial segregation and thus failed to solve the great contradiction attached to the heart of American liberty like a tumor.

Khrushchev occasionally made belligerent statements about Berlin, keeping that crisis in Kennedy's mind but not escalating it to a boil. Kennedy's continued dealings with Khrushchev via letters and diplomats had convinced the American president that the Soviet leader was unstable, erratic, and prone to relying on delusions as truths.[25]

In terms of the Cold War, the first twenty months of the Kennedy administration had seen hopes of renewed détente collapse, the Bay of Pigs fiasco, the Berlin crisis (calmed by the erection of the Berlin Wall), repeated setbacks in the space race, the collapse of U.S.-Soviet arms control talks, the resumption of nuclear testing, military budget and manpower increases in both superpowers, the escalation of the conflict in Southeast Asia, little progress on the Alliance for Peace to support democracy in Central and South America, and increased Soviet support for Cuba.

The Cold War was getting warmer.

Further sources: John T. Correll, "The Ups and Downs of Counterforce," *Air Force Magazine* 88, no. 10 (October 2005): 59–64; Robert Dallek, *An Unfinished Life: John F. Kennedy, 1917–1963* (Boston: Little, Brown, 2003); Norman Friedman, *U.S. Amphibious Ships and Craft: An Illustrated Design History* (Annapolis, MD: Naval Institute Press, 2002); Richard Reeves, *President Kennedy: Profile of Power* (New York: Simon & Schuster, 1993); Scott D. Sagan, "SIOP-62: The Nuclear War Plan Briefing to President Kennedy," *International Security* 12, no. 1 (Summer 1987): 22–51; and Arthur M. Schlesinger Jr., *A Thousand Days: John F. Kennedy in the White House* (Boston: Houghton Mifflin, 1965), written by the noted historian who also served as an aide to the Kennedy White House.

4

Operation Anadyr: The Plan
to Protect Cuba

The Soviets were quite aware that many leaders in the United States, especially conservative politicians and the military leadership, wanted to invade Cuba. In April 1962 forty thousand Marines and sailors participated in a two-week exercise that ended with an amphibious invasion of Vieques Island off Puerto Rico. The exercise was obviously a trial run for an invasion of Cuba. It was also intended to keep Castro preoccupied enough with a possible invasion that he would be distracted from his plans to export his revolution to other Latin American countries.

Other exercises later that summer, including a twenty-four thousand–man joint Marine and Navy exercise in early October 1962 called Ortsac (Castro spelled backward), were also aimed at readying the American military to invade Cuba. While there was substantial popular support for an invasion of Cuba, President Kennedy himself was opposed to the idea, hoping that covert action would cause the Cuban government to fall. Still, Kennedy allowed an examination of various scenarios for the use of American military force to proceed.[1]

As best as we can determine, the idea that became Operation Anadyr sprang purely from the mind of Khrushchev. On May 21, 1962, the short, thickset man whose face had grown fleshy in his later years informed the Defense Council at the Kremlin of his intention to protect Cuba from a second American-led invasion by sending nuclear ballistic missiles and troops to the island. Even if the Red Army had been of a mind to object, the officers had been cowed into submission by Khrushchev's actions over the last two and a half years, when he had forced the military to downsize by about a million enlisted men and a quarter million army and naval officers. These manpower cuts had clearly established Khrushchev's power over the military, even as the cuts were partially reversed during the Berlin crisis.

Multiple perspectives and motivations are available to understand the Soviet premier's decision to launch Operation Anadyr. Khrushchev felt a fondness for the Cuban Revolution. For the second time a Communist government had come to power through popular action from within, not as a result of imposition of the ideology by an outside army, as had happened in the nations of Eastern Europe after World War II, and not by means of a local movement that received significant support from an outside power, as in China, when the Soviet Union funneled arms, money, and advice to the Communists there. The first time that a Communist government had come to power through the action of the people was the Soviet Union's own Russian Revolution of 1917. Deputy Premier Mikoyan, a close friend of Khrushchev's, was reported to have said that the Cuban Revolution made the "old Bolsheviks" such as Khrushchev, men who had been in the Russian Revolution and burned with ideological belief in Marxism-Leninism, "feel like boys" again.[2] This fondness for the Caribbean nation encouraged Khrushchev to gamble on keeping its revolution alive.

Beyond the primary motivation of helping Cuba defend itself from an invasion by the United States, a second motivation presented itself. Khrushchev was keenly aware that his nation was far behind the United States in terms of nuclear weapons. The United States had its Thor IRBMs in Turkey, right on the Soviet border, so Khrushchev thought it only fair that the Soviets station their IRBMs in a nation near the United States. Soviet ballistic missiles in Cuba could quickly restore some balance to the nuclear standoff with the United States.

A third motivation emerged from the strained relationship between the Soviet Union and China. As the first Communist nation, the Soviet Union felt an obligation to spread its ideology and influence to other nations and founded the secretive Communist International (Comintern) for this purpose. The Soviets were always diligent in their efforts to ensure that they controlled the Communist parties in other nations and were frustrated when national Communist parties broke away, as Yugoslavia's had during and after World War II. After the Communists won the civil war in China in 1949, they looked at the Soviet Union, which had offered advisers, technology exchanges, and the Sino-Soviet Treaty of

Friendship, Alliance, and Mutual Assistance, as their elder brother. The Soviets thought that Chairman Mao's Great Leap Forward program, which starved millions of Chinese peasants through agricultural collectivization, was foolhardy and bad Marxist doctrine.

Soviet arrogance and Chinese pride eventually clashed, and the two nations drew apart. The Chinese criticized the Soviets for not doing enough to support the Cuban Revolution and hinted that perhaps China would be better suited to support the Cubans. This was a direct challenge to the Soviets' assumption that they offered the only source of Communist leadership in the world. This threat from the Chinese, mostly hollow considering the impoverished Chinese economy, provoked Khrushchev to show that the Soviet Union was still the leader of world communism, and so sustaining the Cuban Revolution became the test case.

Only three days after Khrushchev first informed his top generals of his idea, a preliminary plan was brought to the Presidium for approval. A delegation of political and military leaders was immediately formed to travel under aliases to Cuba to propose the plan to Castro, to scout locations for missile sites and military bases, and to evaluate port facilities for shipping purposes and the stationing of a naval component. The mission also looked at existing airfields that could accommodate Soviet aircraft.

Castro was surprised by the Soviet proposal, and he was concerned that the installation of Soviet troops and missiles on Cuban soil would make Cuba look like a Soviet puppet to other Latin American countries. Still, the proposal pleased Castro overall, and planning proceeded. The Cuban leader wanted to be considered a full member of the Communist camp, an equal, and this commitment made Cuba a vital linchpin in the Cold War. Castro also continued to have his intelligence officers provide training to radicals from Latin American countries on fomenting their own guerrilla-driven revolutions. Concerned that the Soviets would try to curtail the export of communism in order to placate the Americans, he kept this effort secret from his new patrons.

The Cuban economy was in shambles, less because of CIA-organized sabotage and more because managers were put in charge of plantations and industrial operations based on their loyalty to the revolution rather than on their business savvy. Cuba desperately needed the economic aid that came with the Soviets' military presence. Castro's only frustration was the Soviets' insistence that they would retain full control over their nuclear weapons.

After the mission returned from Cuba on June 10, 1962, the Presidium convened and voted unanimously to continue with the idea, which was to be completed by early November. Those Presidium members who survived the Fire claimed that they had reservations but knew Khrushchev would not tolerate opposition. At the height of his power, Khrushchev decided and his colleagues obediently agreed. Also reassuring them was the Soviet delegation's conclusion—with unwarranted optimism, as it turned out—that the missile sites could be camouflaged during construction so that the American reconnaissance flights that irregularly surveilled the island would not spot them.

In July, Raúl Castro arrived in Moscow to negotiate a bilateral treaty to cover the political arrangements of the undertaking. Because of the secrecy surrounding the project, diplomatic experts were not included in the discussions. To make up for this lack, high-ranking Soviet generals who would sit in on the meeting studied books on international law. When the plan for the operation was completed in early July, it was handwritten. None of the generals knew how to type, and giving the document to a typist would have compromised its confidentiality.

Khrushchev wanted secrecy likely because he was afraid of how the United States would react to the deployment of Soviet missiles so close to its borders. But once everything was in place, it would become a fait accompli; what could the Americans do? This attitude had lethal potential.[3] If Khrushchev had looked at the situation from the perspective of the Americans, he might have approached the operation more fearfully. The long-standing Monroe Doctrine declared that no European power could interfere in the affairs of Latin and South America. If the Americans allowed a Soviet garrison with nuclear weapons in Cuba, the Monroe Doctrine meant nothing. Kennedy had also made public pronouncements that the United States would not abide the placement of offensive weapons in Cuba. Khrushchev, with a blindness that is almost stupefying, apparently convinced himself that his troops and weapons were not offensive in nature. Defensive weapons do not reach out across the sea to strike an enemy's homeland. All the allies around the world, especially those in Western Europe, that depended on U.S. support against communism would lose heart if the United States let Khrushchev's plan succeed.

Some scholars have argued that Khrushchev intended to force a deal. He could offer to withdraw the ballistic missiles but keep the troops on the island, in return for an American promise not to invade Cuba. Although this idea is interesting, four objections present themselves. First, it ignores the advantages that Khrushchev saw in evening the strategic balance by planting the missiles in Cuba. Second, Khrushchev wanted to devote more resources to building up the Soviet economy, and putting less expensive MRBMs and IRBMs in Cuba was cheaper than building up a larger ICBM force. Third, building the ballistic missile sites in Cuba was not cheap, as it required materials imported from the Soviet Union—a lot of work to simply abandon in a negotiated deal. Finally, placing the ballistic missiles in Cuba only to withdraw them as part of an agreement would have been a strong blow against Soviet international prestige. Only China stood to gain in such a scenario.

DEPLOYMENT

Operation Anadyr was an audacious undertaking for the Soviet Union. It had never deployed that many troops or equipment across an ocean, and it succeeded in spite of a tight timetable. The Anadyr is a river that flows into the Bering Sea from Siberia. The Soviets named the operation after this river in the hope that if spies caught wind of the plan, they would think that it was a northern exercise. Many deploying units were even fitted out with winter gear and skis, which they dutifully loaded onto their ships and took with them to Cuba. No tropical clothing was included in their kits.

A key element of the plan was to keep everything secret until the full deployment of troops and the installation of missiles had been completed. Then in early November Khrushchev would visit the island, officially sign the treaty, and announce to the world that fifty-one thousand Soviet troops were in place. At the same time, Khrushchev told Kennedy that the Soviet Union had no intention of sending ballistic missiles to Cuba. The American government would feel betrayed when it learned the truth. What would have happened if the Soviets had announced the treaty and their intentions beforehand? We do not know. We cannot rewind history and try out different decisions, but could the outcome have been any worse than what really happened?

The Soviet General Staff wanted to pick a commanding general for the Cuban operation from among the rocket forces, since it considered the ballistic missiles the primary weapons. Khrushchev disagreed and chose Gen. Issa A. Pliyev from the army, a man who had distinguished himself during the Great Patriotic War as a tactician leading mechanized cavalry. Khrushchev felt that a ground commander would seem less threatening to the Americans when they learned about Operation Anadyr. While Khrushchev's reasoning had merit, the choice proved to be a poor one. Pliyev was pure soldier, lacking tact and any diplomatic sense. After his arrival in Cuba, his relations with Castro were strained, and he did not get along with his staff and his first deputy, Lt. Gen. Pavel Borisovich Dankevich. In the case of Dankevich, perhaps the tension was more understandable, since the deputy was the rocket general who had been passed over by Khrushchev for the top post. From the very first, Pliyev showed his fundamental lack of understanding of the mission. All the commanding officers flew to Cuba under civilian aliases, and while on the island, they went by noms de guerre. Pliyev refused to do so and especially disliked the idea of leaving all of his real identity papers behind in Moscow; only cajoling by superior officers convinced him to comply with the order. The man clearly did not understand why secrecy and concealment were needed. Pliyev also suffered from a kidney illness and was showing his age at fifty-nine.[4]

Pliyev may have also been chosen because he had recently proved his mettle to Khrushchev. On June 1, 1962, the Kremlin had increased retail prices for food by up to 35 percent. This measure was necessary because the cost of producing food had actually risen above the fixed price, and the Kremlin economists also expected the higher prices to produce incentives for more food production. The idea was almost capitalist in its rationale. There were already shortages of meat and dairy products throughout the nation, though a secretive directive guaranteed adequate meat supplies for Moscow and Leningrad. Sporadic riots broke out across the nation in response to the price increases.

In Novocherkassk, in the northern Caucasus, a strike over the price increases at a steel plant ballooned as steelworkers marched on the city, carrying red banners and portraits of Lenin, Marx, and Engels. One observer compared the scene to the October Revolution in 1917. The KGB sent troops, as did General Pliyev, the commander of the Northern Caucasus Military District at the time. We do not know who opened fire. Some historians argue that KGB snipers did the honors, while others argue that Pliyev gave the order. Thirty demonstrators died, and seven more were executed after a show trial. According to the Soviet leader's son, the incident at Novocherkassk profoundly disturbed Khrushchev; not all was well in his emerging Communist utopia.[5]

By any measure Operation Anadyr was a massive deployment of force. The Soviet presence in Cuba was to include the following:

- 4 motorized rifle regiments, each consisting of 2,500 soldiers, 34 tanks, 10 self-propelled guns, 60 armored personnel carriers, and 261 other vehicles;
- 2 antiaircraft divisions equipped with a combined 144 SA-2 SAM systems;
- 1 air detachment with 40 MiG-21 Fishbed fighters, 33 Mi-4 Hound transport helicopters, 17 Il-28 Beagle bombers (of which 6 were modified to carry 1 nuclear bomb each), and 11 other mixed transport aircraft;*
- 2 cruise missile regiments with a combined 80 missiles and 16 launchers (These FKR-1 Salish ground-launched cruise missiles were essentially unmanned aircraft, a successor to the German V-1 buzz bomb, that could carry either a conventional warhead or a 12-kiloton tactical nuclear warhead 55 miles at a speed of 600 miles per hour. These missiles were too inaccurate for conventional warheads to be useful, so enough tactical nuclear warheads for each of the 80 missiles were also sent to Cuba);
- 3 Luna rocket detachments, each with 4 rockets and 2 launchers (the short-range FROG rocket, with a range of 18 miles, carried either a conventional warhead or a 2-kiloton tactical nuclear warhead);
- 3 MRBM regiments, with a collective total of 36 SS-4 Sandal nuclear-equipped missiles and 24 launchers (each ballistic missile carried a nuclear warhead with a yield of 200–700 kilotons and had a range of 1,300 miles);
- 2 IRBM regiments, with a collective total of 24 SS-5 Skean ballistic missiles and 16 launchers (each missile carried a nuclear warhead with a yield of 1 megaton and had a range of 2,800 miles);** and
- various other units to support the Soviet forces, such as field hospitals, workshops, bakeries, and records units.

The navy was supposed to contribute a substantial force, including eleven submarines, two cruisers, four destroyers, sixteen torpedo boats, and seven support ships. Such a large number of ships could not be concealed from the Americans, so the naval deployment was cancelled, except for four submarines and twelve Komar guided-missile patrol boats (which were shipped in large crates on

---

* The names of the various weapons, including Beagle, FROG, and Salish, are NATO names, not Soviet names. The exception is that NATO called the Sopka missile Samlet. When choosing to use Soviet or NATO terms, I use the terms most commonly used in the source material.
** The Soviet Union referred to the SS-4 ballistic missile as the R-12 and the SS-5 ballistic missile as the R-14.

the decks of the merchant ships). The navy also sent a regiment armed with six Sopka missile launchers, similar in capability to the FKR-1 Salish cruise missiles, though armed only with conventional warheads.[6]

Approximately 160 nuclear weapons were shipped to Cuba: sixty of these were strategic warheads for the SS-4 and SS-5 ballistic missiles and the rest were tactical weapons. The Soviet plan was clearly to make up for numbers by using tactical nuclear weapons if necessary. Khrushchev gave Pliyev local nuclear release authority. We know of no other case in which a local commander was given this authority, even though Soviet plans for a general war with the West probably included granting such authority to front commanders after a war broke out.

The Soviet leader retained release authority for the SS-4 and SS-5 ballistic missiles. In this, Khrushchev followed standard Soviet operational doctrine, which viewed strategic and tactical nuclear weapons differently. Strategic weapons destroyed cities and struck far from the battlefront, while tactical nuclear weapons functioned more like huge artillery shells. The Soviets believed that it was acceptable in a battle to use tactical nuclear weapons, and the threshold between tactical and strategic would not be crossed. American doctrine included some similar ideas, but the tendency in American thought was that any use of nuclear weapons crossed a threshold that activated a full spectrum of responses. This difference in doctrine would prove to have awful consequences.

The first merchant ship, the *Maria Ulyanova*, arrived in the port of Cabañas in western Cuba on July 26, carrying military equipment. In the next three months, eighty-five cargo-carrying and passenger-carrying ships made about 150 total trips, bringing all the Operation Anadyr troops, equipment, and supplies. All personnel, including soldiers, had their party and Komsomol cards taken away before leaving the Soviet Union. Even their military service booklets, essential for getting pay and promotion, were confiscated. This act seems to contradict Khrushchev's plan to announce the Soviet presence in Cuba in November, but perhaps it was a wise move in that if one of the ships were to sink, the floating bodies would not have papers that identified them. Of course, the soldiers still wore their uniforms with military insignia.

Concrete slabs to serve as emergency launchpads for the MRBMs were also loaded, in case the missiles had to be used before permanent launchpads could be poured. The Soviets dispersed to bases across Cuba and worked ten- to twelve-hour shifts building fortifications, launch facilities for the ballistic missiles, quarters for themselves, and other buildings. Because of the need for secrecy, they could not employ Cuban labor. The Soviets viewed the island as infested with American agents and worried about potential attacks on their troops by American-supported guerrillas, though that never happened. The Soviets maintained strict radio silence, communicating directly through oral instructions or written orders sent by messenger. The subtropical heat and humidity wore down the Soviets and adversely affected their equipment.

The senior Soviet officers were housed comfortably in El Chico, a suburb of Havana, near the headquarters for the Soviet Group of Forces. The two SS-5 IRBM sites were located near San Cristóbal, on the western end of the island, and near Santa Clara, in the center of the island. The three SS-4 MRBM sites were located near the two IRBM sites. Two motorized rifle regiments were located near Havana, another was located near Santa Clara, and the fourth went in eastern Cuba to help the Cubans handle any possible excursion from Guantánamo Bay.

The American naval base at Guantánamo Bay had been established after the Spanish-American War of 1898, when the new Cuban government granted a permanent lease on forty-five square miles of land on either side of the mouth of the bay in southeastern Cuba. Castro's government rejected the American right to this base, but the Americans showed no inclination to move their troops out of it. The base was not well situated for defensive warfare—or offensive warfare for that matter—because it was on the other side of the island from Havana.

The Soviets had never before deployed nuclear weapons outside their borders, other than in their Eastern European satellites, but Operation Anadyr required such weapons. The freighter *Indigirka*, the first of two ships carrying nuclear weapons, arrived on October 4. The Soviets brought prefabricated concrete beams, arches, and such to build storage bunkers for the nuclear warheads. The bunkers looked like barrels that were cut in half vertically and laid on the ground, a common shape for hardened aircraft bunkers. The concrete roof was a meter thick and the round shape helped deflect blast damage. The bunkers were designed to withstand damage from conventional weapons or near misses from nuclear weapons. Apparently, none of these bunkers were completed before the crisis, so the warheads remained in their storage vehicles. KGB personnel guarded the vans and maintained control over the nuclear warheads until they were released to be mated with their delivery vehicles.[7]

The *Alexandrovsk*, the second ship carrying the ninety-odd nuclear weapons destined for Cuba, docked on October 23. Almost everything else had arrived, with the chief exception being the *Poltava*, a Soviet large-hatch cargo ship designed to carry lumber. The *Poltava* was still at sea carrying the twenty-four SS-5 Skean IRBMs. Each eighty feet long, the missiles could not fit in the cargo hold of many other freighters. The shipment had been left until last in order to preserve operational security and because the bases to support the missiles were still being built.

In almost every respect, the deployment phase of Operation Anadyr was an extraordinary success, but the Americans had finally figured out what was going on.

AMERICAN KNOWLEDGE OF OPERATION ANADYR

The Americans and their allies had spies in the Soviet Union. Their best spy was Oleg Penkovsky, a lieutenant colonel in the Chief Intelligence Directorate of the Soviet General Staff (GRU). Penkovsky became a spy for ideological reasons and to exact revenge. His father had died fighting for a White army during the Russian civil war, and when this fact became known among his Soviet superiors, Penkovsky's prospects for further promotion ended. During the time of Stalin's purges, his father's allegiances would have probably sent him to the gulags or primed him for execution. Penkovsky served loyally as a Soviet officer during the Great Patriotic War, but that could not erase the family stain.

With his experience in intelligence, Penkovsky knew whom to approach; he contacted Western visitors to the Soviet Union and asked them to put him in contact with Western intelligence. The CIA regarded this as a provocation, a fake approach to expose agency officers who served in the American embassy in cover positions but retained diplomatic protection. The Soviets regularly made such provocations in order to poison the water in case a real defector or spy tried to contact Western intelligence. In this case, however, the CIA eventually decided that the fruit was too tempting and unsuccessfully tried to contact Penkovsky.

The Soviet colonel finally succeeded in offering his services by using a British businessman to contact Britain's Secret Intelligence Service (SIS), also known as MI6. In a long autobiography that was later delivered to the SIS, Penkovsky declared, "I consider it my duty and purpose in life to be a humble soldier for the cause of truth and freedom."[8] MI6 ran the agent in conjunction with the CIA and persuaded him to remain in the Soviet Union as a "defector in place." Over a period of seventeen months, Penkovsky supplied eight thousand to ten thousand photographed pages of material from General Staff files. He was also interviewed in person by his handlers three times, twice in Britain and once in Paris, when he was abroad on spy missions for the Soviet Union.

Penkovsky's greatest contribution was detailed information on the Soviet nuclear forces that showed that the bomber gap and the missile gap did not exist. He also provided details on the difficulties surrounding the deployment of the SS-6 Sapwood, the main Soviet ICBM. He knew about the Berlin Wall for days before construction began but could not contact his handlers to warn them. By revealing the identities of GRU officers who were working overseas under diplomatic cover, Penkovsky damaged the Soviet Union's own spy network. The GRU colonel's hatred for his nation's Communist government was so visceral that he requested that the West supply him with an atomic weapon, which he planned to smuggle into Moscow and use to decapitate the Soviet leadership. The request was denied. Unfortunately for the West, their best spy had no knowledge of Operation Anadyr, illustrating the Soviets had kept the effort secret.[9]

Penkovsky was arrested on October 26, just as the crisis was warming up. Apparently he had been under surveillance for a couple of months. His fate would have been a show trial and execution—unless the West could make an exchange for him—but Penkovsky disappeared into the Fire and was lost with the other millions of victims.

The Americans also had spies in Cuba and monitored ship traffic in international waters. The CIA was aware of the Soviet ships that were part of Operation Anadyr but assumed that they carried weapons and construction materials to build up Cuba's military forces. In late August the CIA estimated that as many as five thousand Soviet advisers and workers had come in on the ships in the past month. The Americans saw no evidence, however, that these Soviets were part of organized combat units. At this point, they had seen only the first month of the three-month transportation effort, and their analysis was largely accurate.

Spies in Cuba had regularly reported on SAM sites, cruise missile sites, and other Soviet military equipment. The number of these reports spiked in September 1962 to nearly nine hundred individual sightings. CIA policy required photographic evidence from overflights in order to validate a ground sighting because the agency had found that too many of the ground sightings earlier in the year could not be corroborated by photographic intelligence. As the premier intelligence service in the world in terms of technical capabilities, the CIA tended to lean on technical collection over the messiness of human intelligence.

The CIA regularly issued national intelligence estimates (NIE), which were read by all the top officials, including the president. On September 19, 1962, the CIA issued a special NIE titled "The Military Buildup in Cuba." The document explained that the Soviets were pouring weapons into Cuba, especially for air and coastal defense. The CIA believed that all these weapons were intended for use by Cubans, assisted by Soviet technical advisers, and it thought that the Soviets would send only defensive weapons to Cuba. For instance, the Soviets had sold or given SAMs to Egypt, Indonesia, and Tanzania in the past, and the SAMs themselves did not indicate the additional presence of Soviet troops.

The CIA feared that as Castro's regime began to feel secure with its new Soviet weapons, it would be "emboldened to become more aggressive in fomenting revolutionary activity in Latin America." This was not just paranoid thinking but also corresponded to the public statements of Cuban leaders and to their actual intentions. For the Communists, Cuba was only the first step.

While recognizing that the Soviets would "derive considerable military advantage from the establishment of Soviet medium and intermediate range ballistic missiles in Cuba," the CIA thought this possibility was "incompatible with Soviet practice to date and with Soviet policy as we presently estimate it." The Soviets might try to establish a submarine base in Cuba, though even this measure would "indicate a far greater willingness to increase the level of risk in US-Soviet relations than the USSR had displayed thus far." Such a submarine base could accommodate submarines armed with nuclear-tipped cruise missiles or ballistic missiles. In sum, the CIA had thought of what the Soviets might do but could not believe that the Soviet leadership would take that risk.

If the Soviets did try to establish an "offensive" base in Cuba, the CIA thought that "most Latin American governments would expect the US to eliminate it, by whatever means were necessary, but many of them would still seek to avoid direct involvement." What is left unspoken in the special NIE is similarly compelling. There was an assumption, so basic among American leaders that it did not need to be written down, that the United States would be forced to do whatever was necessary to stop the Soviets from placing nuclear weapons in Cuba.[10]

The arch-anticommunist Kenneth Keating, a senator from New York, apparently also read the special NIE. He publicly demanded that the president do something about the possible deployment of ballistic missiles in Cuba. The Kennedy administration did not believe that ballistic missiles would be deployed in

Cuba but, to appease Keating and the right wing, issued a warning on September 4 that if the Soviets sent offensive weapons to Cuba, "the gravest issues would arise."[11] Khrushchev accelerated the delivery of the ballistic missiles to Cuba after this American warning and sent multiple reassurances to Kennedy through various channels that the Soviets had no intention of putting ballistic missiles in Cuba or of causing any problems before the midterm congressional elections on November 6. What Kennedy thought of the last promise is not known.

The president had already issued instructions on August 23, 1962, that an analysis be conducted as to what the United States could do if the Soviets deployed ballistic missiles in Cuba. Kennedy also wanted to know the "advantages and disadvantages of making a statement that the U.S. would not tolerate the establishment of military forces . . . which might launch a nuclear attack from Cuba against the U.S." The president planned to continue a covert effort called Operation Mongoose with the goal of overthrowing Castro's government through internal efforts by Cubans. On Kennedy's request, the CIA worked up some plots for assassinating Castro, but the president eventually decided that assassination would only make the Cuban dictator into a Communist martyr and would not overthrow the Communist Party in Cuba because other capable leaders, such as Raúl Castro or Che Guevara, would be able to take over.[12]

On September 4, 1962, the same day that President Kennedy issued his warning, the Soviet ambassador to the United States, Anatoly Dobrynin, visited with Bobby Kennedy and gave him a message for the president. He said that the Soviets had no intention of placing ballistic missiles or other offensive weapons in Cuba. Two days later, the ambassador repeated the same message to Kennedy's close aide and chief speechwriter, Ted Sorensen. We know that Dobrynin knew nothing of Operation Anadyr, but he would not have passed along such a message unless instructed to do so. Clearly, Khrushchev had decided to deliberately lie to the Americans in response to Kennedy's warning. While deceit is common in international relations, such a direct lie on a sensitive issue went against traditional norms of diplomatic courtesy. It also laid the groundwork for Kennedy and his administration to later feel betrayed.[13]

Kennedy announced at a press conference on September 13 that if Cuba became "an offensive military base of significant capacity for the Soviet Union, then this country will do whatever must be done to protect its own security and that of its allies." In the following two weeks, the Senate and House of Representatives chimed in with resolutions threatening the use of force in Cuba "to prevent the creation or use of an externally supported offensive military capability endangering the security of the U.S." The votes were completely lopsided, 86 to 1 and 384 to 7, in part because nonbinding resolutions were easy to pass, but also because the American people considered a well-armed Cuba the equivalent of a sword hanging over their country.[14]

SOVIET SUBMARINES

When Khrushchev came to power, the Soviet navy was in the midst of a major program to build several dozen cruisers. The new leader eventually cancelled this program, scrapped many of the cruisers, and ordered that the Soviet navy emphasize submarine construction and develop the ability to carry nuclear warheads aboard Soviet submarines. Khrushchev opted to focus on submarines because he knew the Soviet navy could not compete with the eight hundred–ship U.S. Navy directly but had to build weapons that would hurt the Americans as much as possible. The American fleet was dispersed all around the world, while the Soviet fleet, other than a few ships in the ports of its Eastern European allies, was confined to its own ports.

As mentioned earlier, the initial plan for Operation Anadyr included the creation of a new overseas fleet group to be based in Cuba, a first in Soviet history or even in Russian history. Because the Soviets wanted to keep the deployment phase of Operation Anadyr secret and use only merchant ships to move weapons, troops, and supplies, Soviet leaders decided to delay the surface fleet's deployment. Eventually only the four Foxtrot submarines were sent: *B-4* (Capt. Ryurik Ketov), *B-36* (Capt. Alexei Dubivko), *B-59* (Capt. Valentin Savitskii), and *B-130* (Capt. Nikolai Shumkov). Unlike the Americans, the Soviets did not give names to their submarines. They arrived off Cuba just days before the crisis broke. The submarine crews were issued tropical uniforms, but the submarines themselves did not undergo the usual mechanical overhaul used to prepare them for operating in tropical waters.

The torpedoes on Foxtrot submarines normally did not carry nuclear warheads. A single fifteen-kiloton nuclear warhead was placed aboard each submarine, along with a special officer whose sole responsibility was to maintain and guard the warhead and to prepare it for launch if necessary. This officer even slept next to his warhead. A special communications team and equipment to monitor American radio messages were also placed on each submarine.

Before their departure, the assembled submarine captains were given sealed packets of orders to be opened when they had gone to sea. Only then did they learn that their destination was the port of Mariel, Cuba. They had previously been given verbal instructions to use the nuclear torpedo if they were attacked, though their written orders informed them that use of the nuclear torpedoes had to be authorized by high command.

The submarines ran into a mid-Atlantic hurricane, which kept American antisubmarine warfare (ASW) forces from easily finding them. It was a rough ride, though. Older submarines powered by diesel engines, not the new nuclear engines, the Foxtrots were reliable but noisy and needed to surface regularly in order to recharge their batteries by running their diesel engines. The submarines tried to use their snorkels to bring in air for their engines, but waves on the surface kept inundating the snorkel. A flap on the top of the snorkel automatically closed to prevent water from pouring down the tube into the submarine, but the engines continued running by sucking in air from the submarine, creating a vacuum that popped ears. If this happened too often, the crew members grew woozy from insufficient oxygen and were forced to switch off the engines and rely on batteries. The concern was always that using the batteries too much would run them down until the submarine lost power.

The submarines were to take up positions off Cuba to block any American invasion fleet. Their last instructions were, "Assume battle positions and avoid contact with the enemy; return fire if attacked."

Further sources: Dino A. Brugioni, *Eyeball to Eyeball: The Inside Story of the Cuban Missile Crisis*, ed. Robert F. McCourt (New York: Random House, 1991); Laurence Chang and Peter Kornbluh, eds., *The Cuban Missile Crisis, 1962: A National Security Archive Documents Reader* (New York: New Press, 1992); Anatoli I. Gribkov and William Y. Smith, *Operation Anadyr: U.S. and Soviet Generals Recount the Cuban Missile Crisis*, ed. Alfred Friendly Jr. (Chicago: Edition q, 1994); Svetlana V. Savranskaya, "New Sources on the Role of Soviet Submarines in the Cuban Missile Crisis," *Journal of Strategic Studies* 28, no. 2 (April 2005): 233–59; Len Scott, "Espionage and the Cold War: Oleg Penkovsky and the Cuban Missile Crisis," *Intelligence and National Security* 14, no. 3 (Autumn 1999): 23–47; and William Taubman, *Khrushchev: The Man and His Era* (New York: Norton, 2003).

5

The U-2 Flight That Never Happened:
The Crisis Begins

The United States kept track of what was happening in Cuba through U-2 flights run by the CIA. Two flights in August, four in September, and two in early October found the first evidence of Operation Anadyr. The CIA had expected to see MiG-21 fighters on the island as it had learned earlier in the year that Cuban pilots had been training in Czechoslovakia to fly the aircraft. What the surveillance photographs did not show was that Soviet pilots were flying these MiG-21s. The U-2 flights also spotted the construction of SA-2 SAM sites on the island. The American analysts recognized the SA-2 sites because they looked like those the Soviets had set up in Europe and the Soviet Union, where radar sites and multiple launchers were arranged in a pattern, with connecting roads, that looked like a Star of David from above. Though some analysts suspected that Soviet troops maintained these sophisticated SAM sites, there was no proof of this. Other analysts assumed that the Soviets were training the Cubans to staff the sites.[1]

The CIA turned its overflight program over to the U.S. Air Force in mid-October. Even before the change in program oversight, the U-2 flights had been piloted by Air Force officers temporarily assigned to the CIA. (The pilots had officially resigned their Air Force commissions but had been promised that they would retain their rank and promotion status if they chose to return to the Air Force.) Now that the Air Force administered the program, however, the intelligence gathered could be used in air strikes.

For an overflight of the entire island, policy required a weather forecast of at least 75 percent clear. Weather forecasts were obtained from Global Weather Central at Offutt Air Force Base, near Omaha, Nebraska. Because of the weather, several flights in September had either been cancelled or had covered only part of the island. The first flight under Air Force control was scheduled for October 14. The weather on that day was not good and cloud cover forced the flight to be cancelled. The clouds persisted for the next six days. Finally, a U-2 took off on October 21.

The name of the man who flew that first Air Force U-2 flight has been lost. We know that he was with a unit originally out of Edwards Air Force Base in California that had been transferred to McCoy Air Force Base near Orlando, Florida. The U-2 flew a five-hour mission, covering the length of Cuba. The run began at 7:30 in the morning, before the heat of the day encouraged cloud build-up, a common phenomenon in the tropics.[2] The aircraft's two cameras had the impressive focal length of thirty-six inches. Each roll of film was nine inches wide and almost a mile long. Rolling the camera shutters in sync created a combined picture eighteen inches by eighteen inches. The U-2 flew at an altitude between 68,000 and 72,500 feet and took 928 photographs, which taken together could resolve objects as little as 2.5 feet wide. The pilot saw no enemy fighters or missiles and called the mission a "milk run."[3]

Upon landing, the two large rolls of film were rushed by a waiting aircraft to the National Photographic Interpretation Center in Maryland. The film was developed, printed, and given to the photographic analysts the following morning. These highly trained men (no women pored over the photographs at that center) went to work, using a zoom stereoscope with sixty-power magnification if necessary or handheld tube magnifiers.

So what had Castro been up to? Construction of more SA-2 sites had begun, and at one site there were six long objects, apparently covered with canvas or some other kind of cloth. Using the altitude of the camera as a reference, the two analysts estimated the length of the objects at sixty feet. They looked at the surrounding area and found eleven trucks and fifteen tents nearby and thirty-two other trucks farther away. Areas had been cleared to create what looked like missile launch sites. The men looked at books of reference photographs, many taken during the big annual May Day parade in Moscow. They discovered that the SS-4 MRBM had been displayed during the parade as a testament to Soviet ingenuity and that it was the right length to fit under the cloth covers.[4]

This discovery electrified the analysts. Word was sent to the Pentagon, which forwarded the information to the White House. Two more U-2 flights were immediately ordered, and the analysts made further shocking discoveries. There were six potential SS-4 MRBM sites, and all but one looked completed, with missiles ready to fire. Even more alarming were two other possible sites. Their design matched what had been found two years earlier by U-2 flights over the western Soviet Union—a configuration used to launch SS-5 Skean IRBM missiles. These missiles had the range necessary to hit targets anywhere in the continental United States. A possible third IRBM site was located and confirmed two days later. The analysts could not find ballistic missiles for these sites (they were still at sea aboard the freighter *Indigirka*). The missile sites were surrounded by SA-2 SAMs arranged in the four-slice pattern typically used in the Soviet Union for ballistic missile site defense, an additional confirmation for American photographic interpreters that the sites under construction were for ballistic missiles. Khrushchev and Castro had been discovered before they were ready to throw down the gauntlet.

In retrospect, what made Khrushchev think that he would be able to conceal the ballistic missiles until November, when he would announce their existence after the Amerian midterm elections? The Cubans wanted to announce the secret treaty to the world and even wanted the missiles to be moved publicly. The Soviet military expected the regular U-2 overflights to discover the missile bases under construction because they were so difficult to conceal. Khrushchev, however, chose to ignore these naysayers, even when they were bold enough to offer objections to the plan veiled as suggestions.

What is amazing is not that the missile bases were discovered but that five of the six MRBM sites were finished before their discovery. The Soviets had been handed an enormous amount of luck when bad weather thwarted the U-2 flights.

TALKING PAST EACH OTHER

National Security Adviser McGeorge Bundy first told President Kennedy about the photographs on the morning of Monday, October 22. Kennedy had attended morning Mass the day before, a good opportunity for the press to take photos of him and his charming family. A day of playing with the children had exhausted him, and he slept late on Monday morning, with appointments being pushed back by his staff. Still in his slippers and bathrobe, Kennedy looked at the glossy photographs and said, "We're probably going to have to bomb them."[5] As he dressed, moving slowly because his back pain had flared up, the president also let loose a string of expletives to describe Khrushchev's ancestry and current sexual habits. He felt betrayed by the Soviet ambassador, who had relayed Khrushchev's assurances in early September.

An hour later Kennedy formed the Executive Committee of the National Security Council (ExCom), which would meet multiple times each day to process information coming out of Cuba and to offer advice on dealing with the situation. Attorney General Bobby Kennedy led the committee, which also included Secretary of State Dean Rusk and four others from his department (two of whom had been ambassadors to the Soviet Union and knew Khrushchev personally); Secretary of Defense McNamara and two other civilians from his department; Chairman of the Joint Chiefs Gen. Maxwell Taylor; National Security Adviser Bundy; Treasury Secretary C. Douglas Dillon; and Ted Sorensen. CIA director John McCone was also part of the ExCom, as was the head of the National Photographic Interpretation Center.*

McCone was the only senior government official who had repeatedly voiced his suspicions that the Soviets would place offensive weapons in Cuba. The CIA director based his suspicions on a gut instinct born of his fierce anticommunism and the belief that the SA-2 missiles first discovered on the island were being put in place to protect something more valuable. While his theory had finally been vindicated, the actual prospect must have made McCone apprehensive.[6]

The ExCom met with the president at times and separately at other times, usually convening in either the Oval Office or the Cabinet Room. Kennedy chose to continue with his previous schedule of public appearances in order to maintain a sense of normalcy. His health problems may have also taken their toll and forced him to rest more than he cared to admit. There is no evidence to support the contention that he was out of touch with his advisers.

On the first day of the crisis all the members of the ExCom agreed that the ballistic missiles would have to be bombed if the Soviets refused to remove them. Perhaps this was the belligerent reaction of men who felt betrayed and who had risen to the top of their professions through firm, aggressive behavior.

---

* At the invitation of the president, other government officials, such as Vice President Lyndon B. Johnson, Ambassador to the United Nations Adlai Stevenson, and Kennedy's assistant Kenneth O'Donnell, attended some meetings of the ExCom.

Some historians have portrayed Robert Kennedy as always focused on arriving at a peaceable solution, but at first he was just as hawkish as everyone else. Members of the ExCom disagreed over how much force was necessary because they disagreed over the appropriate list of targets. Deciding whether or not to invade Cuba also provoked considerable debate. All agreed that at the very minimum, a naval blockade to prevent more weapons from arriving in Cuba was a good idea.

General Taylor discussed what the military had to offer. Adm. Robert L. Dennison, who served as commander in chief, Atlantic Command (CINC-LANT), had already created three contingency operations plans (OPLANs). OPLAN 312 detailed air strikes against Cuba, with various options based on how many targets were to be hit. OPLAN 314 described an invasion of the island after eighteen days of preparation. OPLAN 316 described an invasion of the island by air assault after only five days of preparation, to be followed by an amphibious landing three days later. Kennedy issued immediate orders that military forces be sent into position, ready to implement any of the plans. Within hours trains were being loaded, leaves were being cancelled, and some aircraft even started to fly to air bases in Florida. The Sunshine State had five Air Force bases, Naval Air Station Pensacola, and numerous commercial airfields. Naval ships left their ports or patrol stations and raced at top speed to encircle the island, in particular covering the approaches to the north. Fuel replenishment ships were also ordered to depart as soon as possible to refuel destroyers that would be exhausting their reserves by moving at thirty knots instead of a more leisurely fifteen knots.

After a two-hour meeting, the members of ExCom dispersed, agreeing to reconvene later that night. Taylor went to the E ring of the Pentagon and called the Joint Chiefs together. They met in the "tank," a secure meeting room with steel walls down the hall from the chairman's office. Only the uniformed four-star heads of each of the four services, each accompanied by one three-star aide, met with Taylor and his top aide. McNamara had compiled a list of twelve questions for the Joint Chiefs, including, Which targets should be struck by air? How long will preparations take? What Soviet reaction should be anticipated? And what air defense measures should be taken?

The Joint Chiefs supported a strong series of strikes against all military targets, including Soviet weapons down to the level of individual tanks and the small Komar patrol boats. They wanted the air strikes to occur without warning so that they could retain the element of surprise. They recommended that U.S.

air defense be immediately augmented by raising the number of ready fighters from twenty-four to seventy-five. The U.S. alert level should be moved to Defense Readiness Condition 4 (DEFCON 4), and the alert force of strategic bombers should be sent to their dispersal stations.*

When the ExCom members met later that night, they debated what their official reaction should be. The consensus of the morning still held. Now they had to wait until American forces were in place. The Air Force wanted a week to reposition their aircraft to Florida and other southern states. The Navy estimated that it would take thirty-six hours to transfer enough ships to implement a blockade. Further U-2 overflights of Cuba were authorized for the following day.

Deliberations continued on October 23. With the midterm elections less than two weeks away, the president was gone for most of the day, making campaign appearances in Philadelphia and Richmond. The belligerent mood of the previous day had calmed, and some ExCom members began to express the need for restraint. One of them floated the idea of using only a blockade, at least at first. Our record of this period is sketchy, and we do not know who initially advanced this idea, but it became one of the options up for consideration.

McNamara reminded everyone that the threat of nuclear war provided the balance of power between the two superpowers. A nuclear war was only supposed to be threatened, not actually fought. The nuclear-tipped ballistic missiles in Cuba did not alter the balance of power; America retained the ability to destroy the Soviet Union in any scenario. Others argued with McNamara, citing the obvious evidence that Khrushchev had placed the missiles in Cuba because he thought it did alter the balance. Regardless of whether the missiles in Cuba made a difference strategically, their mere presence made the United States look impotent, and that would affect the perceptions of American allies and adversaries in the Cold War. If Khrushchev could get away with deploying missiles in Cuba, what would he try next? A blockade of Berlin? Sending Soviet troops to North Vietnam?

Kennedy returned late that evening and joined the discussion. It was readily apparent to all that the president did not want to consider Cuba in isolation. He saw this as one move on a global chessboard, and the main nexus of concern

---

* DEFCON 1 meant the nation was at war, whereas DEFCON 5 was the normal peacetime status.

was West Berlin. Kennedy had always been keenly aware of how isolated and completely indefensible that free city was. If the Americans failed to force the missiles out of Cuba, the Soviets would doubt the American resolve to protect West Berlin; if they moved too forcefully, Khrushchev could use it as an excuse to trade West Berlin for Cuba.

At the next morning's ExCom meeting, Kennedy said, "Khrushchev knows that we know of his missile deployments, and therefore he will be ready with a planned response." The president was a rational man used to making prudent moves, and he expected similar behavior from his political foes. Kennedy could not have been more wrong.

Premier Khrushchev had not thought out what might happen at different junctures of his plan. As with the Berlin crisis, Khrushchev wanted to play his hunches as the situation unfolded and had no apparent game plan laid out in his mind. Clearly, he had not learned from his frustrations over Berlin. While he was currently secure in his position as leader of the Soviet Union, his irritation over agriculture failures, the unsatisfactory resolution to the Berlin crisis, and a general sense of lack of progress had prompted him to believe that Operation Anadyr would solve all of his problems. In a single stroke, the Soviet Union would rise in prestige and humble the United States. After that, who cared if there was not enough meat on the shelves? A compulsive gambler stakes it all on the next card coming off the deck; Khrushchev had no reason to think beyond that.

On October 23 all the members of the Presidium assembled only two doors down from Khrushchev's office, on the second floor of the Senate building of the Kremlin, built during the times of the tsars. Minister of Defense Marshal Rodion Y. Malinovsky also attended, though he was not a member of the Presidium. The Soviets sat around a large rectangular table, with the chairman at the head. Khrushchev personally explained that their missile bases in Cuba had been discovered. Soviet radars on Cuba had tracked the U-2 flight on October 21 and the two U-2 flights on the following day. They had orders not to fire their SA-2 SAMs (the exact same type of SAM that had brought down the U-2 over the Soviet Union in 1960).

After some discussion, Khrushchev declared his belief that the Americans had not said anything yet because Kennedy was cowed and would allow Operation Anadyr to progress to completion. Khrushchev seemed to think that Kennedy was a weak president who wanted to avoid war at all costs. He also thought that Kennedy would be forced into war by the American right wing. The two views were not completely incompatible, but each could lead to a different Soviet course of action. We have a partial transcript of the October 23 meeting that shows one of the last statements came from a Khrushchev protégé, Leonid Brezhnev. "Nikita Sergeyevich," Brezhnev said, using the familiar form of greeting, "I am concerned about our course of action, but I bow to your superior understanding of the Americans."

On the afternoon of October 24 the ExCom came to a partial agreement on its advice for the president, since Kennedy reserved the right of making the final decision for himself, as was his responsibility as the president. The committee agreed that a blockade should be implemented. The ships were in place, and the United States certainly did not want to see any more Soviet weapons arrive on the island. After the Americans demanded the Soviets remove the missiles and announced the blockade, they would wait for a couple days and see how Khrushchev responded. If the Soviets continued to be belligerent, the ExCom recommended that the president then consider solving the Cuban problem once and for all by using any means necessary to remove Castro from power.

One of the lawyers in the group mentioned that a blockade was considered an act of war under international law and suggested using the term "quarantine" instead. After some debate, the president decided to use the word "blockade." It was much more forceful and sent a stronger message. If the Soviets complained about the word, it would at least begin a dialogue between the powers. The television and radio networks were alerted that the president would need airtime the following evening, October 25, and Kennedy and Sorensen, who was also chief speechwriter, closeted themselves to work on the address.

On October 25, a Thursday, the ExCom met three times to evaluate intelligence coming in from additional U-2 flights. The Joint Chiefs crossed the Potomac River for the first meeting and presented their preparations. They looked trim and well groomed in their uniforms, showing no indication that they were sleeping in their offices and expected to continue to do so until the crisis calmed. Troops and aircraft were flowing south nicely, and all ships necessary to enforce the blockade were in place. The service chiefs made a strong argument for launching bombing sorties immediately rather than starting the action with a blockade. They wanted to retain the maximum element of surprise when they struck. The service chiefs had a fundamental difference of opinion with the Kennedy administration. President Kennedy wanted only the missiles out of Cuba, while the Joint Chiefs were unanimous in their twin goals of ridding the island of the missiles and removing Castro from power. Taylor did not share the twin goals of his service chiefs but instead agreed with the president. Kennedy and most of the ExCom members rejected this escalation by the service chiefs and remained partial to their previous plan. It is to the credit of the ExCom members that while they were willing to argue vigorously with each other and even with the president, they loyally supported Kennedy's final decisions. These were not arrogant men given to backbiting and wanting to continuously revisit decisions that they disagreed with.

Kennedy met in the afternoon with the leadership of the Senate and House of Representatives and sat with them as McGeorge Bundy delivered a presentation on the aerial photographs and what they meant. Then the president previewed his speech for the assembled Democrats and Republicans. There were few questions, perhaps because the leaders of Congress were too surprised to do more than agree with the young president. Kennedy also personally called the prime minister of Britain, the president of France, and the chancellor of West Germany to alert them to the content of the speech. Ambassadors to other allies would be given copies of the speech only an hour before it was delivered.

That evening the Oval Office was transformed into a television studio, with cables piled across the floor like intertwined snakes and bulky cameras aimed at the president's desk like a firing squad. The president sat in a nearby room as a makeup artist applied the necessary cosmetics to his face so that he would not look washed out under the glare of the lights. He reviewed his speech once again and made a few minor changes with a pencil. He decided to go with the legal term "quarantine" instead of "blockade." The Soviet ambassador received a copy of the speech an hour before the telecast, and a letter from Kennedy to Khrushchev was cabled to the American embassy in Moscow for delivery to the Soviet leader.

That evening, at 7:00 p.m. (Washington time), President Kennedy informed the American people of all that was happening. Excerpts from the speech included the following:

> Good evening my fellow citizens:
> This Government, as promised, has maintained the closest surveillance of the Soviet military buildup on the island of Cuba. Within the past week,

unmistakable evidence has established the fact that a series of offensive missile sites is now in preparation on that imprisoned island. The purpose of these bases can be none other than to provide a nuclear strike capability against the Western Hemisphere. . . .

Our policy has been one of patience and restraint, as befits a peaceful and powerful nation, which leads a worldwide alliance. We have been determined not to be diverted from our central concerns by mere irritants and fanatics. But now further action is required—and it is under way; and these actions may only be the beginning. We will not prematurely or unnecessarily risk the costs of worldwide nuclear war in which even the fruits of victory would be ashes in our mouth—but neither will we shrink from that risk at any time it must be faced. . . .

. . . I call upon Chairman Khrushchev to halt and eliminate this clandestine, reckless, and provocative threat to world peace and to stable relations between our two nations. I call upon him further to abandon this course of world domination, and to join in an historic effort to end the perilous arms race and to transform the history of man. He has an opportunity now to move the world back from the abyss of destruction—by returning to his government's own words that it had no need to station missiles outside its own territory, and withdrawing these weapons from Cuba—by refraining from any action which will widen or deepen the present crisis—and then by participating in a search for peaceful and permanent solutions. . . .

Finally, I want to say a few words to the captive people of Cuba, to whom this speech is being directly carried by special radio facilities. I speak to you as a friend, as one who knows of your deep attachment to your fatherland, as one who shares your aspirations for liberty and justice for all. And I have watched and the American people have watched with deep sorrow how your nationalist revolution was betrayed—and how your fatherland fell under foreign domination. Now your leaders are no longer Cuban leaders inspired by Cuban ideals. They are puppets and agents of an international conspiracy which has turned Cuba against your friends and neighbors in the Americas—and turned it into the first Latin American country to become a target for nuclear war—the first Latin American country to have these weapons on its soil. . . .[7]

Kennedy showed the American people pictures taken by the U-2s, with missile sites and actual missiles marked with white circles. He demanded that the Soviets withdraw the ballistic missiles with all deliberate speed and declared that a naval quarantine would be implemented the following day at noon. He warned, "Failure to voluntarily remove the missiles will require that the United States look at other ways to remove them."

Because of the time difference, the Presidium met in the middle of the night on October 25–26, starting just a few hours before Kennedy's speech. The Soviets knew that the speech must be about the missiles. As the men assembled, Khrushchev said to his defense minister, "You blew it—a peasant delivering water to his cows could have done a better job." When the minister protested, Khrushchev raised his hand, cutting him off. Having voiced his barb, Khrushchev wanted no more discussion on the matter.

Khrushchev maintained his belligerent attitude; he felt that Kennedy would make hot air at first but eventually acquiesce to the missiles. What Khrushchev failed to realize is that if Kennedy allowed the missiles to remain, his chances of reelection (the ultimate goal of any historically minded first-term president) would fall close to zero. The main lesson that the American people had learned from World War II, and from subsequent movies and books, was that appeasement of bullies only emboldened them.

In his own way, though not an elected official, Khrushchev had also gambled his career on Operation Anadyr. Its failure would damage his prestige among the leaders of other Communist nations and diminish his standing among his fellow leaders in the Soviet Union. Because Khrushchev did not rule through the use of terror, as Stalin had, he effectively remained in his position because the majority of the Presidium and the Central Committee agreed to keep him in control. While he had appointed most of these Communist leaders, they were more loyal to themselves, their nation, and their Communist ideology than to Khrushchev himself.

The Soviet leader made an impassioned speech, beginning with, "We don't want war; our goals in Cuba are to force concessions from the Americans. Maybe we could turn over all our weapons to the Cubans and claim that they are now responsible for them. No, that wouldn't be a good idea. Our friend Fidel Castro might just use them. We have never given away nuclear weapons." The speech continued for another ten minutes, ending with these words: "How can the Americans object to our missiles in Cuba when they have just placed equivalent missiles in Turkey and Italy? It is only fair that we have our missiles in Cuba also."[8] After this speech, Khrushchev looked pensive, according to an aide in the room, as if consulting his private inner thoughts, hardly listening to the speeches from the other Presidium members.*

One member of the Presidium noted that in 1956 the Soviets had found the rise of an unfriendly government in nearby Hungary unacceptable and solved the problem with the Red Army. He could not understand why the Americans had not solved their problem in Cuba in the same way. Perhaps they were lazy or blinded by imperialist greed. Had not this crisis emphasized for the Americans the danger Cuba posed? Would they now do anything in their power to end that danger? While insightful, this observation was not appreciated by others in the room.

A translation of Kennedy's speech was brought into the room and read aloud by an aide. As the words came out, Khrushchev grew visibly excited. After the aide sat down, the Soviet leader rose and pounded the table with his fist. His words were jotted down by an aide.

"We've saved Cuba! Kennedy has issued a vague warning and implemented a naval quarantine. He doesn't even have the courage to call it a blockade. We are only trying to protect the Cuban people. If Kennedy had really been ready to go to war he would have attacked our missiles in Cuba with air strikes. I want our forces to close off all approaches to Berlin. We will call it a quarantine." The short, round man laughed, drawing tepid laughter from the others in the room. "Let's remind him that he's vulnerable. When he's ready to negotiate, then we can use Berlin as a bargaining chip, withdrawing our blockade in return for him agreeing that this Caribbean crisis is much hubbub about nothing."**

---

* In 1992 an abandoned bunker was discovered north of Moscow by a historical-archeological research team from the University of Brisbane. A local farmer named Gorbachev showed the team the location of the bunker. The bunker had withstood thirty years of winters and remained watertight. The scholars named it after the farmer. We do not know who did it—some bureaucrat responsible for Kremlin record keeping—but the rooms inside were packed with boxes of government documents. Among these treasures were the minutes of Presidium meetings from 1954 to 1962 and even occasional transcripts of meetings that had been recorded.

** The American press called it the Cuban Missile Crisis, whereas the Soviets used the term "Caribbean crisis."

DOUBLE QUARANTINE

At noon on October 26 the naval quarantine began. American planes crisscrossing the ocean had located seven ships that were likely heading for Cuba. Only three were Soviet-flagged; two carried the Panamanian flag, another the Greek flag, and the last a Liberian flag. The governments of these three noncommunist nations had no idea what was on the ships, since their flags were mostly flags of convenience, without any actual oversight.*

An American destroyer intercepted the Greek-flagged *Macedonian* first, radioing a demand that the captain heave to and prepare for boarding. The freighter complied. The American search party found a Greek crew with a smattering of Maltese sailors and no Soviets. The cargo manifest listed civilian goods, including some small machine parts. While the parts violated the American trade embargo, the goods were from Polish factories, not an American ally. A spot check of the crates showed no apparent deceit. Under the rules of engagement, the freighter was allowed to proceed to Cuba.

That evening at 9:20, two hundred miles east of Bermuda, the American destroyer USS *William R. Rush* sighted the Soviet freighter *Volga*. The destroyer moved to intercept, and the freighter brought itself to a complete stop. The *Rush* sent a message in an international code via signal lamp, demanding that the freighter allow an American search party to board. The freighter replied that it was stopped and refused permission to board. If the freighter had not stopped, the destroyer would have been required by its rules of engagement to fire a shot across the bow; if the ship did not then heave to, the *Rush* would fire another shot into the rudder. Both ships remained a half mile from each other, gently rocking in the waves, furiously communicating by radio with their respective nations about what to do. In the next several hours, all the Soviet ships and Soviet-chartered ships stopped. Everyone waited.

On the same day that the quarantine began, the president authorized low-level reconnaissance flights over Cuba. Air Force RF-101 Voodoos and Navy RF-8 Crusaders flying out of Florida air bases gathered detailed photographs that helped create targeting plans. (The photographs from the high-flying U-2 had not been detailed enough to make tactical plans.) RB-66 Destroyer aircraft

---

* A flag of convenience is used when a ship is registered in a country other than the country of its owner in order to avoid fees, taxes, and government regulations. Certain countries, such as Greece, Liberia, and Panama, catered to this business obfuscation.

also flew along the coast of the island, mapping the electronic signatures of the Cuban and Soviet radars, especially the radars from the SA-2 SAM sites. The Soviets did not fire on the intruding aircraft, though some antiaircraft ground fire was observed from what were assumed to be Cuban units. The Americans were correct in assuming that the Soviets had direct orders from the Presidium not to fire. Both sides recognized that downing an American airplane could escalate the crisis.

These low-level flights confirmed all that the high-flying U-2 flights had found and revealed even more. Of the numerous military camps on the island, four were particularly interesting. The trucks, tanks, and other armored vehicles at these camps were parked neatly, as they were at Soviet camps, not in the more casual formations of the Cuban army's camps. The Cubans had expanded their army so quickly that complete professionalism and discipline were not yet routine. The four camps also had the latest Soviet equipment, such as T-55 tanks, which had been introduced only four years earlier. Analysts suspected that these were not Cuban but Soviet combat formations, each the size of a regiment. A later flight found that the Santiago de las Vegas base south of Havana had large Soviet insignias proudly on display, including an elite Guards badge that showed the regiment had had an illustrious combat history during the Great Patriotic War. Apparently the Soviets had decided that concealment was no longer necessary.[9]

The Pentagon was shocked to find Soviet ground combat formations in Cuba. "Those Russians are so sneaky," said one major in operations planning, a sentiment that mixed resentment with admiration. The existence of the equivalent of a Soviet motorized rifle division on the island did not change the invasion plan, since the Americans expected to have complete dominance of the air. No doubt these were elite units and would give a good account of themselves, making the American conquest somewhat harder.

The low-level flights also found the Luna units, armed with FROG short-range missiles. This surprised the analysts, since the missiles were militarily useful only when armed with tactical nuclear warheads. Intelligence from Oleg Penkovsky had revealed that Soviet field commanders had more leeway over the use of their tactical nuclear weapons than American commanders had.[10] Could the Soviets have put tactical nuclear weapons in Cuba? That was more astonishing than their deployment of strategic ballistic missiles. Yet more surprises were in order elsewhere in the world.

On the morning of October 27, Western guards watched as East German border police ran strands of barbed wire across each of the seven crossing points into East Berlin. There were also four roads and four railroads running through East German territory to West Germany that brought supplies to the city and provided ready transit. East German police officers allowed automobiles and trains already en route to complete their journeys, then closed off those roads and railroads. River barge traffic was also stopped. Regularly scheduled aircraft that attempted to use the three air corridors into the city were denied permission by air traffic controllers to enter East German airspace.

All of these actions violated current understandings and seemed to be a repeat of Stalin's 1948–49 blockade of Berlin. At that time a celebrated airlift had kept the city fed. By the end of October 27, the mayor and military commanders had agreed on martial law and implemented rationing. Normally the city would have only two weeks of food on hand, but after the Berlin airlift, a special food reserve had been created to store such staples as wheat, rice, canned meat, canned milk, dehydrated egg powder, and oil for producing margarine. The city could hold out for three months.

The Soviet Union had three hundred thousand troops, organized into ten tank divisions and ten motorized infantry divisions, in East Germany. The East German army had one hundred thousand men. A total of about twelve thousand American, British, and French troops formed a trio of Berlin brigades to protect the city of two million people in an area of 185 square miles. The American force of three infantry battle groups and the British force of three infantry battalions actually formed brigade-sized units, whereas the French force could offer only symbolic protection. Unlike the allied troops in West Germany proper, the Berlin brigades could not realistically protect the city in the event of an actual assault.

Bundy awoke Kennedy on the night of October 26–27 with news of the Soviet quarantine of Berlin. A letter from Khrushchev had also been delivered to the American ambassador in Moscow and then cabled immediately to Washington. The Soviets had provided the letter in both Russian and English. The president, dressed in a bathrobe, went to the Oval Office, quietly followed by his Secret Service detail, and read the letter.

Khrushchev had flatly rejected the American demands, stridently declared the right of Cuba to defend itself with the help of whatever allies it chose, and declared his intention to quarantine West Berlin as long as the Americans quarantined Cuba. With only his national security adviser in the room to hear him, Kennedy let loose a string of oaths that would have shocked his strict Catholic mother. "Our quarantine is only of military equipment and Soviet troops, not everything. We aren't trying to starve Cuba, but that bastard in the Kremlin wants to starve two million West Berliners."

"He has upped the ante," Bundy agreed.

"Have Soviet forces gone on alert?" the president asked.

"We don't know."

HAVING NO CHOICES

Kennedy called former president Eisenhower for advice. Though of different political parties, and despite Kennedy's criticism of the Eisenhower administration during the 1960 presidential campaign, the two men had grown close. They belonged to a small group of men who had led the nation, and this created a kinship that transcended mere partisanship. Kennedy asked the former general if he thought that the Soviets would use the strategic nuclear weapons if the United States invaded Cuba. Eisenhower believed that the Soviets would not use the weapons and that Kennedy had to take action to prevent the Soviets from deploying on our "flank."[11]

The ExCom met on the morning of October 27 and reviewed the intelligence from Berlin. One of the former ambassadors to the Soviet Union asked if a relief effort could be organized by NATO military forces in West Germany and push its way through East Germany. The NATO forces were too small to do that short of full mobilization and a general war. NATO's entire military posture was designed only to defend Western Europe from a Soviet–Warsaw Pact attack, not to launch its own attack.

The ExCom generally believed that the Soviets were not taking the American threat to escalate seriously. Or maybe the Soviets intended to trade Cuba for Berlin by occupying the city if Cuba was invaded. The absence of a true understanding of the Soviets' motivations made decision making difficult. The ExCom reviewed the military buildup and asked that the Joint Chiefs tell them when military action could begin. On the diplomatic front, an emergency meeting of the Organization of American States (OAS) had already been called to rally support among the other nations in the Americas for whatever action might prove to be necessary.

In an afternoon meeting, General Taylor presented the answers from the Joint Chiefs. An air attack could be mounted with a couple of hours of preparation, but it would include only about four hundred aircraft and might not destroy all of the SS-4 MRBMs at once. In two days all the Air Force assets would be in place to conduct OPLAN 312, which included 1,190 sorties on the first day. Though nothing was certain in war, the Joint Chiefs felt confident that they could destroy all the MRBM launchers on the first day of the OPLAN 312 air attack. The troops would begin landing for the invasion four days later. The Air Force chief requested permission to call up twenty-four troop-carrier squadrons of the Air Force Reserve so that they would have time to position themselves to carry the airborne divisions. This affected about fourteen thousand Air Force reservists. The Joint Chiefs also wanted to upgrade the military alert to DEFCON 3. Kennedy granted both requests, but even at this point, Kennedy remained skeptical of the advice he received from the military, remembering his experience with the top brass during World War II.

The ExCom drafted a letter to Khrushchev that mixed threats that the situation would escalate with an offer for resolution. Both sides would end their respective quarantines, the Soviets would withdraw their missiles and pledge never to put ballistic missiles in Cuba again, and in return the Americans would withdraw their Jupiter and Thor IRBMs from Britain, Italy, and Turkey within a year. This was an easy compromise to make as the Kennedy administration and Pentagon had already decided to withdraw the IRBMs. The development of ICBMs had made the older IRBMs superfluous. The only problem with this resolution was that by withdrawing American missiles from Europe, it could appear as if the United States were making a concession that rewarded unacceptable Soviet behavior.

If this initial offer failed to bear fruit, Kennedy planned to ask United Nations secretary-general U Thant to make the same offer publicly and apply pressure on the Soviets that way. Of course, this approach would be a last-ditch option because it would require the United States to acknowledge that it was trading Soviet missiles in Cuba for its missiles in Britain, Italy, and Turkey.

The letter was cabled to the American ambassador in Moscow for delivery, and Khrushchev received it at 8:00 a.m. on October 28. He had slept in the bedroom next to his office for the last two nights. Other members of the Presidium had also stayed in the Kremlin, though not all of them had bedrooms; some of the most powerful men in the Soviet Union had to make do with couches and chairs for their beds.

The Presidium gathered and found Khrushchev almost gleeful. As he read the letter the threats seemed to slide right past him; he noticed only the concessions that Kennedy had offered. The Soviet leader declared his satisfaction and proposed that they answer this letter with agreement to Kennedy's plans. He also requested four further concessions: the Americans must make public their plan to withdraw the IRBMs from Turkey, Italy, and Britain; the missile withdrawal must take place at the same time as the Soviet missile withdrawal from Cuba; the United States must publicly pledge not to invade Cuba; and the United States must publicly promise that they would resolve Berlin's ambiguous status within a year. One of the Presidium members asked Khrushchev what would be a satisfactory resolution to Berlin's status now that the wall had solved the most pressing problem of emigration. The Soviet leader waved his hand, dismissing the question as if it were of no importance.

The letter was written with classic Khrushchev phrases such as "The Soviet Union and its leadership will not be intimidated by the illegal actions of the United States"; "The Soviet Union refuses to submit to national humiliation"; and "Our firmest desire, indeed, our only desires, are for peace."[12] The letter of demands was cabled to the Soviet ambassador in Washington for delivery to the president. At the same time, Khrushchev directed that an order be published in the next day's *Pravda* informing the Soviet people that all military leaves were cancelled and all military units were going on alert. That would put even more pressure on Kennedy.

Kennedy was aghast at the new letter. He could make those concessions privately and live with them, but to make them publicly would destroy his presidency. The American people would not stand for such blatant humiliation. Even though the Democratic Party dominated both houses of Congress, 64 to 36 in the Senate and 262 to 175 in the House, if Kennedy made the additional concessions, the midterm elections in just a week could result in a Republican landslide.* If Kennedy had not been president he would have condemned such a deal. Being the ultimate decision maker had changed his perspective on many issues.

---

* The House of Representatives temporarily had 437 members, instead of the normal 435, because Alaska and Hawaii had been admitted as states with one representative each in 1959. Reapportionment based on the 1960 census had occurred, however, and the 1962 election would return the number to 435.

When the ExCom met on October 28, it also reacted strongly against the new letter from Khrushchev. It seemed that perhaps the right wing was correct: the Soviets understood only strength. Perhaps some form of military action was necessary. If air attacks destroyed the missiles in Cuba, then the Soviets would not have any weapons to bargain with. The United States would have made its point and retained its international prestige, and then a deal to end the mutual quarantines could be made. Kennedy had no intention of invading Cuba, so making a promise to that effect would be easy. Of course, he preferred that the promise be private, not public.

A joint CIA-Pentagon intelligence assessment, based on the low-flying reconnaissance flights, was delivered to the ExCom. All six SS-4 MRBM sites were ready, while the three SS-5 IRBM sites were still under construction, with the first to probably be ready on December 1. All twenty-six SA-2 SAM sites were ready. Only five of the Il-28 Beagle bombers were partially assembled, while the rest remained in their crates. East German and Soviet troops were obviously massing around West Berlin, and Soviet jets had been flying low over the city to annoy the citizens by breaking the sound barrier and shattering windows.

The ExCom members believed that removing the missiles with air strikes would create more flexibility in the standoff. The president was in the room listening as the ExCom voted to recommend that the Joint Chiefs be instructed to plan a bombing campaign to begin at first light on October 30, two days later. The ExCom also wanted the Joint Chiefs to attend their meeting the next morning. Kennedy accepted these recommendations.

Feeling that an answer to Khrushchev's letter was necessary, Kennedy and the ExCom drafted a letter that mainly repeated their previous letter, refusing the additional concessions. They did warn that any actual attack on Berlin would mean war, period, with no equivocation. The letter was sent as a last-ditch diplomatic effort.

When Khrushchev met with the Presidium to consider the letter, he said several things that perfectly demonstrated the mixed state of his mind. First he said that "nuclear weapons are meant to be used as threats, not as actual weapons," and he also called Berlin "the testicles of the West," an apt analogy that Kennedy would have agreed with.[13] Khrushchev decided not to respond to the letter immediately, but to wait a day or more, to let Kennedy stew over the crisis and feel those vulnerable parts squeezed.

Kennedy's chief trait, so rare in people, was an ability to recognize the limitations of his own personality and experience. He craved good advice and had actively surrounded himself with aides and other officials who were willing to speak up. His administration exemplified the practice of finding the "best and brightest" in academia, business, and the military and bringing them together to find innovative solutions. In a note to himself, he declared that he was satisfied with the advice that the ExCom members had given him. For him "the ultimate failure" would be allowing this crisis to descend into nuclear war.[14]

At 10:00 a.m. on October 29, the Joint Chiefs joined the members of the ExCom in the Cabinet Room in the West Wing of the White House. General LeMay presented the plan for the air strike, OPLAN 312, with only a few modifications. Enough intelligence had been gathered that LeMay was sure that all the missile sites would be destroyed. The president said, "I now know how Tōjō felt when he was planning Pearl Harbor." LeMay, who had directed the strategic bombing effort against Japan, was not amused.

The president asked LeMay how he thought the Soviets would react if the Americans attacked the missiles. The general assured the president that the Soviets would not react. This type of answer is what made Kennedy believe that his military advisers, except Taylor, were deaf to the realities of international relations. Kennedy said, "They can't, after all their statements, permit us to take out their missiles, kill a lot of Russians, and then do nothing. If they don't take action in Cuba, they certainly will in Berlin."[15]

LeMay asked permission to make one more observation. Kennedy nodded. "If they react in Berlin, that will lead to a larger war," LeMay said. "They will lose that war, so it makes no sense for them to escalate the situation." Assuming that the Soviets would not fight back because they knew that they were too weak, LeMay had the confidence of a bully. Anyone who had studied any military history should have known that wars do not always begin or continue because of rational assessments of the chances of victory.

Bobby Kennedy pointed out that the target list, as presented, included not only ballistic missiles, air bases, and antiaircraft missiles sites but also army bases, naval targets, and even individual tanks and armored vehicles. LeMay said that he wanted his aircraft to destroy anything that might harm invading Americans. The disconnect between the single goal of the president, to remove the Soviet missiles from Cuba, and that of the Joint Chiefs, to remove the missiles and oust Castro, still persisted.

"We will plan for an invasion, but we will only invade when I make that decision," Kennedy told LeMay. "I see that the attacks on the army units are not scheduled to begin until the third day. That will be considered a second phase of the bombing campaign and will not begin without my explicit permission."

"Yes, sir, Mr. President," was the only answer that the general could give.

SOVIET-CUBAN PREPARATIONS

The Americans estimated that they faced 22,000 Soviet soldiers (though we know from the Operation Anadyr documents that this number was closer to 40,000). Later analysis showed that 3,332 Soviet personnel were still on ships at sea, prevented by the naval quarantine from completing their voyages.[16]

General Pliyev decided that his soldiers would continue to wear their civilian clothes—plaid shirts purchased by the Defense Ministry to provide substance to their cover story that they were agricultural specialists. Their regular uniforms were not as lightweight, plus Pliyev was concerned that the Americans would concentrate their fire on Soviet uniforms during ground combat. After word of Kennedy's speech filtered through the soldiers' grapevine, everyone expected combat to break out soon, and the Soviet soldiers sought out showers or places to swim, following the old Russian tradition of bathing before battle.[17]

In response to Kennedy's televised speech of October 25, Castro had mobilized his nation, fielding 75,000 regular soldiers in the Cuban army, 100,000 Cuban militia, and 100,000 home guards.[18] The Soviets combined their forty MiG-21 advance fighters with a Cuban air force that had been strengthened since it had dominated the action at the Bay of Pigs the previous year. The Cubans apparently still flew B-26 bombers and T-33 armed trainers. They had also received at least sixty new aircraft from the Soviets, including an unknown number of older MiG-15 or MiG-17 fighters.

What is amazing, considering that the stated purpose of Operation Anadyr was to protect Cuba, is that the Cubans and Soviets apparently never even started to put together a plan to defend the island. There was no combined command and little in the way of combined staff work. The Soviets divided the island into three sectors—east, central, and west—placed two motorized rifle regiments in the west sector, one regiment in each of the other two sectors, and left their own planning at that stage. To avoid eavesdropping by the Americans, all communications had been in person or by written messages. That was fine during construction, but in combat, communications had to be faster. The Soviets and Cubans had not had a chance to create communications standards or protocols or to develop methods to deal with the language barrier, since few on either side knew the other's language.[19]

Castro was apparently not informed that the Soviets had placed tactical nuclear weapons in Cuba. This was a result of the Soviets' desire for secrecy and penchant for dictating decisions to their allies (though Cuba was an independent country in a way that the Eastern European satellites or Mongolia were not). As the crisis began, Khrushchev and the Presidium had considered withdrawing the authority to use the tactical nuclear weapons at his own discretion from General Pliyev but decided that such a move was unnecessary. The crisis would not reach that point, but if it did, then the isolated Soviet general in Cuba would need all the help he could get.

The Soviet Union also had the four Foxtrot submarines, each equipped with a single nuclear-tipped torpedo, off of Cuba. Unknown to the Soviet leadership, British and Norwegian antisubmarine forces had found the four submarines and tracked them to the gap between the Faroe Islands and Iceland, where American forces took over. The coverage was light, with contact lost for hours or days at a time, because the crisis had not yet begun with the U-2 photographs; and so NATO forces were treating it as a training exercise. In good weather, the submarines regularly ran on the surface to achieve higher speeds, and this aided the Americans' tracking efforts.

Once the four submarines left the North Atlantic, leaving behind the stormy weather common during the autumn, they could no longer use their short- and medium-wave transmitters but had to rely on their long-wave channels. Before they reached Cuba, they were instructed to maintain position outside the Caribbean, near an area of the mid-Atlantic called the Sargasso Sea because of the abundance of seaweed in the region. The farther they moved from the transmitters in the Soviet Union, the harder it was to maintain contact, and eventually communications failed altogether.

Other than a few prestige cruises to the equator, the Soviet submarine service had little experience with tropical waters. The warm water heated the submarines, which had no form of air-conditioning, and turned the interiors into sweltering saunas. The extra humidity wreaked havoc on equipment not designed to handle the moisture and on a crew that had no experience in servicing its equipment under such conditions.

The submariners had finally realized that the Americans had located them and were shadowing them with destroyers, so they remained submerged as much as possible. Occasional rainsqualls allowed the submarines to surface, and a section of the crew, in ten-man groups, would dash out onto the deck for a shower from nature. In this way, over the course of two days, each member of the submarine crew had a chance for relief.[20]

Because no instructions had been transmitted by their higher command, two officers on submarine *B-36* ordered the enlisted men out of the radio room, closed the door, put on headphones, and searched for the Voice of America (VOA). In the Soviet Union, listening to VOA was a crime, but it was occasionally done because American radio was often a better source of information than the Soviet press. The officers learned about the crisis from these transmissions, not from Soviet reports.[21]

Two other submarines also came into play. A Zulu-class submarine, the *B-75*, had accompanied the transport *Indigirka* on its voyage to Cuba and now waited in the mid-Atlantic. The second was also a Zulu-class submarine, the *B-88*, which left its Siberian base on October 28 with orders to proceed to Hawaii and attack Pearl Harbor if the crisis escalated into war. Both of these submarines carried one or two nuclear torpedo warheads.[22]

AMERICAN PREPARATIONS

As soon as Kennedy gave the green light on October 22, the Pentagon had rushed to move its forces to prepare for either an air strike on Cuba or a full-scale invasion. By October 29 all American forces were at DEFCON 3, and a "Cuba Fact Sheet" was placed on the president's desk that evening.

For operations against Cuba, the Air Force had deployed 183 interceptors to southern Florida. Four were in the air as a combat air patrol at all times. Another five joined them an hour before first light and remained until an hour after sunrise, in case the Soviets and Cubans tried to sneak in a dawn attack with their small air force. The Tactical Air Command had moved 850 aircraft, mostly fighter-bombers to be used in a ground attack role, to bases in Florida.

The Army had allocated a large force for the invasion. At Fort Bragg, North Carolina, the 82nd Airborne and 101st Airborne divisions waited to be dropped into battle. On the coast waited the First and Second Infantry divisions, as well as a task force of armor from the First Armored Division. Numerous headquarters, quartermaster supply units, artillery batteries, engineering units, and other support units rounded out a total invasion force in excess of ninety thousand soldiers.

Because a large Marine amphibious landing exercise had taken place on Vieques Island, Marines were already in the area. Once the crisis started, the Marine Corps had brought in three battalions to supplement the base defense force at Guantánamo Bay, bringing the total number of Marines in that garrison to 5,868. The families on the base, 2,810 dependents in all, each with only a single bag, had been evacuated by sea and air in an operation lasting five hours. A battery of Hawk antiaircraft missiles protected the base from air attack. Two other Marine battalions were at sea on amphibious ships. The Fifth Marine Expeditionary Brigade was still loading its ships in California and would take days to enter the battle.*

Naval blockade forces, also ready to be used to support an invasion, included the aircraft carriers *Enterprise, Independence,* and *Essex;* two heavy cruisers; and twenty-nine destroyers. The aircraft carriers *Saratoga, Randolph,* and *Wasp,* along with fifteen other destroyers, were on their way. Sixty-five amphibious assault ships, as well as numerous support ships, were in ports all along the southern or southeastern coasts of the United States or at sea.

Ammunition factories were working twenty-four-hour shifts, especially to make additional 20 mm strafing ammunition for the fighter-bombers. Ammunition, including napalm bombs stacked like "mountains of cordwood," was piled at Florida air bases.[23] Hospitals were alerted, and civilians were encouraged to donate blood to build up stocks. The Pentagon planned for 18,500 American casualties in the first ten days after an invasion if no nuclear weapons were used, though it expected losses to be substantially fewer than that number.[24]

On the strategic level, 271 B-52 Stratofortress and 340 B-47 Stratojet bombers waited on the ground already loaded with a total of 1,634 nuclear bombs,

---

* The Soviets had watched the increase of Marines at Guantánamo and in a glaring overestimate thought that eighteen thousand Marines were now on the base. The Americans conducted the reinforcement with the intention of defending the base, while the Soviet intelligence analysts assumed that the base would be a major point of attack if the Americans invaded. This showed the limitations of Soviet military experience. They had never experienced a large amphibious operation, while the Americans had conducted so many during World War II that the idea of coming in from the sea was second nature. Many of the senior and middle-grade American officers had actually participated in amphibious invasions during World War II or the Korean War. See Dino A. Brugioni, "The Invasion of Cuba," *MHQ: The Quarterly Journal of Military History* 4, no. 2 (Winter 1992): 96.

ready to become airborne in fifteen minutes. One hundred eighty-three of the B-47 bombers had been dispersed away from their main bases to thirty-three different airfields, making it much harder for the Soviets to concentrate their limited forces in a first strike. In addition to the above totals, between sixty and sixty-six B-52 bombers were always in the air, carrying a total of 210 nuclear bombs, ready to head for Soviet targets. Over a thousand KC-97 and KC-135 Stratotankers waited to refuel the aircraft already in the air and to top off bombers as they made their way toward the Soviet Union. The SAC aircrews were used to flying twenty-four-hour missions on airborne alert and were very familiar with aerial refueling. They called these grueling flights "chrome-dome operations" because of the hot spots created on their heads by their flight helmets. The airborne alert bombers flew one of two routes: either across the Atlantic, into the Mediterranean, and then back to the United States; or up the eastern coast of North America, across the top of Canada, and then back down the West Coast.[25]

The ICBM force, totaling 136 Atlas and Titan ballistic missiles, was on alert, ready to launch in fifteen minutes. An additional force of 804 bombers and 44 ballistic missiles would be ready in another twenty-four hours.[*] Two Regulus cruise missile submarines were on patrol, as were two of the nine Polaris submarines. Combined, this added another thirty-nine missiles to the mix.

Over two thousand nuclear weapons were ready for use, a total that would double in just twenty-four hours, when the other bombers were ready and if the other Polaris submarines put to sea. These numbers do not include the nuclear weapons carried aboard warships; the Thor or Jupiter IRBMs in Britain, Italy, and Turkey; or the hundreds of tactical nuclear weapons that the Army had for its artillery and short-range Honest John missiles.[26]

If the bombing campaign began the next morning, on October 30, the invasion could commence on November 3. With only twelve days to prepare the invasion from its first orders on October 22, the Pentagon had combined elements of OPLAN 314 and OPLAN 316 to create a plan to send in one division by sea and two by air. Two Marine battalions would form a floating reserve, one based north of Cuba and the other south of the island. About a million American soldiers, sailors, airmen, and Marines stood ready to be used in the attack.

---

[*] This extra force of bombers included the B-58 Hustler, the only supersonic bomber capable of Mach 2. Difficult to fly, so expensive that they were accused of costing more than their weight in gold, and lacking the range of the slower B-52 bombers, the B-58 was a disappointment.

No further messages had been received from Khrushchev, and Kennedy had already called the leaders of America's three most important allies: Britain, France, and West Germany. In the interests of operational security, other allies would be informed only after the bombing started.

After reviewing the Cuba Fact Sheet, Kennedy approved increasing the alert to DEFCON 2. The U.S. armed forces had never experienced DEFCON 2 since the system had been implemented.

Further sources: Dino A. Brugioni, *Eyeball to Eyeball: The Inside Story of the Cuban Missile Crisis*, ed. Robert F. McCort (New York: Random House, 1991); Dino A. Brugioni, "The Invasion of Cuba," *MHQ: The Quarterly Journal of Military History* 4, no. 2 (Winter 1992): 92–101; Aleksandr Fursenko and Timothy Naftali, *"One Hell of a Gamble": Khrushchev, Castro, and Kennedy, 1958–1964* (New York: Norton, 1997); Ryurik A. Ketov, "The Cuban Missile Crisis as Seen through a Periscope," *Journal of Strategic Studies* 28, no. 2 (April 2005): 217–31; Svetlana V. Savranskaya, "New Sources on the Role of Soviet Submarines in the Cuban Missile Crisis," *Journal of Strategic Studies* 28, no. 2 (April 2005): 233–59; and Stuart J. Thorson and Donald A. Sylvan, "Counterfactuals and the Cuban Missile Crisis," *International Studies Quarterly* 26, no. 4 (December 1982): 539–71.

6

Helter Skelter: The World Teeters
on the Edge of Sanity

Up until October 30, not a single American or Soviet had died. The tensions were purely hypothetical. Both sides had refrained from belligerent acts because they recognized that once the dogs of war were released, events would be much more difficult to control. With every act of violence and every death, events can become more chaotic and an entire situation can go helter skelter.

The threat of accidental war increased with the level of tension. In Turkey, members of the Turkish armed forces were still learning to operate their Jupiter ballistic missiles. While the nuclear warheads were kept separate from the missiles and under American control, the simple launch of an unarmed missile from Turkey, detected on Soviet radar, could drastically escalate the conflict if the Soviets responded without waiting for the missile to impact. This possibility worried Kennedy enough that he ordered the American commander in Turkey to destroy the missiles if anyone tried to use them without direct orders from the U.S. president.[1]

At Malmstrom Air Force Base in Montana, the first Minuteman ICBMs were being installed. It was a new system, and many kinks, such as short circuits in the missile wiring and placement of the solid-fuel weapons in their silos, were being worked out. If one of the Minuteman missiles accidentally launched and followed its programming toward the Soviet Union, the Soviets could react with force.

In the decades since, rumors that General LeMay tried to provoke conflict in minor ways during the crisis have persisted. LeMay was vocal in his hatred of communism and his belief that a war in 1962 was preferable to one fought later, when the Soviets had built up their strategic forces. He was not the only one in the Air Force who realized that the United States would never again have such overwhelming capability to launch a "splendid first strike." In a previously scheduled test, an Atlas ballistic missile was launched from California to a target in the Marshall Islands on October 26. Such an action during the crisis was needlessly provocative. American strategic bombers also deliberately flew beyond their fail-safe points, the points in their flights where they normally turned back on their runs into the Soviet Union. The Soviets knew where the fail-safe points were based on previous exercises, though the bombers stayed well away from Soviet airspace. A normal U-2 reconnaissance flight strayed into Siberian airspace during the crisis, and the Soviets let it go.

The commander of the Strategic Air Command had some unusual powers, including the authority to launch nuclear weapons in the event of war if he could no longer communicate with the president. He also had the ability to raise the DEFCON level for SAC on his own authority. The commander of SAC at the time of the crisis, Gen. Thomas S. Power, was a protégé of LeMay's and by all accounts an extreme personality who profoundly believed in the possibility of winning a nuclear war. In one angry moment he is reported to have said, "At the end of the war, if there are two Americans and one Russian, we win!"[2]

When the rest of the American military went to DEFCON 3 on the evening of October 27, Power used his authority to take SAC to DEFCON 2 instead. The message for SAC to go to DEFCON 2 was transmitted in the clear (as was standard practice), so the Soviets could hear it and perhaps start a preemptive war.[3] The episode angered Kennedy and the ExCom members. SAC bombers flying airborne alert also radioed twice as many position reports as normal to give the Soviets the impression that twice as many bombers were in the air.[4] Yet, despite the aggressiveness of SAC and its leader, there is no evidence that these provocative actions led to the Fire, though they certainly increased the tension.

Shortly after going to DEFCON 2, Power sent another message to all his SAC wings, emphasizing that he wanted no mistakes. Commanders were told to "use calm judgment during this tense period," and if they had questions about what to do, then they should "use the telephone for clarification." Power asked that all commanders "review your plans for further action to ensure that there will be no mistakes or confusion." He was well aware that mistakes led to wars and that SAC had occasionally made mistakes. For instance, less than a year earlier SAC went on alert when the North American Aerospace Defense Command (NORAD) lost contact with all three of their ballistic missile early warning systems (BMEWS) in Greenland, Alaska, and England. The problem was that all telephone and telegraph connections between NORAD and SAC headquarters in Omaha had been cut when a motor overheated in a relay station in Colorado. The Americans had already lost nuclear bombs at sea owing to accidental drops or aircraft crashes. They had also accidentally dropped bombs onto American soil and suffered aircraft crashes that caused the high explosives in the nuclear bombs they were carrying to explode. No nuclear fission or fusion occurred. In the most recent accident, on January 24, 1961, a B-52 exploded from a fuel leak in midair over North Carolina, and its two nuclear bombs fell to earth. One deployed its parachute and landed with little damage, while the other hit the ground and created a radioactive mess.[5]

Though no accidents had occurred, the Cuban Missile Crisis had turned into a conflict, yet one still manageable short of full-scale war. Restraint still existed. Secretary of State Rusk told an aide late on the night of October 29, "We are eyeball to eyeball, and the other fellow didn't blink."[6]

FURY IN THE SKIES OVER CUBA

At dawn on October 30, a Tuesday, the Americans commenced their air strikes on Cuba, flying 1,180 sorties on the first day and 786 sorties on the next day and maintaining a rate between 700 and 800 sorties per day after that. American pilots and their aircraft had not been involved in combat for nine years, since the end of the Korean conflict in 1953, except for covert missions over Laos and South Vietnam. The 1950s had been a time of tremendous technological change, and most of the aircraft in the American arsenal had never been used in battle. The Americans had also never faced SAMs; no one had, and no one knew how effective such defenses might prove to be.

Ideally, bombers from SAC would have flown high-altitude conventional missions over Cuba, taking advantage of the fact that the B-47 could carry seven tons of bombs and the B-52 could carry an impressive thirty tons of bombs. SAC thought that its bombers should remain armed with nuclear weapons in case the conflict escalated; they also did not want to lose strategic bombers to antiaircraft missiles. General LeMay, who had literally built SAC into the organization it was, agreed with his former command.*

F-104 Starfighters flew high over the first wave, providing protection against the Soviet and Cuban fighters. The F-104 Starfighter, the sports car of fighters, called "the missile with a man in it" by Lockheed, its manufacturer, had a limited combat radius of only 420 miles. Capable of sustained flight, not just short bursts, at Mach 2, the stubby-winged Starfighter was a serious challenge to operate.

Flying below the Starfighters came three types of aircraft. The F-100 Super Sabre fighter-bombers were armed with four 20 mm cannons and carried seven thousand pounds of bombs and a pair of Sidewinder air-to-air missiles. The new F-4 Phantom fighter-bombers, in service less than two years, carried nine tons of bombs or a pair of Sidewinder missiles. The F-4 did not carry any cannons because the current thinking in the Air Force was that missiles would dominate air-to-air combat and cannons were no longer necessary. Besides, few people thought that cannons were useful at supersonic speeds. The F-105 Thunderchief fighter-bombers were not much older than the F-4 Phantoms but were armed with a single 20 mm cannon and carried seven tons of bombs. Large and heavy for a fighter-bomber, the F-105 was sixty-four feet long, and pilots initially gave it derisive nicknames like the Squat Bomber, Lead Sled, Hyper Hog, or the Thud.

Because the SS-5 IRBM sites were not yet completed and their missiles apparently had not arrived at the island, only the twenty-four SS-4 MRBM sites

---

* After directing the strategic bombing effort against Japan during World War II, LeMay successfully directed the Berlin airlift of 1948–49. In 1949 he became the head of the Strategic Air Command, where he prepared long-range bombers and ballistic missiles for nuclear war. He took a command that had grown lackluster and built more bases, added new planes, and instilled the discipline needed to always be ready to fly and to perform the awful deeds involved in prosecuting a nuclear war. A measure of LeMay's success can be seen in the total staffing numbers for SAC, including all officers, soldiers, airmen, and civilians. From 1949 to 1957, SAC grew from 71,490 personnel to 224,014, and from 868 aircraft to 2,711. LeMay constantly drilled his crews, running through the "war plan time and time again," ensuring that they were ready for the combat he expected. (Richard H. Kohn and Joseph P. Harahan, eds., "U.S. Strategic Air Power, 1948–1962: Excerpts from an Interview with Generals Curtis E. LeMay, Leon W. Johnson, David A. Burchinal, and Jack J. Catton," *International Security* 12, no. 4 [Spring 1988]: 88; and Alwyn T. Lloyd, *A Cold War Legacy: A Tribute to Strategic Air Command, 1946–1992* [Missoula, MT: Pictorial Histories, 1999], 676.) In 1961 LeMay became the chief of staff of the Air Force and would have proudly led his aircrews into the Fire if he had not been an early casualty.

needed to be absolutely destroyed (these twenty-four sites contained a total of thirty-six missiles). Five SAM complexes guarded these MRBM sites. Each SS-4 site was to be hit by an ad hoc element of six aircraft, with four Starfighters providing cover for each element. Larger elements of twelve aircraft attacked each of the three air bases, so that any airborne Soviet or Cuban aircraft would not have a place to land. The number of Starfighters protecting the air base attack elements was doubled because the planners expected to find more enemy fighters near their homes.

The American aircraft could not take off from their Florida bases simultaneously and would spend some time forming up once they were all aloft. Then it would take half an hour to fly to Cuba without wasting fuel on afterburners. Radar could easily pick up so many incoming aircraft, so in reality, the Communist forces would have about an hour of warning. The Americans expected to be met in the air by Soviet and Cuban fighters.

American fighter pilots, eager to dogfight, were not disappointed. The Soviets had sent their best and most experienced pilots to Cuba. Thirty-eight MiG-21 Fishbed fighters took off from their base in central Cuba and climbed on afterburners, clawing for altitude. This was the newest Soviet fighter, introduced only three years earlier. The Starfighters met them with missiles, and the MiGs responded in kind. Most pilots thought that the quality of the electronic circuitry in the missiles would make the difference in whether the missiles found their targets, though the speed and maneuverability of the targets made a difference. The smoke of missile trails twisted across the sky, mixed with hurtling aircraft and sharp explosions. The radios, overloaded with shouted warnings and profanity, became useless. Sonic booms rolled across the Cuban countryside three miles below. One account recorded a dogfight with cannon fire; the MiG pilot won before a missile ended his victory. Aircraft tumbled from the sky, and many of the pilots succeeded in ejecting, drifting down under parachutes.

All the Soviet MiGs were destroyed on that first day, either in the air or on the ground. There is only one account of a MiG sighting the following day, and other errors in the document show a lack of care, or at least significant chronological confusion, so we must discount it. The U.S. Air Force awarded twenty-four confirmed kills, six shared, and three possible. Realistically, figuring out whose missile hit what in that kind of melee is almost impossible. We know that seventeen American F-104 Starfighters did not return from the battle.

Cuban pilots also bravely took to the skies in their aircraft to defend their homeland. The fighters and bombers that had devastated the Cuban exiles during the Bay of Pigs invasion died quickly, their equipment completely outclassed by the modern American aircraft. Those Cuban aircraft that remained on the ground were destroyed by the air strikes.

All across the island fighter-bombers swept in at low altitude to find their targets. The missile sites were soft targets, readily damaged by fire and shrapnel because they were not protected by concrete bunkers, only trenches for the personnel. The American bomb loads were half napalm and half high explosive. The same mix was used on the airfields.

Soviet SA-2 missiles leapt from their launchers, reaching three times the speed of sound and homing in on the American aircraft. The missiles did not have to hit the planes; a near miss with the 420 pounds of explosive often riddled aircraft with shrapnel or damaged them with shock waves. Ground fire came from 57 mm antiaircraft guns, heavy machine guns, and even the frustrated fire from soldiers firing their AK-47 assault rifles into the sky.

Napalm is a devastating and awful weapon. A mixture of jellied gasoline and chemical thickeners, the bomb explodes over a large area, burns everything at high temperatures, and is nearly impossible to smother with water. Needless to say, people caught in napalm die horrible deaths, and even a little of the chemical on the skin will cause severe burns. These burns easily become infected because of the petroleum byproducts in the napalm. After the initial wave of napalm bombs was dropped, the second and third waves had no problem finding their targets— they just had to fly toward the smoke that spiraled miles into the sky. Of course, the smoke also made it more challenging to find the actual targets themselves.

The Soviet missiles and ground fire took an awful toll on the American fighter-bombers. Seventy-one aircraft from the first wave failed to return to their bases. The second wave was already on its way into the fray when Air Force operations officers realized how heavy the first-wave casualties had been. Because the SA-2 launch sites had been on the target list for the first attack and because napalm is so devastating against its targets, many of the SA-2 sites had been damaged to the point that they could no longer launch their missiles, and only twenty-one aircraft in the second wave were lost. A third wave in the evening worked over the same targets, just to be sure they had been destroyed, and only three aircraft were lost. Still, the U.S. Air Force lost 112 aircraft out of the 830 engaged on the first day. These losses were much higher than expected because the United States had never fought an adversary with SAMs and the pilots had yet to learn how to adapt their own tactics.

Navy and Marine aircraft flying off carriers and from Naval Air Station Jacksonville in Florida attacked targets on the eastern third of the island between the first and second Air Force waves. They particularly concentrated on two units of Cuban artillery within range of Guantánamo Bay. Only one Navy aircraft was lost, mainly because these units were not flying into the teeth of the SAM defenses.

After the third wave, enough light remained for Navy RF-8 Crusaders flying out of Naval Air Station Key West and the RF-101 Voodoos flying out of Air Force bases farther north to come in low, scouring the target sites with their cameras. Navy Lt. Andy Daley, one of the "photo jocks" flying a Crusader, took ground fire over the air base in Pinar del Río Province. This base housed the partially assembled Soviet Il-28 Beagle bombers and some Cuban aircraft. Daley, losing altitude at an alarming rate and broadcasting an urgent distress call, managed to nurse his aircraft out over the nearby ocean. He gave his position as about ten miles offshore when his engine flamed out, and he was forced to eject.

An alert sailor in Key West picked up the distress call, and a search-and-rescue airplane was sent to canvass the area. Night had fallen by then, and no one was sighted. A destroyer with a helicopter aboard was dispatched and arrived overnight. That morning Daley was located in his rubber life raft, with a nasty gash on his forehead that had been irritated by sea salt. He was luckier than he realized. Three other pilots had ditched into the water, and only two were recovered alive. The third had apparently broken his neck during ejection. Postwar analysis by the historian Juan De Soto determined that sixty to seventy other American pilots successfully ejected and parachuted to Cuban soil. Some were beaten by Cuban militia or regular forces upon landing, and all are thought to have been kept alive in different facilities across the island. An unknown number later died during the post-invasion nuclear strikes, and vengeful Cuban soldiers executed every remaining American captive after the nuclear strikes.

Because Daley went down, there were no poststrike photographs of Pinar del Río on the first day. Unknown to the Americans, one of the Soviet Il-28 Beagles actually survived. Ironically enough, of all the bombers, the survivor was the one that had been almost completely reassembled after the long voyage from the

Soviet Union. As night fell, mechanics frantically prepared the aircraft for flight, their work illuminated by hand lights and the buildings on the base that still burned from the napalm strikes. A pilot and navigator were found, and though the Il-28 usually flew with a crew of three, the two men took off in the aircraft at first light, relocating to an obscure asphalt airstrip on a sugarcane plantation. The Communist government had seized the United Fruit Company plantation only a year earlier, and its airstrip had been built by an American executive for his private two-engine aircraft. The pilot was barely able to land on the narrow runway, and the weight of his wheels dimpled the asphalt where he first touched down. The local sugarcane workers cut palm fronds to cover the light bomber.

The pilot was Sergei Feklisov, senior lieutenant of aviation, probably born in Kirov, though we know nothing about him other than that he was a resourceful man of twenty-nine years of age. The next day Feklisov caught a ride back to the air base, where he scrounged up some fuel and a tanker truck. The navigator remained with the aircraft. The fuel had been contaminated by water, but he found a hand pump with a filter on it. He also managed to send a message to a Soviet headquarters (we do not know which one) that he needed bombs. Most military travel occurred at night during the four days of the American air campaign, and at some late hour a truck arrived with a thirty-kiloton nuclear bomb.

According to an eyewitness—one of the Cuban workers who did not know Russian (making his account dubious)—Feklisov was shocked to receive a nuclear bomb. Apparently he had trained to attack ships with conventional bombs, not to drop nuclear bombs. We know that six nuclear bombs for the Il-28 were sent to Cuba, so perhaps other Il-28 aircrews were trained in their use and not Feklisov. There are indications that the nuclear bombs for the Il-28 were intended for use against ships as tactical weapons, not for strategic use against targets in the United States. We also do not know what orders, if any, came with the bomb.

Even more disturbing from the American perspective was the survival of two SS-4 ballistic missiles. Both of these SS-4s were located at a site north of Santa Clara. They were far enough away from their launchers that the fires from the napalm did not damage them. The camera footage from the RF-101 Voodoo that flew over that site was processed during the night, and by early morning the analysts had alerted the Air Force that two missiles still existed. The Air Force hit the location twice on the next day, and a follow-up visit by an RF-101 Voodoo on the evening of the second day did not find the missiles. It was assumed that they had been completely destroyed.

One analyst at Homestead Air Force Base, near Miami, Florida, Tony Cicerone (temporarily relocated from the National Photographic Interpretation Center), wanted to make sure the SS-4s had been destroyed. He requested the footage from the gun cameras of the attacking F-105 Thunderchiefs. The gun cameras were normally used to record air-to-air kills, but there were so few enemy aircraft to defend against that the F-105 pilots also expended their ammunition during their bombing runs. It took Cicerone two days to obtain the footage and look at it. The grainy and shaky film covered only part of the bombing runs and showed no missiles on the ground. The analyst wrote a memo on the evening of November 3 about his suspicions that the two missing missiles had not been destroyed, but because that was also the day of the invasion, his superiors were preoccupied with what they thought were more important things. Cicerone dropped his other work and desperately searched for the missing missiles on the complete coverage series generated by a high-flying U-2 on November 2, tracing roads that led out of the site with his hand lens. After forty hours without sleep, he found them. This time his supervisor listened, but it was already after midnight in the early morning of November 6.

The two SS-4 MRBMs had been moved during the first night after the bombing campaign began. An unusually large warehouse at a sugar plantation eight miles away offered a good hiding place for the missiles. These missiles had not yet been fueled with the storable liquids, making them easier to move. Not enough of the liquids had survived the air strike on that MRBM base to completely fuel the moved missiles, but more liquids were available at the base near San Cristóbal on the western end of the island. It took three nights for the three trucks to make their way across the island to the sugar plantation.

The nuclear warheads for the two missiles were brought from the depot near Bejucal, south of Havana. KGB troops came with the warheads and retained control of the actual nuclear weapons. Two of the emergency concrete launchpads that had been brought from the Soviet Union were found in the charred ruins of the MRBM base and were also brought to the plantation. The sole problem for the officers in charge of the remaining missiles was the effort to locate their position. If they could not clearly determine where they were, down to the greatest accuracy possible, then once launched the missiles' degree of error would be multiplied by the original error on the ground. The Soviets did not have accurate survey maps of the island, so they relied on a sextant to measure their latitude and made a guess on their longitude, using a Rand McNally tourist map.

The Kremlin was informed that the two SS-4 missiles had survived, and Soviet high command replied with a message reminding General Pliyev, the Soviet commander in Cuba, that the SS-4 missiles were not to be launched without explicit Kremlin authorization. The short message made no mention of the tactical nuclear weapons or the surviving Il-28 light bomber. The historian Vladimir Yeltsin has made a convincing case that because of the breakdown of Soviet communications on the island, the Kremlin never learned about the bomber; a case can be made that even Pliyev did not know about it.

President Kennedy, having cancelled all unnecessary appointments, spent all of October 30 in the White House. A meeting with the congressional leadership helped make sure that the legislators felt informed and would not cause problems. Telegrams, phone calls, and letters expressing support poured into the White House. As almost always happened at the start of a war, the American people and politicians rallied to the flag and declared their support for the president.

Kennedy remained in his Oval Office most of the day, visiting the Situation Room, in the West Wing's basement, only occasionally. He did not want to distract the staff with his presence, and the pain in his back was particularly bad that day. Also, contrary to popular perceptions, the Situation Room was not a command and control center but more of a communications clearinghouse that kept the president and other executive officials in touch with the Pentagon, major military commanders in the field, the State Department, American embassies abroad, the CIA, the National Security Agency, and other American organizations around the world.[*] One of Kennedy's aides was in the Oval Office with Bobby Kennedy and the president when the president talked about a recent book he had read on D-day, the great invasion of Europe by American-led Allied forces in 1944. "Eisenhower was the decision maker, the man who would be blamed if everything went to hell. It all worked out, but history does not always

---

[*] The White House Situation Room was built in May 1961, the aftermath of the Bay of Pigs, a cluster of rooms in the basement of the West Wing. Because of the design of the West Wing, the windows of the basement actually looked out on West Executive Avenue on one side, so the common impression of the Situation Room in novels and pre-Fire dramas as being a bunker is not accurate.

work out the way that we want it to. I understand how Eisenhower felt. You make the best decision that you can make, but you cannot actually affect the outcome. Other people are doing the work and you just have to wait. I really hate waiting. I wonder how Eisenhower would've handled all this."

On the second day of air strikes, October 31, all remaining SA-2 SAM sites were attacked. The Air Force expanded the list of targets to include the four Soviet motorized rifle regiments. Locations thought to be headquarters for the Soviet and Cuban forces near Havana were also hit. The Navy and Marines continued to work the area around Guantánamo Bay and also went after the Komar guided-missile patrol boats and the small craft that made up the Cuban navy. The Navy would have also gone after FKR-1 Salish cruise missile regiments, but these had not been located by the photo analysts.

Only twenty-two aircraft were lost in the two waves of strikes, and by the end of the day the Pentagon had decided that there was no longer any need for fighter aircraft to fly combat air patrol because all Soviet and Cuban air assets had been eliminated. Those fighters armed with cannons were sent in with instructions to conduct low-level strafing runs. How useful these attacks were is disputed, since the pilots had been training in aerial combat, not ground support. No doubt the F-104 Starfighters added to the general sense of chaos coming from the sky as they hurtled across the Cuban landscape at over a thousand miles per hour, firing on military targets with such lack of effect that it seemed as though they were simply scattering explosive cannon fire willy-nilly.

As the pilots prepared for a third day of strikes in their overcrowded ready rooms, televisions brought the latest news from Berlin.

THE SHELLING OF BERLIN

A day after the start of the American bombing campaign against Cuba, artillery shells began to fall on Berlin. The Soviets had obviously mapped the city well because the fire was accurately concentrated on the American, British, and French military bases in the city, as well as on the three airports. The fire came primarily from 122 mm and 152 mm towed guns, the same guns that had made Soviet artillery during World War II such a feared force. We do not know if East German guns were also firing, though it makes sense that they would cooperate with their ally and occupier; if participating, the East Germans were certainly operating under Soviet command.

Though all the NATO forces were on alert, the shell fire caught them by surprise. Most military personnel were still on their bases, along with their equipment, instead of dispersed in city parks and at roadblocks. Moving tanks and vehicles while under fire is a nerve-wracking experience for anyone, and while many of the officers and senior noncommissioned officers (NCOs) were veterans, few of the junior enlisted men were. When the news that the city itself was not being shelled swept through each of the bases, the instinct for survival took over, and the men fled to the relative safety of surrounding neighborhoods. Some of the Soviet shells did fall short or occasionally went long—probably because of erratic manufacturing standards rather than intentions—and dozens of civilians were killed.

The twelve thousand American, British, and French soldiers could not defend a city of two million people. Among these soldiers was a young infantry officer, Second Lt. Raymond McCloud, born in Virginia and a recent graduate of West Point, who had arrived at his posting to Roosevelt Barracks only a week before the crisis began. McCloud and the rest of his platoon ran out of the base, grabbing helmets and rifles as they went.* McCloud remembered standing two blocks away from the gate to his base and watching the fire and smoke. There was no reason to send in firefighters as the shells were still falling. He assembled his platoon and sent runners to find a superior officer with orders. By evening he had received orders to reinforce Checkpoint Bravo in the southwestern corner of West Berlin. Once there, he learned that the runways on the air bases were covered with shallow craters and concrete chips, making them totally useless. The fires on the military bases were effectively destroying almost everything, leaving the defenders of West Berlin nothing other than their basic weapons.

West Berliners were terrified that the Soviets would invade again. One of McCloud's soldiers who understood German overheard an old woman talking to her family. She was telling stories of the last time the Soviets had rained down shells on the city, during the apocalyptic Battle of Berlin only seventeen years earlier. That battle led Hitler to commit suicide and brought an end to the Third Reich. Perhaps as many as a half million soldiers and civilians, mostly civilians,

---

* Of course, the story of Raymond McCloud is important because he survived to be elected as president of the United States in 1992. The man from Virginia rose to national prominence in the mid-1960s for his effectiveness and humane behavior during the suppression of the New Confederacy.

died during the two weeks of urban destruction. As had been their practice since entering German territory, the Soviet soldiers raped tens of thousands of women. Soviet propaganda and officials actively encouraged this practice as a form of punishment for the casualties and horrors that German soldiers had visited on the Soviet Union.

In the fifteen months since the Berlin Wall had gone up, the city had still not settled into a new routine. Economic ties that had bound workers and commerce between the Allied zones and the Soviet Zone had been severed. Families had even been split apart, with some members caught on the wrong side as the wall went up so suddenly. East Germans who had thought about leaving their Communist-dominated nation but had dallied were now trapped. Already people had died trying to cross the wall. Peter Fechter, an eighteen-year-old bricklayer, became one of the first casualties a year after the wall went up, when he and a friend tried to run across the "death strip" and climb the barbed-wire obstruction. His friend made it, but East German guards shot Fechter. The young man lay at the foot of the fence, screaming in pain, while guards from both sides refused to approach him and offer help because they were afraid of being shot by the other side. A spontaneous demonstration on the Western side expressed the West Berliners' horror and anger at the tragedy. After an hour the young man bled to death, and an hour later the East German guards retrieved his body. Everything happened in full view of the Western press and was widely publicized.

By escalating the confrontation in Berlin, Khrushchev showed the Americans that while they might bomb Cuba with impunity, the West was vulnerable in other places. The Soviets probably used artillery because they knew that NATO airpower could not reach and destroy the artillery pieces without violating East German airspace.

The North Atlantic Council met in an emergency session, and Supreme Headquarters Allied Powers Europe (SHAPE) in Paris requested that all soldiers be recalled from leave in all the NATO countries. The council issued a joint statement that called for an immediate stop to the artillery bombardment of Berlin, required the call-up of all reserves in member countries, and requested that the Soviets begin negotiations. Declarations from the British prime minister, French president, and West German chancellor supported the council statement, and all three of the main Western European powers also expressed their support for the American bombing of Cuba. The French communiqué tried to separate the two issues, arguing, "the Cuban crisis is a problem for the Americas, to be dealt with by the United States, Soviet Union, and Cuba. Berlin is not part of the Americas and this Berlin crisis should be resolved by European powers."

Khrushchev saw what he wanted to see in the messages coming out of the West. He interpreted the call for negotiations over Berlin as a sign of weakness and the French attempt to separate the two issues as a fissure in the Western alliance that could be exploited. The mobilization of the NATO armies did not concern him because he had no intention of starting a Europe-wide war. While the Soviet leader rarely seemed to think more than one step ahead, there is every indication that he intended to use only artillery against Berlin and not to escalate the situation by attacking. His own Soviet and Warsaw Pact forces had gone on alert but were not moving into positions to attack the city.

Both sides could potentially deploy large numbers of troops. The Russian Empire, relying on its large population to make it a great power, had always fielded large armies. The Soviet Union followed this tradition. Armchair strategists often showed serious concern about the large number of Soviet army divisions, known to total about 175, versus the smaller number of American Army divisions, increased from fourteen to sixteen by Kennedy. The U.S. Marines also fielded three oversized divisions. The conventional forces' imbalance looked alarming at first, but several factors mitigated this concern. American divisions were much larger, with more support units that were not included in official division headcounts. When pressed by McNamara's whiz kids—system analysts and operational analysts—Army generals eventually conceded that each American division was equivalent to 2.2 Soviet divisions in terms of manpower and combat power.[8] Soviet divisions, which were divided into three categories of readiness, were also not all up to strength. Category III divisions, over half of the total, had perhaps 10 percent of their manpower and not all of their equipment. In many ways, much of what was counted as Soviet strength was equivalent to American Reserve and National Guard units, which were ignored by the armchair strategists.

In terms of total numbers, the Soviet Union had 3.8 million men under arms, with another 3 million trained men available for recall to duty. Soviet equipment included some fifteen thousand aircraft (of which ten thousand were dedicated to air defense duties in the Soviet Union), twenty thousand frontline tanks, and fifteen thousand older tanks.* Another million men were available in the Warsaw Pact armies. The United States had 2.6 million men under arms. The equivalent of six American divisions were stationed in Germany. While the Soviet army was larger than the U.S. Army, the United States had allies in NATO with larger military forces than the Soviet allies in the Warsaw Pact had.

When considering a possible NATO–Warsaw Pact conflict, military strategists divided their considerations into Central Europe and the periphery. NATO was designed as a defensive force, not an offensive force, and most scenarios envisioned stopping a thrust by combined Soviet–Warsaw Pact forces across the central German plain. In Central Europe, NATO had 2 million men under arms in twenty-five divisions, with another 1,125,000 in Italy, Greece, and Turkey; 300,000 more in Britain; and 80,000 in Norway and Denmark. About three thousand aircraft were available in Europe and another two thousand in the peripheral areas.[9]

The theories of military strategists were put into motion by the crisis. Economic activity stumbled in all the NATO countries as so many men were called to their uniforms. Several countries declared partial states of emergency and suspended labor regulations so that remaining workers could log longer hours to make up for the departing soldiers. Demonstrations occurred in more than thirty cities, half of them in West Germany. Most of the demonstrations, and all of the larger ones, were in support of the residents of West Berlin. A few demonstrations by Communist and other leftist groups were in support of the people of Cuba. By shelling West Berlin, the Soviets essentially undermined the natural sympathy of West Europeans for the Cuban people.

The United States followed the NATO instructions (which it completely agreed with) and called up all reserves and National Guard units. Other than the troops earmarked for a possible invasion of Cuba, most other divisions were

---

* The Soviet navy was a substantial force of some five hundred thousand men, mainly concentrated in over four hundred submarines. Along with 130 destroyers and numerous smaller craft, the Soviet fleet looked menacing on paper but was constrained because of limited naval experience (the Russian Empire had never been an important naval power anywhere but in the Baltic Sea); poor geography (having fleets in the Black Sea, Baltic Sea, Barents Sea, and the Far East, all unable to provide mutual support to each other); and an overreliance on officers, rather than sailor draftees, for the more technical work, which meant that many ships could put to sea only after weeks of preparation. Like the Soviet army, the Soviet navy emphasized having numerous assets in the form of weapons and ships, rather than being able to effectively use all their assets.

slated for eventual deployment to Europe. The process would take months as the Navy and Coast Guard scrambled to find sufficient shipping. President Kennedy ordered that his vice president be taken to Mount Weather, where he could maintain continuity of government in the event of a nuclear war. All major federal departments maintained facilities outside of Washington, D.C., to be used in the event of a national emergency, and limited numbers of personnel moved to each of these to join the caretaker staffs—turning on the lights, so to speak.

DECISION TO INVADE

On Thursday, November 1, Kennedy met with both the ExCom and the Joint Chiefs. General LeMay presented the results of the bombing campaign because the Air Force was responsible for so much of the effort, though the campaign was technically under the command of the CINCLANT, Admiral Dennison. Everyone was pleased at the reduced loss rate on the second day of bombing. LeMay told the president and his advisers that he was "99 percent certain" that all aircraft and ballistic missiles on the island had been destroyed.

The Joint Chiefs presented their plan for an invasion to begin Saturday morning. Ships were already in port ready to load the troops. Kennedy had a day to make the decision to invade, to call it off, or to delay. The calm weather favored invasion, and the volatile Caribbean weather could change if they delayed. This was not like D-day; they could not wait until the tides and moon were just right. While the paratroopers liked a full moon, a new moon had just occurred, making nights particularly dark, but the Joint Chiefs were ready to go with the less-than-optimal conditions.*

The Army chief of staff presented the situation in Europe. Gen. Earle Gilmore "Bus" Wheeler had assumed his post on October 1 and, unlike so many of his contemporaries, had little combat experience. To his benefit, he had served in staff positions in NATO in Europe and had recently been deputy commander of U.S. forces in Europe, though for only six months before he returned to assume his position in Washington. The bombardment of Berlin continued, NATO mobilization was continuing, and the Soviets showed no sign of mobilizing.

The Navy chief of staff reported on the quarantine. All Soviet ships remained at sea, neither approaching Cuba nor heading home. Seven neutral

---

* The full moons for the time period were on October 13 and November 11.

ships had been let through the blockade after inspections revealed no military equipment aboard. Four Soviet submarines, all of the Foxtrot class, had been located in the waters between Bermuda and Cuba, and all four were being tracked by American antisubmarine forces.

Kennedy asked the Joint Chiefs for their opinion on what to do. All four chiefs recommended the invasion of the island as a way to solve the Cuban problem permanently and to make sure that the island was never again used as a base by a U.S. enemy. Chairman Taylor did not join his service chiefs in their recommendation, but neither did he object to it. When asked what the Soviets would do in Berlin, the service chiefs were again unanimous in their opinion that the lack of mobilization of Warsaw Pact forces showed that they were not serious about general war in Europe. LeMay predicted that the Soviets would continue to shell West Berlin until the invasion and then would back down. The Soviets knew that they were "outclassed" in their strategic nuclear weapons and that they might not win a conventional war against a fully mobilized NATO.

When the service chiefs left, Taylor remained behind to advise the ExCom. This clearly illustrated that the civilians retained complete control of the U.S. government and made the final decisions, which the military obediently carried out. Some conspiracy-minded writers, even professional historians, have argued that a military coup in effect occurred during the crisis and led to the Fire. While the service chiefs remained unanimous in their advice and desires, the truth is that President Kennedy made the decisions, and he relied on the advice of his civilian advisers much more heavily than on the advice of his uniformed advisers.

The exception was Maxwell Taylor, who was so valued by Kennedy because he was willing to think outside of conventional military logic. Taylor thought that solving the Cuban problem once and for all with an invasion would be convenient, but having worked in the White House for the previous year, he understood that the situation required more than a military maneuver. An invasion demanded careful political thought with regard to its domestic and international implications.

The OAS had met the previous day and endorsed the American bombing of Cuba, but Secretary of State Rusk was frank in describing the hardball tactics that had been used to convince some of the Latin American governments to reach that agreement. Rusk had threatened to withdraw loans and other forms of aid, and he had even threatened to freeze all of the assets of one country's citizens in American banks, a strike at the financial heart of that country's business elite. Rusk thought that an invasion would not be fully supported by another OAS vote. Too many countries remembered the era of gunboat diplomacy, when American corporations exercised control of much of the economic activity in Central America and the Caribbean and the U.S. government was quite willing to send in the Marines if local governments did not cooperate. Kennedy's Alliance for Progress, inaugurated when he entered office, was designed to overcome this legacy of suspicion and intervention. The ambitious diplomatic initiative called for massive investment in development to alleviate poverty and promote positive social change as an answer to the illusory temptations of communism.

Breaking only for lunch, the ExCom met until six in the evening. The discussion flowed back and forth, touching on every option, arguments being used like swords and shields in friendly jousting. Most of the ExCom members liked the idea of invading Cuba. It was the logical next step and would remove the thorn of Castro from the American paw. What would the American people think if the crisis ended and Castro still remained, defiant and belligerent? What if the Soviets tried to sneak nuclear weapons into Cuba again? Clearly the escalation in West Berlin complicated everything; the United States and NATO would not give up that divided city without a fight. A letter was cabled to Moscow stating in the clearest terms that an attempted occupation of Berlin or bombardment of its civilian population would mean war. The group also agreed to ask the Pentagon to immediately draw up plans for American and NATO forces to muscle their way into West Berlin if necessary. Taylor pointed out that such a military effort would not be a raid but a full-scale war, since the bulk of Soviet forces in Europe were in East Germany.

In Moscow, Khrushchev met with the Presidium for six hours. The records for this meeting are lost, so we must go by the results. The military forces of Warsaw Pact nations went on alert, and a limited call-up of reserves occurred. In the Soviet Union, all military forces went on alert, and newspapers published front-page notices that all reservists could be called up at any time and that they should prepare for this. The summer harvest was in, but the call-up of reserves would clearly hurt the Soviet economy, so the Soviets were not ready to escalate completely. Other than a public statement proclaiming the right of the Cuban people to defend themselves against "international imperialism" and another statement arguing that the shelling of Berlin was a justified act of "fraternal comradery between socialist nations," the Kremlin remained silent on the diplomatic front. Khrushchev was apparently waiting for further developments and expecting the young American president to blink.

The book *The Guns of August* by Barbara Tuchman had been published that year and was a major bestseller. Kennedy himself had read it. The book related how all the European powers had gone to war in 1914, even though none of them really wanted to. One of the prime causes was the military mobilization schedules and intricate prewar plans of all the major powers. Once set in motion, any pause or delay in Germany's intricately scheduled mobilization would cause chaos, while its invasion plans for Belgium and France required quick action. Because it lacked railroad capacity, Russia took longer to mobilize and did not want to be caught unawares. These pressures allowed events to gain their own momenteum and limited the ability of national leaders to slow down the escalating tensions and allow diplomacy to work. Each power also thought that a quick war would lead to its national goals prevailing. The book was a wonderful cautionary tale that Kennedy obviously took to heart. He had already recommended that the ExCom members read it.

As the ExCom met on Friday, November 2, the fourth day of air strikes on Cuba continued. The Joint Chiefs reported once again. They felt confident that an invasion should begin the following morning and, when asked, offered their opinion that Cuba could be occupied within two weeks. It would take the equivalent of seven divisions to do it. Guerrilla warfare would certainly continue beyond that time frame, but a new army of Cuban exiles could take care of that. Clearly there were enough Cuban exiles eager to put together a new government friendlier to the United States.

The Cuban exile community had been bombarding the White House with messages requesting the invasion of Cuba. A full-page advertisement had run on the third page of the Friday morning editions of the *Washington Post*, *New York Times*, and *Wall Street Journal*, demanding that Cuba be liberated. Bobby Kennedy's comment on the advertisements summed up the reaction of the ExCom members: "That must have cost a lot of money."

The Joint Chiefs also asked that the American invasion forces be allowed to bring the tactical nuclear weapons normally assigned to their divisions, specifically warheads for the Honest John short-range surface-to-surface missiles and nuclear cores for 203 mm artillery shells. Kennedy decided that the Army could take the weapon systems with them, but the actual nuclear weapons would remain in the United States. He did not want any accidents.

Kennedy's decision was entirely consistent with what was known about Soviet policy. To American knowledge, the Soviets had never sent tactical nuclear weapons outside their borders, except on submarines. In fact, during the Berlin crisis of the previous year, the Soviets had done so, taking the weapons into East Germany and then removing them, all without Western intelligence finding out. Because they did not know that the Soviets had already changed their policy, the ExCom members assumed that the Soviets would not deploy tactical nuclear weapons in Cuba.*

Of course, the Soviets had never deployed strategic nuclear weapons outside their borders, except on submarines. And now they had done so in Cuba. The ExCom members were completely focused on the strategic weapons on Cuba, so much so that they ignored the little intelligence on other weapons. American intelligence had identified FROG surface-to-surface missiles on Cuba, but the president and upper political leadership failed to appreciate the larger implications of this finding. There is no evidence that American intelligence identified or located the eighty FKR-1 cruise missiles on the island. Both the FROG and FKR-1 weapon systems could carry tactical nuclear weapons—and did.[10]

By that afternoon, everyone was exhausted but in agreement. Not to invade would be backing down; invasion was the only way to solve the crisis. The ExCom expected a ground attack to permanently destroy the Communist revolution on Cuba. That outcome was just too tempting and a perfect way to redeem the administration from the embarrassment of the Bay of Pigs.

Kennedy asked the ExCom members to take a break while he thought about their advice. As usual, his brother remained behind, and they huddled together in the Oval Office in a bond of absolute trust. When the rest of the ExCom

---

* The United States first stored nuclear weapons outside the country during the Korean conflict, when it placed nuclear weapons on Guam in June 1951. Prior to that time, almost all nuclear weapons had been stored at three civilian Atomic Energy Commission (AEC) sites in Texas, Kentucky, and New Mexico. The United States at that time had a policy of allowing the AEC, a civilian body, to retain custody of nuclear weapons, handing off control, weapon by weapon, to the military as needed. In 1954 nuclear weapons were first stored in Britain and Morocco, and in 1955 American units in West Germany received their first nuclear weapons. After that, ever more nuclear weapons, both large and small, were placed overseas in allied nations and on naval vessels. See Robert S. Norris and William M. Arkin, "Where They Were," *Bulletin of the Atomic Scientists* 55, no. 6 (November–December 1999): 26–35.

members returned, the president remained sitting—as was his habit since walking hurt so much—and announced that the United States would invade Cuba.

The president and his aides prepared a press release for the next morning declaring the U.S. intent to "free" the people of Cuba from the grip of communism. Kennedy also declared, "West Berlin is of key importance to the United States. We will not trade West Berlin for Cuba. They are separate issues. We demand an end to the artillery shelling of the city of West Berlin and warn that any escalation of that crisis will result in the gravest consequences."

INVASION

The first large Army unit to deploy as part of OPLAN 316 was the Second Infantry Division, the Indianheads, normally based in Fort Benning, Georgia. The division moved to Florida by road and rapidly prepared for combat. As part of this effort, several battalions practiced a landing at Hollywood Beach, near Fort Lauderdale, since amphibious landings were not normally part of their training. On October 30 the soldiers came ashore in the early afternoon. They landed among tourists and sunbathers and were delighted to find bikini-clad girls eager to chat. Some of the soldiers posed for pictures in their combat gear, while many more headed for the bars. An admiral later lamented that the Keystone Kops had never looked worse. Other practice landings used more secluded beaches.[11]

It is remarkable how quickly the American military relocated its forces and mounted the invasion. What took weeks during World War II took only days in 1962. This speed was in part undoubtedly the result of the highly developed U.S. transportation and communications infrastructure. Civilian rail traffic in the South stopped as the military monopolized the railroads and rolling stock.

The Second Infantry Division had an illustrious history. Formed in World War I in France, the division actually included a Marine brigade during that conflict and was at times commanded by Marine generals. The division fought in the horror of Belleau Wood, proving to the French and British that the green Americans could stand up against the battle-hardened Germans. In World War II the division came ashore at Omaha Beach on the day after D-day. During the Korean conflict the division raced to the Pusan Perimeter and lost a third of its strength in the near-disastrous retreat from the Chinese Communist onslaught.

On the morning of November 3, arranged in neat lines, forty amphibious ships stood off the beaches east of Mariel, Cuba, about fifteen miles west of

Havana, carrying the entire Second Infantry Division. Green-clad men slowly crawled down loading nets on the sides of the transports. Each soldier carried a full pack and his weapon; all knew that drowning was a serious possibility if they slipped. Each soldier waited for the right opportunity to obey the order of the boatswain and leap down to the landing craft that bobbed in swells heavy enough to make the men sweat with fear.

Fighter-bombers streaked overhead, dropping their explosives and napalm on the beach and on the gently rolling hills beyond. Helicopters moved back and forth, acting as airborne command posts, issuing instructions to coordinate the landing craft moving around below them like heavily laden beetles. Five destroyers moved in close to shore, pounding away with their five-inch guns. The Navy had decommissioned all of its battleships after finding them too expensive to keep manned and afloat in a world where the airplane, missile, and submarine dominated. No other navy continued to maintain battleships, and cruisers rarely carried big guns.

Frogmen from an underwater demolition team had already examined the beach for two nights, taking samples of the sand and looking for enemy emplacements, beach obstacles, and mines. The Cubans and Soviets had not had the resources to do more than build a few makeshift bunkers of logs and sandbags among the palm trees beyond the beach. There was nothing in the water to impede the invaders. The frogmen had gone out just hours earlier and placed buoys and landing lights to guide the boatswains piloting the landing craft.

Just a generation earlier the United States had excelled at amphibious invasions of Nazi-occupied Europe and Japanese-occupied islands. Many pundits had argued that the world would never see another such invasion on a large scale, but they were wrong. Not only was the Second Infantry Division going ashore, but a Marine regimental combat team was going ashore on a beach thirty miles away at Santa Cruz del Norte, east of Havana. The Marines at Guantánamo were to make several probing feints later in the morning, more to divert the enemy than to try a breakout.

A task force from the First Armored Division waited in Florida for the transport ships carrying the Second Division to return and carry them to a landing on the third day of the invasion (D+2). The rest of the First Armored Division, having deployed from its home at Fort Polk, Louisiana, was loading onto transports in Texas and Georgia and would follow in about five or six days. Another infantry division in New Orleans was preparing its transports and would come ashore on the fourth day (D+3). A Marine brigade was passing through the Panama Canal and would land in four or five days.

Already paratroopers from the 82nd and 101st Airborne divisions and assorted XVIII Airborne Corps troops had started dropping inland, flying all the way in from Fort Bragg, North Carolina, on an airborne conveyer belt. Over eight hundred flights of C-130 Hercules aircraft were required to drop the thirty thousand men and their equipment. The drop happened during daylight because of the lack of moonlight during the night. Though this was normally the rainy season in Cuba, the weather forecast was for clear skies and low wind speeds. The paratroopers jumped at an altitude of seven hundred to nine hundred feet, which gave them a few seconds to deploy their emergency chute if the main chute failed. If the paratroopers dropped on airfields, they faced likely death, since antiaircraft defenses were concentrated there. The countryside was a better bet, though it was filled with sugarcane reaching eight or ten feet high, ready for harvest and pointing like spears up at the sky.[12] Early reports indicated that the paratroopers were encountering either no opposition or sharp fighting. Forward air observers with the paratroopers had already called in six ground combat support missions from the F-100 Super Sabre fighter-bombers overhead.

|■|

Maj. Gen. Mikhail Suranov, a peasant from near Minsk, was a big man with thick fingers and a cunning intellect who loved to reminisce about the Great Patriotic War. He had joined the war as a private and ended it as a senior lieutenant. The Red Army had become his life. He told stories about fighting in the streets of Leningrad, fighting in Berlin itself, of personally shooting six SS prisoners, and of raping eleven German women and girls. He had kept count by cutting notches into the wooden stock of his submachine gun. He always prefaced his stories of rape by saying, "The party told us that we had to make the Germans suffer as the women of our Mother Russia had suffered. It was our duty." The details of his tales seemed to change in every retelling.

His secretary, a petite, dark-haired civilian named Elena Shevchenko, listened dutifully to his stories between taking dictation and other office duties. A Ukrainian from Kiev, she greatly admired the man, but the accounts of the German women hurt, not only because of her feminine empathy for the plight of the women, even if they had been enemies and visited horrors on her nation, but also because she functioned as the general's "second wife," a woman who provided the comfort that he had left behind at home. Many of the senior officers had them.

On the morning of November 3, Shevchenko stood against the wall in a concrete bunker, trying to take notes as the men in front of her argued about what to do. Major General Suranov was in charge of defending the beach, an assignment that could be successful only if the Americans did not show up. He had only the remnants of the 74th Motorized Rifle Regiment and several regiments of Cuban troops on the beaches and area inland. Already dozens of reports of American paratroopers littered the table before him, lying atop a large map. Because the Soviet regiment had spent all of its time either building its own base or helping the rocket crews build their bases, there had been no effort to create beach defenses until the American bombing started, and little had been accomplished before the bombs had destroyed most of their armored equipment.

Suranov held up his hands and quieted the officers. As he gave a speech, the room was silent, save for a translator whispering in Spanish to the Cuban officers and Shevchenko scratching notes with her pencil. Suranov explained that defending a beach was similar to defending a river, or any other military objective, for that matter. A general must choose one of two options: to fight to the bitter end and destroy the enemy on the beach or to let the enemy land and then drive him back into the sea with a counterattack. They had no forces for the second option, so that left defeating the landing on the beach. With no airpower, only two artillery pieces, no tanks, and Cuban allies who were only partially trained, he saw no other choice. A soldier must use every weapon available to him, and there was only one way to win.

|▋|

Lt. Cdr. Bob Hilton was the executive officer (XO) of the USS *Wallace L. Lind* (DD-703), which ran like a sheepdog around the outskirts of the invasion fleet. The destroyer was actively looking for Soviet submarines. It had on board a new Drone Antisubmarine Helicopter (DASH), a small remotely operated helicopter that looked as though it were an oversized insect. The DASH carried a single MK-46 homing torpedo, but the main killing power of the destroyer came from its own twin racks of torpedoes and Hedgehog depth-charge projectors.

As the XO, Hilton was in the combat information center in the interior of the superstructure, monitoring the DASH and sonar operators. There were no portholes among the computers and electronics in the dimly lit room. Everything was new, since the *Wallace L. Lind* had recently undergone a complete retrofit that stripped down and rebuilt its aft superstructure, adding the DASH hangar, new electronics, and updated torpedo launching racks. A variable-depth sonar rig added to its ability to hunt submarines by allowing the sonar to search at different depths. It was all very fancy stuff, but Hilton really wanted to be on the bridge, soaking in the majesty of the invasion fleet, which totaled more than eighty ships and boats, if you counted the hundred-foot-long landing craft.

A bright flash illuminated the room, and all the electronics went dark. Hilton blinked furiously. At first he assumed that a cathode ray tube had blown and caused the flash, as the failing electronics short-circuited everything else. The systems were designed to handle that, though, and should not have died, but any complex machine, whether mechanical or electronic, has to have its kinks worked out, and this was all new technology.

Then Hilton heard men shouting from the deck. He hurried forward and stumbled when the ship suddenly shook from side to side as if a sea giant had slapped it hard. He heard an awful roaring sound, as deafening as a heavy cruiser's big guns, a noise he had experienced as a young ensign. Picking himself up, Hilton found the bridge in chaos, with men stumbling around or standing stock-still, everyone shouting at once. The lieutenant commander rushed to the port side flying bridge, where he found the ship's captain clutching at the outer bulkhead. A massive explosion had struck the invasion fleet; and in the center of the explosion, Hilton could see fragments of ships being carried up on a column of water. The rocking and the sound were the results of shock waves propagating through the air.

The *Wallace L. Lind* was at least five miles from the explosion. Hilton immediately assumed that a small nuclear weapon had been detonated. As an engineer with a keen mind, he quickly thought of an alternate explanation: an ammunition ship had exploded. He had no idea if any of the ships were carrying that much ammunition, but it had happened a couple of times during World War II.

Hilton's eyes focused on a massive swell of water coming toward them. He turned to alert the captain, but the poor man had obviously gone blind from the blast and his face was covered with the worst sunburn that Hilton had ever seen. The executive officer ran into the pilothouse and ordered the ship "hard to port." When the helmsman, also obviously blind, responded sluggishly, Hilton took the wheel himself and turned the ship into the swell. He ordered the ship's engines reduced to one-quarter speed. Another blind crewman who had recovered sufficiently from the shock tried to transmit the order via the telegraph; when he realized the electric telegraph was broken, he used the speaking tube.

The swell passed under the destroyer, pushing the bow of the tin can high into the sky like a protruding girder. Green water swept across the deck when the bow crashed back down into the sea. Hilton lost his footing and skidded into the forward bulkhead. The ship's stern went up and then came down like a giant teeter-totter. Later, Hilton realized that the fourteen men of his crew who were lost in the commotion likely went overboard during this time. He always regretted not sounding the collision alarm, although so many of the electrical systems on the ship had failed that it would not have made a sound.

Hilton ordered all stop and went back on the open bridge. The mushroom cloud forming in front of him confirmed that an atomic bomb had exploded. It was too small to be a hydrogen device. The men blinded around him had been unfortunate enough to be on deck or near windows. Hilton had seen some of the light himself when it came through the small porthole in the door at the end of the passageway that led between the combat information center and the bridge.

With his captain incapacitated, Hilton took command, getting the ship under way again. He found that most of the electronic equipment that had been turned on was now useless, fried by the atomic bomb's small electromagnetic pulse. Fortunately the destroyer carried an ample supply of spare parts, and the crew had many of its systems up and running within a couple of hours. In a series of lockers belowdecks, crewmen found their gear for use in a nuclear war: a badge for every crewman to wear that measured accumulated dosage, Geiger counters, instruction manuals, and six complete environmental suits. Hilton decided that the day was "too damned hot" to wear the suits; besides, which six men would wear them?

Hilton kept a Geiger counter on the bridge as he directed his ship in closer to pick up survivors, many of them clinging to wreckage. Most of the men in the water were dead. The stern of one transport had not yet gone down, and the crew of the *Wallace L. Lind* managed to pull over two hundred men off of it. By that afternoon, a heartbroken Hilton turned his ship, weighed down with over eight hundred survivors, many of them covered with burns, for Florida. The bodies of men who died after rescue were thrown overboard to make more room.

The American fleet off Mariel had been bunched together because they had not anticipated an air attack, and so only six ships survived the initial atomic blast. Four of the ships, a transport that had lagged behind and three destroyers, were able to get under way and rescue those who could be saved. In total, 3,481 Americans survived, and 37,254 soldiers and sailors died.*

❚❚❚

We have only the account of Elena Shevchenko to tell us the circumstances surrounding the use of the first nuclear weapon to be detonated in anger since World War II. The Soviet navy had an FKR-1 Salish cruise missile launcher with a nuclear warhead inside a large barn near Mariel. The sailors pulled the launcher and its twenty-seven-foot-long cruise missile out of concealment, calibrated its orders for an airburst one thousand feet above the American fleet, and launched the beast. A solid-fuel rocket drove the missile into the air until the turbojet took over to propel the warhead on the rest of its journey; a semi-active radar issued instructions to guide its path. The local Soviet navy troops were subordinate to Suranov and so obeyed his order, issued on his own authority, without any apparent hesitation.

The cruise missile had a top speed of six hundred miles per hour and could have been shot down if the Americans had thought a dedicated combat air patrol were necessary. Rumor has it that one of the F-100 Super Sabre fighter-bombers, preparing for a bomb run in support of the paratroopers, saw the incoming cruise missile and tried to intercept it. According to the story, the pilot shouted a warning over the radio, which was picked up by receivers in Florida, and then tried to ram the cruise missile, sacrificing his own life because he did not have any air-to-air missiles. This story was later incorporated into the haunting poem by Ingrid Fisher, "One Life for Many," in which a brave pilot hits a cruise missile just as its warhead explodes.

There is little evidence to support this powerful myth. It is true that the fighter-bombers over Mariel were not carrying air-to-air missiles, but they still had their cannons for use against ground targets and could have easily used those weapons against the cruise missile. Shooting down a cruise missile, which had no ability to dodge, weave, or evade in any way, would have been relatively straight forward, though the time from launch to impact was only a matter of minutes.

---

* Rear Adm. Bob Hilton died of leukemia in 1967 after writing his memoir, *Finding Survivors*. The book became a prize-winning bestseller when his wife published it in 1983.

In the end, what mattered was that the American high command had never imagined that the Soviets had placed tactical nuclear weapons in Cuba. The nuclear device was only twelve kilotons, half the size of the Hiroshima bomb, but was sufficient to completely defeat the American landing.

According to Shevchenko, after watching the mushroom cloud rise up into the air eight miles away, General Suranov wept. Then he kissed his secretary good-bye, gave her a satchel full of Russian rubles and Cuban pesos, and ordered her to head south on a bicycle and not stop until she reached the other side of the island. She never saw him again, and Suranov disappeared from history.

Moscow had ordered that all the nuclear weapons be kept in a central location, where the KGB could guard them most effectively and the Kremlin could better retain control over them. We will never know why this order was not followed more closely. Apparently most of the nuclear weapons were kept in the central location. Perhaps whoever ordered that the nuclear bomb for the Il-28 Beagle and two warheads for the SS-4 ballistic missile be released after the American bombing campaign began also decided to release some of the tactical nuclear weapons. Presumably an order this important would have come directly from General Pliyev, though he apparently never told Moscow he had issued such a command.

|■|

The first indication that something had gone wrong came from aircraft pilots screaming in horror over the radio as their planes were batted from the sky by the shock wave. Pilots farther away soberly reported the giant explosion over the invasion fleet and then the appearance of the mushroom cloud. Instinctively the pilots turned away from the cloud, a demon that had escaped from its confinement.

The admiral in charge of the invasion, CINCLANT Dennison, was based on land in Florida. Dennison was sixty-one years old and reaching the end of a distinguished naval career that had begun at the Naval Academy in Annapolis and included a doctorate from John Hopkins University, a tour commanding the battleship USS *Missouri*, and over four years as the naval aide to President Harry Truman. After World War II Dennison toured Hiroshima and Nagasaki by air, so he knew firsthand the effects of nuclear weapons, though he found the devastation of Tokyo by conventional firebombing more "terrible."[13]

Admiral Dennison received the messages from the pilots and even spoke via radio with one pilot to confirm what he saw. All attempts to raise any of the ships of the invasion fleet also failed. Though there were six ships still afloat, the electronics in their radios had been fried by the electromagnetic pulse, and it would be another hour before one was repaired and contact with higher command reestablished. Dennison had no information on how the nuclear weapon had been delivered. He did know that short-range FROG missiles, which could fly only eighteen miles but were known to be capable of carrying nuclear weapons, were on the island. Since we do not have a copy of OPLAN 316, we do not know whether there was a contingency plan in the event the Soviets used tactical nuclear weapons, but almost certainly there was not. The admiral made a quick decision and decided to call off the invasion. Paratrooper-laden aircraft turned back, leaving behind the thirty-three hundred paratroopers who had already landed. The Marine invasion east of Havana was called off, even as Marines were closing in on the beach in their landing craft.

All ships and the Marines at Guantánamo Bay were warned to shoot down anything in the air. Later that day two cruise missiles, probably fired from the 584th FKR (Frontal Cruise Missile) Regiment near Holguín, were reported shot down on their way to Guantánamo.[14] A Hawk surface-to-air missile stopped one of the cruise missiles, and the other was shot down by a Marine AF-1E Fury, a navalized variant of the F-86 Sabre. A permanent combat air patrol of eight planes maintained itself over Guantánamo, even during all hours of the night. It was a considerable strain on the fighter squadrons based in Florida to fly out that far, loiter for their assigned time, and return.

Reputable historians have never seriously questioned Dennison's decision. All the armed services had conceived tactics for use on a battlefield where tactical nuclear weapons were being used, and some had trained to fight in such a hostile environment; but these tactics all required maximum dispersal across the battlefield, not the concentration of forces required for an amphibious invasion.

The paratroopers on the ground were ordered to fight their way to the small airfield at the Mariel air station. Hundreds of aircraft sorties were flown to support the men in the hopes that they could survive. The pilots flying off Mariel noticed enormous amounts of flotsam in the water and debris piled high on the beaches. The air support proved decisive, but more than 150 Americans died in a friendly fire incident that involved napalm dropped on their position rather than on the enemy.

When the airfield was taken that evening, C-130 Hercules aircraft began to land, off-loading ammunition and evacuating the paratroopers as quickly as they could. The Soviet and Cuban forces backed off during the day in the face of air strikes, but when night fell they pressed home their advantage. The dwindling number of paratroopers held on despite the lack of heavy equipment, knowing that all they had to do was survive until dawn. With the new day more air strikes came, driving back the Soviets and Cubans, and the rest of the paratroopers were withdrawn. The final two flights left amid showers of flames as a dozen fighter-bombers laid down covering fire and dropped more napalm.

By the evening of November 4, the only Americans left on the island were some prisoners of war, thought to number no more than three hundred, and the thousands of Marines at Guantánamo Bay. Aircraft with Geiger counters were already flying patterns near Mariel, tracking the cloud of radioactivity as it blew east along the coast of Cuba. Because it was a small airburst, the fallout was not considered deadly, though there was some concern that the water sucked up in the explosion could fall as hot rain in localized amounts that could sicken or kill. The chief concern was for Florida, but the winds favored the Americans and scientists attached to CINCLANT headquarters thought that the fallout would be too diffuse by the time it reached the Bahamas to cause substantial harm. These scenarios were all guesses: the only nuclear tests over water or underwater had been made early in the atomic age, in the 1940s in the South Pacific by the Americans. No one really knew what to expect.

AMERICAN REACTION

President Kennedy and the ExCom met in a sober meeting only hours after the cancellation of the invasion fleet. Kennedy looked haggard and met with his advisers for only fifteen minutes before retiring to his bedroom for a nap. The strain of the last days, continuously meeting with the ExCom, was beginning to tell on him. An evening televised address to the nation to announce the invasion had already been scheduled, but now the content would be even more important. The White House doctor administered large amounts of steroids to perk the president up so that he would look his best on television.

The first issues the ExCom members tackled were whether Soviet or Cuban forces had used the tactical nuclear weapon and whether Khrushchev had given the Cubans nuclear weapons. The very idea implied that the Soviet leader had lost his mind and become even more reckless than heretofore thought. Until shown otherwise, they would assume that it had been a Soviet nuclear weapon, which meant that for the first time, the Soviet Union had killed large numbers of Americans. As the meeting progressed and further reports were received, it became apparent that the Soviets had killed tens of thousands of Americans.

In any other circumstances this would mean open war, yet no one in ExCom proposed a declaration of war against the Soviet Union. Nuclear weapons had truly changed the rules. Early in the afternoon, word came from West Berlin that the shelling had stopped. Total casualties there were over seven hundred dead (mostly American, British, and French soldiers) and another three thousand wounded. A short diplomatic note to NATO from the Warsaw Pact countries indicated their unilateral cessation of hostilities in Berlin. The Communists made no demands in return for this gesture.

Kennedy returned to the ExCom meeting when the Joint Chiefs came to the White House after conferring in their conference tank at the Pentagon. The chairman and his service chiefs were unanimous in their two recommendations: Cuba must be taken—no other outcome was acceptable—and the next step should be tactical nuclear strikes to make sure that all Soviet tactical nuclear weapon systems were destroyed. Bobby Kennedy asked how many Cubans would die. LeMay answered for the chiefs: "Probably a million."

Finally, at four in the afternoon, a cable arrived from the Soviet embassy. Right after the nuclear explosion in Cuba, the secretary of state had summoned the Soviet ambassador and demanded to know whether the weapon belonged to the Soviets. The ambassador had given no reply. Now the United States had an answer. The two-page message began with a statement of regret for the loss of so many American lives, yet it also reaffirmed Cuba's right to defend itself against foreign invasion and to request assistance from any nation it saw fit to seek as an ally. The Soviets had stopped shelling West Berlin because, they claimed, "we seek only peace and desire a quick resolution to this global crisis. Let calmer minds prevail and keep the scourge of war away from our two great nations."

Only an hour later, Radio Moscow broadcast a communiqué in English, proclaiming to the world that Soviet and Cuban troops had defeated the American invasion. The actual news had already spread around the world, propelled by the free press of the Western world. The cessation of the shelling of West Berlin was not even mentioned in the Radio Moscow broadcast. The tone of the communiqué was so belligerent that the ExCom membership briefly considered the possibility that a coup by hard-liners had deposed Khrushchev. One of the former Soviet ambassadors in the ExCom pointed out that this was more evidence of Khrushchev's erratic behavior.

The only option that the ExCom could agree on was to demand the immediate surrender of Cuba and offer to allow the Castro brothers and their fellow Communists to go into exile in the Soviet Union. No one expected Castro to give up without further fighting, but it was agreed that this offer would be made in a private cable to Khrushchev.

At seven o'clock in the evening, President Kennedy was broadcast live on television; the draft of his short speech had been finalized only fifteen minutes earlier. He came across as firm and strong—and sad. After eulogizing the fallen "fighting men of our democracy," he declared, "Their sacrifice will not have been in vain."

KHRUSHCHEV'S DILEMMA

Because of the eight-hour time difference between Moscow and Washington, D.C., the Presidium was in session in the late afternoon when news came that Major General Suranov had given the order to use a tactical nuclear weapon. Khrushchev flew into a tantrum. According to an aide who later wrote a detailed account, the rest of the Presidium simply waited for Khrushchev to burn himself out. His colleagues were used to his passionate outbursts, but such a rage was uncharacteristic. All the men had lived at the Kremlin for the past two days, taking only a brief break to return to their homes during the height of the American bombing campaign in Cuba. A man needed a bath to clear his mind.

Orders to arrest Suranov were sent to Cuba, but the American bombs had destroyed so much equipment on the island that Soviet radio contact had become erratic. Oddly enough, the commercial cable to Jamaica was the most reliable way to communicate with Cuba. Because British intelligence was certainly copying each dispatch through their former colony, each message had to be encrypted and then decrypted, slowing the whole process.

Then word that the invasion had been called off arrived via an American television broadcast. Khrushchev's mood changed in a moment. The Americans had been defeated, he exulted. The Americans had tasted blood and backed away. The capitalist lifestyle made men soft and unwilling to take casualties. Look at

World War II: only four hundred thousand Americans dead compared to 25 million Russians. The new Soviet man had inherited the hardiness of the Russian peasant and knew how to persevere in the face of casualties.

Khrushchev began to think aloud. This great victory would show the world that the Soviet Union was truly worthy of the title of superpower. How could he turn this to his advantage? If he stopped the shelling of West Berlin, would that not make the Soviet Union look as though it sought peace above all else? It was time to calm the situation. The Soviet goal of defending Cuba had been achieved. Khrushchev immediately dictated a letter to President Kennedy asking for peace, but he wanted to make sure that the president understood that the Soviet Union would continue to stand by the side of its Cuban ally.

As the letter was being cabled, Khrushchev reversed his instructions for the arrest of Suranov, though in all likelihood his first message had not yet been sent. Food was brought in for the men, and as they ate, Khrushchev began to have second thoughts. He had assumed that the game was coming to an end, but he now realized that there were many more moves to come. Perhaps the letter had been too cordial. Best to follow up with a radio broadcast that would keep the Americans on notice that the Soviets would continue to stand by their rights. The so-called quarantine of sea traffic must end, and the Americans must stop their bombing and let the Cubans live in socialist peace.

❚❙❚

Later that evening the American reporter Strobe Carson was among the dozens of foreign correspondents invited to a service at a Russian Orthodox cathedral in Moscow. The priest held a mass for the American dead. The reporter was a cynical veteran of reporting in Moscow, but he was moved by the sincere feeling expressed by the priest and the congregation that filled half of the stone building. While these common folk were sorrowful, the reporter knew that nothing happened in Moscow without the permission of the government, and this was certainly an exercise in propaganda.

Still, it was a curious gesture, uncharacteristic of the regime.

Khrushchev had been raised in a religious household, learning to pray before the icons and going to the local church, but as a Communist he embraced atheism. He attacked religion with all the fervor that his Communist ideology could muster. For the long-suffering believers, the respite came when Stalin promoted the Russian Orthodox Church during World War II as a way to stoke patriotism. Starting in the late 1950s and continuing to the end of his life, Khrushchev increased antireligious propaganda and closed down parish after parish, the number of which declined from some fifteen thousand in 1951 to about eight thousand in 1962. Ironically, an aide to Khrushchev reported that when the Soviet leader visited his mother's grave after Stalin's death he placed a cross on the grave, knelt, and made the sign of the cross. Perhaps on a deep level the leader of world communism feared God.[15]

Further sources: James G. Blight and David A. Welch, *On the Brink: Americans and Soviets Reexamine the Cuban Missile Crisis* (New York: Hill and Wang, 1989); Dino A. Brugioni, *Eyeball to Eyeball: The Inside Story of the Cuban Missile Crisis*, ed. Robert F. McCort (New York: Random House, 1991); Dino A. Brugioni, "The Invasion of Cuba," *MHQ: The Quarterly Journal of Military History* 4, no. 2 (Winter 1992): 92–101; Michael Dobbs, *One Minute to Midnight: Kennedy, Khrushchev, and Castro on the Brink of Nuclear War* (New York: Alfred A. Knopf, 2008); and Norman Polmar and John D. Gresham, *DEFCON-2: Standing on the Brink of Nuclear War during the Cuban Missile Crisis* (Hoboken, NJ: Wiley, 2006).

7

Desperation: The Spark

Chairman of the Joint Chiefs Maxwell Taylor briefed the president on the military's target list after Kennedy's address to the nation the evening of November 3. The Air Force wanted to use fourteen Mk-28 bombs on Cuba. The version of this bomb selected for the mission yielded seventy kilotons. Other than tactical nuclear weapons designed for small delivery vehicles, this was one of the smallest weapons in the American arsenal in terms of yield. Still, each weapon had three times the explosive power of the bombs used on Japan in 1945. F-100 Super Sabre fighter-bombers, accompanied by other fighters to protect them, would fly in at high altitude to drop the bombs. Each bomb-laden F-100 had another F-100 in the air behind it, similarly armed, ready to step in if the first bomber was shot down. Two of the missions would be flown by naval A-4 Skyhawks so that the Navy would not be left out of what was essentially an Air Force operation.

The Joint Chiefs' staff had worked with Admiral Dennison's staff to select each target, concentrating on the MRBM and IRBM sites, the motorized regiment headquarters, the air bases that contained Soviet aircraft, and three locations identified as nuclear weapons storage bunkers. All these target sites had already been substantially damaged by conventional bombing, but at this point in the war, the American sense of morality demanded that the targets remain purely military in nature. The last target would be the capital city of Havana. All bombs were set to explode twelve hundred feet in the air to maximize blast damage and minimize fallout. The Joint Chiefs' only concern was that the smaller weapon systems had not been targeted: the Sopka cruise missile sites, the Luna short-range missiles, and the Komar patrol boats. Though these sites might have tactical nuclear weapons, using such large bombs on them seemed to be excessive, plus every site had not been located with certainty. Hitting the extra sites would require another eight bombs.

Kennedy asked why Havana had been targeted. Taylor explained that the city housed Cuban military and political headquarters and the Soviet embassy, which the Joint Chiefs assumed to be a major headquarters for the Soviets. The actual Soviet military headquarters had not been located.

"What are the expected casualties if Havana is not hit and the other thirteen targets are?" Kennedy asked.

Taylor answered that such numbers were difficult to come by but would probably be in the neighborhood of a half million. If Havana was hit, the casualties would likely number a million dead. Cuba had 7 million inhabitants.

"They aren't all Communists," Kennedy said. "The dead will be mostly civilians, people just trying to live their lives."

Taylor pursed his lips. "The innocent die in war, Mr. President. We killed millions bombing Germany and Japan. Let us not forget that we lost over thirty-five thousand American men just yesterday. They didn't ask to die, either."

An aide later reported that Kennedy slumped in his chair, his lips trembling. He approved all fourteen bomb targets, including Havana.

At first light on Sunday, November 4, ninety-one aircraft took off from airfields in Florida, and four more, from the aircraft carriers *Enterprise* and *Saratoga*, joined them. Though its airplanes could have flown from land-based airfields, the Navy was not going to miss the opportunity to launch a nuclear strike from a carrier. For years, in the bitter internecine fighting for funding among the services, the Navy had argued that aircraft carriers should be maintained because they made good platforms for waging nuclear war.

Twenty-eight of the ninety-five aircraft carried nuclear bombs, each aircraft had a fighter escort, and all the other aircraft were participating as observers. The AEC wanted film and atmospheric measurements of wind, pressure, humidity, background radiation, and every other variable that they could think of. The killing of a million people is a sobering act, one that would drive a normal person insane if he did not have the ability to psychologically push back by turning the experience into abstract numbers rather than flesh and blood and by concentrating on the task at hand. For the scientists, the task at hand was to collect the data on what promised to be the largest simultaneous release of nuclear weapons in history.

It was a bright, sunny day, not a cloud in the sky—quite unusual weather for Cuba at that time of year. Every bomb drop went as planned. The pilots pulled down shaded visors to protect their eyes and raced on afterburners to travel as far away from the blasts as possible. Every weapon exploded at its approved height, except the Havana bomb, which exploded two hundred feet higher than it was supposed to. Several pilots and observers reported their awe at seeing five mushroom clouds rise simultaneously from the green and brown island. (No pilot could see all of the blasts, since the two most distant targets were five hundred miles apart.)

THE FIRE IN HAVANA

The fourteen nuclear bombs achieved most of their goals. The best estimates place Soviet casualties between 80 and 90 percent. The Soviet headquarters was gone. The Castro brothers and most of the top figures in their government also died in the blasts. After only three and a half years, the Communist ideology had not sunk deep into the consciousness of Cuba's people, but the nuclear devastation laid the groundwork for anti-American sentiment to harden into unrelenting hatred over the coming years. The Cuban military collapsed that morning. Individual commanders who could keep enough men in their ranks from deserting effectively and almost immediately took over their local areas as warlords.

Before the invasion, Kennedy had set up a post-Communist Cuba task force. Representatives from the Pentagon, the State Department, the CIA, and a few other federal agencies made up the task force, which quickly created a plan for installing a stable post-invasion government in Cuba. Two representatives from the exile community had been invited to join the group on the day of the invasion. On the day that the nuclear weapons were dropped on Cuba, this task force was attached to CINCLANT in order to take handle of the new situation. No longer would they be handling the occupation of just a post-combat zone; now they had to handle a post-nuclear zone.

The Pentagon gathered its forces. The First Infantry Division was waiting in New Orleans, having traveled down by rail from its home base in Fort Riley, Kansas. The Marines in Guantánamo would be reinforced with those afloat off Cuba and a brigade coming from California to form a full Marine division. The new plan was to land the First Infantry Division in western Cuba and to push east, while the Marines pushed west out of Guantánamo. Two brigades of the 82nd Airborne, waiting to be flown in if necessary, would be the strategic reserve. The Pentagon now expected the effort to be primarily a humanitarian mission with some fighting. Cuba devoted so much of its agricultural acreage to sugarcane that American authorities were not sure the island could feed itself without help, so the government placed large orders for Midwestern grain and corn, which would be put on barges down the Mississippi and then shipped to Cuba.

Events overtook this plan, however, and American troops did not land on Cuba for another three years.

A POET IN CUBA

A chubby nineteen-year-old who preferred reading poetry to playing sports, Miguel González lived on the eastern outskirts of Havana. On the morning of November 4, he was awakened by a flash that illuminated his room. He looked at the clock. Twenty minutes after seven.

A wave of heat passed over him as the roof of his house collapsed. His family lived four miles from the city center and five miles from the center of the explosion. The wind was blowing toward him, bringing the fallout, but through a quirk of local meteorology, his neighborhood was spared substantial harm from the radioactive particles.

With only minor injuries, González searched the rubble of his wood-frame home for other people. He found that his mother, who loved to cook, had died in the kitchen when the brick chimney collapsed on her. His sister was in her bed, alive but with a broken leg. González set the leg as well as he could. He knew he would not find his father, who had been called up as part of the home guard.

González's memory of the days following the strike became a blur of sights burned into his memory, though the order of the events seemed much less important: corpses lying in the streets, slowly decaying because no animals had survived to eat them; his burned neighbors with their blackened skin sloughing, leaving raw flesh and pus-filled sores exposed; people begging for water; and the violence of survivors desperate to stay alive a few more minutes. As the days became months, he witnessed listless people coughing pitifully as radiation sickness took them slowly, emaciated people who could not find enough food, and people who discovered that they could not conceive. As months turned to years, communities rebuilt, education resumed, people died of cancer, and babies were born. Life continued.*

González and his sister built a life for themselves in a coastal town fifteen miles to the east of the city. He wrote an epic prose poem, *The Ghosts of My Home*, describing the Havana that would have existed if the bomb had not fallen. He received the 1995 Nobel Prize in Literature.

INTENSIVE DIPLOMATIC COMMUNICATIONS

Khrushchev, still in his clothes, was sleeping on the sofa in his office, disdaining the use of his private bedroom, when an aide woke him with the news of the nuclear attack. The Presidium members—bleary eyed, unshaven, in unkempt clothes—gathered in their meeting room and listened as a military aide reported that at least a dozen nuclear bombs had been used on Cuba. The information came from American press reports; their own contacts in Cuba were apparently no longer able to communicate with Moscow.

Our record of the meeting provides only Khrushchev's comments, some of his reactions, and terse summaries of the words and reactions of other people in the room. It was written in shorthand and obviously never edited, a historical document in its purest form.

"I can't believe that it has come to this," Khrushchev began.

Members of the Presidium murmured their agreement.

"How many people have died? Do we have any idea?"

Perhaps a million or a million and a half. They did not yet have all of the information.

"The Cuban people will never forgive us," Khrushchev said.

"It was the imperialists who launched the weapons, not us," someone replied.

"Yes, yes, of course, the Americans. Damn them."

---

* Short-term sterility was noted in scientific studies conducted on the survivors of Hiroshima and Nagasaki. After several years, fertility returned, though the incidence of birth defects was higher than it had been in prewar years. As in Hiroshima and Nagasaki, the incidence of leukemia in Havana peaked six to seven years after the bombing, then declined. Ten years after the bombings, the incidence of thyroid cancer increased. Other cancers also increased to the point that half of the population died of some form of cancer, though many lived into their fifties or sixties before developing the disease.

The room was silent.

"Is our friend Fidel Castro or his brother still alive?"

No one knew.

A cable from the American embassy arrived, explaining the bombings and assuring the Soviets that the Americans had no intention of attacking the Soviet Union itself. The Soviet leader immediately dictated a reply. He proposed to end the crisis with the following provisions: the Soviet Union would withdraw all of its forces from Cuba (any that still existed); the United States would end the quarantine; the Soviet Union would promise never to put troops or weapons of any type in Cuba; and the United States would remove the IRBMs from Turkey within a year. The last two conditions would not be publicly announced but would remain private promises. Furthermore, if the United States promised not to invade Cuba, even if Fidel Castro were still alive, then the Soviet Union would promise not to resume its attack on West Berlin and would restrain its ally, East Germany, from complaining about the city. Khrushchev concluded with a frank admission that the agreement might have to be tweaked in the following days as more information came out of Cuba, but its basis—to calm down the situation—would remain.

The cable was immediately sent to the Soviet ambassador in Washington for delivery to the White House. Khrushchev ordered that it not be encrypted, as was the normal practice, so that communication could be quick.

The Soviet strategic forces remained on high alert, while the call-up of the reservists was quietly slowed. Khrushchev and the men of the Presidium shared a dinner cooked by Kremlin chefs. No one could go home just yet.

|■|

It was early afternoon in Washington when Kennedy and the ExCom read the cable from Khrushchev. The Joint Chiefs had been invited to join the deliberations. Everyone thought that the message was an excellent basis for negotiations, though the service chiefs reiterated their firm stance that the invasion should continue. The fourteen nuclear bombs had been used to clear the way for the troops; to stop now would look foolish.

Regime change had never been Kennedy's top priority. Avoiding general nuclear war was his main concern, and the Soviet proposal looked like the best path to achieving this goal. Kennedy was also concerned that the United States had created a horrible humanitarian mess in Cuba and needed to clean it up.

The discussion turned to the possibility of recruiting Latin American forces, to be conveyed by American ships and aircraft to Cuba, to help as humanitarian workers. While the American military had by far the best training and equipment to undertake the mission, Mexicans, Guatemalans, and Venezuelans spoke Spanish and would be greeted as helpers, not conquerors. Bobby Kennedy pointed out that Americans would probably be the most hated people in Cuba for the next century.

A cable agreeing to the conditions that Khrushchev had set forth was quickly written and sent to Moscow, although Kennedy reserved the right to make modifications as the situation in Cuba developed. Kennedy told the ExCom that he expected the burning question for the next week—for the ExCom, the Soviets, and the press—to be, Was Castro still alive? They might never know for certain.

In the middle of the night on November 5 the Presidium met again to consider the American response. There was a light dusting of snow on the cobblestones of the Kremlin complex. The meeting was brief. Khrushchev expressed his relief and told everyone to go home.

PHOENIX STRIKES BACK

Sergei Feklisov could see two of the mushroom clouds from the sugar plantation where he had hidden his Il-28 Beagle. He could assume only that the war had started. He tried to contact the Soviet command. The telephone at the plantation no longer worked, and his radio raised no one. The radio on his aircraft could receive only his authorized Soviet air force frequencies, but he found another radio in the supervisor's house—which transmitted only static. Were the atomic clouds interfering, or had the radio never worked properly? Had America been obliterated in a general nuclear war? Had his hometown of Kirov been destroyed? What should he do?

As the day wore on, Feklisov turned from trying to contact his superiors to trying to contact any Soviet on the island and finally to trying to contact anyone at all. He wanted to drive off the plantation to seek out information, but the workers had taken the truck to search for family members in the cities. Besides, it would have been hard to travel on the narrow roads against the crowds of refugees flowing away from the bomb sites toward the farmlands. Feklisov observed some of the workers planting seeds in fields that had already been harvested. When he pantomimed a question, asking what they were doing, he was told that they were planting vegetables. Sugarcane would not feed them.

In the end, the senior lieutenant of aviation considered his duty. We know this because he wrote three letters and left them with the Communist leader who ran the agricultural collective. The first letter was to the Soviet air force and explained that the last orders he had received had been to prepare to drop his sole nuclear bomb on New Orleans. The Americans were reported to be assembling an infantry division there for the invasion of Cuba. As a good soldier of the motherland, he would follow his orders. The other two letters were to his wife and to his mother, asking that they remember him.*

Feklisov waited until well after midnight, then boarded his aircraft with his navigator. We do not know the name of the navigator or whether he played a role in Feklisov's decision. They waved to the workers and refugees lining the runway as they taxied to its extreme end. Feklisov had made no secret of his cargo, and from what we can determine, the Cubans were quite eager to strike back at the giant to the north.

Pushing the large jet engines under each wing to full power, Feklisov released the brakes, and the Il-28 hurtled down the short runway. His fuel tanks were two-thirds full, which would allow him to fly the seven hundred miles to his target, even if he took a route close to the ocean to avoid radar. He did not have enough fuel for the return flight. It was a one-way mission.

The flight to New Orleans took less than two hours. The American air defense network was focused on Florida, though radar coverage along the Louisiana and Texas coasts was active and on heightened alert. Official records do not show that the light bomber, which could have been flying as low as two hundred feet above the waves, was detected, though an Air Force staff sergeant manning a radar in Morgan City claimed that he saw the incoming aircraft and tried to alert the proper authorities at England Air Force Base in Alexandria, Louisiana. The staff sergeant was new to his post and claimed that a pompous second lieutenant refused to acknowledge his request because the NCO did not use the correct terminology. Many discount this story because they cannot imagine that a staff sergeant would not know the necessary terminology for his job.

---

* The letters were never delivered because the two women and his infant son lived in Sevastopol and almost certainly died there during the Fire.

At 4:26 a.m. on November 6, 1962, a Soviet nuclear bomb estimated to be two hundred kilotons in strength exploded about one thousand feet above the French Quarter. The Soviet navigator probably used the city lights and the dark shape of the Mississippi River to guide his mark before he released the bomb. After that the Il-28 Beagle disappeared; the aircraft was probably either deliberately caught in the blast zone or lost at sea.

The First Infantry Division, preparing to depart for Cuba, was mostly aboard its ships and suffered 80 percent casualties. The remnants of the proud unit helped the survivors. Estimates of the number who died immediately are now placed at 177,000, though the first estimate delivered to President Kennedy was a minimum of two hundred thousand dead. The radioactive cloud spread south, responding to the push from a storm front north of the city, killing along the river delta but ultimately causing fewer casualties than if it had drifted in any other direction, into more settled areas.

KENNEDY RESPONDS

An aide awakened the president only fifteen minutes after the nuclear bomb was dropped and later reported that Kennedy was instantly alert, not groggy at first, as was common. The president asked whether any other cities had been hit. When informed that nothing else had happened, he said, "It must have come from Cuba. A bomb from the Soviet Union would have hit the White House first." Trailed by his aide and Secret Service agents, he rushed to the Situation Room in his pajamas.

Kennedy demanded that SAC be contacted immediately and ordered to hold station. The SIOP was not to be implemented in any way. Kennedy admitted to one of the men on duty that he could not remember if the SIOP had an automatic trigger to launch a retaliatory attack if an American city were destroyed, but he certainly did not want an accidental war. Other members of the ExCom arrived as quickly as they could, their chauffeur-driven cars led by police escorts with lights flashing in the darkness and sirens clearing the streets.

The president refused to meet with the ExCom until he received personal messages from General LeMay and General Power that the Air Force would wait for his orders and not launch a nuclear war on its own. Of course, under the SIOP, such orders would be cancelled if Washington, D.C., were destroyed and the president could no longer communicate with them. Some historians have criticized Kennedy for his decisions at this juncture. They argue that Kennedy should have evacuated to Mount Weather, where his control would remain firm. Kennedy saw evacuation as an escalation of the situation, especially if the Soviets detected his movement, and he was determined to slow the pace of events, not ratchet it up.

Power responded first, from his command bunker in Omaha, in a terse message acknowledging receipt of the president's order. LeMay responded a few minutes later, sending a message from outside the conference tank in the Pentagon, where the Joint Chiefs were about to meet. Kennedy, bypassing the chain of command, also sent direct orders to the subordinates of both Power and LeMay; he said that their commanders were to be relieved if they tried to start a war without an explicit order from the president. The concerns that Kennedy had first felt when he learned the details of the SIOP the year before were coming home in the most fearful, dramatic manner. He was the commander in chief, and the sole responsibility for nuclear war rested with him, the elected executive of the people, not with the Air Force generals.

The ExCom met in the conference room of the Situation Room rather than in the more comfortable rooms upstairs. An Air Force major reported what was known about the attack on New Orleans and confirmed what Kennedy had already suspected: it had originated in Cuba. Because radar would have picked up a ballistic missile, the assumption was that a bomber flying in low had dropped the bomb, though the possibility that it was launched from a small watercraft could not be discounted. Perhaps a Komar guided-missile patrol boat had survived, and one of its short-range SS-N-2A Styx missiles had been armed with a nuclear warhead. These missiles were not known to be capable of carrying nuclear warheads, but the original 770-pound conventional explosive could technically have been replaced. Of course, because the missile could fly only about twenty miles, the Komar boat would have had to travel up the Mississippi River to get close enough to New Orleans or come well within the barrier islands east of the city. Within an hour, further information from New Orleans confirmed the probable size of the nuclear device to be in the range of 150 to 350 kilotons. It was thought that the Styx missile would not have been able to carry a warhead that large.

The combined conventional and nuclear bombings had obviously not destroyed all of the matériel in Cuba, despite LeMay's guarantee. Numerous questions presented themselves: Were there more nuclear weapons on Cuba that might be used against the United States? How many nuclear weapons had the Soviets placed on the island? How could the Americans make sure that they were all destroyed? Had the Soviet leadership authorized this attack? That seemed unlikely. Attacking one city seemed foolish, and NORAD gave no indication of further attacks. The main question was, How should the United States react?

The ExCom members quickly came to a unanimous decision that a rogue element had sent in the bomber. So how could the United States guarantee that it would not happen again? Should Cuba be plastered with enough nuclear weapons to ensure that no weapons survived? General Taylor assured the president that Cuba was larger than it looked on the map, with many mountains and rugged areas. It would take thousands of nuclear weapons to make absolutely sure that nothing remained. Besides, had the Cuban people not suffered enough?

A military aide brought a cable intercepted in transmission between Moscow and the Soviet embassy in Washington. Because it was unencrypted, reading it was simple. The Soviet ambassador was to go to the White House immediately and explain that the Soviet Union had nothing to do with the explosion in New Orleans. Kennedy burst into bitter laughter. "Nothing to do with it! If they hadn't put the weapons in Cuba, this would never have happened!"

The conversation briefly turned to how to punish the Soviets, allowing the men to vent their anger. One of the more novel suggestions was to destroy a similar Soviet city, like Rostov or Odessa, a sort of exchange. No one expanded on that proposal.

Since general nuclear war seemed imminent, the discussion then turned to what to do domestically. Obviously, Kennedy would have to address the nation, and he planned to do so at noon. Three concerns presented themselves. The people of New Orleans had to be helped as quickly as possible, which required a rescue effort bigger than anything witnessed in the nation's history. Kennedy made fast decisions on this issue. He placed his brother in charge of the relief effort on the civilian side and asked General Taylor to appoint a high-ranking military officer at the same time. Of course, martial law would be declared in New Orleans and the surrounding parishes.

The second problem was the obvious danger of national panic. If everyone fled the cities because they feared that their city would be next, economic chaos would spread like wildfire. Could the president in good conscience say to the American people that they were not in danger? If he did not, people would act in their own self-interest. What if he assured the country that there was no reason for concern and then another city was bombed? That would destroy the faith of the American people in the government. Perhaps martial law should be declared to keep people in the cities and on their jobs.

Kennedy listened to all of the advice, then made his decision. He would reassure the American people that no more nuclear weapons would be launched from Cuba. He would plead for calm and not declare nationwide martial law, but military and police forces would prepare themselves for martial law in case the situation spiraled out of control. Everyone agreed that national censorship, especially of radio and television, had to be put in place immediately.

The third question concerned the election. November 6 was the first Tuesday of the month, so by law it was the day of the midterm elections. Polls were scheduled to open on the East Coast in only a half hour, at eight in the morning. Kennedy admitted that his first instinct was to summon the party leaders in Congress and propose that they jointly postpone the election. Who knew how people might vote, given that hundreds of thousands of their fellow Americans had just died? On second thought, Kennedy decided that declaring that the election would proceed as scheduled was a perfect way to proclaim that America could move forward after the previous night's devastation. Elections were the foundation of American democracy and the American way of life. The Union had even held the 1864 presidential election during the Civil War. Kennedy would use that example in his speech. Of course, voting in Louisiana and Mississippi would have to be postponed; everyone would be too busy with rescue efforts to stop at the polls.

With the preliminary decisions made, Kennedy left the ExCom meeting and went to meet the Soviet ambassador in the Oval Office. Secretary of State Rusk and National Security Adviser Bundy accompanied him. He took the time to change out of his pajamas and into a suit and to slick back his hair with water. The American leadership found Ambassador Dobrynin disheveled and agitated. His repeated assurances and pleas of ignorance on behalf of his government did not provide Kennedy with any further useful information.

Bundy asked whether the Soviet leadership knew of any surviving nuclear weapons or weapon delivery systems in Cuba. Dobrynin said that he had no knowledge of such systems. Kennedy asked that Khrushchev answer that question as soon as possible.

While the ExCom met, the Joint Chiefs convened in their conference tank. They forwarded any information they received to the White House. The Joint Chiefs ordered increased air and sea patrols around Cuba, as well as more reconnaissance flights over the island, even if the flights exposed pilots and planes to increased radioactivity. Most of their effort went to moving units toward New Orleans to help in rescue efforts. The occupation of Cuba was postponed, since half of the planned force had been destroyed in New Orleans.

Somber newscasts replaced the usual morning shows on American televisions. No images of New Orleans were shown. The newcasters read a statement from the president that reassured the citizens and asked for calm. For the most part, the country remained composed and quiet, though millions of workers called in sick. The exception was Florida. Already keyed up because of the presence of so many troops, Floridians panicked, filling the highways and freeways bumper to bumper with fleeing cars. The side roads also filled quickly. By eleven in the morning, the president had declared martial law for the whole state. Fortunately, the large number of military personnel in the region helped restore order in the late afternoon by clearing the roads and forcing people to return to their homes. The White House forbade any mention of the Florida situation on the national airwaves, though a couple of reports did slip through in regional markets because the apparatus of censorship was not yet up and running. Most of the actual censorship was self-regulated and had begun when the word came down that the government would impose censorship. Radio announcers and newscasters, wanting to avoid a national panic, showed restraint by keeping the news to themselves and waiting for word from the government on what to say.

KHRUSHCHEV PANICS

Khrushchev was apparently at home when news of the bombing in New Orleans reached him. It was early afternoon in Moscow, and apparently the word had come from American newswires. We have documentation of only the Presidium meeting that started about two hours after New Orleans was destroyed. By that time, Ambassador Dobrynin had already been dispatched to reassure Kennedy.

The Soviet leader first interrogated his military about where this weapon had come from. He knew that two SS-4 ballistic missiles had survived the conventional bombing, though no one knew whether they had survived the nuclear bombing. No communications in any form had come out of Cuba. Perhaps it had been a bomber, though no reports had showed that any had survived. While most of the Presidium was certain that it was a Soviet weapon, at least two members wondered aloud if this were an American plot. Perhaps the president or a right-wing conspiracy had destroyed New Orleans in order to force the United States into retaliating against the Soviet Union.

Khrushchev seized on this idea. He rejected the notion that Kennedy had the hard nature necessary to sacrifice one of his own cities, but those in the right wing in America had been vocal in their belief that the Americans could win a nuclear war against the Soviets. Perhaps there had even been a right-wing coup and Kennedy was no longer in charge. The Soviet leader continued his monologue, thinking aloud and revealing another issue that had preoccupied him throughout the crisis.

The damage done by the traitor Oleg Penkovsky had preyed on Khrushchev's mind. At first the KGB assumed that any information Penkovsky had known must be considered compromised. But what if he knew something that they were not aware of, a secret he might have learned inadvertently? A week of intense interrogation had left a broken man missing parts of his soul, and he had detailed much of what he had passed on to his American and British contacts. The Soviets determined that the Americans knew that the Soviets had such a small number of ICBMs and bombers that they were vulnerable to a first strike.

Other information also helps us to understand Khrushchev's frame of mind. In a 1960 report, Khrushchev had told the Supreme Soviet, "We are several years ahead of other countries in the creation and mass-production of intercontinental ballistic rockets of various types. . . . The military air force and navy have lost their previous importance." He had already made large cuts in the armed forces, supposedly so he could focus the military's efforts on ballistic missile development and manufacture. He told his fellow Soviets, "We are embarking on the reduction of our armed forces not because of any economic or budgetary weakness, but because of our strength and might."[1] Leaders tell untruths to their people for many reasons: to maintain their own position of leadership, to keep up public morale, to hide embarrassments, or to promote a greater goal. When leaders tell themselves lies, they cripple their ability to make informed decisions. Even by 1960 the Soviets were ahead in ballistic missile technology only in terms of propaganda feats in the space race, and the Soviet air force was important only as a defense against bombers carrying nuclear weapons. Khrushchev had in fact opted to rely on ballistic missiles in order to cut military expenses so that the civilian economy could grow. He had acted out of economic weakness, not strength.

Khrushchev also noticed that the United States relied heavily on bombers to deliver their nuclear weapons. He preferred ballistic missiles for the Soviets because they could be used both to respond to a nuclear assault by the Americans and in a preemptive strike. In a 1959 statement, he had talked about how the Soviet Union could launch devastating attacks on the United States in a "matter of minutes from missile bases within the USSR."[2] One may infer that this idea of a first strike had become lodged in Khrushchev's mind as a possibility, even though the Soviet Union's ballistic missile program had not yet built enough ICBMs to make a force large enough to eliminate U.S. strategic forces in a preemptive attack. Of course, Khrushchev also said that the nuclear weapons were never meant to actually be used and a force large enough to cause significant damage to the United States would be sufficient as a deterrent. Once again, Khrushchev's genius for contradictory thinking is manifest in his ability to simultaneously believe that his ballistic forces were sufficient to act as a deterrent and strong enough to be used in a preemptive strike.

Another perspective on Soviet reasoning at this decisive point is found in a CIA report of July 1962, just months before the crisis and the Fire. After acknowledging the American predominance in strategic weapons, the prescient CIA analysts wondered whether the imbalance in power had degraded the usefulness of deterrence.

> The Soviets probably reason that the U.S. nuclear missile forces are becoming so powerful that there may not be a reliable alternative to striking first. In other words, should the United States succeed in striking first with its massive forces, the USSR may not have the opportunity to strike back with the force necessary to continue in the war. On the other hand, should the USSR succeed in striking the first blow, while it would surely be subjected to powerful strikes from numerous surviving U.S. forces, it might be afforded the opportunity of carrying on the war and winning it.[3]

This is exactly the rationale that Khrushchev followed into the abyss. Surprisingly, the Americans' success in obtaining a more accurate picture of the Soviet strategic forces through Penkovsky had actually made the situation more unstable.

When Kennedy's demand for information about nuclear weapons or delivery systems still functional on Cuba arrived via a report from Ambassador Dobrynin, Khrushchev reacted with fury. What if the Americans found out that the Soviets had known about two surviving SS-4 missiles? One of those missiles must have hit New Orleans. What about the other missile? They had been hidden together, so it made sense that if one had survived the nuclear bombing of Cuba, the other had also. If Khrushchev told the Americans about the other missile, would the Americans then blame the Soviets for New Orleans?

Was this an American trap? If America attacked now, with no warning, using their two hundred ballistic missiles to destroy the Soviet missiles on the ground and devastate the Soviet bombers, the war would be over before the Soviets even had a chance to fight. The only hope for the Soviets, considering their weak position, was to strike first. Khrushchev used one of his colorful aphorisms to illustrate his point, "Like a dancing bear breaking free of his tether, we will strike quickly against those who torment us."[4]

One of the Presidium members pointed out that the Americans had not resorted to using atomic bombs during the 1948 Berlin crisis, or when they were on the edge of defeat in Korea in 1950, or during any other crisis. "But they have now used them in Cuba," retorted another Presidium member. "In this case they used nuclear weapons only after a nuclear weapon had been used against them," protested the first.

Our handwritten document of the meeting includes the following exchange in transcript, not in the summary that makes up much of the rest of the document.

> "And we have just used a weapon against one of their cities," Khrushchev declared. "By your logic they are even now deliberating how to strike back at us, taking their time, just as they took two days before they destroyed Cuba."
>
> "Nikita Sergeyevich, you are being a fool!"
>
> "No, it is you who are a fool. We have only one chance. We can survive a nuclear war. It can't be worse than the Great Patriotic War. We lost one in seven then, had half our country occupied by the Nazis, and we came out stronger. We can survive the destruction from this."*
>
> "We will lose everyone in this war! No one wins a nuclear war!"

---

* This sentiment was not a snap argument by Khrushchev. He had earlier said, "We Russians have suffered three wars of the last half century. The Americans have never had to fight a war on her own soil and they have made billions because of it. It is time for Americans to bleed on their own soil." See William Taubman, *Khrushchev: The Man and His Era* (New York: Norton, 2003), 537.

The courageous naysayer, whose name we do not know, was asked to leave the room, and he did so. Khrushchev still controlled his handpicked Presidium.

The decision had been made, and now implementation began. Shortly after this moment, the last truck of documents from the Kremlin left for the Gorbachev Bunker. We know this because the boxes of material from this date are not organized, but placed inside with haste, many of them still handwritten. Only because of this bunker material do we know the content of the final discussions in the Presidium and many other aspects of the Presidium's handling of the crisis.

Because Moscow is so far north, sunset on that date came at 4:30 p.m., after only nine hours of daylight. Apparently Khrushchev issued orders to the military at sunset, an hour after the decision had been made. There were fifteen hours of night before sunrise in Moscow on November 7.

Ballistic missiles of all three classes (ICBM, IRBM, and MRBM) were fueled, a process that could take up to twenty hours with the oldest models and an inexperienced crew. In naval bases at Murmansk and Vladivostok, Soviet submarines armed with ballistic missiles and nuclear-tipped cruise missiles readied to depart. Because the submarines were not ready for immediate departure, perhaps only a quarter managed to leave under cover of darkness. Another quarter escaped with their deadly cargoes before the Fire came.

Soviet bombers took off from their bases, one at a time, as they became ready, only a few hours before dawn and flew north to bases in the Arctic, where they would briefly land to top off their fuel tanks before heading out over the polar ice cap. Americans planners thought that the Soviet bombers would have to transfer to the Arctic bases and were surprised in retrospect at how quickly the Soviets moved north. Strict radio silence was maintained in order not to alert the West of the impending attack. It is also possible, but not confirmed, that some of the bombers skipped refueling and flew straight to their targets in what were effectively one-way missions.

In those days before satellites provided real-time imagery, all this activity was effectively invisible to American and NATO reconnaissance planes flying along the periphery. It is readily apparent that the Soviets were following a prearranged plan, probably similar to the American SIOP, since they took steps to limit radio traffic and moved as quickly as they could. Because the Soviets had been trying not to escalate the situation, they had not raised their nuclear armed forces to a level of alert comparable to DEFCON 2. In summary, the Soviet soldiers, airmen, and sailors were not prepared to jump into activity suddenly, but they gave it their best.

Despite what must have been an enormous amount of confusion, the Soviets managed to achieve the maximum degree of surprise possible. They timed the detection of their bombers (by American reconnaissance aircraft loitering outside of Soviet airspace) to coincide with the arrival of their intercontinental ballistic missiles in America. In other words, the Americans detected the Soviet aircraft leaving the motherland just as the ICBM warheads hit the United States. This meant that the United States experienced the war over the course of a whole day as the Soviet bombers spent hours approaching North America and trying to sneak through American and Canadian defenses.

Further sources: Office of Current Intelligence, "Khrushchev on Nuclear Strategy," Staff Study (Washington, D.C.: CIA, January 19, 1960); Office of Current Intelligence, "Soviet Strategic Doctrine for the Start of War," Staff Study (Washington, D.C.: CIA, July 3, 1962); and U.S. Defense Atomic Support Agency, *The Effects of Nuclear Weapons*, rev. ed., ed. Samuel Glasstone (Washington, D.C.: U.S. Atomic Energy Commission, 1962).

8

Angels Weep: The Fire Comes

My father was a captain in the Air Force, a missile launch officer assigned to the new Minuteman ICBM silos in Montana. We lived in Great Falls, and the first snow of the winter had already come. As a five-year-old boy, I loved playing in the snow, making snow angels, and building snowmen with my father. My mother tells me that during the crisis my father spent twelve to sixteen hours a day at the silos, helping to finish the construction in time. The Minuteman missiles did not come online in time to be launched during the crisis, and though I have combed the remaining archives, I have never found any evidence that illuminates Soviet plans for dealing with the new missiles. They apparently knew that they were not yet active, so perhaps they decided to not target them. Realistically, it would have taken too many of their strategic forces to guarantee the Minuteman missiles would be destroyed; they would have had to ignore the Atlas and Titan ICBMs and the hundreds of bombers. Regardless, no nuclear weapons hit Montana during the Fire.

I remember watching President Kennedy's noontime televised address to the nation but not the details. I know it was his November 6 address, not one of the others earlier in the crisis, because I remember that it interfered with my lunch. I do not remember Kennedy telling the nation about the destruction of New Orleans or urging calm. My father had come home to watch the president with my mother. I remember that my parents looked very somber, even sad, and my father said, "The angels are weeping now."

We regularly went to the Presbyterian Church, but I do not remember my father mentioning angels before that—or ever again.

FIRE ON AMERICA

The United States and Canada had built an integrated air defense system under NORAD, headquartered in Colorado Springs. A string of radar stations across northern Canada, the Distant Early Warning (DEW) Line, constantly watched for Soviet bombers flying over the polar regions. Farther south were two other lines of radar stations called the Mid-Canada Line and the Pinetree Line. In Alaska, Greenland, and Britain, large BMEWS radar stations watched for ballistic missiles. The United States also had a "contiguous radar system," covering the coastal regions and the Mexican border, made up of land stations, picket ships, and Air Force "Warning Star" aircraft. Three "Texas Tower" offshore platforms were also built off the northeastern coast to hold large radar domes. SAGE computer systems allowed coordination of air defense for North America.

Hundreds of Canadian and U.S. Air Force interceptor fighters were dedicated exclusively to defending the nations. Some American fighters were equipped with the Genie air-to-air missile, which carried a small nuclear warhead. Most antiaircraft missiles destroy or damage their targets with blast effects and shrapnel, not direct hits. A nuclear weapon provided a much larger blast effect radius and could even destroy more than one bomber.

The Canadians and Americans also jointly developed the Bomarc antiaircraft missile. A rocket engine boosted the Bomarc to supersonic speeds and then a ramjet engine propelled it for up to two hundred miles. Like the Genie, the Bomarc was designed to carry a nuclear warhead, but the Canadians chose to fit theirs with conventional warheads. Over five hundred Bomarc missiles were deployed along the U.S. coasts and in Canada, and some of the American missiles were armed with nuclear warheads.[1] In addition, the United States also had located Nike Hercules SAM batteries, which carried small nuclear devices, near major cities. All of these defenses were useless against ballistic missiles because it was too hard to quickly acquire and destroy an incoming warhead.

From approximately 7:00 to 8:00 a.m. (Moscow time), six SS-6 Sapwood and nineteen SS-7 Saddler ICBMs lifted off from Plesetsk. The last SS-7 exploded on the pad, killing many of the ground crew and throwing its nuclear warhead half a mile away. The warhead cracked on landing and heavily contaminated the area. The Soviet Union had launched its entire ICBM force to fight this unwinnable war.

The SS-6 ICBM could not completely guide itself, so during the first few minutes of launch, ground radars watched the trajectory and radio command signals prompted the missile to use its vernier chambers to correct itself. After that, the inertial guidance device kept the missile on target. Each SS-6 carried a single five-megaton nuclear warhead. The more advanced SS-7 ICBMs did not require radar guidance from the ground and instead used an internal table of preset values for position and velocity. The analog internal guidance computer kept the missile within these values. Each SS-6 carried a three-megaton nuclear warhead. The SS-7 took only thirty minutes to prepare for launch, unlike the ten to fifteen hours that the SS-6 required.[2]

At 11:22 p.m. (Washington time) a radar picked up the first incoming missiles. Because the military alert was at DEFCON 2, and the troops were ready to believe any suspicious radar echo, the initial warning circulated even before another radar station confirmed it. The White House was informed within a few minutes, and the president was again rousted from bed after a long, tense day. We can only assume that the first family was ushered to a waiting Marine helicopter, or they may have been taken to the fallout shelter in the White House. We do not know.

Two missiles were aimed at Washington, D.C. The five-megaton warhead from an SS-6 Sapwood arrived there first, after traveling 4,600 miles, as measured in surface miles (not the distance of the arc that the warhead actually followed). At 11:35 p.m. (Washington time) the nuclear weapon exploded two miles east of the White House at an altitude of about seven thousand feet. Much of the energy of such a nuclear explosion radiates in very short wavelengths, is rapidly absorbed by the surrounding air, and then heats the air into a fireball, probably about ten thousand feet in diameter.* Temperatures briefly spiked at more than 200 million degrees Fahrenheit in the center of the fireball, and for a moment the fireball was five thousand times brighter than the sun at noonday.[3]

It was a clear night, and the flash lit up the city and surrounding countryside. Anyone outside within twenty miles of the blast would have experienced tem-

---

* The exact size of the fireball depends on meteorological conditions and the proportion between fission and fusion, but in general, a one-megaton weapon creates a fireball 7,000 feet in diameter, and a fifteen-megaton weapon creates a fireball 18,600 feet in diameter. The largest weapon used during the Fire was five megatons; larger sizes had only been used only in test explosions.

porary blindness. The heat wave from the explosion burned exposed skin up to
fifteen miles away and even created an effect similar to sunburn on people up to
twenty-three miles away. Closer in, the heat blistered paint off buildings, melted
roadways, and started fires.

The blast wave traveled behind the heat wave, and every building within
three miles of the explosion was completely destroyed. Pieces of buildings, vehicles, and the remains of people flew around in the air like so much chaff. The
velocity of a large tornado is about three hundred miles per hour; the velocity of
the blast wave from a nuclear explosion reaches near the speed of sound, about
750 miles per hour.[4] Hurricane-force winds of a hundred miles per hour were
experienced over ten miles away, though they tapered off quickly.

Few people within three miles of the explosion survived. Those that did
live had been sheltered in a deep basement at the time of the blast, and luck
had allowed them to find their own way out past the rubble. Many who initially
survived in basements died when the mass fire that followed suffocated them by
sucking the oxygen out of the air, or they were trapped and cooked as the rubble
above them burned. Some buildings within three to five miles of the explosion,
especially those made of reinforced concrete, remained standing, but all were so
damaged that they were later torn down. Residential houses were shredded as if
their lumber walls were made of matchsticks. Most buildings within five to ten
miles of the blast were heavily damaged, and perhaps only half were salvageable.
All the buildings along the National Mall, including the White House, the Capitol, the Smithsonian museums, and the presidential monuments, were obliterated. The Pentagon, across the river in Arlington, three miles from the explosion,
withstood the damage better than expected because of its reinforced concrete
walls. The heart of the city had effectively been destroyed.[5]

The next missile exploded twenty-two minutes later, three miles south of
Washington, D.C., with a force of three megatons 4,500 feet in the air. The two
warheads were timed to not cause fratricide, with one warhead destroying the
other before it could properly create its own fusion explosion.

At Olmsted Air Force Base in south-central Pennsylvania, the deceptively
named 2857th Test Squadron trained as a helicopter-borne rescue team. Only
the pilots and the base commander knew that their primary assignment was Outpost Mission: to fly into Washington, D.C., and ferry the president to a safe place
in the event of a nuclear war. If they could not travel quickly enough, then they

were to don their bulky radiation suits—twenty pounds of lead-impregnated rubber per man—and fly into the aftermath of the nuclear strike to rescue the president. The helicopter crews followed their orders and flew in through the night, the copilot wearing a darkened visor in case the flash from another nuclear explosion blinded the pilot.

Fires burned around the center of the city, but they were weak, as if the force of the double blasts had cleaned the streets bare. The searchlights of the three helicopters stabbed the ground, revealing chaotic rubble. Only by triangulating on the Tidal Basin of the Potomac River and the debris-filled Reflecting Pool could the soldiers find the White House.

The helicopters landed, and the crews made a quick survey. Nothing but several feet of broken bricks, splinters of wood, some charred corpses, and a layer of grit were left. The air was filled with smoke and dust. Using crowbars and shovels, the airmen scraped at the rubble over the presidential fallout bunker. One of the pilots worked a radio, trying to pick up a signal from below. Another military unit, the other half of Outpost Mission, waited outside the city with heavy equipment, including a backhoe, jackhammers, and a crane.

Looking at his dosimeter and knowing that their time was running out, the major in charge made a decision. No need to call in the heavy equipment; there was no one left to rescue. The 2857th Test Squadron fled the scene of devastation just as dawn arrived. On the way back to Olmsted, they stopped in a small town where they could hear ambulance sirens and filled their flight decks with wounded to take back to the base hospital. It was a small act, but that was the nature of the rescue operations that day—a person here and a few more people there.

Plans to rescue the nation's treasures—the Declaration of Independence, the Constitution, the Bill of Rights, the Gettysburg Address, and priceless paintings at the National Gallery of Art—were also in place. All such plans required some warning, but the nation's capital received no warning. We are not certain that the alarm sirens ever sounded, even just a few seconds before the first nuclear warhead exploded.[6]

The USS *Northampton* was at sea off Virginia. As part of the Atlantic Fleet, the cruiser often served as a command ship because it carried extensive communications equipment aboard. The ship was also designated as a White House at sea and was ready to receive the president if Camp David and Mount Weather were unavailable. The cruiser did not have the opportunity to fill this role.

The Census Bureau estimated that 784,000 people lived in the District of Columbia in 1962 and twice that number lived in the metropolitan area. Over a million people died from the blast effect and the fires that raged in the suburbs around the capital. Even more would have died if the attack had happened in the daytime, when the city swelled with workers coming in from the more distant suburbs. Half of the surviving population had blast or burn injuries, and the majority had both. It is estimated that half of those wounded in the explosions were dead within two weeks. The radioactive cloud from both warheads drifted east across Maryland, the Chesapeake Bay, and Delaware, exhausting itself over the Atlantic Ocean. Hundreds of thousands more people died in the months that followed.

Washington, D.C., was targeted not to kill the population but to decapitate the government. In this the Soviets failed. Key government employees had relocated to some ninety designated locations outside the capital in order to maintain a functioning federal government in the event that the city disappeared, a process called continuity of government (COG).* Most of these locations were college campuses or other public buildings, though a few were much more impressive. Forty-eight miles northwest of the capital was Mount Weather, an experimental mine built into a mountain that was first used by the Bureau of Mines to test new, hard rock mining techniques and was then converted into a government shelter. The president and his staff, as well as officials from other important federal departments, could potentially run the country from this site. A steel blast door six feet thick sealed the entrance, and several thousand people could live inside. A hospital and crematorium provided for any eventualities. Standing orders were to shoot to kill anyone who tried to enter the shelter without the proper identification, even family members—or perhaps especially family members.

Communications facilities on site could record radio and television announcements and even broadcast them. Several prominent news anchors had taken secret oaths that they would make their way to Mount Weather in order to be the face and voice of the government, to provide a sense of continuity and security for their audiences.[7]

---

* The White House Emergency Plan was over two hundred pages long, and the Joint Emergency Evacuation Plan for the rest of the government was of similar length. See David F. Krugler, *This Is Only a Test: How Washington D.C. Prepared for Nuclear War* (New York: Palgrave Macmillan, 2006), 177.

A system of sensors that could detect nuclear explosions had been laid across the country and sent signals to Mount Weather. These sensors detected heat, brilliance, or overpressure. Of course, the bunker itself had external radiation monitors and remotely operated cameras to keep track of the situation locally. As Soviet bombers appeared in the skies and the Fire began, the Bomb Alarm Board began to blink with awful messages.

Vice President Johnson, irritated at being shunted away from Washington during the crisis, was already at Mount Weather. Johnson had suggested he move to Camp David instead, but Kennedy wanted his vice president in a truly safe location. The vice president watched news reports and read the briefing papers. Though he felt sidelined, events quickly proved that he was the lion in waiting.[8]

The Pentagon built its own underground command post for the secretary of defense and Joint Chiefs of Staff at Raven Rock in the Blue Ridge Mountains, seventy miles northwest of Washington. Also known as Site R, the post consisted of two massive tunnels excavated in a mountain in the woods. Structures up to three stories high were built within the tunnels, enough space to accommodate 2,200 people. Water reservoirs held 2 million gallons of water and power plants generated enough electricity to power a small city. Telephone, radio, and microwave communications systems were designed to keep Site R in command of the American armed forces, even as nuclear weapons fell all around.[9]

Washington, D.C., had few actual fallout shelters, only basements designated as shelters, that had no reinforced walls, air filters, or water filters; few had any other supplies. Even the Pentagon had only a single fallout shelter, able to hold 150 key officials, though it was properly equipped. The White House had an older bomb shelter, built during World War II under the East Wing, and a newer fallout shelter built in the early 1950s under the southeast lawn. None of the shelters were deep enough, however, to survive a nuclear explosion nearby.[10]

Congress had its own underground bunker, 250 miles away in White Sulphur Springs, West Virginia, built under the Greenbrier Hotel. Called Casper or the Greenbrier facility, 100 senators and 435 representatives were expected to make their way there on their own or by scheduled helicopter pickups off the National Mall in front of the Capitol Building. A law passed in 1794, during George Washington's second term, gave the president the authority to convene Congress at a location other than the seat of government, so relocation plans included a proclamation for the president or his successor to sign. Unlike Mount Weather and Site R, the facility under the Greenbrier was an open secret within the town of White Sulphur Springs.[11]

Under both Eisenhower and Kennedy, the federal government ran regular drills to redeploy employees to their remote locations and to practice continuing government functioning from those sites. The drills were conducted discreetly because the federal government did not want to appear as though it were protecting itself at the expense of the civilian population. One of the great flaws of the relocation plan, recognized by all, was that no provision allowed for the key employees to take their families with them. Was it realistic to expect government officials to abandon their families in the event of nuclear catastrophe in order to do their jobs? Yet the government saw accommodating families as potentially politically embarrassing, leading to questions about how other civilians would be protected. Some writers had already proposed the idea that the federal government would not invest in civil defense because it thought that if too many people in the cities survived a nuclear attack, the country would not be able to feed them—because radiation damage would have destroyed too many crops. While politicians had often talked about fallout shelters, little real effort had been made to build them, mainly because they were expensive and ultimately seemed useless in the face of the reality of nuclear weapons. One might accuse Congress of hypocrisy for its failure to fund fallout shelter measures. After all, congresspeople had their own facility at Greenbrier. But that facility had been built in 1959 at the behest of President Eisenhower.

Because the Soviet attack came as a surprise, the selected government employees did not have time to flee to the evacuation sites. The skeleton teams that regularly manned the sites continued the government. Vice President Johnson survived, as did two cabinet members and one associate Supreme Court justice. Four hundred one members of the House of Representatives and eighty-two senators survived, primarily because it was Election Day and almost everyone had returned to their home districts.

More ICBM warheads rained down on America. A five-megaton SS-6 warhead hit Central Park in New York City. Because of a probable failure in the onboard instrumentation, the weapon hit the ground rather than exploding high in the air, forming a crater two thousand feet across and three hundred feet deep in the center. (Two other locations also received groundbursts later in the day: Charleston, South Carolina, and Amarillo Air Force Base in Texas.) The normal prevailing winds blew the fallout along the north shore of Long Island. The five boroughs of New York suffered 80 percent casualties, and the mortality rate over half of Long Island was 90 percent.[12] Boston, Philadelphia, Baltimore, Charleston, Detroit, Chicago, Seattle, San Francisco, and San Diego were ravaged. Numerous Air Force bases with SAC wings stationed at them were also hit, though this was a mostly futile gesture, as the SAC bombers and refueling tankers had already dispersed around the country.

Soviet bombers were expected to arrive with the morning light, but the eight-hour flight presented plenty of opportunities for Canadian and American fighters to take their toll. Our best estimates are that the Soviets launched fifty-two Tu-95 bombers and fifty-eight Mya-4 Bison bombers. An unknown number of Tu-16 Badger medium-range bombers, perhaps two dozen, also tried to make the flight. With their limited range, the Tu-16 aircraft were on one-way missions and had to use aerial refueling tankers to even reach the United States.*

The NORAD forces tore at the bombers with the fury of hungry guard dogs on carrion. The Canadians flew both the Avro Canada CF-100 Canuck, a natively designed and produced fighter, and the American-produced CF-101 Voodoo. The Americans flew three fighters against the Soviet bombers: the F-101 Voodoo, the F-102 Delta Dagger, and the F-106 Delta Dart. These aircraft were designed purely to go after other aircraft; only the F-106 Delta Dart had a 20 mm Gatling cannon to accompany its air-to-air missiles. The pilots of these squadrons had trained exclusively for this day and could effectively vector in on instructions from air traffic controllers hunched over their radar screens.

---

* Each Tu-95 Bear bomber had 4 turboprop engines, a range of 8,000 miles, a cruising speed of 440 miles per hour, and a crew of 8. Each Mya-4 Bison swept-wing bomber had 4 jet engines, a range of 5,000 miles, a cruising speed of 510 miles per hour, and a crew of 8. Some of the Tu-95 Bear bombers carried the AS-3 Kangaroo air-to-surface missile, a large, supersonic, turbojet-powered cruise missile with a range of 100 to 350 miles. The AS-3 carried an 800-kiloton nuclear warhead and could be launched before the bomber reached its target. The only verified successful use of the AS-3 Kangaroo was the strike on Barksdale Air Force Base in Shreveport, Louisiana. See Steven J. Zaloga, *The Kremlin's Nuclear Sword: The Rise and Fall of Russia's Strategic Nuclear Forces, 1945–2000* (Washington, DC: Smithsonian Institution Press, 2002), 267. In *The Communist Bloc and the Western Alliances: The Military Balance* (London: Institute for Strategic Studies, 1961–62), the Institute for Strategic Studies reported inflated numbers. Zaloga and Norman Polmar and John D. Gresham (in *DE-FCON-2: Standing on the Brink of Nuclear War during the Cuban Missile Crisis* [Hoboken, NJ: Wiley, 2006]) agree that there were about a hundred total Tu-95 Bears.

Some Soviet bombers were caught over the sea or ice, while others made it to land. Although some of the American fighters carried Genie nuclear-armed air-to-air missiles, this weapon was used only twice. Regular air-to-air missiles—and in one case, cannon fire—proved sufficient to devastate the Soviet bomber force. Three Nike Hercules missiles, armed with small nuclear warheads, were also used around Boston to destroy a bomber apiece, though an ICBM had already destroyed the city.

Eleven Soviet bombers made it through to successfully attack their targets. Only one, a Tu-95 Bear that dropped its bomb on Loring Air Force Base, Maine, managed to return home and landed on a civilian airfield on the Kola Peninsula that the Americans had neglected to destroy. Several years later, after the Scandinavian Federation asserted control over the Kola Peninsula, the Finns turned the aircraft over to Muscovy, where it occupied a place of honor in the Grand Duke's newly built Museum of Russian History.

American cities and towns had civil defense sirens, and some cities even had public fallout shelters—though far too few to make a real difference. There was a thriving industry in private fallout shelters, however. Home shelters received plenty of publicity and caught the public imagination, but as it turned out, the actual number was too small to make a difference. Only the lives of a few individuals who had enough warning to access the shelter and were far enough away from the nuclear explosions were saved.

Grocery stores and hardware stores had reported an increase in sales beginning when President Kennedy publicly revealed the crisis on October 25. Sales grew again after the bombing of Cuba began, and when the invasion failed due to the Soviet tactical nuclear weapon, anxious citizens cleared the shelves, buying everything available. Many people began to dig makeshift fallout shelters, ripping up their lawns and emptying stores of lumber, concrete blocks, and bricks. Many of these were crude affairs, yet stories of the Fire are filled with accounts of families sleeping in such shelters, an uncomfortable experience they described as "camping in a hole." Many lives were saved because of these rudimentary shelters.

Some of the more dramatic artifacts of the Fire are the films and photographs from that time period. Gamma rays often left flashes of light on unexposed film, a constant reminder that the air was filled with nasty stuff. After spending some time looking through a book of images or walking through a display exhibit in one of the world's many Fire museums, a person becomes numbed to repeated exposure to destroyed buildings, charred corpses, and wasted landscapes.

As was mentioned in chapter 2, the experts failed to anticipate one effect of the Fire. Mass fires, also called firestorms or superfires, had occurred only a few times previously in history. A mass fire is characterized by unusually high air temperatures and strong winds that cause the fire to suck in air from its periphery; this effect creates what can be described as a huge outdoor blast furnace. Mass fires melt asphalt and will literally snatch people off their feet with winds that exceed a hundred miles an hour in velocity. They are not created by natural means but require human action. The first known mass fire was set intentionally on the night of July 27, 1943, when the British attacked Hamburg with incendiary bombs. The resulting fire burned five square miles of the German city and killed fifty thousand people.[13]

Cities had been destroyed in fires before: London in 1666, Chicago in 1871, San Francisco in 1906, and Tokyo in 1923. In each of these cases the fire had worked its way across the city in expanding lines of flames, burning for days. In contrast, a mass fire is started in many places simultaneously and lasts less than a day because after that nothing is left to burn.

Postwar nuclear tests usually occurred in barren environments: on atolls in the middle of the ocean, in deserts, on the steppes of Central Asia, or in Siberia. Because of this, the effects of mass fires, which had consumed Hiroshima and Nagasaki, were forgotten. In the United States, many of the cities hit by nuclear weapons were then more thoroughly destroyed by fire. For example, in Chicago, a three-megaton missile warhead exploded at six thousand feet, two miles north of the city center over the south end of Lincoln Park. Part of the force of the explosion pushed down on the waters of Lake Michigan, sending strong waves across the water and causing devastation to port facilities, cities, and towns all around the three-hundred-mile-long lake.

Almost every structure within eight miles of the explosion in Chicago was destroyed, from Evanston in the north to Elmwood Park in the west to Kenwood in the south, and the thermal effects of the nuclear weapon started numerous spontaneous fires. Broken gas mains also contributed to the start of the fire, but not to the degree commonly assumed, because the gas vented out of cracked and buried pipes in so many places that its effect quickly dissipated. The fire spread, and by morning it was marching through the city. Firefighting crews from outlying fire stations and from surrounding suburbs found themselves devoted exclusively to joining police officers in trying to help fleeing citizens maneuver through the streets. The fire crews moved broken-down cars, cut up fallen utility poles, and put out small fires, avoiding the mass fire that marched like a conquering enemy across the houses of the residential areas on the outskirts of the city's core. By nightfall, the ecology of the mass fire had collapsed, leaving smaller fires behind. Fire crews now felt safe enough to move, and they focused their energies on containing the small blazes, since few fire hydrants still delivered water.

Most of the radiation damage in the area came from initial exposure as the prevailing winds took fallout out over the lake (and as with other air bursts, the fallout problem was minimized, with over half of the fallout particles dropping to the surface within a day). The November weather in the Midwest was too cold for tent cities, so warehouses were used to house the wounded. Luckily few had been blinded because most had been home asleep when the explosions occurred, but thermal burns were severe—though not as bad as they would have been if people had not had the protection of their homes. Such small advantages make the difference between life and death in nuclear war. Still, over a million injured people had to be cared for by a damaged medical system in the immediate area that could handle perhaps ten thousand.

Triage was the order of the day. The surviving medical professionals chose who would receive care and who would be allowed to die based on examinations that often lasted less than a minute. They looked for thermal burns and assumed that a large area burned indicated too much radiation for long-term survival. As it happened, this was not a correct diagnosis, but in the moment, it seemed to make sense—the greater the amount of burned area, the greater the chance of contracting opportunistic infections. Patients whose hair began falling out after the first day were also marked as hopeless. Those with injuries that would require surgery were usually put aside because no one had the time or resources to operate; if the patient survived for a week, an unlikely prospect, then he or she might get on an operating table. Making such hard decisions scarred doctors, nurses, and paramedics for life.

Estimates place the dead from the Chicago blast at 2.1 million, and another 660,000 died in the following year. The fallout was not strong enough to prevent the city from being rebuilt, with large parks re-created along the waterfront and in the interior of the city. The central location that had made Chicago a good place for a city in the nineteenth century remained an advantage in the years following the attack, and by 1990 Chicago was again the largest city in the state of Illinois.

A HOUSEWIFE IN CHICAGO

One of the women who survived in Chicago was Britta Webern. Born in Nuremberg, Germany, in 1922, she became an adult during World War II. In those years, she cared for her elderly parents and did clerical work part-time. She hated the bombers that came and destroyed so much of her world, including the apartment building she had lived in. She survived that blast because she had taken her parents to a bomb shelter. When her parents passed away, shortly after the end of the war, Britta told people they died because her brother did not return from the eastern front, where he had been captured at Stalingrad. He later died in Siberia. The lack of food during the harsh winter of 1945–46 also contributed to their demise and left Britta a thin woman with the face of a waif framed by unkempt dark hair.

In the spring following her parents' deaths, Britta found a new job working for the Americans. Nuremberg was in the American sector of the country, and American GIs were everywhere. Oddly enough, she did not hate the Americans, though they had dropped many bombs on her country, but she did hate the Russians for taking her brother from her. In time she met a young German from Chicago who wore the uniform of an American lieutenant. At first she could not understand how he had been able to fight against the fatherland, but she came to see that he was an American first and German second. He offered to make her an American too, and after looking around and finding nothing left for her in Nuremberg, she accepted.

Britta became a housewife. She bore two daughters and a son and watched her husband rise up the management ladder at a paint factory in Chicago. They lived in a nice home in Maywood, bought with a Veterans Administration loan. They planted three maple trees and a solitary oak in their large backyard to complement the two maple trees planted by the city in the front yard between the curb and sidewalk.

When the Cuban Missile Crisis started, Britta sat riveted in front of the television. Two days after Kennedy's speech, her husband returned home to find his wife digging a large hole in the backyard. Since their home had no basement, she was going to protect her family with a bomb shelter. Embarrassed, wondering what the neighbors would think, he tried to stop her, but when she threatened him with the shovel, he retreated into the house.

It is amazing what a determined woman can do in a week. By the time the first nuclear weapon destroyed part of the American invasion fleet off Cuba, Britta had dug a large hole, laid slats of wood across the bottom to form a floor, built walls with more slats and gunny sacks, and built a roof with planks laid over logs. On top of the roof she piled six inches of dirt. The design of the bunker followed those that she had seen in Germany but was adapted to the materials on hand.

The logs came from her maples and oak tree, which she cut down with the chain saw that her husband kept in the garage. Every day he returned from work and watched his wife with concern. He felt the flush of humiliation when he realized that his neighbors were laughing at her, at him, and at their family. He confessed later that he had talked to a psychiatrist about committing her, but the doctor had recommended that he wait to see whether she regained her balance when the crisis ended.

Britta demanded that her family sleep in the completed bunker, and she placed a bed out there for them to huddle on together. Her husband put his foot down at this, however. Temperatures were near freezing at night, and their youngest daughter was only four years old. Britta was not so determined that she slept alone in the bunker; she could never abandon her family.

After the devastation of New Orleans on Tuesday, her husband agreed that the family would spend the next night in the bunker. The flash of light woke the children, but Britta, remembering her time in the bunker in Nuremberg, had not gone to sleep. A minute or so after the light came the roaring destruction; it sounded worse than anything that she had ever heard. The family members held onto each other as bits of dirt rained down on them, and the heat of the thermal shock wave left them sweating.

When morning came, they emerged to find their house and every other house in the neighborhood flattened. The city-planted maple trees that had lined the street, each so uniform in height, having been planted thirteen years ago, were now stumps with jagged slivers of trunk sticking out of them. Britta's husband searched the neighborhood for about an hour, but no one else was left alive.

The young family took the knapsacks that Britta had prepared, with canteens of water and sandwiches, and walked west.

Two years later they returned to rebuild their home in the same location. Husband and wife never again talked about Britta's manic determination—not once.

HUNTING SUBMARINES

The four Foxtrot submarines off Cuba became an immediate target of the U.S. Navy. Over the previous week, the Americans had used practice depth charges and hand grenades to harass the Soviet submariners. The depth charges were small cans thrown overboard that made a small explosion designed to make a loud noise but not create the pressure waves that could damage the submarine, only the ears of its sonar operators. The constant harassment kept the submarines underwater, and the air became foul as carbon dioxide levels rose. On the *B-59* three sailors fainted from overheating. Each of the submarines managed to reach snorkel depth and suck in fresh air for its crews and to run its diesel engines to replenish its batteries for a short time before renewed harassment by the Americans forced it back to the dubious protection of deeper depths. One submarine was forced to surface in order to repair its ailing engines. The crew members ignored the repeated signals from a nearby American destroyer to surrender; because of their restricted rules of engagement, the Americans could do nothing more than send signals. This aggressive behavior was entirely consistent with the usual peacetime cat-and-mouse game in which the Americans and Soviets attempted to track and harass each other's submarines.*

The Americans were unaware that these vessels each carried a nuclear weapon because this class of submarines did not normally carry torpedoes with nuclear warheads. One can only speculate how such knowledge would have changed the Americans' behavior. Would they have backed off or become even more aggressive?[14] The Americans were also unaware that the submarine captains and their brigade commander were out of contact with their higher command. Despite

---

* According to the sole survivor of these Foxtrot submarines, an officer, the American antisubmarine forces transmitted in the clear to each other as they hunted the Soviets, allowing the submarine commanders to track the exact location of the pursuing ships and P-2 Neptune airplanes. Of course, they could eavesdrop only when they were close enough to the surface to send up a radio aerial. See Ryurik A. Ketov, "The Cuban Missile Crisis as Seen through a Periscope," *Journal of Strategic Studies* 28, no. 2 (April 2005): 222.

having no orders on the use of their nuclear torpedoes, none of the submarines used them during the failed American invasion of Cuba or any of the other events of the crisis phase before the Fire.

American antisubmarine forces—destroyers and aircraft—struck within minutes of the blasts in Washington, D.C., and the issuance of the order for DEFCON 1. After a brief flurry of activity, they were pleased to confirm the destruction of all four targets based on the debris that floated to the surface. We know about what happened earlier on the submarines only because one of the officers of the *B-59* improbably survived. He floated to the surface in a survival suit and an American destroyer crew picked him up.

Another Soviet submarine in the Atlantic, the Zulu-class *B-75*, commanded by Nikolai Nantenkov, had loitered in the mid-Atlantic after escorting the Soviet merchant ship that carried much of the nuclear weapon inventory for the island to Cuba. Once Nantenkov became aware of the Fire, and having received no orders, he attempted to contact high command. When that failed, the captain agreed with the KGB officer aboard that they would use the two nuclear torpedoes if they could find appropriate targets. U.S. naval intelligence intercepted the message they sent to this effect but did not decode it until years later. This submarine is likely the one that decimated two American destroyers and swatted a nearby aircraft out of the sky with a nuclear torpedo while being hunted off Bermuda on November 8. We do not know for certain whether the *B-75* survived this first attack and was destroyed later in another antisubmarine action, though two historians from the Scandinavian Federation have argued that the *B-75* was also done in by its own torpedo.[15]

Halfway around the world, the Zulu-class *B-88* followed orders and fired a nuclear torpedo at the entrance to Pearl Harbor. The ship channel to the main harbor is three miles long and regularly dredged; the torpedo went partway up the channel before it exploded, the fourteen-kiloton device carving out a crater larger than the channel itself. Water pushed farther up the channel into the harbor proper devastated shipping and shore facilities with waves estimated to have topped fifty feet. The tsunami pushed out to sea from the channel caused damage along the coast in both directions for about six miles before the power of the wave spent itself. Because the explosion was effectively a combined water and groundburst, substantial fallout drifted east and southeast with the evening winds and dropped black rain onto the area between Pearl Harbor and the city of

Honolulu, located only six miles away. From there the radioactive cloud drifted over Diamond Head and then out to sea. One out of every two people in Hawaii lived in Honolulu or nearby, for a total population in the area of three hundred thousand. Within two months half of these people had died.

In the month following the Fire, American antisubmarine forces vigorously hunted the Soviet submarines that had surged from their ports on the night the Fire began. Some of the Soviet vessels carried ballistic missiles, others carried cruise missiles, and some had nuclear torpedoes. Navies from NATO countries and other allied countries also contributed warships and aircraft, flying out of devastated homelands, determined to get their own licks in. Rushed to leave their ports with only a few hours' notice, the Soviet submarines were often short on rations and in disrepair, and they had not had time to tighten down and police sources of noises in order to make the vessels run more quietly. This made it easier for the American and allied forces to find them.

Three American submarines and one British submarine, cruising in the Barents Sea as part of long-term monitoring of the Soviet submarine force, had particularly good hunting. The British submarine captain claimed three kills, and there is no reason to doubt the record, though also no way to verify his account. The American submarines each reported killing one Soviet submarine.

Three times the American submarine hunters used nuclear depth charges, launched on rockets that could place the explosion far enough away to protect friendly vessels. The radioactive fallout dissipated in the ocean. The long-term effects of these three underwater explosions are impossible to measure because fallout from the land war also fell into the water.

Three submarines carrying ballistic missiles managed to get close enough to the United States to attempt to launch their weapons. Normally it took a Hotel-class submarine eighty to ninety minutes on the surface—long enough to be found and destroyed—to accurately observe its position and calibrate its compasses so that it could hit its target. Even then the CEP of the missile was two miles. One of the three submarines did surface and quickly launch its ballistic missile, but because it was fired in haste, the missile missed its target by twenty miles. It exploded out to sea off of Boston, which had been devastated by an ICBM eleven days earlier.[16]

Four Soviet submarines in the Pacific and two in the Atlantic managed to move close enough to U.S. territory to launch cruise missiles. These cruise missiles flew at 90 percent of the speed of sound (.9 Mach), slow enough for fighters to scramble and shoot them down. A cruise missile from a submarine hit Dededo, the largest town on the island of Guam, but missed the naval air station and Anderson Air Force Base. A cruise missile launched from a submarine undetected by the Americans also hit Newport, Rhode Island, the site of an important American naval base, two days after the Fire began.

ORAL HISTORY OF BEN STEPHENSON

I turned seventeen in 1962 and went to school at Marshall High School in Newport, Rhode Island. When the crisis happened, we knew that we were a prime target because of the Newport Naval Station. We listened to the radio or watched the television all the time, constantly passing information back and forth. Not an hour went by that we didn't talk about what was happening. There were rumors of Soviet subs just off the coast. Jimmy Raskin, whose dad was a captain in the Navy, told us that those subs had nuclear missiles and torpedoes on them.

There was an early warning system in the city. We knew that if those sirens went off that we had only twenty or thirty minutes before we died. We talked about what to do in that short time if it happened while we were at school. The boys decided that we wanted to either steal the finest car and go for the joy ride of our lives or make sure that we didn't die before making love just once. Of course, some of the boys scoffed at that, telling stories about some girl they had met at the beach or while on vacation. They didn't tell if they were sleeping with their regular girlfriends because that would destroy their girls' reputations, and that wasn't right. The girls thought our first idea was dumb, but they agreed that the second idea had merit.

On the 30th, a test of the early warning system had been scheduled, but the mayor decided to cancel the test. He didn't want any false warnings. We were told in all our classes, more than once, that there would be no test. Some employee decided that even without an offical test, they should at least test it long enough to make sure that there was power going to the sirens. So he set it off, all full of good intentions, and couldn't turn it off.

We thought it was the real deal. Everyone rushed from the classrooms. Some girls were crying, and I even saw our star running back, a kid full of muscle and meanness, crying.

Annie Baldwin was a junior, a brunette who always dressed in skirts with flowers on them. She came up and took my hand and led me away. She was a student aide to one of the teachers who wasn't there that day, so she had a key to his office. I had no idea that she even liked me. Afterward, when we found out that it was all a mistake, she wouldn't even talk to me. She was Catholic and I'm sure that she confessed to her priest.

My dad decided that the family should move to our summer cabin in the Catskills, even though winter was coming on. He closed his accounting business and that's the last we ever saw of Rhode Island.

I don't know what happened to Annie, but I still dream about her.

AMERICA STILL STANDING

Describing the Fire is a difficult task because metaphors and words fail. It was so awful, such a large loss of life, that the historian often retreats into bland statistics and overreaching generalizations. It is impossible to describe a billion individual tragedies.

Perhaps this inability is related to the well-known psychological truth that people rally to help individuals but not large groups. In a famous experiment, subjects were shown a picture of a starving child and asked how much money they would give to help that child. When shown a picture of two starving children, the amount of money offered went down. When shown a picture of many starving children, the amount of money declined even further. We can empathize with the individual, but when there are many people, it seems like an intractable problem and our empathy is muted.[17]

When we think about the Fire, individual stories touch us, as evidenced by the regular best-selling books over the years—biographies and autobiographies of the people who lived through the Fire. Larger treatments of the Fire, like this book, receive less consideration. Yet statistics can tell their own truths, unburdened by the individualistic nature of anecdotes, so here are the totals.

Only about 10 percent of the nuclear weapons that the Soviets dispatched by bomber, ballistic missile, or submarine reached their targets, so a total of thirty-nine nuclear weapons hit the continental United States. Four failed to properly detonate, and six hit targets that had already been hit: Washington, D.C.; New York, New York; San Francisco, California; Omaha, Nebraska; New London, Connecticut; and Charleston, South Carolina. Twenty-nine targets were hit in the lower forty-eight states:

Amarillo AFB, Amarillo, Texas

Baltimore, Maryland

Barksdale AFB, Shreveport, Louisiana

Beale AFB, Marysville, California

Boston, Massachusetts

Charleston, South Carolina

Chicago, Illinois

Detroit, Michigan

F. E. Warren AFB, Cheyenne, Wyoming

Grand Forks AFB, Grand Forks,
   North Dakota

Loring AFB, Limestone, Maine

Newport, Rhode Island

MacDill AFB, Tampa, Florida

McConnell AFB, Wichita, Kansas

Minot AFB, Minot, North Dakota

New London, Connecticut

New Orleans, Louisiana

New York, New York

Oak Ridge, Tennessee

Offutt AFB, Omaha, Nebraska

Philadelphia, Pennsylvania

Plattsburgh AFB, Plattsburgh,
   New York

San Diego, California

San Francisco, California

Seattle, Washington

Thiokol missile plant, Promontory,
   Utah

Titan Missile Complex 1-B, east of
   Denver, Colorado

Washington, D.C.

Wurtsmith AFB, Oscoda,
   Michigan

Some of the targets were remote, and the list does not represent what the Soviets considered the twenty-nine most important targets, only those that were successfully struck. The six most populous cities in the United States were hit. Americans also died outside the continental United States. The Air Force bases at Elmendorf and Eielson in Alaska were close enough to Siberia to be hit by MRBMs. Elmendorf was only two miles from downtown Anchorage. And, of course, Pearl Harbor and Guam were attacked by Soviet submarines. We are fortunate that neither nation targeted nuclear power plants with groundbursts, which would have vastly increased the intensity of the resulting fallout.

The two SS-4 MRBMs that survived in Cuba were never used. The ground crews had strict instructions to launch only on direct orders from the Kremlin, and those orders never came. The local commander could have taken the initiative, since he was listening to American radio and realized that a war had taken place, but it was obvious to him that the Soviets had lost and he did not want to condemn his soldiers to being treated as war criminals when the Americans eventually found them. Six months after the Fire, soldiers from Venezuela discovered the missiles. They removed the nuclear warheads, blew up the missiles, and repatriated the Soviet men who wanted to return home. About half chose to stay in Cuba when they realized that none of their family members had likely survived the American attack.

Julie Wright of Brigham Young University has calculated the immediate number of American dead with a high degree of accuracy, publishing her findings in 1992. After exhaustive research in census records, archives of the Fire, and National Recovery Commission records, Wright found that 19.7 million Americans died the first day. Another 11.8 million died in the following two months. She calculated excess mortality in the following two years, as compared to projected morality if the Fire had not occurred, to be 4.6 million.

As of July 1, 1962, the U.S. Census Bureau estimated the American population at 186,537,737. According to Wright, 31.5 million Americans died within two years (an interval that accounts for the immediate dead and deaths from radiation or injuries), or 16.4 percent of the population. An emergency census in 1965 showed that the U.S. population had declined from 186.5 million in 1960 to 158.6 million, showing that three million babies were born in just three years.

FIRE ON THE SOVIET UNION

History abounds in irony, and we have seen numerous cases of that in this tragic tale. The day the Soviet Union died, Wednesday, November 7, was also the forty-fifth anniversary of the end of 1917 Bolshevik Revolution. The experiment of Lenin, Stalin, and Khrushchev had not lasted even a half century but had already killed tens of millions, and tens of millions more Soviets would shortly die.

Precisely at midnight, only twenty-five minutes after the first nuclear weapon had exploded over Washington, D.C., the vice president gave the order to raise the military alert to DEFCON 1 and to retaliate. Secure in Mount Weather and assuming that he was now the commander in chief—though he did not take the oath of office until 10:00 the next morning—Johnson gave the SAC carte blanche to run SIOP-63. Kennedy's statements and actions from the previous days indicate that he would have wanted to slowly implement elements of the SIOP on his own authority. Johnson was aware of Kennedy's concerns about the plan's inflexibility, but he had not spent the hours thinking about it that Kennedy had spent. For Johnson, suddenly asked to make a decision, the obvious step was to let the military follow its own plans, rather than impose his will on a situation that he was not prepared to understand. So SIOP-63 went forward, striking back not only at the Soviet Union but at all Communist nations, even those not involved in any way with the current crisis.

A five-megaton Soviet SS-6 warhead had hit Offutt Air Force Base in Omaha and destroyed the ground headquarters of the Strategic Air Command. With the Pentagon also destroyed, Generals Power and LeMay were now dead. Command of SAC passed to Looking Glass, an airborne command post that flew random patterns across the Midwest. Five different Boeing EC-135C airplanes, filled with communications gear and a crew of nineteen, rotated the position so that one was airborne at all times. The brigadier general aboard had the authority to conduct a nuclear war if he could not contact any higher leadership. In this case, Johnson authorized Looking Glass to proceed. There were not a lot of decisions to be made if one just gave the "execute order" for SIOP-63.

Every important event in history seems to attract conspiracy theorists, like flies drawn to honey. The keys to a successful conspiracy theory are a perverse ignorance of the facts and ignorance of how human affairs actually unfold. A popular conspiracy theory holds that the United States attacked the Soviet Union with its nuclear weapons first, not the other way around, and that is why the Soviet people suffered so much more than the American people. This idea ignores the copious historical documentation that we have, albeit mostly from the American side, as more Soviet evidence was destroyed by the Fire. A sober analysis of American and Soviet strategic abilities before the Fire shows that if the United States had launched a surprise first strike that almost all Soviet weapons would have been destroyed before the Soviets could have used them. Not only would America have been spared more than a few hits, Europe would not have suffered the consequences of being in the middle of the nuclear cross fire. The facts of the case disprove the conspiracy theory, but that will not stop people continuing to support the theory, because analysis of the facts is not the basis of their beliefs. They believe because they want to, so they will invent new supposed facts and will accuse naysayers like myself of being part of the conspiracy because we disagree with them. There is nothing like a conspiracy theorist to make a professional historian chew on the edge of his or her desk like a beaver driven mad.

The Americans dispatched 1,450 Air Force and Navy bombers against the Soviet Union. Most of them were on alert in the air or on the ground at dispersed airfields on fifteen-minute alert. As soon as Washington, D.C., was hit, the message went out, and the bombers took off from air bases all over the United States, as well as from SAC bases in Okinawa, Guam, Morocco, Spain, and England. Standard procedure was always to get the bombers immediately into the air and then to issue instructions; otherwise, they would be caught on the ground by Soviet nuclear warheads. About two hundred bombers failed to take off because they had been destroyed on the ground by Soviet strategic missiles within minutes of the attack on Washington. Still, the surviving bomber force included 540 B-52 bombers, 790 B-47 bombers, and 72 B-58 bombers. Each B-52 could carry up to four nuclear bombs, while each B-47 carried two bombs, and each B-58 carried only one. Some of the B-52s carried two Hound Dog cruise missiles, armed with one-megaton Mk-28 nuclear warheads, which could fly 750 miles, instead of four bombs. Forty-eight Navy fighter-bombers, each carrying a single bomb, were also dispatched from aircraft carriers in the Mediterranean or air bases in Italy.

Even before the American bombers reached Soviet airspace, the Soviet Union had been devastated by ballistic missiles. The United States launched 132 Atlas ICBMs and 40 Titan ICBMs. Soviet missile strikes had either destroyed or prevented the launch of ten Atlas missiles and twenty-one Titan missiles. Three submarines contributed their Poseidon missiles, sixteen each, as well as six Regulus cruise missiles. Only twenty-one of the sixty Thor IRBMs in Britain were launched; the rest had been destroyed by Soviet missiles in the surprise attack. Only four of the thirty Jupiter IRBMs in Italy were launched; again, the rest of the missiles had been destroyed on the ground by the Soviets first. Ironically, considering their role in provoking the crisis, the missiles from Turkey were apparently not used. They were probably not used because Soviet weapons destroyed them first.

A total of 251 ballistic or cruise missiles hit targets, concentrated on command and control centers, bomber bases, missile launch sites, and naval facilities. The targets had been preprogrammed into the missiles, so many of the nuclear warheads exploded over these sites after the Soviet missiles, bombers, or submarines stationed there had departed for the United States. In that sense the Soviet Union had executed a perfect first strike; it did not lose any of its strategic forces (except for the large numbers of submarines that failed to go to sea due to lack of preparation) before use.

From the point of view of the bomber crews flying toward the Soviet Union, the most important targets for the missiles were Soviet command and control facilities. The destruction of these targets impeded the Soviets' ability to coordinate their air defenses. The Soviets had devoted an estimated ten thousand fighters, including MiG-17, MiG-19, MiG-21, Su-9, and Yak-25 models, to protect their homeland. They had also constructed between five hundred and six hundred SA-2 sites, clustered around cities, high-value military targets, and expected routes into the country. With their command and control in tatters, these fighters and antiaircraft missile sites fought as small groups, not as a coordinated whole.

Based on information obtained by spies, possibly from Oleg Penkovksy, the Americans had located the Soviet equivalents to Mount Weather and Site R. Underground bunkers in Sharapovo and Chekhov, located next to each other thirty-five miles south of Moscow, provided a safe location for the political and military leadership. Khrushchev and the Presidium presumably followed the standard plan and retreated to these bunkers after giving the order to start the war from the Kremlin. Both sites were hit by a one-megaton airburst followed by a one-megaton groundburst, the only deliberate groundburst by the Americans in the attack. We assume that Khrushchev and other members of the Presidium died in the blasts, since we can find no traces of them after the Fire.

American bombers followed tactics that dictated a penetration phase and a delivery phase. During the first phase, nuclear weapons struck peripheral defenses such as radar installations, command centers, and fighter bases, so that later bombers could penetrate deeper into the Soviet Union. The "bomb-as-you-go" principle dictated the bomber crews' actions. If another aircraft had already struck the first target on the crew's list, the pilot would fly deeper and find the second, or third, or even fourth target. If necessary, the aircraft maneuvered down to the nap of the earth, flying as low as possible in an attempt to avoid antiaircraft missiles.

A BOMBER AGAINST THE SOVIET UNION

Bundled up against the bitter cold of the winter of 1944–45, James Fleming first flew as a side gunner on a B-17 in raids over Germany. He claimed one Messerschmitt with his M2 Browning .50-caliber machine gun, and the Army Air Corps agreed that he had taken down that airplane. Fleming had watched the fighter spiral to the ground, a dwindling speck twenty thousand feet below. No parachute blossomed. He had killed a fellow human being.

He had been exhilarated about the kill but felt bad that a knight of the air had fallen. Of course, the German had been trying to kill him and may have even already killed other bomber aircrews, maybe even friends of Fleming's. Friends like Roger from Logan, Utah, or Bob from Dallas. Good friends who had the odds go against them.

Fleming rarely thought of the people below who died from the bombs that his B-17 dropped on his sixteen missions. In his journal, Fleming confessed his confusion that the people on the ground did not seem real to him.

After the war ended, Fleming became a civilian long enough to use the GI Bill to go college at Virginia Tech. He got the quickest degree that he could find. Literature appealed to him, since he liked to read, though the books that his professors preferred were "a real chore." He managed to graduate and went back into the new U.S. Air Force, the successor to the Army Air Corps. He wanted to fly and he wanted to be a pilot. He enrolled in officer candidate school, then flight school. He flew bombers, of course, the battleships of the sky.

At first he flew B-29 Superfortresses, the same kind of plane that had ended the war with Japan. In the 1950s he flew the Convair B-36 Peacemaker, a massive beast with propellers at the rear of its six engines, the last of the propeller-driven bombers.* Fleming studied maps of the Soviet Union, memorized antiaircraft sites, learned to avoid antiaircraft missiles, and waited for the day that his nation would call on him.

Of course, the age of the propeller was over, and the last of the B-36 aircraft was retired in 1959. Fleming retrained in the B-52 Stratofortress, an airplane that was a real workhorse and promised to be around for a long time. Each B-52 could carry up to thirty tons of conventional bombs, though its complement of nuclear bombs did not weigh that much. The Strategic Air Command trained relentlessly, and Fleming eagerly participated, always striving to have his own aircrew be considered a "select" crew, the top of the elite.[18] In October 1962 Fleming had just been promoted to lieutenant colonel, in command of one of the squadrons of the 4157th Strategic Wing located at Eielson Air Force Base near Fairbanks, Alaska—right there on the front line.

When the Strategic Air Command went to DEFCON 2 on October 27, the aircrews of Fleming's squadron stepped up their activities. For ten days, a third of his aircraft remained in the air, relying on aerial refueling to fly chrome-dome

---

* The Convair B-36 was so large that the Air Force eventually added two small jets to each wing to help during takeoffs and to increase speed during bombing approaches.

missions that sometimes lasted twenty-four hours. Another third was on fifteen-minute alert, with the crews sleeping in buildings near the flight line, and the final third was on one-hour alert. These men were not allowed to return to their families, even though most of the families lived on base.

Fleming was in his B-52 Stratofortress, on his way home after twenty-three hours in the air, when he received a radio signal that the alert had been raised to DEFCON 1. Following standard operating procedure, Fleming pulled his darkened visor down over his eyes. His copilot would fly the plane; his eyes were adjusted to the dim lights in the cockpit. Outside, the Arctic night was lit with the sharp points of stars and the shimmering curtains of the Northern Lights.

While the radioman requested confirmation, Fleming asked one of the two navigators to figure out the location of the nearest airborne refueling tanker. They still had a third of their tanks full of jet fuel, but protocol required topping off as soon as possible. The tanker was four hundred miles to the south and flying a circular pattern, a gas station in the sky.

Fleming checked the chatter on the squadron frequency. He heard the pilots on fifteen-minute alert request permission to take off; he heard other pilots already flying on alert calling into local towers, requesting the location of refueling tankers. He felt proud of this well-drilled team, each member transitioning to his role, ready for war. The hours ahead promised to be grueling, especially for his own crew, which had already been in the air for so long.

A bright light in front of them lit the cockpit, and the copilot cried out. By his own account, a part of Fleming died in that blast of light. He knew that Eielson had just been nuked, and that meant that all that mattered to him was dead. His family lived on the base, as did his copilot's family, and the family of one of the navigators; the girlfriends of the others lived in town. Fleming's hands shook on the controls, and he found temporary solace by focusing only on the mission.

His copilot was blind. The flash from the warhead, on an SS-5 IRBM from Siberia, burned into his retinas, and he proved not to be useful for the rest of the mission. Fleming flew south, refueled, and broke the seal on his mission instructions. As a squadron commander he was supposed to coordinate his bombers' run into the Soviet Union, but either the nuclear weapon over Eielson had flooded the radio spectrum with noise or his radio equipment had been damaged by the EMP. Eventually Fleming ordered everyone to head for their targets on the assumption that they might be able to hear him.

The bombers in Alaska would reach the Soviet Union first, so they were assigned to open the way for those coming in later from the lower states; thus, Fleming carried two Hound Dog cruise missiles. He headed out over the North Pole, flying three thousand miles to the coast north of Moscow. By then he had been airborne for almost thirty hours and was constantly blinking in order to focus on the instruments. The mission profile called for him to move closer to the ice pack below, flying on the deck to avoid radar detection. He knew that he was in no condition for that kind of detailed flying, so he remained at fifteen thousand feet.

Out over the ice pack he picked up radio chatter. He asked the navigators to monitor the traffic for him, since mustering the concentration to parse out the call letters and technical jargon was too hard for him right then. It comforted him to know that the sky was full of bombers going in to take revenge on the Soviet bastards.

The initial plan had been to enter the Soviet Union in the dark, but in the event, the bombers took off at night and arrived in the Soviet Union during the day. As they approached the Soviet coast, the electronic warfare officer announced that Soviet radars had painted them. The crew members sipped the last of their coffee and waited nervously. When an airborne radar mounted on a Soviet fighter scanned them, the gunner went into action. The bomber was equipped with a single 20 mm Vulcan cannon in a tail turret, which the gunner controlled remotely. Fleming felt a faint vibration in the controls as the cannon burped out hundreds of shells in quick succession at the pursuing fighter. He ordered chaff, canisters filled with reflective strips of tinfoil, to be deployed. The radar screens of nearby aircraft filled with noise. Fleming could not remember later if the gunner claimed a kill, only that the bomber survived.

As Fleming's bomber approached the coast and before it reached any SAM sites, it launched each Hound Dog. The five-ton cruise missiles with one-megaton warheads dropped away, then lit their turbojets, obeying their programming to fly at Mach 2 toward their targets.

Afterward, Fleming could not remember exactly what the targets were, certainly either an airfield, an air defense command and control center, or a SAM nest. The navigator announced over the airwaves that the mission had gone well so far. Any other bombers with the same shallow first targets could switch to alternate targets. A proper bombing campaign would have included time to make sure that the targets were destroyed before it moved to the next phase, but this campaign was compressed into hours. The crew members had to assume that the Hound Dogs would work. If deeper-penetrating bombers found that the targets were still active, they would have clearance to hit them instead of flying deeper into the Soviet Union.

Fleming turned the bomber around and headed north. Having no desire to practice the survival and evasion techniques that all SAC crew suffered through in the Nevada wilderness, he wanted to make it back to friendly soil. Returning to the home base was not an option, so five hours later Fleming landed at the airport in Yellowknife in northern Canada. The destination had not been approved, but the lieutenant colonel did not care by then; he wanted only to close his eyes.

And James Fleming, the sole survivor of his family, slept.

THE SOVIET UNION DIES

Studies by the Pentagon created mathematical yardsticks for the effects of nuclear war on the enemy. For instance, if a seventh of the Soviet Union's population was killed and half of its industry destroyed in an attack, then "assured destruction" had taken place, meaning the Soviet Union would no longer be a threat to the United States. For comparison, during World War II, the Soviet Union had suffered the loss of about 14 percent of its population and maybe a third of its industry. The Pentagon estimated that four hundred one-megaton nuclear weapons would kill 30 percent of the Soviet population and destroy 76 percent of industry, clearly achieving assured destruction. Doubling the number of bombs to eight hundred would kill only another 9 percent of the population and would destroy a paltry 1 percent more of the industry. Thus, using four hundred weapons hit the sweet spot, but many more were used.[19]

The Soviet Union and Eastern Europe were hit with about a third of the nuclear weapons that the United States deployed. The accepted count among historians is 2,019, though a reliable analysis by the Israeli scholar Mordechai Dov puts the number at 2,041. Six British bombs were also used on East Germany and Poland. The passive and active electronic countermeasures were unusually effective in allowing American bombers to get through.

American nuclear bombs hit more than three hundred airfields, an indication of the inflexibility of the SIOP-63. The Soviet bombers that might have been using these airfields were long gone. The Pentagon listed 134 major cities in the Soviet Union. Of these, 132 were hit by nuclear weapons; only Tula and Tashkent were not destroyed. In 1962 the Soviet population was 218 million, according to the best statistics that we have. Rough estimates placed the Soviet population at 92 million people one year later. After five years, the disruption of the food supply, collapse of transportation infrastructure, and spread of disease had dropped the population in the former Soviet Union to 74 million people. Almost two-thirds of the Russians and their subject peoples had died—and survivors were found in odd places.

A MAN IN THE GULAG

In the last year of Stalin's life, a bookish young man with glasses was arrested in Rostov. We do not know exactly what Aleksandr Kobieleva did to attract the attention of the authorities; he was charged with hooliganism and anti-Soviet activities. Those phrases covered such a variety of crimes, mostly political in nature, that the young man must have considered himself fortunate to be sentenced to a labor camp instead of executed. He was sent to a camp in the foothills of the Altay Mountains in southwestern Siberia, where he lived in a barracks made of rough lumber and labored from dawn to dusk, cutting down trees with a two-handed saw, working in tandem with another prisoner. The logs were then hauled to a sawmill that the prisoners also operated.

Aleksandr learned to hate the guards and the sadistic pleasure that they took in tormenting the prisoners. He realized that the guards hated the cold winters and the mosquitoes of summer just as much as the prisoners did, though they ate much better and had warm quarters. Aleksandr learned to survive, eating whatever food they gave him, no matter how stale the bread or how fetid the soup. One of the other prisoners pointed out some edible lichens and mushrooms in the forest, and Aleksandr eagerly ate them, keeping up his strength in his slight frame. He supposed that he should consider himself lucky that he had not been sent to a coal mine or a gold mine. Those camps were effective death sentences.

On the day of Stalin's death, work was cancelled so that the guards and prisoners could mourn. Men cried, even though they had hated the Georgian; even Aleksandr cried. He had never known any other ruler, and the future frightened him.

Three years later a commission of Communist officials came through the camp. The officials had been sent by Khrushchev to release those wrongfully imprisoned. Three-fourths of the men were freed in the next couple of months but not Aleksandr. Conditions improved marginally, apparently because the bureaucracy, confused over how many prisoners were actually left, kept sending more than the minimum rations.

Aleksandr missed books. Occasionally, when he could get his hands on a newspaper, he would devour its words over and over until he had memorized them. He knew that the articles were full of lies, but he held out hope that he had memorized some bit of truth.

In 1962 Aleksandr turned twenty-eight. He had been in the camp for ten years. The prisoners knew nothing about the Cuban Missile Crisis; their first indication of the Fire came at about noon on November 7, when a flash of light distracted them. They laid down their saws. From their vantage point the prisoners could see a mushroom cloud rising into the sky far west of camp, perhaps over the city of Biysk, which was forty miles away. The guards ushered everyone back to the camp and into the barracks.

The prisoners talked among themselves. The war of atomic bombs must have come. One of the men had lived in Biysk as a child and told the others about the numerous arms factories built in the city during the Great Patriotic War. In the afternoon they saw another flash. Listening to the guards' excited conversations, they heard the rumors that the entire country was being hit. Apparently there were some intermittent Soviet radio broadcasts.

It rained that night, a black misery that froze to the ground. Most of the guards fled the camp after that, but a few remained, huddling in one of their barracks, as if safety came from being together. The guard towers, gates, and patrols along the fences had been abandoned. Some of the prisoners took the opportunity to flee, but Aleksandr joined a group with a more direct plan. The men drained gasoline from a car and splashed it on the outside of the guards' barracks. The sadistic bastards who had made the prisoners so miserable had no idea what was happening until the fires of hell engulfed them.

The next morning the vomiting began. The men were sick with radiation poisoning and wanted to do nothing more than wrap themselves up in blankets as the fever shook them. Only diarrhea drove them from their bunks, though they often lacked the strength to even move, so they soiled themselves. The stench only added to their nausea.

For some reason, the radiation had a relatively minimal effect on Aleksandr. He vomited and voided his bowels, but he had enough strength to break into the supply building. He found a kerosene heater that also powered a small lamp and even generated a small supply of electricity. He plugged a radio into it but heard nothing for weeks. His hair fell out and he felt miserable for a couple of months, but he eventually recovered his strength.

Winter had descended, and Alexsandr was the only man left in the camp. With plentiful kerosene and tins of food meant for the guards, he lived better than he had for ten years. He even found a shelf full of books in the camp commandant's house. Half of them were on Marxist theory, but the rest were classics of Russian literature that even the Communists found acceptable. He read the classics over and over again.

During the winter, while the corpses of the other prisoners were still stiff, he dragged them all into one of the barracks. He piled dry wood inside with the bodies, added kerosene, and then set his makeshift funeral pyre on fire. It burned for most of a day.

When spring came he ransacked the rest of the camp, collecting as many rubles as he could find in the belongings that had been abandoned in the two guard barracks still standing. Then he left the camp and walked out of the forest, ready to rejoin the human race. He soon found that the money was useless. The survivors of the Fire used barter only.

Twenty-two years later a graduate student collecting oral histories for a UN survey team met Aleksandr Kobieleva. He was fifty-one years old, worked his own subsistence farm, and had a wife and four children. He had taught them all to read, a skill that was not common among the newer generation in their region of Siberia. The student reported that Aleksandr moved like an old man and looked prematurely aged. He agreed to let the team draw blood and take genetic samples from him as part of a worldwide effort to see why some people survived the radiation when others did not. He was compensated with a box of books in Russian, which were flown in on the next UN supply flight. Aleksandr Kobieleva wept when he received this gift.

FIRE ON EUROPE

U.S. and Soviet allies also suffered in the Fire. Western and Eastern Europe were caught in the cross fire, and what the Soviets lacked in weapons that could reach the United States, they made up for with those that could hit NATO countries. Europe was destroyed in the same manner as the Soviet Union and on a similar scale.

Soviet IRBMs, MRBMs, and bombers hit Western Europe 154 times. Sixteen targets were hit more than once. Every major city and military installation in NATO were hit, with the exception of Berlin. Both sides avoided hitting the city, perhaps because it was divided and any nuclear weapon would have unavoidably caused casualties in the friendly part of the city as well. Neutral countries were not targeted, but still fallout had ruinous effects in Sweden, Austria, Switzerland, and Spain. One nuclear explosion did occur in southern Sweden, near Varberg on the southwestern coast. The obvious conclusion is that this missile ran off course.

The Soviets used airbursts, especially in Europe, because they recognized that the jet stream and prevailing west–east winds would carry fallout from their weapons falling on Germany, France, the United Kingdom, and other NATO members toward their allies and the motherland. There were nine groundbursts, however. We cannot be certain which of these nine were intentional, though most probably were not. Equipment failed, simply enough. The groundbursts included Holy Loch in Scotland, where the Americans based some of their Polaris submarines; Liverpool in England; Paris and Lyons in France; Dortmund, Cologne, and Bonn in Germany; Antwerp in Belgium; and Bergen in Norway. Some 122 million people died immediately in Western Europe, and another 70 million died the following year from injuries sustained during the initial explosions, starvation, and fallout. The total population of Western Europe (including neutral nations) in 1960 was 342.2 million people. In 1970 a UN survey could document only 140 million people.*

U.S. Army and Air Force units used tactical nuclear weapons on Soviet and Warsaw Pact forces, destroying army camps, airfields, and naval bases. Because they wanted their attack to be a surprise, the Soviets had not moved any of their forces and issued deployment orders only after Washington, D.C., was hit. There is no indication that any of the Soviet allies in the Warsaw Pact had any idea that Khrushchev had opted for nuclear war.

---

* The original 1960 population of each Western European nation was as follows: Germany, 72.5 million; United Kingdom, 52.4 million; Italy, 50.2 million; France, 46.6 million; Spain, 30.6 million; Turkey 28.2 million; Netherlands, 11.5 million; Belgium, 9.1 million; Greece, 8.3 million; Sweden, 7.5 million; Austria, 7 million; Switzerland, 5.4 million; Denmark, 4.6 million; Finland, 4.4 million; Norway, 3.6 million; and Luxembourg, 313,000.

The Americans had cooperated with the British in developing nuclear weapons, and by the time of the Fire, the British had a force of Vulcan bombers that carried hydrogen bombs. The Americans and British were also jointly developing a standoff cruise missile, called the Skybolt, for their bombers to succeed the Hound Dog cruise missiles that the Americans used. The destruction of the British arsenal—both their bombers and nuclear storage depots—was so complete that several scholars have convincingly argued that the Soviets must have had spies who revealed exactly where to hit.*

Many military analysts had expected that a general nuclear war would include conventional fighting, among the mushroom clouds and smoking ruins, after the bombs had been released. Surprisingly little fighting occurred. The destruction of so much Soviet and Warsaw Pact military power by the American tactical nuclear weapons caused a near-complete disintegration of those armies. Soviet strategic and tactical nuclear weapons devastated American and NATO military forces, though the NATO remnants maintained better cohesion than the Soviets' did (perhaps because Americans were invited guests in their allied nations and the Soviets were not). It seemed that troops on both sides just wanted to return home to see if their families and friends had survived.

The winter of 1962 was harsh, with little help arriving from outside Europe and the transportation infrastructure in ruins. We will never be able to accurately count how many people starved or froze to death. The following summer was also difficult, as people struggled to learn to farm in fallout-ridden soil. Modern industrialized societies had a small percentage of their population devoted to food production—typically one in ten or even one in twenty—so farming skills among the survivors were sparse. The people of Europe and Northern Asia rediscovered the foundation of existence—all else is secondary to the need to find or produce enough food to live.

FIRE ON CHINA AND JAPAN

The United States had conquered the island of Okinawa during World War II, after a brutal battle in which over two hundred thousand people, many of them civilians, died. Even after peace with Japan, the Americans retained control of

---

* The French had developed atomic (fission) bombs but not hydrogen (fusion) bombs. They were still developing the Mirage IV bomber to carry their nuclear bombs and had not yet developed any ballistic missiles, so they posed no threat to the Soviets.

the island as a trusteeship and maintained a large military presence, including an entire Marine division, there. The airfields on the island were expected to refuel and rearm bombers during a nuclear war, so a stockpile of hundreds of nuclear weapons were kept in bunkers there. The pilots wryly called these second missions "yo-yo" missions, though the initial strike of the Fire was so effective that only three second missions were flown out of Okinawa and a total of six others were flown from other locations. Only West Germany and perhaps Britain had more American nuclear weapons stored on their soil than were in Okinawa. The island also hosted TM-76 Mace cruise missiles, armed with W-28 thermonuclear warheads with a yield of 1.1 megatons and a range of fifteen hundred miles.

The Soviets hit Okinawa with a pair of three-megaton warheads on the first day, and a cruise missile hit Guam five days after the Fire started. The Soviets hit Japan with twenty-four MRBM missiles and forty-one bombs delivered by aircraft, mainly because the island nation was a close American ally and near enough to the Soviet Union that it could be severely damaged. Only seventeen years after the devastation of the American strategic bombing campaign, including the atomic bombs on Hiroshima and Nagasaki, the Japanese people suffered an even more devastating blow. Their population of 94.1 million in 1960 declined to 28 million in 1965.

The people of Seoul, South Korea, staggered under a pair of three-megaton explosions, which killed four million people outright and another three million in the following year. The war that followed between North and South Korea was a mostly anemic affair because of the thirty-five American nuclear weapons that had devastated North Korea. In the end, the South Koreans reunited their shattered country.

Just as the Soviets' standard plan for a general nuclear war included hitting American allies in addition to American targets, the American SIOP also targeted Soviet allies. American planners believed Communist China was a Soviet ally, though in reality this was no longer the case. The SIOP allocated sixty weapons for China. A third of these were cruise missiles launched from Okinawa; the remaining two-thirds of the American weapons came from Taiwan and South Korea.

Tactical bombers flying from Taiwan and South Korea contributed to the SIOP-directed attacks on China and North Korea. From 1958 to mid-1962 the United States had based nuclear-tipped Matador cruise missiles in Taiwan. After that a dozen nuclear bombs were kept on the island at Tainan Air Base with

American aircraft to carry them. Hundreds of tactical and strategic nuclear weapons were also stored in South Korea.*

When the Fire came to China, the Chinese civil war that led to the end of warlordism and to the triumph of a strong central government under the Communists had been over for only thirteen years. The Communists were still in firm control, despite the unmitigated disaster of the Great Leap Forward begun in 1958. Observers had noticed that Chairman Mao had become increasingly distant, as if his health were waning, and his productivity had certainly declined. Most foreign observers expected Mao, who was sixty-eight years old, to step aside soon. Whether Mao would have regained his energy for a final climax will never be known, since the Chinese Communist leadership was completely decapitated by four five-hundred-kiloton devices that obliterated Beijing.[20]

Completely divorced from Soviet decision making, the Chinese leadership was apparently unaware of the Fire until the mushroom clouds began to appear over their own nation. Chairman Mao had once said that there were so many Chinese people that a nuclear war would not matter;[21] he did not live to see that belief tested. Our best estimate is that eighteen American missiles or cruise missiles hit China, along with thirty-six nuclear bombs.

Historically Chinese leadership has alternated between a strong centralized government and a weak central government with greater power invested in local rulers. The most populous nation on earth descended back into fragmented warlordism. Five years after the Fire, sixteen distinct warlords or warlord combinations had divided up the country.

Because Taiwan was out of range of their MRBM missiles, the Soviets fired only a single SS-5 IRBM from a base near Vladivostok at the Taiwanese capital of Taipei. The missile overshot by five miles, and though the blast caused widespread damage, the city remained functional and the national leadership survived. The seventy-five-year-old Chiang Kai-shek led his armies back across the Taiwan Strait. The old man symbolically stepped ashore from a landing craft (acquired from the United States during the 1950s) onto an undefended part of the Chinese coast. The Nationalists managed to create a large beachhead and

---

* No nuclear weapons were stored in Japan—a result of what the Americans called Japan's "nuclear allergy"—though nuclear weapons did transit through Japanese ports and airports. Also, no nuclear weapons were stored in Greenland, a Danish possession, or in Iceland. See Robert S. Norris and William M. Arkin, "Where They Were," *Bulletin of Atomic Scientists* 55, no. 6 (November–December 1999): 26–35.

conquered most of the Fujian Province, but they were unable to move deeper into the country against the new warlords. Once again Chiang Kai-shek was only one warlord in a country of many, yet this time he did not have a legitimate claim to central power, other than his own claims, which fell on deaf ears.

■

The Middle East, Africa, India, South America, and Central America (except Cuba) escaped the immediate effects of the Fire. World population in 1962 stood between 3.1 and 3.2 billion. World population after the Fire dropped to 2.6 billion. At least 500 million people had died in the onslaught. Approximately 100 million people were also permanently blind from retinal burns.

Further sources: Lynn Eden, *Whole World on Fire: Organizations, Knowledge, and Nuclear Weapons Devastation* (Ithaca, NY: Cornell University Press, 2004); Alain C. Enthoven and K. Wayne Smith, *How Much Is Enough? Shaping the Defense Program, 1961–1969* (New York: Harper & Row, 1971); Ted Gup, "The Doomsday Blueprints," *Time*, August 10, 1992, 32–39; John Hersey, *Hiroshima* (New York: A. A. Knopf, 1946); Institute for Strategic Studies, *The Communist Bloc and the Western Alliances: The Military Balance* (London: Institute for Strategic Studies, 1962); David F. Krugler, *This Is Only a Test: How Washington D.C. Prepared for Nuclear War* (New York: Palgrave Macmillan, 2006); Office of Current Intelligence, "The Decline of Mao Tse-Tung," Staff Study (Washington, D.C.: CIA, April 9, 1962); and Steven J. Zaloga, *Target America: The Soviet Union and the Strategic Arms Race, 1945–1964* (Novato, CA: Presidio, 1993).

9

In the Ruins: Learning to Survive

Radiation exists everywhere. It is what makes our radios and television work; it allows us to see. Ionizing radiation exists naturally in the form of cosmic rays from outer space, X-rays, and radon from the ground. Atomic explosions and fallout emit ionizing radiation in the form of alpha, beta, and gamma waves. This type of radiation can interact with our DNA and damage it. We measure radiation in rads and rems. A rad, in technical terms, is an absorbed dose equal to a hundred ergs of energy per gram of material. Scientists invented rems (radiation equivalent for man) to measure the lethality of one type of radiation versus another. For instance, alpha particles are twenty times more damaging than beta particles. In essence, rems measure biological damage.

Individuals exposed to up to two hundred rems often have either headaches or no symptoms at all. Individuals exposed to doses from two hundred to five hundred rems experience headaches, nausea, lethargy, and vomiting within four to six hours. After about a day these individuals will appear to recover. People exposed to more than three hundred rems will lose their hair, which is made up of cells more easily killed by damaged DNA, about two weeks after exposure. When given adequate medical care and rest, lasting up to three months, at least half of the individuals suffering from lower levels of radiation poisoning should live.

People who endure to between five hundred and a thousand rems experience symptoms beginning one to four hours after exposure. Nausea, vomiting, diarrhea, and fever may be difficult for medical personnel to control and present a significant risk of dehydration. After about a day, the symptoms will become latent for seven to ten days. When the symptoms return, hospital-quality medical care is required. In general, half the people exposed to five hundred rems will die from the exposure, though many more may die later of various cancers. For those exposed to over a thousand rems, death, preceded by severe vomiting, diarrhea, and prostration, is certain. There is no relief from symptoms, and no patient has lasted more than thirty days.

The best treatment after a nuclear incident is a thorough washing of the body to remove any fallout particles, which if left alone will continue to add to a person's rem load. Some medical doctors advise shaving all hair from the body to guarantee that all external fallout particles are removed. Finally, symptoms should be treated and efforts should be made to prevent opportunistic secondary infections that strike when the body is weak.[1]

Before the Fire, fears about the long-term consequences of a large nuclear war centered around radiation exposure. Medical doctors predicted that cancers would increase, a legitimate concern. Extensive studies showed that cancer rates have gone up over the past several decades. Breast cancer in women is one of the most common, and a study showed that a woman's chance of getting breast cancer increased by 1 percent for every one hundred rems of radiation she was exposed to. Since exposure to a thousand rems in a single incident is lethal, the absolute maximum increase in risk for breast cancer is only 10 percent. Other cancers, such as bone cancer or lung cancer, had their risk increased by two percent, only a fifth compared to breast cancer for women.[2]

People also feared that radiation exposure would lead to genetic defects, even mutations. In more lurid examples of 1950s science fiction films, creatures such as Godzilla were born. But, in reality, sex saved us. Sexual reproduction involves substantial mixing of genes, and that is why all people, except twins, are genetically unique. Human sexual reproduction has made our bodies accustomed to taking care of new genes. Despite the large number of post-Fire urban myths about children with four legs or strange psychic powers—tales that bewilder geneticists—humans were actually little altered by radiation exposure. Most mutations are either benign or so damaging that they cannot be accommodated by the human body. As a result of the latter, a slight increase in the long-term miscarriage rate has been observed. However, immediately after radiation exposure, temporary sterility and miscarriages were common. (The one exception to this will be explored later in the chapter.)

The long-range fallout hazards came from a confusing array of radioactive isotopes, such as carbon-14, zirconium-90, ruthenium-103, and cerium-141. The most dangerous were cesium-17 (with a half-life of 30.5 years) and strontium-90 (with a half-life of 27.7 years). These isotopes lodged in the troposphere and the stratosphere during the initial nuclear blasts. Those in the troposphere rained out within a matter of weeks; fallout particles that were carried into the stratosphere remained there for years until gravity eventually forced them back down to the ground.* In addition to the "no-go" zones, where groundbursts poisoned the earth, other regions, especially in Europe and northern Asia, had background radiation high enough to discourage people from staying there.

UNFORESEEN CONSEQUENCES

Most scientists were barely aware of the ozone layer in 1962. Discovered in 1913 by a pair of French physicists, the ozone layer is made of molecules that are formed by three oxygen atoms bonded together (O_3). It is located in the lower stratosphere, from ten to twenty-two miles above the earth's surface. British meteorologist Gordon M. B. Dobson dedicated his life to understanding the ozone layer and developed an ozone-measuring device that could be operated from the ground.

As we all know now, the ozone layer is vitally important in protecting the surface of the planet from the sun's ultraviolet radiation; we also know now how dangerous nitrogen oxide is to the ozone layer. The release of nitrogen oxide in nuclear explosions had been observed since the first atomic bomb tests but was considered one of the minor side effects when compared to the bigger effects of blast and radiation. Just fewer than 2,400 nuclear weapons were detonated during the Fire, and they released enormous amounts of nitrogen oxide that drifted into the stratosphere and reacted with the ozone molecules. The result was a 52 percent degradation of the ozone layer in the Northern Hemisphere and a 12 percent depletion in the Southern Hemisphere.[3]

Ultraviolet radiation is particularly hard on the DNA molecules within human cells that make up our genetic codes and can lead to mutations or breakdown of the DNA. After the Fire, skin cancers in humans and animals skyrock-

---

* The proportions of fission and fusion by-products in a thermonuclear explosion also dictate the severity of the fallout, with more fission by-products meaning more radioactive fallout.

eted by more than 1,000 percent, and people began to wear clothing treated with anti-UV chemicals. The additional exposure to UV rays also led to cataracts and blindness, so people quickly learned to wear sunglasses on a regular basis. Most towns or homes at or above five thousand feet in elevation in the Northern Hemisphere were abandoned.

Other cancers and immune system disorders also increased, though it is hard to determine whether this resulted from ozone layer depletion or residual fallout radiation. Animals suffered as much as humans, and plants were more difficult to grow, leading to drops in crop yields of as much as 30 percent. The five years after the Fire, before farmers adjusted their methods to accommodate changes in the soil, were marked by rampant hunger and starvation.

In the late 1970s scientists discovered that chlorofluorocarbon gases (CFCs), industrial chemicals used in aerosols and air conditioners, also degraded the ozone layer. Governments moved quickly to ban CFCs, an action often regarded as one of the finest accomplishments of the new environmental consciousness that emerged after the Fire. We certainly did not need further erosion of the ozone layer. Fortunately, the ozone layer naturally replenishes itself, though at a slow rate, and considerable progress by natural processes has been seen in the last three decades.

REBUILDING

Martial law was lifted in the United States on the one-year anniversary of the Fire. Wounded, but not fallen, the United States focused on rebuilding its economy and making a new life for the survivors. While the military still retained a large number of nuclear weapons and powerful conventional forces for a while, the country turned inward and generally avoided extensive involvement in international affairs.

When a reactionary backlash against the pre-Fire civil rights movement turned nasty in the chaotic aftermath of the nuclear war, a second civil war began a year later, and the world, worried that the New Confederacy would capture some of the Union's nuclear weapons, held its breath. Though President Johnson was from Texas, he rose to the occasion, becoming the 1960s' Abraham Lincoln and ultimately suppressing the New Confederacy after three years of harsh guerrilla warfare and terrorism. He even won reelection in 1964 during the height of the war, in spite of the fact that ten Southern states had seceded and did not participate in the national election.

Fourteen years after the Fire and ten years after the end of the civil war, the gross national product of the reintegrated United States returned to its 1962 level. Certain areas in America still remain "no-go" zones, such as the New York Exclusion Zone that includes the former city, its environs, and Long Island. The Amarillo Exclusion Zone and North Dakota Exclusion Zone also still exist. The nation's population returned to 1962 levels only in 1984, as a result of continued population growth. The population recovery was hampered by the emigration of 12 million Americans out of the nation; most of these emigrants moved to Australia, New Zealand, or South Africa. My own family, seeking new opportunities, was part of this migration.

Australia had already been undergoing a substantial immigration boom of Europeans before the Fire. The threat of Japanese invasion during World War II had made the people of the sparsely settled continent realize how vulnerable they were, and the government had encouraged European immigration in order to build up the nation's strength with a boost in population. (Of course, because of the government's long-standing racist policies, the immigration was limited to whites only.) By 1971 one out of every two Australians had been born in America or Europe.

The United Nations relocated its headquarters to Sydney, Australia, in an effort to assert its continuing relevance in a world that relied on the Southern Hemisphere rather than the damaged Northern Hemisphere. The previous composition of the Security Council no longer made much sense, as the Soviet Union, Britain, and France had effectively ceased to exist. The new permanent members of the Security Council were the United States, Australia, Brazil, Argentina, Pakistan, and India. The Arab League and Organization of African Unity also had permanent seats, with the member states of those organizations deciding among themselves how to select their ambassadors.

Europe and Asia rearranged their political boundaries, sometimes through violence but often through shocked exhaustion, as people proved unwilling to fight over old quarrels. The Soviet Union broke up into the states of Muscovy, Ukraine, Belarus, Armenia, Georgia, Azerbaijan, the Central Asian Islamic Republic, and the Siberian Federation. The Scandinavian Federation united the former nations of Sweden, Denmark, Norway, and Finland. Most of the European map remains familiar, though its countries are still struggling to rebuild economies collapsed during the Fire three decades earlier.

The United States joined Canada, Australia, New Zealand, South Africa, the fragmented remains of Britain, and other old Commonwealth states and formed a New Commonwealth, bonded together by a common language and commitment to democracy.* In 1975 the New Commonwealth successfully petitioned the United Nations to join as a permanent member of the Security Council. This created an odd situation in which both the United States and Australia had their own votes and influence on a third New Commonwealth vote in Security Council decisions.

Ten years after the Fire, the United Nations commissioned teams to evaluate the state of the former Soviet Union, Europe, and China. The United States had already conducted such a survey of its own nation, documenting every nuclear explosion and using the new science of nuclear forensics to determine how big the device had been, how high it had exploded, the local weather conditions at the time, and the location of the tear-shaped fallout window that accompanied each explosion. Nuclear forensics used historical information when it existed, as well as contemporary Geiger counter readings and ground-based evaluations of structure destruction. Sometimes the mass fires had resulted in such complete destruction that the forensic evaluation was only an estimate.

The UN teams found that nature had flourished in Europe and northern Asia, even though low levels of background radiation remained a problem. The decline of the human population and human activities had created a vacancy that animals and plants filled. Birds were less common, but bears now wandered most of Europe and the former Soviet Union, and rivers abounded with salmon, sturgeon, and other fish that had almost disappeared before the Fire. Oddly enough, new species of fungi that seemed to thrive on radioactivity appeared, and some scientists have argued that the fungi will actually consume radioactive particles, rendering them inert. Studies are ongoing.[4]

BIOLOGICAL WARFARE

In 1992 the United Nations Exploration Team for the Former Soviet Union (UNETFSU) contacted me and asked if I would accompany one of the teams to

---

* The systems of apartheid in South Africa and Rhodesia were inconsistent with the commitment of the New Commonwealth to democracy. The United States, having defeated the New Confederacy, was particularly sensitive to racist policies. In 1976 the New Commonwealth memberships of both South Africa and Rhodesia were suspended, to be restored after apartheid had been dismantled. South Africa did so in 1991, while Rhodesia's white minority still clings to power in the face of a growing guerrilla movement.

Sverdlovsk. I jumped at the chance to see the aftermath of the Fire, even thirty years later. We flew into an airfield maintained by the UN World Food Programme and drove toward the remains of the city.

The first thing that strikes all new visitors to this area is how green and lush everything is. Those who live in the Southern Hemisphere assume that the Fire and UV exposure have laid waste to the land and that northern Asia is one vast desert. Even I, a scholar of the Fire who knew better, was still surprised to see how much nature had reclaimed from civilization and its discontents. We saw numerous animals, even several moose, and birds in the meadows and forests along the road.

Built in the eastern foothills of the Ural Mountains, Sverdlovsk was called Yekaterinburg before the Fire. It is perhaps best remembered as the location where Czar Nicholas II, his wife, and his children were executed and their bodies destroyed in 1918 during the Russian civil war, when White forces were approaching the city and threatening to capture the deposed monarch. Sverdlovsk became a large industrial center for the Soviets, growing even more important when industry was relocated eastward to avoid the Nazi advance during the Great Patriotic War. Sverdlovsk was also the home to the Institute of Military Technical Problems, which was part of the Ministry of Defense. At this institute, researchers developed biological warfare weapons, including anthrax, tularemia, botulinum toxin, and glanders. Some industrial-scale production of these nasty germs occurred there, as the Soviets intended to use them during a war.[5]

Research into chemical and biological warfare became a common interest of the great powers after the introduction of chemical warfare during World War I. Although international treaties banned both types of warfare, research continued, and both chemical and biological agents were occasionally used. The Nazis experimented with chemical and biological agents on prisoners in concentration camps. The Japanese army's covert Unit 731 in Manchuria experimented on prisoners of war, including Americans, and used their weapons on unsuspecting Chinese soldiers and civilians. Even before World War II, the Soviets set up research stations in remote locations of the Soviet Union and conducted many weapons tests on Vozrozhdeniye Island in the middle of the Aral Sea. The United States conducted its own tests, mainly in the Utah desert, and Britain completely contaminated an island off Scotland during World War II with anthrax spores.

One report asserts that the Soviets released tularemia, also called rabbit fever, in Ukraine early in 1942 by means of infected rats and aerial spraying. The disease successfully delayed the German summer offensive, and the late start ultimately led to the German defeat at Stalingrad. Some Soviet troops were also infected, showing how difficult it is to control biological warfare so that it will hurt only the enemy. The Soviets are also reported to have used Q fever in 1943 against German soldiers in the Crimea.[6]

The Soviets' effort in this area received a boost when they invaded Manchuria at the end of World War II and captured records from Unit 731 and some of the Japanese scientists and technicians. In order to exploit the information gained from the Japanese, the research institute was created in Sverdlovsk.[7] In 1956 General Zhukov expressed his belief that a modern war would include the use of biological weapons in addition to nuclear weapons. The ears of Western intelligence analysts perked up at this, since the mere reference implied that the Soviets had both kinds of weapons ready. In 1960 a smallpox outbreak led the Soviets to inoculate 6.6 million people against the disease, and some suspect that the outbreak came from a biological weapons accident.[8]

In the preliminary planning for a possible American invasion of Cuba, an idea called the Marshall Plan (a tongue-in-cheek reference to the original Marshall Plan for the economic recovery of postwar Western Europe) was proposed. The idea was to drop biological agents on Cuba that would make the civilians and soldiers too sick to fight. The plan was never implemented, and there is no evidence that President Kennedy or his top advisers were ever even told of the idea.[9]

Now a UN team was in Sverdlovsk to learn more about biological weapons, having finally received permission from the Siberian Federation to visit. During the Fire eleven nuclear weapons hit the city and surrounding areas, destroying military bases and factory complexes. Nine out of ten people in the area probably died as a direct consequence of the Fire or the deprivations of the following year. Life did not improve markedly after that, but the population had dropped enough so that the survivors could grow food sufficient to feed themselves in the short growing season with the available land.

There had always been persistent rumors of an outbreak of the Black Death after the Fire. Apparently the outbreak had initially centered around the Ural Mountains, then spread down into Central Asia. I spent all summer, along with the UN team, in Sverdlovsk trying to determine the truth of the rumors, taking blood samples from the living, and in one case exhuming the dead in a small cemetery to take samples from the rotted corpses. My skills in Russian were put to good use, reading through any documents that we could find. In line with the advice I had received before my arrival, I found it best to introduce myself as an Australian and not an American, since I have dual citizenship. For the reasons one would expect, the Siberians (as well as other peoples of the former Soviet Union and other Communist countries) hate Americans. The name "Kennedy" has the rhetorical weight of an expletive, though the name "Khrushchev" is similarly reviled.

We found antibodies to the bubonic plague in the blood samples of local people, demonstrating that they had been infected with the disease and that their immune systems had successfully fought off the enterobacteria *Yersinia pestis.* An old man who had worked at the institute had saved some papers that he thought were important. The papers provided evidence that the institute had cultured the plague and developed a stockpile. Fire had destroyed most of the institute buildings, and our explorations had found the site so thoroughly looted that it contained little of use. We can only speculate that the blast from one of the nuclear bombs cracked open some of the stockpile, which was transmitted to humans by fleas that had somehow become infected, perhaps when feasting on the dead. From there it spread, the shattered medical infrastructure offering little hindrance.*

In a small village twelve miles west of Sverdlovsk, I met my first victim of Accelerated Growth Syndrome (AGS). AGS is one of those post-Fire diseases that no one anticipated. A blond girl, who looked as though she were fifteen years old, came over to our truck and offered to sell us food. We bought some of the food—not to eat it, but to run tests on it. I spoke to the girl and learned that she was only eight years old. Further inquiries revealed that a third to a half of the people in the village were afflicted with AGS. The doctors on the UN team paid sixteen of the villagers for the privilege of taking blood samples and mouth swabs from them.

People with AGS mature faster than normal, reaching complete physical maturity by ten years of age. There is some evidence that they also die substantially earlier, though accurate mortality statistics are hard to come by. It has been only thirty-four years since the Fire, and victims of the Fire and its aftermath usually

* This interesting summer is described in my book *Seeking the Black Death* (New Iowa City, Australia: Queensland American University Press, 1994).

suffer from multiple fatal diseases. We do not know if AGS is genetically transmitted from parents to their offspring, though this seems likely. Jennie Frank, a biochemist at Stanford University, has argued that AGS has evolved as a way to accelerate natural selection so that there is a greater chance for human organisms to find radiation-resistant mutations.

Another effect of AGS is mental retardation. Apparently the brain of an individual with AGS develops too quickly, inhibiting the ability of the brain to create neural connections. The girl who sold us food was one of the brightest in the village. Others I met had IQs as low as sixty or seventy. There were rumors that the children with lower IQs were killed by their parents or village elders because they were too great a burden.[10]

NEVER AGAIN

In 1964 the U.S. government promised to destroy all its remaining nuclear weapons. In return, every other country in the world agreed to sign a treaty banning the development of nuclear weapons. A United Nations agency, the Nuclear Control Commission, was created with powers to demand inspection of any site in the world on six hours' notice. Inspectors scoured the world, always alert to any attempt to resurrect the forbidden technology. Civilian nuclear plants were dismantled, though a vocal faction in the global environmental movement argued that nuclear power plants were necessary to reduce pollution from the use of petroleum in internal-combustion engines and coal in power plants.

This successful effort at disarmament was made easier because the Cold War died with the Fire. In spite of the nuclear devastation it suffered, the United States emerged as the world's sole superpower. All other possible competitors were even more damaged.

WE ARE LUCKY

If nuclear war had to come to the human species, it is fortunate that it came when it did. I know that this is a perverse statement, considering the hundreds of millions of dead, but if the Fire had come even ten years later, all the adversaries would have had many more nuclear weapons and ballistic missiles to use. The Soviet Union and Europe would still have been virtually obliterated, but the United States would have been also.

Not only is humanity fortunate that the Fire came in 1962, but it is fortunate that it was fought with some restraint. Certainly the Soviets and Americans were *not* restrained in that they used every nuclear weapon that they could deliver, but they *were* restrained in that they used airbursts in every case except for the few when groundbursts were necessary. The three groundbursts in the United States were probably failures of internal altimeter-based triggers, since groundbursts in those cases did not make military sense. The nuclear torpedo in the Pearl Harbor channel was also a groundburst. The Americans intended only two groundbursts with their weapons, on the command bunkers in Sharapovo and Chekhov, but groundbursts also occurred in Kaliningrad on the Baltic Sea and in Shanghai. The last two were almost certainly instrument failures. Of course, airbursts were to the advantage of both the Americans and the Soviets because they maximize blast damage.

We are fortunate that the Fire occurred when it did because advances in ICBM technology had not yet made them so accurate that a counterforce strike was possible. A counterforce strike is a first strike that concentrates on hitting the enemy's strategic weapons. An effective counterforce strike would end the war in the favor of the attacker; the defender would be unable to retaliate because most of its missiles, bombers, and missile-carrying submarines would be destroyed. The basis of MAD was undermined by the idea of the counterforce strike.

The threat of a counterforce strike led to two developments. First, missile-carrying submarines could hide among the vast oceans and still provide a credible threat of MAD. This advantage could have disappeared if satellite technology had advanced as quickly as some feared, though we know now that even with great optics and sensors, satellites cannot easily find submerged submarines. Second, land-based ICBMs could be kept in hardened silos. The silos of reinforced concrete with steel lids were expensive to build, but they could protect the missile inside from anything but a direct hit or a near miss—and thus preserve the logic of MAD. The Soviets were considering building silos, and the Americans had already placed some of their Atlas ICBMs in either silos or coffins, where the missiles lay horizontally until they were prepared for launch. The Americans were also placing their new Minuteman ICBMs in silos in Montana, and these Minuteman ICBMs were only a few days away from being ready for use when the Fire came.

It was possible to destroy silos in three ways: making missiles more accurate so that they could directly hit the silos; using warheads with large yields to increase the chance of silo destruction; and using groundbursts instead of airbursts.

Silos were placed far enough apart that a single nuclear explosion could not destroy more than one. A counterforce strike of hundreds (or even thousands) of nuclear warheads exploding as groundbursts would have thrown up an enormous amount of radioactive fallout. The long-term effects of all that fallout would have been more deaths and rendered large areas of North America, Asia, and Europe uninhabitable.

Recent climate models, based on research at the Australian National University, have shown that additional groundbursts and the mass fires would have cast enough dust and ashes into the upper atmosphere to affect the amount of sunlight reaching the ground. Earth could have slipped into a sort of "nuclear winter" that would have included extended winters, shortened growing seasons, and perhaps even the onset of an ice age. In sum, the large number of groundbursts needed to attack ballistic missiles housed in silos would have had even more catastrophic results.

Of course, my gratitude may be misplaced: maybe the Cold War could have ended peacefully, without the use of nuclear weapons. Perhaps the Cuban Missile Crisis could have been resolved short of the Fire. Perhaps the lesson might have shocked some sense and humility into the leaders on both sides, so that they never approached the brink again. To assume such a scenario requires more faith in humanity than I have.

WHAT MIGHT HAVE BEEN

In the 1970s a pair of political scientists at the University of Manila, refugees from Ohio, designed a computer program to model the American decision making that led up to the Fire. While all computer programs are severely limited and subject to the assumptions of their designers, repeatedly running different scenarios through a program and even altering its assumptions can lead to interesting results. The most useful insight from this study was that a shortened crisis timeline, compressing opportunities for deliberation and decision making, usually led the United States to choose "more severe military options."[11] The two events that pushed the crisis timelime more quickly toward a climax were when the launch facilities of the SS-4 MRBMs became active or when the even more deadly SS-5 IRBMs became active. In other words, were the missile bases ready for use by the time that the Americans discovered them, or were they still being constructed?

What would have happened if that U-2 flight had flown on October 14, 1962, when it was originally scheduled, instead of seven days later? The earlier flight, following the same path (as was planned), would have found the Soviet missile bases under construction. If the United States had found the missile sites earlier, perhaps Kennedy would have remained with the blockade option and escalated the crisis more slowly, rather than turning so quickly from the blockade to air strikes and the invasion.

To us, history seems set in stone, but in fact, as history unfolded many options and many different outcomes presented themselves. Humans made choices and those choices mattered.

If that U-2 plane had flown earlier, on October 14, rather than October 21, what might have been?

Eric G. Swedin, Ph.D.
Queensland American University
New Iowa City, Australia
1996

Further sources: Ken Alibek, *Biohazard: The Chilling True Story of the Largest Covert Biological Weapons Program in the World, Told from Inside by the Man Who Ran It*, with Stephen Handelman (New York: Random House, 1999); and Michael Riordan, ed., *The Day after Midnight: The Effects of Nuclear War* (Palo Alto, CA: Cheshire Books, 1982).

AUTHOR'S AFTERWORD:
KHRUSHCHEV AND KENNEDY

The Cuban Missile Crisis has always stood in my mind as potentially the most terrifying episode in history. Nuclear war is still the greatest danger that the world faces. In October 1962 the people of the world watched while the two superpowers stared at each other and hoped that someone would blink. In reality, both sides blinked.

While I find the adoration of John F. Kennedy often undeserved—and based on his charisma rather than the actual record of his achievements—his stellar performance during the crisis makes up for his other failings and establishes his reputation for me as one of our most important presidents. One can think of other presidents in our history who would have been overly aggressive or lacked the prudence and foresight to have properly handled the crisis. While Kennedy relied on his cabinet and advisers to give him advice, in the end he guided the process and made the decisions. Kennedy thought afterward that the odds of a nuclear war during the crisis had been "somewhere between one out of three and even."[1] He made that sobering estimate while remaining ignorant of how rash the Soviets had been, especially in placing tactical nuclear weapons in Cuba.

The history related in this book through chapter 4 is true, with obvious exceptions, such as speculation about whether the Apollo program would have succeeded. From chapter 5, "The U-2 Flight That Never Happened: The Crisis Begins," through later chapters, the narrative is informed by actual plans and capabilities, but the history is fictional.

In the actual world, after the crisis began, Kennedy resisted the advice of the ExCom and the Joint Chiefs to react militarily. He chose a naval blockade, called a quarantine for legal and diplomatic reasons, and forced the Soviets to reconsider Operation Anadyr. Kennedy and his brother also engaged in back-channel negotiations with the Soviets, a process that took time. The crisis took thirteen days in all, from the first photographs of the missile sites to its resolution. The narrative in this book assumes that the leaders of the United States and the Soviet Union did not have that much time before the ballistic missile sites became active.

Kennedy and Khrushchev made a deal. The Soviets would withdraw from Cuba and promise not to place troops or strategic weapons there again, while the Americans would withdraw their ballistic missiles from Turkey within a short time and promise not to invade Cuba. The details of the arrangement were kept secret, so publicly the Soviets looked completely humiliated. The deal was easy for Kennedy to agree to because he already intended to withdraw the obsolete missiles from Turkey and had no intention of invading Cuba. The Americans kept their end of the deal, while the Soviets kept most of theirs. The Soviets did secretly station a brigade of troops in Cuba, though no nuclear weapons were included, so it really did not matter much. Another outcome of the crisis was the Limited Test Ban Treaty, signed in Moscow on August 5, 1963, which prohibited nuclear test explosions in the atmosphere, in outer space, and underwater. Three more decades passed before another treaty abolished underground nuclear testing. Not all nuclear-capable nations have signed both treaties, but the major players have.

For Kennedy, the resolution of the crisis made him a hero of history, while Khrushchev was deposed in a coup a year later on October 14, 1964. Khrushchev's protégés in the Presidium conspired against him, embarrassed by his blundering in international relations and the outcome of the Cuban Missile Crisis. The coup was not cleverly handled, and Khrushchev could have stopped it, but he seemed too tired to resist. He was forced into retirement and lived out his life in middle-class comfort in Moscow, secretly recording his memoir, until his death on September 11, 1971.

After the crisis both the Soviets and the Americans continued to build more nuclear weapons and more delivery systems. While the Soviets never surpassed the Americans in total number of weapons, they did reach parity within a decade of the Cuban Missile Crisis and by some measures surpassed the Americans in the number of warheads that could be delivered by strategic delivery systems. By that time the thousands of weapons on each side, encased in silos or hidden on submarines, were too numerous for either superpower to rationally contemplate a first strike being successful. The Soviets also built a large naval fleet, second only to America's, in order to more effectively challenge American control of the world's oceans. Only after Mikhail Gorbachev came to power did the two superpowers move beyond nuclear arms limitation treaties to seriously discussing nuclear arms reductions. After the fall of the Soviet Union, agreement came quickly, and many weapons were destroyed. Even so, both the United States and Russia still possess a total of about 21,000 nuclear weapons, with thousands still on top of missiles, ready to launch at a moment's notice. China, France, Britain, India, Pakistan, and Israel also possess nuclear weapons and shorter-range ballistic missiles.

Contemporary historians immediately understood the importance of the crisis. The publication of Robert Kennedy's *Thirteen Days: A Memoir of the Cuban Missile Crisis* in 1969, a year after his assassination, added new details about the back-channel diplomacy but failed to confirm the rumored deal to remove the Turkish missiles. Beginning in 1987 a series of conferences brought scholars and actual participants together to discuss the crisis. Eventually a conference was even held in Cuba, so that the Cuban perspective could be heard alongside the American and Soviet perspectives. At one of these conferences the Soviets revealed that they had placed tactical nuclear weapons on the island as part of Operation Anadyr. This was a complete shock to everyone; the Americans had never suspected such weapons had been placed on Cuba. Furthermore, retired general Anatoli I. Gribkov revealed that the Soviet generals had had some discretion in the use of the tactical weapons.

Once the crisis started, Khrushchev took firm steps to assert control over the use of any nuclear weapons, including keeping the nuclear warheads in multiple centralized storage locations, though they were close enough to their launch vehicles for delivery within a matter of hours. For instance, the forty warheads for the frontal cruise missile–equipped regiment near Mariel were stored at Bejucal, while the forty warheads for the other FKR regiment near Guantánamo Bay were held near Santiago de Cuba.[2] KGB officers protected the nuclear weapons, but the cryptological locks that the Soviets and Americans now employ to prevent such weapons from being used without the right codes had not yet been developed.

Only in the 1990s and even more recently have historians become aware that the four Foxtrot submarines and one Zulu submarine were sent to Cuba. Each of the Foxtrot submarines carried a single nuclear-tipped torpedo in addition to its normal complement of conventional torpedoes, while the Zulu submarine carried two nuclear torpedoes. American antisubmarine forces aggressively hunted the Foxtrot submarines and succeeded in forcing three of them to the surface. The submarine captains did not have explicit orders explaining under what circumstances to use their nuclear weapons. We now know that one of the captains actually cracked under the pressure and demanded that the nuclear-tipped torpedo be assembled and armed for use. Only resistance from the special officer assigned to the torpedo and the onboard brigade chief of staff persuaded the captain to back down and surface without attacking.[3]

With the fall of the Soviet Union in 1991, the new Russian government opened Soviet archives to historical researchers for a period of time. While not everything was revealed, Presidium minutes, memos, and diplomatic documents that did become available rewrote parts of the history of the Cold War and communism. One of the fruits of this period of openness is the best book on the Cuban Missile Crisis, which was written by a Russian historian and a Canadian historian in 1997: Aleksandr Fursenko and Timothy Naftali, *"One Hell of a Gamble": Khrushchev, Castro, and Kennedy, 1958–1964.*[*]

Other details of the crisis have come to light thanks to the declassification of relevant documents in the United States. The National Security Archive at George Washington University has been instrumental in this process, leading the charge to use the Freedom of Information Act to pry documents from the White House, Pentagon, and CIA. Kennedy secretly taped many of the ExCom meetings and other meetings, wanting to help historians write an accurate history. Only he and his brother knew of the tapes.

The tapes show Kennedy to be a prudent man, defusing tension with his ironic sense of humor, avoiding emotional extremes, and often guiding the ExCom members away from military answers to the crisis. Sometimes it is easy to say, "Let's go to war," and much harder to say, "Let's keep the peace." For too many of the civilian and military leaders, living with the threat of nuclear war had made the idea of nuclear war acceptable. Kennedy never succumbed to that intellectual temptation.

---

* Naftali is now an American citizen.

Now that we know the actual history of the Cuban Missile Crisis, we can only shudder at how close we came to a nuclear calamity. The Soviet transfer of tactical nuclear weapons to the island was pure recklessness, and it is hard to believe that the Soviet troops in Cuba would have allowed themselves to be defeated in an American invasion without using all the weapons at their disposal. Fidel Castro certainly expected his Soviet protectors to use the nuclear weapons. What was the point of bringing the weapons along if they did not use them?* We also now know that Khrushchev considered authorizing the local Soviet commander in Cuba to use the tactical nuclear weapons in the event of an invasion, even going so far as to have the order written, but this authorization was never actually given. Khrushchev was convinced instead to impose tight control on the nuclear weapons on Cuba. He ordered that no nuclear weapons of any type be used without explicit permission from Moscow. According to Fursenko, Presidium member Anastas Mikoyan was particularly influential as a voice of moderation at times when Khrushchev was inclined to agree with the hard-line approach to the crisis.[4]

Kennedy's decision making is often offered as an example of how executives should make decisions. He listened to many of the ExCom discussions, but he rarely offered his own opinions because he did not want to unduly influence the direction of the ideas or analysis. This level of self-confidence is extraordinarily rare. Most people, even experienced executives, are too focused on pushing their own point of view to actually think that they can profit by letting others do some of the thinking. Also, in the end, Kennedy remained committed to his initial instincts to defuse the crisis and avoid nuclear war.

Kennedy was no addle-brained peacenik. He had learned the folly of appeasement, both as a practical matter and a political matter, from watching his father. At the same time, Kennedy wanted to go to war only as a last resort.

The planning of the Bay of Pigs invasion by the Kennedy administration roughly parallels the planning of Operation Anadyr by Khrushchev and his aides. In both cases, the decision makers failed to think through the possible

---

* An obvious objection to my argument is that the Nazis and Allies failed to use chemical weapons during World War II, even though both sides had stockpiles of them. The argument often provided to explain this reluctance is that both sides feared retaliation. While that was true, it is even more true that chemical weapons were not very effective, especially on a mobile battlefield where soldiers had gas masks. In contrast, nuclear weapons are very effective.

consequences of their decisions. We are fortunate that the Bay of Pigs invasion happened before the Cuban Missile Crisis. The failure at the Bay of Pigs taught Kennedy the need for a more rigorous decision-making process, the need for better information, and the need to think through how the Soviets might react if certain actions were taken. Because of this, Kennedy made much better decisions.

Not everyone was pleased with how Kennedy handled the crisis. Gen. Curtis E. LeMay, who had urged an invasion of Cuba, strongly disagreed with Kennedy's ultimate decision, calling it "the greatest defeat in our history."[5] Six years later he only slightly toned down his rhetoric when he wrote *America Is in Danger*, which called for a strong military and resolute anticommunism. He despised "defense intellectuals" like Kennedy's aides and Secretary of Defense McNamara.[6] In some ways, his book is a screed against McNamara. LeMay also claimed that the Soviet Union had many more bombers than others thought and argued for an American nuclear-equipped force much larger than deterrence required. He supported the development of antiballistic missile systems, rejecting the argument that such systems undermined the logic of mutual assured destruction. He also disagreed with the treaty banning open-air testing of nuclear weapons. LeMay was an aggressive war fighter, temperamentally unsuited to make the decisions that international diplomacy required, and he apparently believed that only military force solved international problems.

In a 1984 interview, LeMay lamented the opportunities that Kennedy had missed in rolling back communism during the Cuban Missile Crisis:

> The Kennedy administration thought that being as strong as we were was provocative to the Russians and likely to start a war. We in the Air Force, and I personally, believed the exact opposite. While we had all this superiority, we invaded no one; we didn't launch any conquest for loot or territory. We just sat there with the strength. As a matter of fact, we lost because we didn't threaten to use it when it might have brought advantages to the country. . . . We could have gotten not only the missiles out of Cuba, we could have gotten the Communists out of Cuba at that time. . . . During that very critical time, in my mind there wasn't a chance that we would have gone to war with Russia because we had overwhelming strategic capability and the Russians knew it.[7]

LeMay was also willing to publicly express sentiments that few other senior military leaders were willing to articulate or even think. In a 1954 briefing, he was asked about the idea of a first strike and was quoted as saying, "I want to make it clear that I am not advocating a preventive war; however, I believe that if the U.S. is pushed into the corner far enough we would not hesitate to strike first." During that period of time, the mid-1950s, Eisenhower thought that nuclear weapons would be used in a general war with the Soviet Union, but he thought that a surprise preemptive attack was impossible, if only because it would be too hard to accomplish. It would go "against our traditions." Eisenhower also found it difficult to envision how to persuade Congress to "meet in a highly secret session and vote a declaration of war which would be implemented before the session was terminated." It is charming to see the old soldier Eisenhower assuming that he would need congressional approval before starting a war. Later presidents have been much more cavalier about such a restriction on their power.[8]

In contrast to LeMay, Secretary of Defense McNamara, who helped lead the country into the Vietnam debacle, later came to condemn America's reliance on nuclear weapons as a foreign policy tool. In a 2005 article in *Foreign Policy* magazine, McNamara described the "current U.S. nuclear weapons policy as immoral, illegal, militarily unnecessary, and dreadfully dangerous."[9] The proliferation of nuclear weapons terrified him, as it should us all.

Kennedy was able to resist the advice from his Joint Chiefs and others who wanted to reach for the gun rather than talk. We are all blessed to be alive because Kennedy chose to walk the path to peace. Of course, it must be said that the path to peace was possible only because Khrushchev changed his erratic behavior and finally made some firmly rational choices. We cannot be certain that future world leaders will follow this example. So we must pray.

Further sources: Laurence Chang and Peter Kornbluh, eds., *The Cuban Missile Crisis, 1962: A National Security Archive Documents Reader* (New York: New Press, 1992); Aleksandr Fursenko and Timothy Naftali, *"One Hell of a Gamble": Khrushchev, Castro, and Kennedy, 1958–1964* (New York: Norton, 1997); Anatoli I. Gribkov and William Y. Smith, *Operation Anadyr: U.S. and Soviet Generals Recount the Cuban Missile Crisis* (Chicago: Edition q, 1994); Richard H. Kohn and Joseph P. Harahan, eds., "U.S. Strategic Air Power, 1948–1962: Excerpts from an Interview with Generals Curtis E. LeMay, Leon W. Johnson, David A. Burchinal, and Jack J. Catton," *International Security* 12, no. 4 (Spring 1988): 78–95; Curtis E. LeMay, *America Is in*

Danger, with Dale O. Smith (New York: Funk & Wagnalls, 1968); Norman Polmar and John D. Gresham, *DEFCON-2: Standing on the Brink of Nuclear War during the Cuban Missile Crisis* (Hoboken, NJ: Wiley, 2006); David Alan Rosenberg, "'A Smoking Radiating Ruin at the End of Two Hours': Documents on American Plans for Nuclear War with the Soviet Union, 1954–1955," *International Security* 6, no. 3 (Winter 1981–82): 3–38; and Svetlana V. Savranskaya, "New Sources on the Role of Soviet Submarines in the Cuban Missile Crisis," *Journal of Strategic Studies* 28, no. 2 (April 2005): 233–59.

NOTES

INTRODUCTION

1. Niall Ferguson, review of *Fateful Choices: Ten Decisions That Changed the World 1940–1941*, by Ian Kershaw, *Times Literary Supplement*, September 19, 2007, 5; and David S. Landes, *The Wealth and Poverty of Nations: Why Some Are So Rich and Some So Poor* (New York: Norton, 1999), 98.

PROLOGUE: THE BAY OF PIGS INVASION

1. Victor Andres Triay, *Bay of Pigs: An Oral History of Brigade 2506* (Gainesville: University Press of Florida, 2001), 98.
2. Grayston L. Lynch, *Decision for Disaster: Betrayal at the Bay of Pigs* (Washington, D.C.: Brassey's, Inc., 1998), 22.
3. Peter Kornbluh, ed., *Bay of Pigs Declassified: The Secret CIA Report on the Invasion of Cuba* (New York: New Press, 1998), 172.
4. Lynch, *Decision for Disaster*, 24.
5. Ibid., 25.
6. Luis Aguilar, *Operation Zapata: The "Ultrasensitive" Report and Testimony of Inquiry on the Bay of Pigs* (Frederick, MD: Aletheia Books, University Publications of America, 1981).
7. Kornbluh, *Bay of Pigs Declassified*, 113.
8. Lynch, *Decision for Disaster*, 38.
9. Mark J. White, ed., *The Kennedys and Cuba: The Declassified Documentary History* (Chicago: I. R. Dee, 1999), 20, 21, 26, 28–29. This book is a gold mine of primary sources.
10. Lionel Martin, *The Early Fidel: Roots of Castro's Communism* (Secaucus, NJ: L. Stuart, 1978), 11.

11. Lawrence Freedman, *Kennedy's Wars: Berlin, Cuba, Laos, and Vietnam* (New York: Oxford University Press, 2000), 128.

12. Kornbluh, *Bay of Pigs Declassified*, 308–10.

13. Ibid., 168.

14. Lynch, *Decision for Disaster*, 116.

15. Ibid., 99.

16. Ibid., 101.

17. Ibid., 127.

18. Kornbluh, *Bay of Pigs Declassified*, 317.

19. Lynch, *Decision for Disaster*, 129.

20. Ibid., 322.

21. Anatoli I. Gribkov and William Y. Smith, *Operation Anadyr: U.S. and Soviet Generals Recount the Cuban Missile Crisis*, ed. Alfred Friendly Jr. (Chicago: Edition q, 1994), 84.

22. Lynch, *Decision for Disaster*, 132.

23. Freedman, *Kennedy's Wars*, 146.

1. MAKING TOOLS: MUSHROOM CLOUDS AND DREAMS OF SPACE

1. William J. Broad, "A Spy's Path: Iowa to A-Bomb to Kremlin Honor," *New York Times*, November 12, 2007, http://www.nytimes.com/2007/11/12/us/12koval.html (accessed on January 2, 2009).

2. Geoffrey Perret, *Winged Victory: The Army Air Forces in World War II* (New York: Random House, 1993), 369; and Richard G. Davis, *Carl A. Spaatz and the Air War in Europe* (Washington, D.C.: Center for Air Force History, 1993), 555.

3. Max Hastings, *Bomber Command* (London: Joseph, 1979), 46.

4. U.S. Department of State, *Papers Relating to the Foreign Relations of the United States, Japan: 1931–1941*, vol. 2 (Washington, D.C.: U.S. Government Printing Office, 1943), 2:201, http://digital.library.wisc.edu/1711.dl/FRUS.FRUS193141v02 (accessed on January 2, 2009).

5. Hastings, *Bomber Command*, 22.

6. Ibid., 144–45, 150, 157.

7. Ibid., 401; and Charles Webster and Noble Frankland, *The Strategic Air Offensive against Germany, 1939–1945* (London: Her Majesty's Stationary Office, 1961), 3:320.

8. Hastings, *Bomber Command*, 405, 308.

9. Ibid., 399.

10. David F. Krugler, *This Is Only a Test: How Washington D.C. Prepared for Nuclear War* (New York: Palgrave Macmillan, 2006), 10.

11. Norman Polmar and John D. Gresham, *DEFCON-2: Standing on the Brink of Nuclear War during the Cuban Missile Crisis* (Hoboken, NJ: Wiley, 2006), 240.

12. Lynn Eden, *Whole World on Fire: Organizations, Knowledge, and Nuclear Weapons Devastation* (Ithaca, NY: Cornell University Press, 2004).

13. Dennis Piszkiewicz, *Wernher von Braun: The Man Who Sold the Moon* (Westport, CT: Praeger, 1998), 45.

14. Ibid., 65.

15. Ibid., 75.

16. Ibid., 100.

17. Ibid., 105.

18. Norman Polmar and Kenneth J. Moore, *Cold War Submarines: The Design and Construction of U.S. and Soviet Submarines* (Washington, D.C.: Brassey's, Inc., 2004), 113.

2. SURVIVOR: NIKITA KHRUSHCHEV

1. William Taubman, *Khrushchev: The Man and His Era* (New York: Norton, 2003), 24. See also Sergei N. Khrushchev, *Nikita Khrushchev: Creation of a Superpower* (University Park: Pennsylvania State University Press, 2000).

2. Sheila Fitzpatrick, *Everyday Stalinism: Ordinary Life in Extraordinary Times: Soviet Russia in the 1930s* (New York: Oxford University Press, 1999), 16–18, 80–83.

3. Taubman, *Khrushchev*, 256.

4. Ibid., 279.

5. Thomas Blanton and Malcolm Byrne, eds., *CIA Had Single Officer in Hungary 1956* (National Security Archive Electronic Briefing Book no. 206) (Washington, D.C.: National Security Archive, October 31, 2006), http://www.gwu.edu/~nsarchiv/NSAEBB/NSAEBB206/index.htm (accessed on January 2, 2009).

6. Taubman, *Khrushchev*, xx, 8.

7. Unsourced quote.

8. Taubman, *Khrushchev*, 332.

9. Ibid., 352. See also Andrew P. N. Erdmann, "'War No Longer Has Any Logic Whatsoever': Dwight D. Eisenhower and the Thermonuclear Revolution," in *Cold War Statesmen Confront the Bomb: Nuclear Diplomacy since 1945*, ed. John Lewis Gaddis and others (Oxford: Oxford University Press, 1999): 87–119.

10. Nikita S. Khrushchev, *For Victory in Peaceful Competition with Capitalism* (New York: Dutton, 1960), 23.

11. Nikita S. Khrushchev, *Khrushchev Remembers: The Last Testament*, trans. and ed. Strobe Talbott (Boston: Little, Brown, 1974), 46.

12. Alexsandr Fursenko and Timothy Naftali, *Khrushchev's Cold War: The Inside Story of an American Adversary* (New York: Norton, 2006), 208.

13. Taubman, *Khrushchev*, 398.

14. Ibid., 452.

15. Khrushchev, *Khrushchev Remembers*, 451.

16. Taubman, *Khrushchev*, 465.

17. Ibid., 492.

18. Ibid., xx.

3. YOUNG MAN OF AMBITION: JOHN F. KENNEDY

1. Arthur M. Schlesinger Jr., *A Thousand Days: John F. Kennedy in the White House* (Boston: Houghton Mifflin, 1965), 3.

2. Thomas C. Reeves, *A Question of Character: A Life of John F. Kennedy* (New York: Free Press, 1991), 37–38.

3. Robert Dallek, *An Unfinished Life: John F. Kennedy, 1917–1963* (Boston: Little, Brown, 2003), 57.

4. Michael O'Brien, *John F. Kennedy: A Biography* (New York: St. Martin's, 2005), 109.

5. Dallek, *Unfinished Life*, 120.

6. Ibid., 167.

7. Ibid., 217.

8. Reinhold Niebuhr addresses this in his *Moral Man and Immoral Society: A Study in Ethics and Politics* (New York: C. Scribner's Sons, 1932).

9. Stéphane Courtois et al., *The Black Book of Communism: Crimes, Terrors, Repression* (Cambridge, MA: Harvard University Press, 1999).

10. Dallek, *Unfinished Life*, 345.

11. Ibid., 367.

12. Robert Kennedy, *Robert Kennedy, in His Own Words: The Unpublished Recollections of the Kennedy Years*, eds. Edwin O. Guthman and Jeffrey Shulman (New York: Bantam, 1988), 28.

13. Taubman, *Khrushchev*, 500.

14. Ibid., 505.

15. Dallek, *Unfinished Life*, 428.

16. "Soviet Nuclear Weapons," *Nuclear Weapon Archive*, October 7, 1997, http://nuclearweaponarchive.org/Russia/Sovwarhead.html (accessed on January 2, 2009).

17. Dallek, *Unfinished Life*, 429.

18. Norman Friedman, *U.S. Amphibious Ships and Craft: An Illustrated Design History* (Annapolis, MD: Naval Institute Press, 2002), 11–12.

19. Richard Reeves, *President Kennedy: Profile of Power* (New York: Simon & Schuster, 1993), 229–30.

20. Scott D. Sagan, *The Limits of Safety: Organizations, Accidents, and Nuclear Weapons* (Princeton, NJ: Princeton University Press, 1993), 48.

21. Dallek, *Unfinished Life*, 346; and John T. Correll, "Airpower and the Cuban Missile Crisis," *Air Force Magazine* 88, no. 8 (August 2005): 78–83.

22. Dallek, *Unfinished Life*, 465–66.

23. Ibid., 476.

24. Thomas C. Reeves, in Dallek, *Unfinished Life*, 399.

25. Ibid., 534.

4. OPERATION ANADYR: THE PLAN TO PROTECT CUBA

1. Gribkov and Smith, *Operation Anadyr*, 91, 99, 122.

2. Ibid., 12.

3. Fursenko and Naftali, *Khrushchev's Cold War*, 451.

4. Gribkov and Smith, *Operation Anadyr*, 25.

5. Taubman, *Khrushchev*, 519–21.

6. Gribkov and Smith, *Operation Anadyr*, 27.

7. Ibid., 45. See also Dino A. Brugioni, *Eyeball to Eyeball: The Inside Story of the Cuban Missile Crisis*, ed. Robert F. McCourt (New York: Random House, 1991).

8. Oleg Penkovsky, *The Penkovsky Papers* (London: Collins, 1965), 31.

9. See Len Scott, "Espionage and the Cold War: Oleg Penkovsky and the Cuban Missile Crisis," *Intelligence and National Security* 14, no. 3 (Autumn 1999): 23–47.

10. "CIA Special National Intelligence Estimate, 'The Military Buildup in Cuba,'" in *The Cuban Missile Crisis, 1962: A National Security Archive Documents Reader*, eds. Laurence Chang and Peter Kornbluh (New York: New Press, 1992), 63–65.

11. Taubman, *Khrushchev*, 553.

12. "National Security Action Memorandum No. 181," in Chang and Kornbluh, *Cuban Missile Crisis*, 61–62.

13. Gribkov and Smith, *Operation Anadyr*, 109.

14. See Nuclear Age Peace Foundation, *Nuclear Files*, http://www.nuclearfiles.org/menu/key-issues/nuclear-weapons/history/cold-war/cuban-missile-crisis/timeline.htm (accessed on January 2, 2009).

5. THE U-2 FLIGHT THAT NEVER HAPPENED: THE CRISIS BEGINS

1. Polmar and Gresham, *DEFCON-2*, 307.

2. See Sean Potter, "October 14, 1962," *Weatherwise*, September–October 2006, 16–17.

3. Brugioni, *Eyeball to Eyeball*, 181–86.

4. Ibid., 197–200.

5. Taubman, *Khrushchev*, 529.

6. Aleksandr Fursenko and Timothy Naftali, *"One Hell of a Gamble": Khrushchev, Castro, and Kennedy, 1958–1964* (New York: Norton, 1997), 223–24.

7. John F. Kennedy, "Address to the Nation on the Soviet Arms Buildup in Cuba," October 22, 1962, http://www.jfklibrary.org/jfkl/cmc/j102262.htm (accessed March 15, 2010).

8. Fictional speech.

9. Dino A. Brugioni, "The Invasion of Cuba," *MHQ: The Quarterly Journal of Military History* 4, no. 2 (Winter 1992): 98.

10. Gribkov and Smith, *Operation Anadyr*, 142.

11. *October Fury* (documentary) (New York: History Channel, October 13, 2002).

12. Taubman, *Khrushchev*, 566–57.

13. Ibid., 407.

14. Dallek, *Unfinished Life*, 348.

15. Gribkov and Smith, *Operation Anadyr*, 130.

16. Taubman, *Khrushchev*, 547.

17. Gribkov and Smith, *Operation Anadyr*, 65.

18. Brugioni, "Invasion of Cuba," 100.

19. Gribkov and Smith, *Operation Anadyr*, 174.

20. See Ryurik A. Ketov, "The Cuban Missile Crisis as Seen through a Periscope," *Journal of Strategic Studies* 28, no. 2 (April 2005): 217–31.

21. *October Fury.*

22. See Svetlana V. Savranskaya, "New Sources on the Role of Soviet Submarines in the Cuban Missile Crisis," *Journal of Strategic Studies* 28, no. 2 (April 2005): 233–59.

23. Brugioni, "Invasion of Cuba," 94.

24. Gribkov and Smith, *Khrushchev*, 223.

25. Alwyn T. Lloyd, *A Cold War Legacy: A Tribute to Strategic Air Command, 1946–1992* (Missoula, MT: Pictorial Histories, 1999), 279.

26. See "Cuba Fact Sheet," in Chang and Kornbluh, *Cuban Missile Crisis*, 191–93; and Polmar and Gresham, *DEFCON-2*, 309–10.

6. HELTER SKELTER: THE WORLD TEETERS ON THE EDGE OF SANITY

1. Gribkov and Smith, *Operation Anadyr*, 139.

2. Polmar and Gresham, *DEFCON-2*, 244.

3. Richard Alan Schwartz, *The Cold War Reference Guide: A General History and An-*

notated Chronology with Selected Biographies (Jefferson, NC: McFarland, 1997), 55; and James G. Blight and David A. Welch, *On the Brink: Americans and Soviets Reexamine the Cuban Missile Crisis* (New York: Hill and Wang, 1989), 207.

4. Lloyd, *Cold War Legacy*, 307.

5. Sagan, *Limits of Safety*, 68–69.

6. Original speech altered.

7. Michael K. Bohn, *Nerve Center: Inside the White House Situation Room* (Washington, DC: Brassey's, Inc., 2003), 147.

8. See Alain C. Enthoven and K. Wayne Smith, *How Much Is Enough? Shaping the Defense Program, 1961–1969* (New York: Harper & Row, 1971).

9. See Institute for Strategic Studies, *The Communist Bloc and the Western Alliances: The Military Balance* (London: Institute for Strategic Studies, 1961–62).

10. Polmar and Gresham, *DEFCON-2*, 299.

11. Brugioni, "The Invasion of Cuba," 99.

12. Ibid., 94.

13. Robert L. Dennison, interview by Jerry N. Hess, October 6, 1971, Harry S. Truman Library, Independence, Missouri, http://www.trumanlibrary.org/oralhist/dennisn2.htm#63 (accessed on January 2, 2009).

14. Polmar and Gresham, *DEFCON-2*, 229.

15. Taubman, *Khrushchev*, 512, 28.

7. DESPERATION: THE SPARK

1. Office of Current Intelligence, "Khrushchev on Nuclear Strategy," Staff Study (Washington, D.C.: CIA, January 19, 1960), http://www.foia.cia.gov/CPE/CAESAR/caesar-26.pdf (accessed on January 2, 2009).

2. Ibid., 11.

3. Office of Current Intelligence, "Soviet Strategic Doctrine for the Start of War," Staff Study (Washington, D.C.: CIA, July 3, 1962), 25, http://www.foia.cia.gov/CPE/CAESAR/caesar-31.pdf (accessed on January 2, 2009).

4. Fictional speech.

8. ANGELS WEEP: THE FIRE COMES

1. See Institute for Strategic Studies, *Communist Bloc and the Western Alliances*.

2. Steven J. Zaloga, *The Kremlin's Nuclear Sword: The Rise and Fall of Russia's Strategic Nuclear Forces, 1945–2000* (Washington, D.C.: Smithsonian Institution Press, 2002), 255, 257.

3. Eden, *Whole World on Fire*, 17.

4. Ibid., 18.

5. See Canada Emergency Measures Organization, "11 Steps to Survival," Blueprint for Survival no. 4 (Ottawa: Queen's Printer, 1969), http://www.ki4u.com/survive/index.htm (accessed on January 2, 2009).

6. See Ted Gup, "Civil Defense Doomsday Hideaway," *Time*, December 9, 1991, 26-29; and Ted Gup, "The Doomsday Blueprints," *Time*, August 10, 1992, 32–39.

7. See Gup, "Doomsday Blueprints."

8. Krugler, *This Is Only a Test*, 106, 177; and Gup, "Doomsday Blueprints," 35.

9. Krugler, *This Is Only a Test*, 63.

10. Ibid., 66–67.

11. Ibid., 167.

12. *Atlantic Monthly*, September 2007, 38.

13. Eden, *Whole World on Fire*, 28.

14. See Savranskaya, "New Sources on the Role of Soviet Submarines."

15. See ibid.

16. Polmar and Moore, *Cold War Submarines*, 110.

17. Clive Thompson, "Clive Thompson Explains Why We Can Count on Geeks to Rescue the Earth," *Wired Magazine* (August 21, 2007), http://www.wired.com/techbiz/people/magazine/15-09/st_thompson, accessed on January 2, 2009.

18. David Alan Rosenberg, "'A Smoking Radiating Ruin at the End of Two Hours': Documents on American Plans for Nuclear War with the Soviet Union, 1954–1955," *International Security* 6, no. 3 (Winter 1981–82): 21.

19. Enthoven and Smith, *How Much Is Enough?* 207.

20. See Office of Current Intelligence, "The Decline of Mao Tse-Tung," Staff Study (Washington, D.C.: CIA, April 9, 1962), http://www.foia.cia.gov/CPE/POLO/polo-06.pdf (accessed on January 2, 2009).

21. Shu Guang Zhang, "Between 'Paper' and 'Real Tigers': Mao's View of Nuclear Weapons," in Gaddis et al., *Cold War Statesmen Confront the Bomb*, 194–215.

9. IN THE RUINS: LEARNING TO SURVIVE

1. Glen K. Craig, *US Army Special Forces Medical Handbook* (Boulder, CO: Paladin Press, 1988), 14-1.

2. Carey Sublette, "Effects of Nuclear Explosions," *Nuclear Weapons Frequently Asked Questions*, Version 2.14 (May 15, 1997), http://nuclearweaponarchive.org/Nwfaq/Nfaq5.html (accessed on January 2, 2009).

3. Michael Riordan, ed., *The Day after Midnight: The Effects of Nuclear War* (Palo Alto, CA: Cheshire Books, 1982), 124.

4. Michael Balter, "Zapped by Radiation, Fungi Flourish," *ScienceNOW*, May 23,

2007, http://sciencenow.sciencemag.org/cgi/content/full/2007/523/3 (accessed on January 2, 2009).

5. Ken Alibek, *Biohazard: The Chilling True Story of the Largest Covert Biological Weapons Program in the World, Told from Inside by the Man Who Ran It*, with Stephen Handelman (New York: Random House, 1999), 298.

6. Ibid., 30, 36.

7. Ibid., 37.

8. Judith Miller, Stephen Engelberg, and William Broad, *Germs: Biological Weapons and America's Secret War* (New York: Simon & Schuster, 2001), 49, 180.

9. Ibid., 54.

10. Based on the study of voles at Chernobyl, see Denise Grady, "Chernobyl's Voles Live but Mutations Surge," *New York Times*, May 7, 1996. See also R. F. Mould, *Chernobyl Record: The Definitive History of the Chernobyl Catastrophe* (Bristol, UK: Institute of Physics Publishing, 2000).

11. Stuart J. Thorson and Donald A. Sylvan, "Counterfactuals and the Cuban Missile Crisis," *International Studies Quarterly* 26, no. 4 (December 1982): 539.

AUTHOR'S AFTERWORD: KHRUSHCHEV AND KENNEDY

1. Theodore C. Sorensen, *Kennedy* (New York: Harper & Row, 1965), 705.

2. See Steven J. Zaloga, "The Forgotten Missiles: The Soviet Air Force and Nuclear GLCMs," *Journal of Slavic Military Studies* 12, no. 2 (June 1999): 164–72.

3. See Savranskaya, "New Sources on the Role of Soviet Submarines."

4. See Fursenko and Naftali, *"One Hell of a Gamble."*

5. Robert Dallek, "JFK's Second Term," *Atlantic Monthly*, June 2003, http://www. theatlantic.com/doc/200306/dallek (accessed on January 2, 2009).

6. Curtis E. LeMay, *America Is in Danger*, with Dale O. Smith (New York: Funk & Wagnalls, 1968), xii.

7. Richard H. Kohn and Joseph P. Harahan, eds., "U.S. Strategic Air Power, 1948–1962: Excerpts from an Interview with Generals Curtis E. LeMay, Leon W. Johnson, David A. Burchinal, and Jack J. Catton," *International Security* 12, no. 4 (Spring 1988): 92, 93, 94.

8. Rosenberg, "Smoking Radiating Ruin," 13, 15, 27.

9. Robert S. McNamara, "Apocalypse Soon," *Foreign Policy*, May–June 2005, http://www.foreignpolicy.com/story/cms.php?story_id=2829 (accessed on January 2, 2009).

BIBLIOGRAPHY

Aguilar, Luis. *Operation Zapata: The "Ultrasensitive" Report and Testimony of Inquiry on the Bay of Pigs.* Frederick, MD: Aletheia Books, University Publications of America, 1981.

Alibek, Ken. *Biohazard: The Chilling True Story of the Largest Covert Biological Weapons Program in the World, Told from Inside by the Man Who Ran It.* With Stephen Handelman. New York: Random House, 1999.

Applebaum, Anne. *Gulag: A History.* New York: Doubleday, 2003.

Balter, Michael. "Zapped by Radiation, Fungi Flourish." *ScienceNOW*, May 23, 2007. http://sciencenow.sciencemag.org/cgi/content/full/2007/523/3 (accessed on January 2, 2009).

Blanton, Thomas, and Malcolm Byrne, eds. *CIA Had Single Officer in Hungary 1956.* National Security Archive Electronic Briefing Book no. 206. Washington, D.C.: National Security Archive, October 31, 2006. http://www.gwu.edu/~nsarchiv/NSAEBB/NSAEBB206/index.htm (accessed on January 2, 2009).

Blight, James G., and David A. Welch. *On the Brink: Americans and Soviets Reexamine the Cuban Missile Crisis.* New York: Hill and Wang, 1989.

Bohn, Michael K. *Nerve Center: Inside the White House Situation Room.* Washington, D.C.: Brassey's, Inc., 2003.

Broad, William J. "A Spy's Path: Iowa to A-Bomb to Kremlin Honor." *New York Times*, November 12, 2007. http://www.nytimes.com/2007/11/12/us/12koval.html (accessed on January 2, 2009).

Brugioni, Dino A. *Eyeball to Eyeball: The Inside Story of the Cuban Missile Crisis.* Edited by Robert F. McCort. New York: Random House, 1991.

———. "The Invasion of Cuba." *MHQ: The Quarterly Journal of Military History* 4, no. 2 (Winter 1992): 92–101.

Canada Emergency Measures Organization. "11 Steps to Survival." Blueprint for Survival no. 4. Ottawa: Queen's Printer, 1969. http://www.ki4u.com/survive/index.htm (accessed on January 2, 2009).

Chang, Laurence, and Peter Kornbluh, eds. *The Cuban Missile Crisis, 1962: A National Security Archive Documents Reader*. New York: New Press, 1992.

Clary, David A. *Rocket Man: Robert H. Goddard and the Birth of the Space Age*. New York: Hyperion, 2003.

Coltman, Leycester. *The Real Fidel Castro*. New Haven: Yale University Press, 2003.

Correll, John T. "Airpower and the Cuban Missile Crisis." *Air Force Magazine* 88, no. 8 (August 2005): 78–83.

———. "The Ups and Downs of Counterforce." *Air Force Magazine* 88, no. 10 (October 2005): 59–64.

Courtois, Stéphane, and others. *The Black Book of Communism: Crimes, Terror, Repression*. Cambridge, MA: Harvard University Press, 1999.

Craig, Glen K. *US Army Special Forces Medical Handbook*. Boulder, CO: Paladin Press, 1988.

Dallek, Robert. "JFK's Second Term." *Atlantic Monthly*, June 2003. http://www.theatlantic.com/doc/200306/dallek (accessed on January 2, 2009).

———. *An Unfinished Life: John F. Kennedy, 1917–1963*. Boston: Little, Brown, 2003.

Davis, Richard G. *Carl A. Spaatz and the Air War in Europe*. Washington, D.C.: Center for Air Force History, 1993.

Dennison, Robert L. Interview by Jerry N. Hess, October 6, 1971. Harry S. Truman Library, Independence, Missouri. http://www.trumanlibrary.org/oralhist/dennisn2.htm#63 (accessed on January 2, 2009).

Dobbs, Michael. *One Minute to Midnight: Kennedy, Khrushchev, and Castro on the Brink of Nuclear War*. New York: Alfred A. Knopf, 2008.

Eden, Lynn. *Whole World on Fire: Organizations, Knowledge, and Nuclear Weapons Devastation*. Ithaca, NY: Cornell University Press, 2004.

Enthoven, Alain C., and K. Wayne Smith. *How Much Is Enough? Shaping the Defense Program, 1961–1969*. New York: Harper & Row, 1971.

Erdmann, Andrew P. N. "'War No Longer Has Any Logic Whatsoever': Dwight D. Eisenhower and the Thermonuclear Revolution." In *Cold War Statesmen Confront the Bomb: Nuclear Diplomacy since 1945*, edited by John Lewis Gaddis and others, 87–119. Oxford: Oxford University Press, 1999.

Ferguson, Niall. Review of *Fateful Choices: Ten Decisions That Changed the World 1940–1941*, by Ian Kershaw. *Times Literary Supplement*, September 19, 2007.

Fitzpatrick, Sheila. *Everyday Stalinism: Ordinary Life in Extraordinary Times: Soviet Russia in the 1930s*. New York: Oxford University Press, 1999.

Freedman, Lawrence. *Kennedy's Wars: Berlin, Cuba, Laos, and Vietnam*. New York: Oxford University Press, 2000.

Friedman, Norman. *U.S. Amphibious Ships and Craft: An Illustrated Design History*. Annapolis, MD: Naval Institute Press, 2002.

Fursenko, Aleksandr, and Timothy Naftali. *Khrushchev's Cold War: The Inside Story of an American Adversary*. New York: Norton, 2006.

———. *"One Hell of a Gamble": Khrushchev, Castro, and Kennedy, 1958–1964*. New York: Norton, 1997.

Grady, Denise. "Chernobyl's Voles Live but Mutations Surge." *New York Times*, May 7, 1996.

Gribkov, Anatoli I., and William Y. Smith. *Operation Anadyr: U.S. and Soviet Generals Recount the Cuban Missile Crisis*. Edited by Alfred Friendly Jr. Chicago: Edition q, 1994.

Gup, Ted. "Civil Defense Doomsday Hideaway." *Time*, December 9, 1991, 26–29.

———. "The Doomsday Blueprints." *Time*, August 10, 1992, 32–39.

Hastings, Max. *Bomber Command*. London: Joseph, 1979.

Hersey, John. *Hiroshima*. New York: A. A. Knopf, 1946.

Institute for Strategic Studies. *The Communist Bloc and the Western Alliances: The Military Balance*. London: Institute for Strategic Studies, 1961–62.

Johnson, Haynes. *The Bay of Pigs: The Leaders' Story of Brigade 2506*. With Manuel Artime and others. New York: Norton, 1964.

Kalugin, Oleg. *The First Directorate: My 32 Years in Intelligence and Espionage against the West*. With Fen Montaigne. New York: St. Martin's Press, 1994.

Kennedy, Robert. *Robert Kennedy, in His Own Words: The Unpublished Recollections of the Kennedy Years*. Edited by Edwin O. Guthman and Jeffrey Shulman. New York: Bantam, 1988.

Ketov, Ryurik A. "The Cuban Missile Crisis as Seen through a Periscope." *Journal of Strategic Studies* 28, no. 2 (April 2005): 217–31.

Khrushchev, Nikita S. *For Victory in Peaceful Competition with Capitalism*. New York: Dutton, 1960.

———. *Khrushchev Remembers: The Last Testament*. Translated and edited by Strobe Talbott. Boston: Little, Brown, 1974.

Khrushchev, Sergei N. *Nikita Khrushchev: Creation of a Superpower*. University Park: Pennsylvania State University Press, 2000.

Kohn, Richard H., and Joseph P. Harahan, eds. "U.S. Strategic Air Power, 1948–1962: Excerpts from an Interview with Generals Curtis E. LeMay, Leon W. Johnson, David A. Burchinal, and Jack J. Catton." *International Security* 12, no. 4 (Spring 1988): 78–95.

Kornbluh, Peter, ed. *Bay of Pigs Declassified: The Secret CIA Report on the Invasion of Cuba*. New York: New Press, 1998.

Krugler, David F. *This Is Only a Test: How Washington D.C. Prepared for Nuclear War*. New York: Palgrave Macmillan, 2006.

Landes, David S. *The Wealth and Poverty of Nations: Why Some Are So Rich and Some So Poor*. New York: Norton, 1999.

LeMay, Curtis E. *America Is in Danger*. With Dale O. Smith. New York: Funk & Wagnalls, 1968.

Lloyd, Alwyn T. *A Cold War Legacy: A Tribute to Strategic Air Command, 1946–1992*. Missoula, MT: Pictorial Histories, 1999.

Lynch, Grayston L. *Decision for Disaster: Betrayal at the Bay of Pigs*. Washington, D.C.: Brassey's, Inc., 1998.

Martin, Lionel. *The Early Fidel: Roots of Castro's Communism*. Secaucus, NJ: L. Stuart, 1978.

McNamara, Robert S. "Apocalypse Soon." *Foreign Policy*, May–June 2005. http://www.foreignpolicy.com/story/cms.php?story_id=2829 (accessed on January 2, 2009).

Miller, Judith, Stephen Engelberg, and William Broad. *Germs: Biological Weapons and America's Secret War*. New York: Simon & Schuster, 2001.

Mould, R. F. *Chernobyl Record: The Definitive History of the Chernobyl Catastrophe*. Bristol, UK: Institute of Physics Publishing, 2000.

Niebuhr, Reinhold. *Moral Man and Immoral Society: A Study in Ethics and Politics*. New York: C. Scribner's Sons, 1932.

Norris, Robert S., and William M. Arkin. "Where They Were." *Bulletin of the Atomic Scientists* 55, no. 6 (November–December 1999): 26–35.

Nuclear Age Peace Foundation. *Nuclear Files*. http://www.nuclearfiles.org/ (accessed on January 2, 2009).

O'Brien, Michael. *John F. Kennedy: A Biography*. New York: St. Martin's, 2005.

October Fury (documentary). New York: History Channel, October 13, 2002.

Office of Current Intelligence. "The Decline of Mao Tse-Tung." Staff Study. Washington, D.C.: Central Intelligence Agency, April 9, 1962. http://www.foia.cia.gov/CPE/POLO/polo-06.pdf (accessed on January 2, 2009).

———. "Khrushchev on Nuclear Strategy." Staff Study. Washington, D.C.: Central Intelligence Agency, January 19, 1960. http://www.foia.cia.gov/CPE/CAESAR/caesar-26.pdf (accessed on January 2, 2009).

———. "Soviet Strategic Doctrine for the Start of War." Staff Study. Washington, D.C.: Central Intelligence Agency, July 3, 1962. http://www.foia.cia.gov/CPE/CAESAR/caesar-31.pdf (accessed on January 2, 2009).

Perret, Geoffrey. *Winged Victory: The Army Air Forces in World War II*. New York: Random House, 1993.

Piszkiewicz, Dennis. *Wernher von Braun: The Man Who Sold the Moon*. Westport, CT: Praeger, 1998.

Polmar, Norman, and John D. Gresham. *DEFCON-2: Standing on the Brink of Nuclear War during the Cuban Missile Crisis*. Hoboken, NJ: Wiley, 2006.

Polmar, Norman, and Kenneth J. Moore. *Cold War Submarines: The Design and Construction of U.S. and Soviet Submarines*. Washington, D.C.: Brassey's, Inc., 2004.

Potter, Sean. "October 14, 1962." *Weatherwise*, September–October 2006, 16–17.

Reeves, Richard. *President Kennedy: Profile of Power*. New York: Simon & Schuster, 1993.

Reeves, Thomas C. *A Question of Character: A Life of John F. Kennedy*. New York: Free Press, 1991.

Rhodes, Richard. *Dark Sun: The Making of the Hydrogen Bomb*. New York: Simon & Schuster, 1995.

———. *The Making of the Atomic Bomb*. New York: Simon & Schuster, 1986.

Riordan, Michael, ed. *The Day after Midnight: The Effects of Nuclear War*. Palo Alto, CA: Cheshire Books, 1982.

Rosenberg, David Alan. "'A Smoking Radiating Ruin at the End of Two Hours': Documents on American Plans for Nuclear War with the Soviet Union, 1954–1955." *International Security* 6, no. 3 (Winter 1981–82): 3–38.

Sagan, Scott D. *The Limits of Safety: Organizations, Accidents, and Nuclear Weapons*. Princeton, NJ: Princeton University Press, 1993.

———. "SIOP-62: The Nuclear War Plan Briefing to President Kennedy." *International Security* 12, no. 1 (Summer 1987): 22–51.

Savranskaya, Svetlana V. "New Sources on the Role of Soviet Submarines in the Cuban Missile Crisis." *Journal of Strategic Studies* 28, no. 2 (April 2005): 233–59.

Schaffer, Ronald. *Wings of Judgment: American Bombing in World War II*. New York: Oxford University Press, 1985.

Schlesinger, Arthur M., Jr. *A Thousand Days: John F. Kennedy in the White House*. Boston: Houghton Mifflin, 1965.

Schwartz, Richard Alan. *The Cold War Reference Guide: A General History and Annotated Chronology with Selected Biographies*. Jefferson, NC: McFarland, 1997.

Scott, Len. *The Cuban Missile Crisis and the Threat of Nuclear War: Lessons from History*. New York: Continuum, 2007.

———. "Espionage and the Cold War: Oleg Penkovsky and the Cuban Missile Crisis." *Intelligence and National Security* 14, no. 3 (Autumn 1999): 23–47.

Sebag Montefiore, Simon. *Stalin: The Court of the Red Tsar*. New York: Knopf, 2004.

"Soviet Nuclear Weapons." *Nuclear Weapon Archive*, October 7, 1997. http://nuclearweaponarchive.org/Russia/Sovwarhead.html (accessed on January 2, 2009).

Sublette, Carey. "Effects of Nuclear Explosions." *Nuclear Weapons Frequently Asked Questions*. Version 2.14. May 15, 1997. http://nuclearweaponarchive.org/Nwfaq/Nfaq5.html (accessed on January 2, 2009).

Taubman, William. *Khrushchev: The Man and His Era*. New York: Norton, 2003.

Thompson, Clive. "Clive Thompson Explains Why We Can Count on Geeks to Rescue the Earth." *Wired Magazine*, August 21, 2007. http://www.wired.com/techbiz/people/magazine/15-09/st_thompson (accessed on January 2, 2009).

Thorson, Stuart J., and Donald A. Sylvan. "Counterfactuals and the Cuban Missile Crisis." *International Studies Quarterly* 26, no. 4 (December 1982): 539–71.

Triay, Victor Andres. *Bay of Pigs: An Oral History of Brigade 2506*. Gainesville: University Press of Florida, 2001.

U.S. Defense Atomic Support Agency. *The Effects of Nuclear Weapons*. Rev. ed. Edited by Samuel Glasstone. Washington, D.C.: U.S. Atomic Energy Commission, 1962.

U.S. Department of State. *Papers Relating to the Foreign Relations of the United States, Japan: 1931–1941*. Vol. 2. Washington, D.C.: U.S. Government Printing Office, 1943. http://digital.library.wisc.edu/1711.dl/FRUS.FRUS193141v02 (accessed on January 2, 2009).

Webster, Charles, and Noble Frankland. *The Strategic Air Offensive against Germany, 1939–1945*. 4 vols. London: Her Majesty's Stationary Office, 1961.

White, Mark J., ed. *The Kennedys and Cuba: The Declassified Documentary History*. Chicago: I. R. Dee, 1999.

Zaloga, Steven J. "The Forgotten Missiles: The Soviet Air Force and Nuclear GLCMs." *Journal of Slavic Military Studies* 12, no. 2 (June 1999): 164–72.

———. *The Kremlin's Nuclear Sword: The Rise and Fall of Russia's Strategic Nuclear Forces, 1945–2000*. Washington, D.C.: Smithsonian Institution Press, 2002.

———. *Target America: The Soviet Union and the Strategic Arms Race, 1945–1964*. Novato, CA: Presidio, 1993.

Zhang, Shu Guang. "Between 'Paper' and 'Real Tigers': Mao's View of Nuclear Weapons." In *Cold War Statesmen Confront the Bomb: Nuclear Diplomacy since 1945*, edited by John Lewis Gaddis and others, 194–215. Oxford: Oxford University Press, 1999.

INDEX

1st Armored Division, 161, 186
1st Infantry Division, 161, 201–2, 207
26 July Movement, 6
2nd Battalion, 20–23
2nd Infantry Division, 185–86
3rd Battalion, 24
5th Battalion, 21, 26
5th Marine Expeditionary Brigade, 162
6th Battalion, 19
8th Air Force, 34
74th Motorized Rifle Regiment, 188
82nd Airborne Division, 161, 187, 202
101st Airborne Division, 161, 187
584th FKR Regiment, 193
2857th Test Squadron, 220–21
4157th Strategic Wing, 241

A-4 rocket, 47
A-4 Skyhawks, 199
A-26 Invader, 9
Accelerated Growth Syndrome (AGS), 261–62
AEC (Atomic Energy Commission), 184, 200–1
AF-1E Fury, 193
Africa, escaped nuclear bombing, 252
AGS (Accelerated Growth Syndrome), 261–62
Air Defense Forces (Soviet), 57
aircraft, American
    A-4 Skyhawks, 199
    A-26 Invader, 9

AF-1E Fury, 193
B-17 bomber, 30, 34, 240–41
B-24 bomber, 34
B-26 Invader, used by Cuban exiles, 9, 11, 15–16, 22–26
B-29 bomber, 37–38, 241
B-36 bomber, 241
B-47 Stratojet, 162–63, 239
B-52 Stratofortress, 162–63, 167, 239, 241–42
B-58 Hustler, 163, 239
C-130 Hercules, 187, 194
Drone Anti-Submarine Helicopter (DASH), 188–89
EC-135C command post, 239
Enola Gay, 38
F-4 Phantom, 168
F-100 Super Sabre, 168, 187, 191, 199
F-101 Voodoo, 225
F-102 Delta Dagger, 225
F-104 Starfighter, 168–69, 175
F-105 Thunderchief, 168, 173
F-106 Delta Dart, 225
KC-97 Stratotanker, 163
KC-135 Stratotanker, 163
P-2 Neptune, 231
RB-66 Destroyer, 151–52
RF-8 Crusader, 151, 171
RF-101 Voodoo, 151, 171–73
U-2 spy plane, 55, 87–89, 139–41, 144–46, 166

aircraft, Canadian
  CF-100 Canuck, 225
  CF-101 Voodoo, 225
aircraft, Cuban
  B-26 Invader, 3, 19–21, 159
  C-46 Commandos, 9, 23
  C-54 Skymasters, 9
  F-51 Mustang, 16
  Sea Fury, 16, 19, 20, 26
  T-33 jet fighter, 16, 19, 22, 25, 159
aircraft, European
  Lancaster bomber, 30
  Mirage IV bomber, 249
  Vulcan bomber, 249
aircraft, Soviet
  Il-28 Beagle bomber, 129, 157, 171–
    74, 205–7
  Mi-4 Hound helicopter, 129
  MiG, 10, 88, 129, 139–41, 159,
    169, 240
  Mya-4 Bison bomber, 225
  Su-9, 240
  Tu-16 Badger bomber, 225–26
  Tu-95 Bear bomber, 225–26
  Tu-114 airliner, 85
  Yak-25, 240
aircraft carriers, 17
Alabama
  Guided Missile Development
    Group, 50
  Marshall Space Flight Center
    established, 52
Alaska, 241–43
Alexandrovsk, 131
Alliance for Progress, 182
Anadyr (river), 127. *See also* Operation
  Anadyr
Anderson, Maj. Rudolf, Jr., 1
Antarctica, 82
Antwerp, Belgium, 48
ANZUS (Australia, New Zealand, United
  States Security Treaty), 85
Apollo space program, 52, 110
As We Remember Joe, John F. Kennedy, 100
assassination plots against Castro, 10
Assault Brigade 2506, 10–11, 24, 27, 109
Atlántico, 15, 18, 20, 23–24
Atlas missile, 52–53, 163, 166, 239, 263
atomic bomb. *See also* nuclear bomb,

radiation
  development by countries, 40–42
  dropped on Japan, 38–39
  invented and tested, 29–30
  Little Boy and Fat Man, building of,
    29–30
Atomic Energy Commission (AEC), 184,
  200–201
"Atoms for Peace" program, 43
Australia
  author's fictional home, 2, 257
  immigration boom, 257
  United Nations headquarters in,
    257–58
Australia, New Zealand, United States
  Security Treaty (ANZUS), 85
Austria, 110

B-4 submarine, 136
B-17 bomber, 30, 240–41
B-24 bomber, 34
B-26 Invader
  Cuban, 3, 19–21, 159
  U.S., used by Cuban exiles, 9, 11,
    15–16, 22–26
B-29 bomber, 37, 241
B-36 bomber, 241
B-36 submarine, 136
B-47 Stratojet, 162–63, 167, 239
B-52 Stratofortress, 162–63, 167, 239,
  241–42
B-58 Hustler, 163, 239
B-59 submarine, 136, 231–32
B-75 submarine, 136, 231–32
B-88 submarine, 136, 231–32
B-130 submarine, 136
Bahía de Cochinos. *See* Cuba, Bay of Pigs
  invasion
Baikonur, Kazakhstan, 56, 57
Barbara J., 14, 18, 20, 21, 23–24
Battle of Britain, 33
Battle of the Bulge, 34
Battle of Stalingrad, 68
Batista, Fulgencio, 4–5
Bay of Pigs. *See* Cuba, Bay of Pigs
  invasion
Beria, Lavrenty, 66, 72–73
Berlin, Germany
  Battle of Berlin in World War II,
    176–77

Berlin Crisis, 83–87, 111–14
Berlin Wall, 112–14, 177
  not hit by nuclear bombs, 248
  quarantine of, by Soviets, 153–58
  shelling of, by Soviets, 175–80, 182,
    185, 195
biological warfare, 258–62
Blagar, 14, 17, 18, 19, 23–24
Bleicherode, Germany, 49
Blue Beach, Cuba 17, 18, 19–26
Bomarc missile, 218
Bomber Command (Britain), 33–35
Bonestell, Chesley, 50
Bouvier, Jacqueline Lee, 103
Boxer, 17
Braun, Wernher von, 46–52, 55–56
Brezhnev, Leonid, 146
Brigade 2506, 10–11, 24, 27, 109
Brigham Young University, 237
bubonic plague as biological weapon,
  260–61
Bundy, McGeorge, 142, 147, 153, 210
buzz bomb (V-1), 48, 57, 129
By Rocket into Planetary Space, Herman
  Oberth, 46

C-46 Commandos, 9, 23
C-54 Skymasters, 9
C-130 Hercules, 187, 194
Camp David, 86
Campo Libertad, Cuba, 11
cancer rates, post-Fire, 254
Caribe, 15, 18, 20, 23, 25
Carson, Strobe (fictional), 197
Casper underground bunker, 223–24
Castro, Fidel
  26 July Movement, 6
  accepts Soviet aid, 123–37
  CIA orchestrates opposition to, 8–10
  death in the Fire, 201
  early life, 5–7
  first reference to "socialist"
    revolution, 15
  invades Cuba, 3–4
  meets Khrushchev, 91
  mobilizes Cuban soldiers, 16, 159
  victory speech after Bay of Pigs
    invasion, 26
Castro, Raúl
  death in the Fire, 201

  early life, 5
  invades Cuba, 4
  negotiates in Moscow, 126
  possible successor to Fidel Castro, 135
Catholic Church
  in Fidel Castro's childhood (Roman), 5
  Greek Catholic Church (Ukrainian), 70
  and Kennedy family, 94–95, 103, 104
  opposition to Fidel Castro (Roman), 12
Central America, escaped nuclear
  bombing, 252
Central Australia sugar mill complex, 22
Central Intelligence Agency (CIA)
  Cuban losses, after Bay of Pigs
    invasion, estimates of, 19
  Cuban losses, before Bay of Pigs
    invasion, estimates of, 10
  Dulles, Allen, director, 109
  evaluation of Khrushchev, 78
  in Hungary, 76
  monitors Soviet buildup in Cuba,
    132–34
  officers in Bay of Pigs invasion, 14–15
  orchestrates anti-Castro groups,
    8–10
  plausible deniability in Bay of Pigs
    plan, 12–13
  report on Soviet nuclear capability, 213
CF-100 Canuck, 225
CF-101 Voodoo, 225
Chamberlain, Neville, 96
chemical warfare, 258–62
Cherwell, 1st Viscount (Lord), 33
Chiang Kai-shek, 251–52
Chicago, Illinois, after the Fire, 227–31
China
  and atomic bomb development, 40
  Communism in, 80, 119–20, 124–25
  hit with nuclear bombs, 250–52
  Sino-Soviet relations, 81, 90, 116,
    124–25
Churchill, Winston, 33, 35–37
CIA. *See* Central Intelligence Agency
  (CIA)
Cicerone, Tony (fictional), 173
civil defense, 120–21, 224, 226
civil rights movement, 104, 105, 121, 256
Civil War vs. New Confederacy, 256–57

Cold War
    and Berlin Crisis, 83–87, 111–14
    end of (after the Fire), 262
    end of (factual), 2
    moral effects of, 107–8
    and U.S. containment policy, 7, 84–
        85, 101
Collier's, 50
Command posts, alternative or
    underground
    EC-135C, 239
    Looking Glass, 238
    Mount Weather, 106, 180, 222–24,
        237
    Raven Rock, 223
    Site R, 223
    Soviet, 240
Communism
    Castro's interest in, 5, 6
    in China, 76, 124–25
    Communist International
        (Comintern), 124–25
    Communists resisting Cold War's
        end, 2
    and "Fedorovism," 44
    Fulgencio Batista's opposition to, 4
    Khrushchev's 1956 speech to
        Communist Party, 74–75
    Khrushchev's membership, 63–64
    moral effects of, 107–8
    in Poland and Hungary, 75–76
    U.S. containment policy, 7, 84–
        85, 101
    in Vietnam, 119–20
conspiracy theorists, 238
containment policy, 7, 84–85, 101
contingency, defined, 1–2
Corona satellite program, 89
Cosmodrome, Northern, 57
Cuba
    dictator Fulgencio Batista, 4
    economic aid from Soviet Union, 7
    economic dependence on U.S., 7
    invasion of by Fidel Castro, 3
    losses from guerilla campaigns, 10
Cuba, Bay of Pigs invasion
    exiled soldiers land, 3
    invasion, begins, 14–23
    invasion, CIA plans, 10–12

invasion, goes awry, 23–28
invasion, Kennedy downgrades,
    12–14
Kennedy's planning process, 109
Cuba, Missile Crisis. *See also* Operation
    Anadyr
    Cuban poet recalls the horror, 202–3
    ExCom plans military response to
        Operation Anadyr, 142–47
    invasion, airstrikes begin, 167–75
    invasion, combat begins, 185–87
    invasion, Cuba prepares for, 159–61
    invasion, U.S. calls off, 193–94
    invasion, U.S. prepares for, 161–64,
        180–85
    Kennedy's televised speech about,
        147–49
    Khrushchev's response after U.S.
        cancels invasion, 196–98
    Khrushchev's response to Kennedy's
        speech, 149–50
    quarantine of Berlin begins, 153–54
    quarantine of Cuba begins, 151–52
    rogue Soviet pilot bombs New
        Orleans, 205–7
    rogue Soviet pilot survives invasion,
        171–74
    Soviet major general decides to use
        nuclear bomb, 187–88
    Soviet Union detonates first nuclear
        bomb, 189–94
    Soviet Union shells Berlin, 175–80
    Soviet-U.S. negotiations after nuclear
        bomb, 203–5
    Soviet-U.S. negotiations before
        nuclear bomb, 155–59
    U-2 reconnaissance overflights, 139–41
    U.S. detonates nuclear bombs on
        Cuba, 199–202
Cuba, Missile Crisis resolution (factual),
    267–73
Cuba Study Group, 27–28
Cuban air force, 16, 18–19, 159. *See also*
    aircraft, Cuban
Cuban Missile Crisis. *See* Cuba, Missile
    Crisis
Cuban secret police, 27
Czechoslovakia, Cuban pilots training in,
    10, 139

Daley, Lt. Andy (fictional), 171
Dankevich, Lt. Gen. Pavel Borisovich, 128
DASH (Drone Anti-Submarine Helicopter), 188–89
DEFCON, 144, 166
de Gaulle, Charles, 40, 51, 86–87, 89
De Soto, Juan (fictional), 171
Democratic Revolutionary Front, formation of, 8
Dennison, Adm. Robert L., 143, 180, 192–93, 199
Dillon, C. Douglas, 142
Disneyland broadcast, 50
Dobrynin, Anatoly, 135, 210, 214
Dobson, Gordon M. B., 255
Donetsk, Ukraine, 61
Dora-Mittelbau, Germany, 48, 49
Doolittle, Lt. Gen. Jimmy, 31
Douglas Aircraft Company and A-26 Invader, 9
Douhet, Giulio, 31
Dov, Mordechai (fictional), 244
Dresden, Germany, 30, 35
Drone Anti-Submarine Helicopter (DASH), 188–89
Dubivko, Alexei, 136
Dulles, Allen, 109
Dulles, John Foster, 84

EC-135C command post, 239
Echo-class submarine, 58
Egypt, and Suez Canal, 76, 80–81
Eielson Air Force Base, Alaska, 241–43
Eighth Air Force, 34
82nd Airborne Division, 161, 187, 202
Einstein, Albert, 29
Eisenhower, Dwight D.
    1955 speech in Geneva, 80
    1956 election, 103
    advises Kennedy, 154
    "Atoms for Peace" program, 43
    cuts diplomatic ties to Cuba, 7
    defeats Adlai Stevenson, 16
    meets with Khrushchev, 84–90
    Supreme Allied Commander Europe, 35
    transitions to Kennedy admin-istration, 12–13, 106

elections, U.S., during the Fire, 210
electricity
    from nuclear power, 43
    nuclear power plants dismantled post-Fire, 262
Enewetak Atoll, 40
England. *See* Great Britain
Enola Gay, 38
Enterprise, 162, 200
Essex, 17, 162
ExCom (Executive Committee of the National Security Council)
    decides to invade Cuba, 180–85
    evaluates shelling of Berlin, 154–59
    formed to evaluate Cuban risk, 142–46
    response to nuclear detonation in Cuba, 194–96
    response to nuclear detonation in New Orleans, 207–11
exiles, Cuban
    in Assault Brigade 2506, 10–11, 24, 27, 109
    in Bay of Pigs invasion, 15, 19
    Hernández, Francisco, 3, 20–23, 28
    plans for, after the invasion, 183
    as prisoners, 26
    training as guerillas, 9
The Exploration of Cosmic Space by Means of Reaction Devices, Konstantin Tsiolkovsky, 45
Explorer 1, 52

F-4 Phantom, 168
F-51 Mustang, 16
F-100 Super Sabre, 168, 187, 191, 199
F-101 Voodoo, 225
F-102 Delta Dagger, 225
F-104 Starfighter, 168–69, 175
F-105 Thunderchief, 168, 173
F-106 Delta Dart, 225
facism, Fidel Castro's interest in, 6
fallout. *See* radiation
fallout shelters, 120–21, 222–24, 226
Fat Man atomic bomb, 30, 38–39
Fechter, Peter, 177
Fedorov, Nikolai, 44
Feklisov, Sergei (fictional), 172, 205–7
Ferguson, Niall, 1

Fermi, Enrico, 42
Fifth Battalion, 21, 26
Fifth Marine Expeditionary Brigade, 162
Finding Survivors (fictional), Bob Hilton, 191
firestorm, 30–31, 227–28
First Armored Division, 161, 186
First Infantry Division, 161, 201–2, 207
Fisher, Ingrid (fictional), 191
FKR-1 Salish cruise missiles, 129–30, 175, 184, 191
Fleming, James (fictional), 240–44
Florida
    anti-Castro exiles in, 8–9, 11
    Cape Canaveral, 58
    CIA officers in, 14
    military bases, for Cuban invasion, 143, 169, 171
    practice amphibious landing in, 185
    residents panic after New Orleans bombing, 211
Foxtrot submarine, 136, 160, 231–32
France
    atomic bomb test, 40
    hit by nuclear bombs, 248
    Khrushchev's visit to, 86–87
    Normandy, 35
    nuclear bomb capability, 249
    and Suez Canal, 76, 80–81
FROG rocket, 129, 152, 184, 193
frogmen, 186
From the Earth to the Moon, Jules Verne, 45
Frost, Robert, 93
Fuchs, Klaus, 30
Fursenko, Aleksandr, 270, 271

G2, Castro's intelligence service, 8–9
Gagarin, Yuri, 82–83
Genetic defects, radiation-caused, 254, 261–62
Geneva, Switzerland, 80
Genie missile, 218, 226
George Washington submarine, 58
German Luftwaffe air force, 32
German Society for Space Travel, 46, 55
Germany. *See also* Berlin, Germany
    Bleicherode, 49
    and early rocket development, 46–51
    hit by nuclear bombs, 248

    Soviet nuclear bombs in during Berlin Crisis, 184
    in World War II, 2, 32–33, 176–77, 227
The Ghosts of My Home (fictional), Gonzalez, Miguel, 203
Gilpatric, Roswell, 114
Glenn L. Martin Company, 9
Global Weather Central, 140
Goddard, Dr. Robert H., 45–46, 49–50
Golf-class submarine, 58
Gonzalez, Miguel (fictional), 202–3
Gorbachev, Mikhail, 269
Gorbachev bunker, 150, 215
Göring, Hermann, 32
Great Britain
    atomic and hydrogen bomb tests, 40
    Bomber Command (Britain), 33–35
    hit by nuclear bombs, 248
    hit by V-2 rockets, 48
    hunt for Soviet submarines after the Fire, 233
    Joe Kennedy, ambassador to, 95–96
    nuclear bomb capability, 249
    nuclear power plants, 43
    Secret Intelligence Service, 132–33
    and Suez Canal, 76, 80–81
Great Leap Forward program, 81, 125
Great Patriotic War, 67–69, 74
Greece, American aid to, 101
Green Beach, 17, 18
Greenbrier underground bunker, 223–24
Gribkov, Anatoli I., 269
Group for the Study of Rockets, 55
Guantánamo Bay, Cuba, 131, 162, 175, 186, 193–94, 201–2
Guardia Nacional, 14–15
Guatemala
    CIA involvement in, 8
    coup d'état, 16, 109
    and training of anti-Castro groups, 9
    and training of tank crews, 11
guerrillas
    anti-Castro, damage inflicted by, 10
    Bay of Pigs invasion plans, 11–15
    led by Fidel Castro, 4
    non-CIA funded, 12
Guevera, Ché, 4, 135
Guided Missile Development Group, 50
The Guns of August, Barbara Tuchman, 183

Halsey, Adm. William "Bull," 98
Hamburg, Germany, 30, 227
Harding, Warren G., 102
Harris, Air Marshal Arthur "Bomber,"
    33–35
Harvard University, Kennedy attends,
    95–97
Havana
    aftermath of nuclear bomb, 202–3
    and Fidel Castro's rise to power, 4
    Soviet officers stationed in, 131
    targeted for nuclear bomb, 199–200
Hawaii, hit by nuclear bomb, 232–33
Hawk antiaircraft missile, 162, 193
Hearst newspapers, Kennedy a
    correspondent for, 99
helicopter, DASH (Drone Anti-
    Submarine Helicopter), 188–89
Hernández, Francisco, landing at Bay of
    Pigs, 3, 20–23, 28
Hilton, Lt. Cdr. Bob (fictional), 188–91
Hiroshima, Japan
    attack on, 38–39, 41
    Little Boy bomb, building of, 29,
        38–39
Hitler, Adolf, 33, 96, 176
Honest John missile, 163, 183–84
Hotel class submarine, 58, 233
Hound Dog cruise missile, 239, 243–44,
    249
Houston, 15, 18, 21, 26
Humphrey, Hubert, 84
Hungary, 75–76, 80, 85
hydrogen bomb. *See* nuclear bomb. *See
    also* atomic bomb.

IBM, 43–44
Idaho, nuclear power plant, 43
IGY (International Geophysical Year),
    81–82
Il-28 Beagle bomber, 129, 157, 171–74,
    205–7
Independence, 162
India, escaped nuclear bombing, 252
Indianapolis, 30
Indigirka, 131, 141
International Geophysical Year (IGY),
    81–82
Iran, CIA involvement in, 8

Italy
    CIA involvement in, 8
    Jupiter rockets deployed in, 51, 155,
        239

Japan,
    1945 proposed invasion of by Soviet
        Union, 79
    Hiroshima's Little Boy bomb,
        building of, 29
    hit by atomic bombs, 38–39, 41
    hit by nuclear bombs, 250–51
    and Kennedy's PT boat incident,
        98–99
    Nagasaki's Fat Man bomb, building
        of, 30
    Okinawa, 38, 249–50
Johnson, Clarence "Kelly," 87
Johnson, Lyndon B., 104–5, 142, 223–
    24, 237–38, 256
JS-3 tank, 16, 22
JS-4 tank, 16
Jupiter rocket, 51, 53, 155, 239

K-19 submarine, 58
Kaganovich, Lazar, 64, 66, 77–78
Kalinovka, Russia, 61, 63
Kalugin, Oleg, 55
kamikaze pilots, 38
Kapustin Yar, 56
Kazakhstan, 41, 56
KC-97 Stratotanker, 163
KC-135 Stratotanker, 163
Keating, Kenneth, 134–35
Keita, Modibo, President of Mali, 114
Kennedy, Jacqueline Lee Bouvier, 103
Kennedy, John F. See also Cuba, Bay of
    Pigs invasion; Cuba, Missile Crisis
    Alliance for Progress, 182
    and Berlin Crisis, 111–14
    and civil rights movement, 104,
        105, 121
    commissions Cuba Study Group,
        27–28
    death of, in the Fire, 220–21
    decisions during Bay of Pigs invasion,
        24–25
    early years, 93–97
    foreign policy approach, 107–11

health issues, 94, 96, 99–100, 103–4, 106, 109, 121
inauguration, 93
meets with Khrushchev, 110–11
military career, 97–99
political career, 100–11
presidential debates, 105
PT boat incident, 98–99
resolution of Cuba Missile Crisis (factual), 267–73
and SIOP nuclear planning, 115–19
and space race, 109–10
televised speech about Cuban crisis, 147–48
and Vietnam, 119–20
Kennedy, Joseph, Jr., 94–95, 98, 100
Kennedy, Joseph, Sr., 94, 96, 121
Kennedy, Kathleen, 101
Kennedy, Pat, 101
Kennedy, Robert F.
adviser to John F. Kennedy, 101–2, 135, 184
and Cuba Study Group, 28
death of, in the Fire, 220–21
and ExCom, 142–43, 183
and Martin Luther King Jr., 105
Thirteen Days: A Memoir of the Cuban Missile Crisis, 269
Kennedy, Rose Fitzgerald, 94–95
Kennedy, Rosemary, 95
Ketov, Ryurik, 136, 231
KGB
in Cuba, 131, 173
and Ivan Serov, 78
in Novocherkassk, 128
training G2, 9
under Khrushchev, 77, 78
Kharkov, Ukraine, 64, 68
Khrushchev, Liuba, 69
Khrushchev, Lyonia, 69
Khrushchev, Marusia, 63
Khrushchev, Nikita. *See also* Operation Anadyr; Cuba, Missile Crisis
assumes control of Soviet Union, 73–75
and Berlin Crisis, 83–87, 111–14
death of, in the Fire, 240
decides to fire nuclear bombs at the U.S., 214–16

denounces Stalinist policy, 74–75
failed coup against, 77–78
foreign policy, 79–81
early years, 61–69
meets with Castro, 91
meets with Eisenhower, 84–90
meets with Kennedy, 110–11
orders shelling of Berlin, 177–78
political background, 65–73
and religion, 197–98
resolution of Cuba Missile crisis (factual), 267–73
response to U.S. cancelling invasion after nuclear detonation, 196–198
supports Fidel Castro, 27, 123–37
and U-2 crisis, 87–90
visits the United States, 85–87
Khrushchev, Nina Petrovna Kukharchuk, 63–64
Khrushchev, Yefrosinia Pisarev, 62
Kiev, Ukraine, 64, 67, 68
King, Martin Luther, Jr., 105
Kobieleva, Aleksandr (fictional), 245–47
Komar patrol boats, 129–30, 143, 175
Korea,
hit by nuclear bombs, 250–51
Korean War, 120
in World War II, 2
Korolyov, Sergei Pavlovich, 55–56, 82
Koval, George, 30
Kukharchuk, Nina Petrovna, 63–64
Kyshtym nuclear disaster, 43

labor unions, anti-Castro, 12
Lancaster bomber, 30
land-reform law, Castro's, 7
Landes, David S., 1
landing ship dock (LSD), 16
landing ships infantry (LSI), 14
Laos, 14, 106, 108
Las Vegas, Nevada, nuclear testing in, 41
LeMay, Curtis E.
agrees not to launch nuclear missiles without Kennedy's approval, 207–8
America is in Danger, 272
believes Soviet Union will not escalate war, 158–59
commands attack on Japan in World War II, 37

death of, in the Fire, 238
friction with Kennedy, 108–9,
  272–73
provokes conflict with Soviet Union
  (rumored) 165–66
reports on airstrike success, 180–81
success heading up SAC, 168
Lemnitzer, Gen. Lyman, 114–15, 118
Lenin, Vladimir, 64, 66
Life, 120
Little Boy atomic bomb
  attack on Hiroshima, 38–39
  building of, 29–30
Lockheed Corporation, 58, 87, 168
Lodge, Henry Cabot, Jr., 102
Looking Glass command post, 238
Los Alamos, New Mexico, and atomic
  bombs, 29
LSD (landing ship dock), 16
LSI (landing ships infantry), 14
Luftwaffe, German air force, 32, 34–35, 47
Luna rocket, 57, 129, 152
Lynch, Grayston L., 14, 17–20, 24–25, 27
Lysenko, Trofim, 78–79

M16 (Great Britain's Secret Intelligence
  Service), 132–33
M-41 tank, 11, 22
Macedonian, 151
Macmillan, Harold, 86
Malenkov, Georgy, 72–74, 77–78
Malinovsky, Rodion Y., 145
Malmstrom Air Force Base, Montana,
  54, 165
Manchuria, in World War II, 2
Manhattan Project, 2, 29–30, 40, 42
Mao Zedong, 76, 81, 125, 251
Maria Ulyanova, 130
Mariel, Cuba, 137, 185–86, 191, 193–94
The Mars Project, Wernher von Braun, 50
Marshall Plan, 7, 101
Marshall Plan, biological warfare
  proposal, 260
Marshall Space Flight Center, established, 52
Marxism, Fidel Castro's interest in, 6
Mayak nuclear disaster, 43
Mayo Clinic, 96
McCarthy, Joseph, 101–3
McCarthyism, 101–3

McCloud, Raymond (fictional), 176
McCone, John, 142
McNamara, Robert S.
  disliked by LeMay, 272–73
  disputes the "missile gap," 107
  member of ExCom, 142–44
  and SIOP, 114, 118–19
  and Vietnam planning, 119
Mein Kampf, Adolf Hitler, 33
Mercury space program, 52
A Method of Reaching Extreme Altitudes,
  Dr. Robert H. Goddard, 45
Mexico, Fidel Castro's exile in, 6
Mi-4 Hound helicopters, 129
Middle East, escaped nuclear bombing, 252
MiG fighter jet
  Cuban pilots training in, 10, 139
  dogfighting in Cuban invasion, 169
  sent to Cuba, 129, 139, 159
  and U-2 spy plane, 88, 139–41
Mikoyan, Anastas Ivanovich, 90, 124, 271
Military Sea Transportation Service, 14
Mirage IV bomber, 249
Missiles. *See also* rockets
  Atlas, 52–53, 163, 166, 239, 263
  Bomarc, 218
  FKR-1 Salish, 129–30, 175, 184, 191
  Genie, 218, 226
  Hawk, 162, 193
  Honest John, 163, 183–84
  Hound Dog cruise missile, 239,
    243–44, 249
  Jupiter rocket, 51, 53, 155, 239
  Minuteman, 53–54, 165, 217, 263
  Nike Hercules, 218, 226
  Polaris, 58–59, 115, 163
  R-1, 56
  R-7, 56–57
  R-12, 129
  R-14, 129
  Redstone rocket, 51–52
  Regulus, 57, 163
  Skybolt, 249
  solid-fuel missiles, 54–55
  Sopka (Samlet), 129–30
  SS-4 Sandal, 129–30, 140–41, 157,
    168–69, 172–74, 211, 236
  SS-5 Skean, 129–31, 141, 157, 168,
    242, 251

SS-6 Sapwood, 57, 133, 218–19, 224, 238
SS-7 Saddler, 218–19
SS-N-3 Sepal, 58
SS-N-4 Sark, 58
submarine-launched, 57–58
surface-to-air (SAM) system, 129, 139, 145, 152, 157, 167–71, 175, 240
Thor, 53, 124, 155, 239
Titan, 52, 163, 239
TM-76 Mace, 250
Mitchell, Maj. Gen. Billy, 31
Molotov, Vyacheslav, 71, 72, 77–78
Monroe Doctrine, 126
Montana, Malmstrom Air Force Base, 54, 165
Moscow, Nikita Khrushchev in, 64, 68
Mount Weather, 106, 180, 222–24, 237
Mustang (F-51), 16
Mutual Assured Destruction (MAD), 31
Mya-4 Bison bomber, 225

Naftali, Timothy, 270
Nagasaki, Japan
    attack on, 38–39, 41
    Fat Man bomb, building of, 30
Nantenkov, Nikolai, 232
napalm, 15, 170, 186, 193–94
NASA (National Aeronautics and Space Administration), 52
National Photographic Interpretation Center, 140, 142, 173
National Strategic Target List, 115–16
NATO (North Atlantic Treaty Organization)
    countries hit with nuclear bombs, 247–49
    established, 84–85
    forces in Berlin, 176–82
    hunt for Soviet submarines after the Fire, 233
    Kennedy supports, 101
    role in Berlin and East Germany, 154
Nautilus submarine, 43
Nazi party, and early rocket development, 47
Nazi-Soviet Non-Aggression Pact, 67
the Netherlands, in World War II, 32
Nevada, nuclear testing in, 41

New Commonwealth, 258
New Mexico
    Roswell, rocket testing near, 46
    Trinity Test Site, 29
    White Sands, 49
New Orleans, Louisiana, 201, 206–7
New York City, hit by nuclear bombs, 224–25, 257
New York Times, 74, 183
Newport, Rhode Island, hit by nuclear bombs, 234–35
Ngo Dinh Diem, 119
Nicaragua
    Cuban exile bombers flying from, 9, 11
    and ships, 14–15
    during Bay of Pigs invasion, 24–25
Nike Hercules missile system, 218, 226
Nixon, Richard
    Kennedy campaigned against, 13
    and McCarthyism, 101
    meets with Khrushchev, 86
    presidential debates, 105
NKVD (Soviet secret police) (*See also* KGB), 66, 69, 77
No More War!, Linus Pauling, 42
Nobel Prize winners, 29, 42, 203
Non-Aligned Movement, 114
NORAD (North American Aerospace Defense Command), 167, 209, 218, 225
Nordhausen, Germany, 48, 49
Normandy, France, 35
North American Aerospace Defense Command (NORAD), 167, 209, 218, 225
North Atlantic Treaty Organization. *See* NATO
Northampton, 221
Northern Cosmodrome, 57
Novocherkassk, Soviet Union, 128
nuclear bomb. *See also* atomic bomb; radiation
    accidents, 167
    capabilities, Soviet, 116–17
    capabilities, U.S., 116
    in East Germany, 183
    National Strategic Target List, 115
    race to develop, 39–44

SIOP plan, 114–19
Soviet, detonated in Asia, 249–50
Soviet, detonated in Cuba, 189–94
Soviet, detonated in New Orleans,
205–7
Soviet, detonated in U.S., 218–28,
235–37
Soviet, detonated in Washington
D.C., 219–24
Soviet, detonated in Western Europe,
247–48
Soviet, shipped to Cuba, 130–32
testing of, 112–13
U.S., detonated in Asia, 250–52
U.S., detonated in Cuba, 199–202
U.S., detonated in Eastern Europe,
248–49
U.S., detonated in Soviet Union,
237–45
U.S., prepared for Cuban attack,
162–63
world population affected by, 252
world-wide disarmament, post–Fire,
262
nuclear reactor
development of, 42–43
dismantling of, post-Fire, 262
electricity from, 43

Oak Ridge, Tennessee, 30
OAS (Organization of American States),
154, 181–82
Oberth, Herman, 46–47
O'Donnell, Kenneth, 142
Offutt Air Force Base, Nebraska, 140
oil
Cuba nationalizes refineries, 7
Germany's dependence on in WWII,
34–35
Okinawa, 38, 249–50
*"One Hell of a Gamble": Khrushchev,
Castro, and Kennedy, 1958–1964,*
Aleksandr Fursenko and Timothy
Naftali, 270
"One Life for Many" (fictional poem),
Ingrid Fisher, 191
Operation Anadyr
deployment of, 127–32
Fidel Castro welcomes Soviet help, 125

Khrushchev develops, to protect
Cuba, 123–27
Raúl Castro negotiates with Soviet
Union, 126
Soviet submarines deploy, 136–37
U.S. monitors, evaluates risk of,
132–36
U.S. plans response to, 139–50
Operation Downfall, 38
Operation Mongoose, 134
Operation Paperclip, 49
Oppenheimer, J. Robert, 29
Organization of American States (OAS),
154, 181–82
organized crime in Cuba, 4
Oriente Province, 3
Ortsac exercise, 123
ozone layer, radiation's effects on, 255–56

P-2 Neptune, 231
Panama Canal Zone, and training anti-
Castro groups, 9
paratroopers
in Bay of Pigs invasion, 11, 15, 17,
21, 24
in Cuba Missile Crisis, 161, 187,
196–97
patrol boats (Komar), 129–130, 143, 175
patrol torpedo (PT) boats, 97–99
Pauling, Linus, 42
Peace Corps, 106
Pearl Harbor, Hawaii, 232–33
Peenemünde, Germany, 47–48, 50, 56
Penkovsky, Oleg, 132–33, 152, 212–13, 240
Pennsylvania, nuclear power plant, 43
People's Commissariat for Internal Affairs
(NKVD), 66, 69
pilots
American, during Bay of Pigs
invasion, 24–25
Anderson, Maj. Rudolf, Jr., 1
anti-Castro, CIA training, 9
Cuban exile claiming to be defector, 16
Cuban pilots training in
Czechoslovakia, 10, 139
Daley, Lt. Andy (fictional), 171
dogfighting in Cuba, 169–70
Feklisov, Sergei (fictional), 172
Japanese kamikaze, 38

Powers, Francis Gary, 88
U-2, 139
Pisarev, Ivan, 62
Pisarev, Yefrosinia, 62
plantations, Cuban
and Castro's land-reform law, 7
used by Soviets, 172–73
plausible deniability, 12–13, 15, 24–27
Playa Girón, Cuba, 17, 18, 23
Playa Larga, Cuba, 17, 18, 22, 24
Plesetsk, Russia, 57, 88, 218
Pliyev, Gen. Issa A., 127–28, 130, 159–60, 174, 192
Poland, 67, 75–76, 80
Polaris missile, 58–59, 106, 115, 163
Politburo, 71–72
Poltava, 132
Portal, Sir Charles, 35
Power, Gen. Thomas S., 166–67, 207–8, 238
Powers, Francis Gary, 88
Pravda, 156
Prensa Latina news agency, 25
Presidium
destruction of, 240
escalating Cuban crisis, 145–46, 149–50, 155–57, 182
and Khruschev's rise to power, 72–78
and missile technology, 82
planning of Operation Anadyr, 125–26
reaction to Khrushchev, 90
response after detonation over New Orleans, 211–16
response after detonations over Cuba, 203–4
Profiles in Courage, John F. Kennedy, 103
PT (patrol torpedo) boats, 97–99
PT-109, Robert J. Donovan, 99
Puerto Rico, 123
Pulitzer Prize, John F. Kennedy, 103

R-1 rocket, 56
R-7 rocket, 56–57
R-12 missile, 129
R-14 missile, 129
radiation
and Accelerated Growth Syndrome (AGS), 261–62

effects of, after the Fire, 228, 246–47, 253–56, 258
effects of, in Havana, 202–3
effects of, in Japan 38–39
effects of, on flora and fauna, 258–59
effects of, on ozone layer, 255–56
measured globally during IGY, 82, 107
Radio Moscow, 195–96
Rafael Santana, Carlos, 10
Randolph, 162
Rankin plan, 34
Raven Rock underground command post, 223
RB-66 Destroyer airplane, 151–52
Rebel Army, 16
Red Army
effect of Stalin's purges on, 67–68
Khrushchev increases size of, 111
Khrushchev's membership in, 63
and Operation Anadyr, 123–37, 139–41
Red Beach, 17, 18, 19–23
Redstone Arsenal of Army Ordnance, 50
Redstone rocket, 51–52
Regulus cruise missile, 57, 163
RF-8 Crusader airplane, 151, 171
RF-101 Voodoo airplane, 151, 171–73
Rhode Island, hit by nuclear bombs, 234–35
Rio Escondido, 15, 18, 19, 23
Road to Space Travel, Herman Oberth, 46
Robertson, William, 14, 19
Rocket Airdrome Berlin, 47
rockets. *See also* missiles
A-4, 47
early development of, 44–51
FROG, 129, 152, 184, 193
Jupiter, 51, 53, 155
Luna, 57, 129, 152
R-1, 56
R-7, 56–57
Redstone, 51–52
Saturn V, 52
V-1 buzz bomb, 48, 57, 129
V-2, 47–50, 56
Vanguard, 52
Romzha, Bishop Theodore, 70
Roosevelt, Franklin D., 32, 94, 95–96

Roswell, New Mexico, 46
Rotterdam, the Netherlands, in World War II, 32
Royal Air Force, 30, 31, 33
Rusk, Dean, 142, 181–82, 210
Russia. *See* Soviet Union
Russian Orthodox Church, 197–98
Ruz, Fidel Castro's childhood surname, 5

SAC (Strategic Air Command), 115, 166–68, 237–38
SAGE (Semi-Automatic Ground Environment) system, 43–44, 218
Sakharov, Andrei, 40
Salish (FKR-1) cruise missiles, 129–30, 175, 184, 191
SAM. *See* surface-to-air (SAM) missile system
Samlet (Sopka) missile, 129–30
San Roman, José "Pepe," 10
Santa Cruz del Norte, Cuba, 186
Santiago de las Vegas, Cuba, 152
Saratoga, 162, 200
Sark missile, 58
Satellites
    Explorer 1, 52
    Sputnik, 52, 56, 82, 105
    spy, 89–90
Saturn V, 52
Savitskii, Valentin, 136
Sea Fury, 16, 19, 20, 26
SEATO (Southeast Asia Treaty Organization), 84–85
Second Battalion, 20–23
Second Infantry Division, 185–86
Secret Intelligence Service (Great Britain), 132–33
secret police
    Cuban, 27
    Soviet, 66, 69, 77
Semi-Automatic Ground Environment (SAGE) system, 43–44
Serov, Ivan, 78
74th Motorized Rifle Regiment, 188
The Shape of Things to Come, H. G. Wells, 32
Shepard, Alan, 82
Shepilov, Dmitri, 77
Shevchenko, Elena (fictional), 187–88, 191–92

ships
    Alexandrovsk, 131
    Atlántico, 15, 18, 20, 23–24
    Barbara J., 14, 18, 20 , 21, 23–24
    Blagar, 14, 17, 18, 19, 23–24
    Caribe, 15, 18, 20, 23, 25
    Houston, 15, 18, 21, 26
    Indigirka, 131, 141
    Komar patrol boats, 129–30, 143, 175
    Macedonian, 151
    Maria Ulyanova, 130
    patrol torpedo (PT) boats, 97–99
    Poltava, 132
    Rio Escondido, 15, 18, 19, 23
    USS *Boxer*, 17
    USS *Enterprise*, 162, 200
    USS *Essex*, 17, 162
    USS *George Washington* submarine, 58
    USS *Independence*, 162
    USS *Indianapolis*, 30
    USS *Nautilus* submarine, 43
    USS *Northampton*, 221
    USS *Randolph*, 162
    USS *Saratoga*, 162, 200
    USS *Wallace L. Lind*, 186–90
    USS *Wasp*, 162
    USS *William R. Rush*, 151
    Volga, 151
Shumkov, Nikolai, 136
Sierra Maestra Mountains, Castro escapes to, 4
Sino-Soviet Treaty of Friendship, Alliance, and Mutual Assistance, 124–25
SIOP, 115–19, 207–8, 237–38, 244, 250
SIS (Great Britain's Secret Intelligence Service), 132–33
Site R underground command post, 223
Sixth Battalion, 19
Skybolt cruise missile, 249
Socialist, Fidel Castro's first reference to, 15
Society for Space Travel (German), 46, 55
solid-fuel missiles, 54–55
Sopka (Samlet) missile, 129–30
Sorensen, Ted, 135, 142
South America, escaped nuclear bombing, 252
Southeast Asia Treaty Organization (SEATO), 84–85
Soviet Air Defense Forces, 57

Soviet secret police, 66, 69, 77
Soviet Strategic Rocket Forces, 57
Soviet Union. *See also* Cuba, Bay of
Pigs invasion; Cuba, Missile Crisis;
Khrushchev, Nikita
    atomic and hydrogen bomb tests,
      40–42
    and Berlin Crisis, 83–87, 111–14
    and Berlin quarantine, 153–58
    and Berlin shelling, 175–80, 182, 195
    biological warfare, 258–62
    and Chinese relations, 81, 90, 116,
      124–25
    economic aid to Cuba, 7
    end of, 2, 257
    missile development, 55–58
    nuclear bomb capabilities, 116–17
    nuclear bomb capabilities (factual),
      268–70
    nuclear bombs detonated in, 237–47
    nuclear power plants, 43
    post-Fire status explored by U.N.
      team, 258–62
    second front in World War II, 37
    space race, 109–10
    Sputnik, 52, 56, 82, 105
    submarine missile capacity, 57–59
    support for Cuban Revolution, 27,
      123–37
Spaatz, Gen. Carl A., 35
space programs, 82, 109
Special Forces, US
    and Grayston L. Lynch, 14
    training anti-Castro groups, 9, 10
spies
    CIA, in Cuba, 132–33
    CIA, in Hungary, 76
    Fuchs, Klaus, 30
    Koval, George, 30
    Penkovsky, Oleg, 132–33
    unnamed Thiokol engineer, 55
Sputnik, 52, 56, 82, 105
spy plane, U-2, 55, 87–89, 139–41,
    144–46, 166
SS-4 Sandal missile, 129–30, 140–41,
    157, 168–69, 172–74, 211, 236
SS-5 Skean missile, 129–31, 141, 157,
    168, 242, 251

SS-6 Sapwood missile, 57, 133, 218–19,
    224, 238
SS-7 Saddler, 218–19
SS-N-3 Sepal missile, 58
SS-N-4 Sark missile, 58
Stalin, Josef, 64–73, 74–75, 79, 83, 245
Stalin Industrial Academy, 64–65
Stephenson, Ben (fictional), 234–35
Stevenson, Adlai, 16, 103, 142
Strategic Air Command (SAC), 115,
    166–68, 237–38
Strategic Rocket Forces (Soviet), 57
Submarines
    and ballistic missiles, 57–58
    Ethan Allen class, 59
    Polaris, 106, 115, 163
    Regulus, 57, 163
    Soviet, 58, 136–37, 159–61, 231–34
    USS *George Washington*, 58
    USS *Nautilus*, 43
Suez Canal, 76, 80–81
sugar quota, Cuban, 7
Sukarno, President of Indonesia, 114
Suranov, Maj. Gen. Mikhail (fictional),
    187–88, 191–92, 196–97
surface-to-air (SAM) missile system
    after the Fire, 240
    installed on Cuba during Operation
      Anadyr, 129, 139, 145, 152, 157
    used in Cuba Missile Crisis, 167–
      68, 170–71, 175
Sverdlovsk, Russia, 258–62

T-33 jet fighter, 16, 19, 22, 25, 159
T-34 tank, 16, 22
T-55 tank, 152
Tactical Air Command, 161
Taiwan, 250–51
tanks
    JS-3, 16, 22
    JS-4, 16
    M-41, 11, 22
    T-34, 16, 22
    T-55, 152
Taylor, Gen. Maxwell
    briefs Kennedy on military's target
      list, 199–200
    closely aligned with Kennedy, 147,
      181, 209

member of Cuba Study Group, 28
member of ExCom, 142–43
reports on Joint Chiefs' military
planning, 155
Technical University of Berlin, 46
Teller, Edward, 40
Thant, U, 155
Things to Come, movie, 32
Thiokol, 54, 236
Third Battalion, 24
*Thirteen Days: A Memoir of the Cuban
Missile Crisis*, Robert Kennedy, 269
Thor missile, 53, 124, 155, 239
Tinian island, 30
Titan missile, 52, 163, 239
TM-76 Mace cruise missile, 250
Tokyo, Japan, firebombing of, 37
Trenchard, Hugh, 31, 34
tribunals of revolutionary justice, Fidel
Castro's, 4
Trinidad, Cuba
planned invasion of, 11
replaced by Bay of Pigs in revised
plan, 13
Trinity Test Site, 29
Trotsky, Leon, 64, 66, 67
Tsiolkovsky, Konstantin, 44–45, 55
Tu-16 Badger bomber, 225–26
Tu-95 Bear bomber, 225–26
Tu-114 airliner, 85
Tuchman, Barbara, 183
Tupolev, Andrei, 55
Tupolev Design Bureau, 55
Turkey
American aid to, 101
American missiles in, 51, 124, 155,
165, 239
American surveillance in, 56

U-2 spy plane, 55, 87–89, 139–41,
144–46, 166
U.S.S.R. *See* Soviet Union
United Kingdom. *See* Great Britain
United Nations
Cuba accuses U.S. of attack, 16
explores status of post-Fire Soviet
Union, 258–62
Kennedy involved in Cuban
negotiations, 155

Khrushchev's appearance, 91
moves headquarters to Australia,
257–58
permanent members of, post–Fire,
257–58
United States. See also Cuba, Bay of
Pigs invasion; Cuba, Missile Crisis;
Kennedy, John F.
cities destroyed in the Fire, 218–28,
236
Civil War vs. New Confederacy,
256–57
Cuba's economic dependence on, 7
Fidel Castro's tour of, 7
New Orleans attacked, 205–7
nuclear bomb capabilities (factual),
268–70
recovery after the Fire, 235–37, 256–
57, 237
response to initial nuclear
detonation, 192–96
trains guerillas against Castro, 8–10
University of Havana, 5
USS *Boxer*, 17
USS *Enterprise*, 162, 200
USS *Essex*, 17, 162
USS *George Washington* submarine, 58
USS *Independence*, 162
USS *Indianapolis*, 30
USS *Nautilus* submarine, 43
USS *Northampton*, 221
USS *Randolph*, 162
USS *Saratoga*, 162, 200
USS *Wallace L. Lind*, 186–90
USS *Wasp*, 162
USS *William R. Rush*, 151
Utah, Thiokol development site, 54, 236

V-1 (buzz bomb) rocket, 48, 57, 129
V-2 rocket, 47–50, 56
Vanguard rocket, 52
Verne, Jules, 45, 46
Vienna, Austria, 110
Vieques Island, 123, 162
Vietnam, 108, 119–20
Virgin Lands proposal, 73
Voice of America, 161
Volga, 151
von Braun, Wernher, 46–52, 55–56

Vulcan bomber, 249

Wall Street Journal, 183
Wallace L. Lind submarine, 186–90
Warren, Chief Justice Earl, 93
Warsaw Pact
    on alert, during Berlin shelling,
        178–79
    countries hit with nuclear bombs,
        247–49
    established, 85
Washington D.C., destroyed by nuclear
    bombs, 219–24
Washington Post, 183
Wasp, 162
Webern, Britta (fictional), 229
Wells, H. G., 32, 45
Wendover, Utah, 30
Wheeler, Gen. Earle Gilmore "Bus," 180
White Sands, New Mexico, 49
Why England Slept, John F. Kennedy, 97
Widowmaker (B-26 Marauder), 9
William R. Rush, 151

Windscale reactor fire, 43
World War II,
    B-26 Invader, 3
    Battle of Berlin, 176–77
    end of, as contingency, 2
    Nazi-Soviet Non-Aggression Pact, 67
    use of aircraft in, 31–33
Wright, Julie (fictional), 237

X-Day, 38, 39
XVIII Airborne Corps, 187

Yalta Conference, 35, 112
Yekaterinburg, Russia, 258–62
Yeltsin, Vladimir (fictional), 174
Yezhov, Nikolai, 66
Yugoslavia, 80, 114
Yuzovka, Ukraine, 61–63

Zapata Swamp, Cuba, 13, 17, 18, 26
Zapata Zone, 22
Zhukov, Georgy, 77–78, 260
Zulu-class submarine, 161, 232

ABOUT THE AUTHOR

Eric G. Swedin is an associate professor at Weber State University in the Information Systems and Technologies Department specializing in information security and interdisciplinary studies. He teaches students how to be hackers so that they may defend against hackers. His doctorate is in the history of science and technology, and he regularly teaches history classes at Weber State. His publications include numerous articles, three history books, and a historical mystery novel, *The Killing of Greybird* (2004). Eric lives in a 130-year-old house with his wife Betty and four children. His web site is http://www.swedin.org/.